A CALL FROM THE DEAD

Dalbey couldn't speak. He sat rigid, gripping the phone, a look of disbelief on his face. That gravelly voice, what they used to call a whiskey tenor. He suddenly felt like laughing.

"You there?" asked the voice from out of the past. "You know who this is?"

"I'm here. I know."

The familiar chuckle. "You're supposed to be in Amsterdam. Them folks are pissed. Is this phone secure?"

"I don't think so."

"That's okay. I need your help. This is Crisis One, good buddy. You're the only person I can trust. I'll be in touch."

Dalbey listened to the click and the dial tone. He knew the voice as well as he knew his own—a voice he thought had been long dead. . . .

THE SPY WHO WOULDN'T DIE

Stuart James

BANTAM BOOKS
NEW YORK · TORONTO · LONDON · SYDNEY · AUCKLAND

THE SPY WHO WOULDN'T DIE
A Bantam Book / May 1989

ISBN 0-553-27895-9

Published simultaneously in the United States and Canada

Bantam Books are published by Bantam Books, a division of
Bantam Doubleday Dell Publishing Group, Inc. Its trademark,
consisting of the words "Bantam Books" and the portrayal of a
rooster, is Registered in U.S. Patent and Trademark Office and in
other countries. Marca Registrada. Bantam Books, 666 Fifth
Avenue, New York, New York 10103.

PRINTED IN THE UNITED STATES OF AMERICA

KR   0 9 8 7 6 5 4 3 2 1

THE SPY WHO WOULDN'T DIE

Chapter One

The white-haired man had been watching the Cassidy house for a week. It was an isolated retreat overlooking a quiet cove on Chesapeake Bay, a modern design in wood and glass. Named "Land's End," it was at the end of an unpaved lane that left the paved road through a gateway of high, dense bushes and snaked through a stand of tall pines to end in a turnaround at the house. There were other houses nearby, but they were occupied only on weekends, and even then the trees and plantings gave the Cassidys complete privacy.

There were two cars at the house. A Chevrolet station wagon and a Datsun 280Z. The Chevy was driven by Cassidy and his wife. The Datsun belonged to Cassidy's daughter, an attractive blond woman in her thirties. There was a woman who came by the day to clean and cook. She was dropped off by a pickup truck at eight A.M. and picked up again at six P.M.

A cement walk and a series of stairs descended from the house to the cove. A fifty-foot dock extended from the sandy shore, and at the end of the dock was Cassidy's sailboat, a white C&C 30 with a red sailcover and a jib furled on the headstay. Cassidy spent most of the day puttering around the boat. At a little past noon each day the wife, gray-haired but still trim, would carry a lunch down to the boat.

Posing as a gardener working on the adjacent properties while the owners were away during the week, the man was able to monitor movement at the house without arousing suspicion. The daughter was the only problem. There was no pattern to her movements. He knew the woman lived and worked in Philadelphia. She had been divorced for four years, no children. He had complete dossiers on Cassidy and his family. Having the daughter at the house disturbed him. He didn't feel comfortable without patterns. He didn't like surprises. On the other hand, the possibility of a problem would make him careful, keep him on edge.

He ended his surveillance on Friday, before homeowners arrived for the weekend. He loaded his tools into a nondescript panel truck that was lettered on the side panels:

Bryson & Healey
Landscape Architects
Horticultural Design & Maintenance
113 Main St.   Dover, Del.

With his usual care he had chosen the name of a company that actually existed. He backed out of the driveway where he had parked the truck, turned onto the deserted road, and drove off at a measured speed. When he turned onto the county road he accelerated.

For the first time he realized that it was an oppressively hot day. It was not something that bothered him. He expected it to be hot in Maryland in August. He passed through the rich checkerboard of farms, the neat fields bordered and fenced. The corn was waist high and it made him think nostalgically of a long-ago life and other cornfields that he had been desperate to escape.

He brought his mind back to the present, to the job. Every detail had to be painstakingly analyzed and then challenged. He had to consider every possible intangible. What could go wrong?

When he reached the state highway he turned right

and drove into Chestertown, a quiet, red-brick village mired in the eighteenth century. He passed through the town, crossed the ancient concrete drawbridge over the Chester River, and continued south at a leisurely pace—a workman in no hurry to get to his next job. When he reached U.S. 50, the weekend traffic from Annapolis and Washington was already building. He threaded into the southbound flow, keeping to the right to let the cars rush by. He turned off at Easton and followed the state highway to St. Michaels, where he had rented a cottage on the outskirts of town for the month of August.

It was a small, white house with clapboard siding and a sloping roof of green asphalt shingles. It had the transient, unoccupied quality of the seasonal rental, maintained, but not cared for. The location suited him perfectly. It was on the water. It was close enough to neighboring houses to discourage vandals or curious snooping, but isolated by shrubbery and a stand of pines. Since it was usually rented by the week or month, a lone man with fishing gear did not incite curiosity.

He turned the panel truck into the small, unpaved driveway that skirted the side of the cottage, driving slowly to the single-car garage at the rear of the property. He climbed down, then leaned back inside and made a show of removing his fishing equipment and carrying it to the steps at the rear of the cottage. He unlocked the garage door and opened it. Then he drove the truck inside, closed the door, and locked it. He went to the rear of the cottage, and let himself inside.

The air was close, stale, unpleasantly musty. He pulled back a kitchen chair and sat at the bare table. He was as ready as he was going to be, so he had a long weekend to himself. He had decided to move on Tuesday. There was always the possibility that weekenders might stay over for a Monday. He wanted as few people as possible in the vicinity of the Cassidy house.

He leaned back in the chair, took a deep breath, and

expelled it. His head tilted back, eyes closed, he swiveled his head back and forth to ease the muscle tension. He pushed up from the chair with a grunt and went to the refrigerator, pulling it open. There was no food inside, just a half dozen bottles of wine that he had brought with him. He removed a 1976 Chassagne-Montrachet and carried it to the sideboard to remove the cork.

The wine was cold and he sipped it slowly, turning the glass in his fingers and savoring the tartness. He felt weary. He would have liked to sleep, but instead he took the wine to the bathroom and showered. He dressed in casual clothes, then returned to the kitchen still sipping the wine. He corked the half-empty bottle and returned it to the refrigerator.

He walked the half-mile into town and had dinner at a popular seafood restaurant that overlooked the busy yacht harbor. He had a beer at the bar, making small talk with the bartender. He had eaten there every night since arriving in St. Michaels. He wanted to be a familiar face, just another vacationer.

He walked back to the cottage, finished the wine, set the alarm clock, and slept. In the morning he rented a fishing skiff, bought bait, and spent the day fishing. Relaxing, he read a paperback of Pushkin short stories. He returned in late afternoon, had his catch filleted and wrapped, stopped for a beer, then walked to the cottage, where he put the fish in the freezer compartment. He fished again on Sunday, and on Monday he bought a flowering plant that he had gift-wrapped and carried back to the cottage.

On Tuesday he arose before sunrise. He dressed quickly, then went into the kitchen and made coffee. The cottage was equipped with an electric percolator, so he was forced to make eight cups.

While the coffee was brewing, he left the cottage and walked slowly to the water's edge. The sky was gray, the dawn quickly coming on. He stepped onto the small pier that was supported by pilings driven into the sand. He flexed his knees, unconsciously moving up and down to test the weathered decking.

The air was warm, already rich with salt smell and marsh. He took a deep breath, savoring it.

A pair of swans drifted by, riding the gentle swells off the bay. He took a sight on them with thumb and forefinger, but quickly lost interest. He had once shot a deer and found the experience disquieting and pointless. Except for the chatter of awakening birds, it was silent. He glanced at his wristwatch: 5:15. He had to get moving.

He returned to the house and poured a cup of coffee. He drank it black, sipping it as he went through the house, checking that everything was locked. He returned to the kitchen, placed the half-empty cup on the bare table, unplugged the percolator, then went to a corner of the room and picked up his fishing rod and well-worn tackle box.

Taking a last look around the kitchen to make sure that all was as it should be, he backed through the screen door, holding it open while he pulled the kitchen door closed and carefully locked it, double-checking by turning the doorknob. He didn't expect any curious kids, but he took no chances. He pulled at the padlock on the garage door. It was secure. Then he walked into town.

He ate breakfast in a small café on the main street, then walked the block to the harbor and the boat livery where he had rented a fishing skiff over the weekend. He rented the same aluminum boat with a fifteen-horsepower outboard. He bought fresh bait for a day's fishing.

The weathered owner of the livery recognized him and made the usual pleasantries. He jotted down the information for his rental form, then warned, "Don't get out too far. Get squalls in this kind of weather. They come up on ya afore ya know it."

He thanked the man. He climbed into the skiff, secured the tackle box and rod, then gave the outboard starter-line a sharp tug. It started on the first pull, which meant that the plugs were clean, the magneto functioning properly. He had two spare plugs and a few tools in his tackle box, but he still glanced at the floor of the boat to make sure there was a paddle on board. He motored slowly out of the harbor, then turned left and increased the power until the boat rose onto plane and skimmed over the gentle chop.

Following the shoreline he watched for his cottage. It was almost eight o'clock before he spotted it hidden by the pines and pulled in toward the pier. He secured the boat with a chain, then carried the fishing gear and bait into the cottage.

He was moving now, getting into it. His senses were sharp. He was on schedule. He liked the feeling. The weeks of planning were suddenly compressed into hours. He knew there was no substitute for detailed preliminary study, but there was something unreal about it, something childish, as though he were playing a game. Now he was working.

Unlocking the garage door, he carried the padlock to the pier and used it to lock the skiff. It had to be there when he returned. He returned to the cottage.

He went to a closet, reached up, and pulled a black attaché case from the top shelf. He started for the kitchen, then changed his mind and went into the bedroom, where it would be more natural to have the shades drawn.

Placing the case on the bed, he opened it to reveal an Ingram M-11 machine pistol, two loaded clips, and a noise suppressor nestled in sponge-rubber compartments. He removed the gun. It was a homely piece, the size and shape of a jumbo toothpaste carton. It was plain metal, stark and deadly in its simplicity. The noise suppressor screwed onto the stubby barrel, a six-inch extension that looked like a small billy club. The assembled weapon was only fifteen inches long. He lifted one of the thirty-shot clips, tested the spring tension with his thumb, then carefully inserted it into the receiver and slammed it home with the heel of his hand. He turned the weapon over, admiring it. Ugly and efficient. It could burp out sixteen shots a second with the soft recoil and accuracy of a .22 match pistol.

For backup he would carry a 9mm Makarov, a small, flat automatic that was two-thirds the size and half the weight of the U.S. Army Colt .45, and twice as accurate. With one slug levered into the chamber and a full clip, it gave him a reserve of nine shots, enough to bail out of most situations.

Wearing a jacket in eighty-degree heat would seem odd, might draw attention to him, but he still had to conceal the weapons. The M-11 was equipped with a metal clip, so he could carry it on his belt at the small of his back. He had already tried it before a mirror. Nothing showed from the front. The Makarov slipped into a rear pocket. Though not the way he liked to carry a loaded pistol, it would do if he was careful.

Satisfied, he dismantled the M-11 and returned it to the case, snapping it closed. He took the Makarov from a drawer, checked the safety carefully, and slipped it into his pocket.

He left the house, again locking it carefully behind him. He went to the garage. He stepped inside and closed the door.

Placing the case behind the driver's seat and the pistol in the glove compartment, he took two rolled sheets of vinyl from the rear of the truck. He spread one of the sheets. It was hand-painted with the inscription:

CAROUSO'S FLOWERS
Decorative Plants & Flowers
We Deliver   Chestertown, Md.

He carefully peeled the backing from the white vinyl panels, then stuck them on the sides of the truck, covering the previous inscription. In the rear of the truck was the gift-wrapped plant with a card attached.

He opened the door and backed the truck out of the garage, letting it idle while he got out to close the garage door. He backed out of the driveway, turned onto the road, and drove away.

It was forty miles to Chestertown. He glanced at his wristwatch: 9:05. He drove carefully. He wasn't going to have his meticulous planning blown by a traffic accident or speeding ticket.

His watch read 10:03 when he drove through Chestertown. Cassidy would be at his boat. The hired woman would be in the kitchen cleaning up the breakfast dishes. Mrs. Cassidy would be somewhere in the house. He couldn't place the daughter. This nagged at him. Perhaps she would have returned to Philadelphia.

He continued north, passed the small airport, then turned left onto the county road. It was another twenty minutes before he reached the two brick pillars, turned left, and drove slowly through the quiet, grass-lined streets of Avon Meadows. When he reached the dirt driveway with the hand-painted sign that said "Land's End," he stopped the truck.

Climbing down from behind the wheel, he went to the right front wheel and pretended to examine the tire. He listened for sounds. There were no cars in the neighboring driveways. The houses seemed to be unoccupied.

Back in the truck he opened the attaché case and assembled the weapon. He took the small automatic from the glove compartment, checked the safety, and slipped it into his pocket. He took several moments to adjust an expensive dark wig over his hair. He took a pair of white gloves from his pocket and slipped them on, then reached for the plant and pulled it forward.

He gripped the wheel with both hands and stared straight ahead. He took a deep breath, lifting his shoulders; held it for several beats, then blew it out audibly. He started the motor, shifted into first, and followed the rutted lane past the border of trees and unkempt bushes.

The Chevy wagon was parked in the turnaround. The Datsun was not there. He would know in a minute if that was good or bad news. He pulled up behind the station wagon, placing the truck so that he would be hidden from the kitchen window when he got out, and cut the engine. He knew the hired woman would be looking at the truck from the windows over the kitchen sink.

He climbed down, slipping the weapon onto the belt at his back. He reached in and brought out the gift-wrapped plant. Moving around the front of the truck, he kept the weapon hidden and went straight for the back door. He mounted the several steps, pressed the doorbell, and waited, facing the door, the plant extended in both hands. He heard footsteps, a rustle of movement, and the door opened. The hired woman stood in the doorway.

"For Mrs. Ellen Starrett," he said.

"She's not home."

"Do you expect her?"

"She's gone into town." The woman stared, eyes narrowing. If he was local, she assumed she should know him. She didn't.

"This is for her." He took a step forward and the woman instinctively backed off a step as he knew she would. He pushed the plant into her hands, moving to the side and through the door. He pulled a pad of forms from his pocket.

"What is it, Mrs. Bolton?"

The voice came from the top of the stairs. It was rich, melodic, an educated voice, much traveled. He positioned himself so the weapon was obscured from both the hired woman and the stairway.

"Flowers for Mrs. Starrett," the woman said, looking up.

Sarah Cassidy appeared. She wore a flowered T-shirt and white shorts. She was a handsome woman, trim for her years. When she saw the flowering plant she smiled. "How nice," she said, descending the stairs, her eyes on the plant.

He took a step back, his right hand slipping behind his back. He dropped the receipt book and brought the M-11 up in a smooth arc, releasing the safety as it moved. The woman stopped her descent on the third step. Her right hand rested lightly on the banister. An expression of puzzlement crossed her face. He noticed the crinkling of the lines at her eyes and forehead. He pointed and pressed the trigger.

It was like the sound of a pellet gun: *brrrt-phffrt!*

The burst of subsonic .380 slugs hit her in the face, passed through her brain, and she was dead before she fell. The hired woman let the plant slip from her hands and it crashed to the floor. He turned and shot her before she could make a sound. She collapsed against the wall and slid to the floor slowly, her legs folded oddly under her, her body canted to one side.

He retrieved the receipt book from the floor and slipped it into his pocket. He moved quickly through the house, out through the sliding glass door that opened onto the deck, down the steps, across the small lawn, and down the steps to the dock. He was careful to maintain an unhurried, measured step. Cassidy would feel the footsteps, and he wanted him to assume that it was his wife. He didn't want him alarmed.

He reached the boat. The hatch was open. There was music coming from the cabin. He recognized the dramatic crescendos of the Franck Symphony in D.

Stepping into the cockpit, he moved carefully to the open hatch. Over the music he heard the tapping of a hammer.

"Cassidy!"

The tapping stopped. Cassidy came to the hatchway. His head and shoulders were framed in the opening. His expression was questioning, then he took in the man standing over him, recognizing the M-11. Some old instinct made him start to dodge in the cramped space and bring up the hammer in his hand. It was wasted effort. The M-11 was already pointed. *Brrrt-phffrt!* Cassidy leapt as though stung. He banged his head on the cabin roof and fell out of sight.

Moving quickly, the man climbed into the cabin to make certain that Cassidy was dead, then emerged, moved briskly off the dock, and returned to the house.

The sliding door off the deck was still ajar. He slipped inside. The sound of a hysterical female voice made his pulse race. *Merde!* he muttered to himself.

"Don't you understand what I'm saying? They're shot! Killed!"

He slipped silently through the room. He entered the front hallway from the kitchen. The daughter was on the telephone.

"I just found them! My God, don't you believe me?"

She saw him and caught her breath. "Oh, no," she gasped. "Oh, my God!"

He stepped in quickly, firing as he moved. She whirled away. Her arm flew up and she flung the telephone. He caught it in midair and held it to his ear.

"Hello, hello. Damnit, she's off. Hello! Where are you? Where are you calling from? Jesus Christ, what—"

He cradled the phone, breaking the connection. He bent over the young woman. She still had a pulse. He placed a gloved hand over her mouth and pinched her nose until the pulse died away. He rose to his feet and looked around.

The plant was on the floor. The clay pot was shattered, but the dirt and shards were still contained by the plastic wrapping. He snapped the M-11 to his belt and lifted the plant, taking care not to leave a thing, not a speck of dirt.

He left the house, letting the door lock behind him, and carried the broken plant to the truck. He placed the guns inside, then climbed in behind the wheel, removing the white gloves and the wig. He sat for a moment, letting the details run through his mind one last time, then, satisfied that he had left no loose ends, he started the truck.

He drove for ten minutes, then turned off onto a dirt farm road that stretched like a straight yellow line between two green fields. He drove slowly to keep the dust down. When he was far enough from the county road, he stopped and turned the truck around, then parked. He sat, listening to the quiet. He got out and walked around the truck. He could see everything in every direction. When he was satisfied that he was unobserved, he reached up and peeled the vinyl panels from the sides of the truck. He crumpled them and tossed them into the back. He climbed in behind the wheel, closed the door, and sat for a moment listening. Then he started the engine and drove back to the county highway.

He drove through Chestertown, and down Route 213 to Interstate 50. When he was on the highway south, he was able to relax. It was done. Cassidy silenced. No witnesses. Too bad about the women, but it couldn't be helped. He didn't dwell on it.

When he reached the cottage in St. Michaels, he put things away, took the skiff, and went fishing. He returned the boat to the livery about the time the pickup truck arrived at Land's End to take the hired woman home.

Chapter Two

It was difficult to tell Dalbey's age. He looked about fifty, maybe fifty-five. His hair was gray; the laugh lines around his eyes were permanent, and what looked like freckles showing through the tan on the backs of his hands were liver spots. But he was hard-muscled, lean, on a tall frame, and his movements were so naturally easy, so youthful, it was hard to pin him down to an exact year.

He was shooting a round of skeet with Harry Markham. He preferred to shoot trap because he considered it more difficult, but skeet was Markham's game, and Dalbey enjoyed competition.

They were even through station six, then Markham missed his second target at station seven. He stepped back, swearing to himself, and Dalbey moved into position. "Pull!"

Dalbey leaned forward, the shotgun extended. The clay targets rose from the houses at opposite ends of the skeet course, a low straightaway outgoer and a right-quartering incomer. Dalbey took the low target first, got under it, held and fired. He didn't wait for the break, but was already on the second target, pumping a new shell into the chamber. He followed the black disc arcing overhead. It was still on the rise. He stayed under it, patiently holding fire until it peaked, then fired as it began the descent, enjoying the rush of exhilaration as the gun blasted and the target shattered.

The two men walked to the next station. Markham grumbled about the wind coming off Long Island Sound. They both broke their targets and moved on.

Dalbey watched a sailboat that had come out of Black Rock Harbor. It had run before the wind—wing-on-wing—along the Connecticut shoreline to make the red buoy, and was now rounding, sheeting in for a close reach. A man stood at the wheel, hauling in the main, and a woman in a white bikini winched the sheet for the genny. Dalbey watched the boat, admiring the sure, athletic movements of the woman, but mentally criticizing the sail trim. Markham fired, breaking the target, and Dalbey brought his attention back to the skeet match.

They finished with Markham two down. Dalbey said, "Your tip."

"Thanks," Markham grumbled. He handed five dollars to the target boy, then broke his gun and followed Dalbey across the grass to the gun room.

It was hot, even for August. There was a breeze blowing off the water, but Dalbey was still sweating. He wore an old brown shooting vest with a padded right shoulder, the large pockets bagged from the weight of shotshells over the years. He wore a white polo shirt beneath the vest, faded chinos, and chukka boots—his shooting costume, Marianna used to call it.

He climbed the steps to the small porch and opened the door to the gun room, breathing deeply of the air-conditioned cool as he stepped inside. He held the door for Markham to enter, then closed it.

It was an unpretentious, functional room. Lockers along two walls. An empty gun rack. A stone fireplace at one end that was never used. Several vinyl-covered armchairs patched with gray tape. A long bench between the lockers, and a counter at the far end. Behind the counter were more racks for shotguns, boxes of shells, and the assorted paraphernalia of shooting. A bald-headed man with a gray mustache and an unlit pipe clenched in his teeth sat on a high stool behind the counter. He was bent over a gun stock with a checkering tool. He looked up when the two men came into the room.

"Mr. Dalbey," he said, making it sound like *Dah-bey*. "There's a message from your wife at the clubhouse."

"Thank you, Louis," Dalbey said.

Markham placed his shotgun on the counter. "Would you run a patch through this?" he said to Louis.

"I surely will Mr. Mah-kum," he said in his thrifty Yankee accent. He took Markham's autoloader and pressed the reject button to make certain the chamber was cleared and left it open. He reached for a cleaning rod and fitted a clean patch into the slot.

Dalbey always cleaned his own gun, a legacy from the Judge. *"Take care of your tools, boy, and they'll take care of you."* He hung the vest in the locker and removed a long, aluminum gun case, placing it on the bench. He took out the cleaning rod, oil, and patches and went to work.

Markham watched him for a minute, then said, "See you in the club."

"Right." Dalbey looked up as Markham left. He felt relief. He had known Markham for ten years, had already listened to the endless complaint about the advertising business, how the Democrats and lawyers had ruined the country, how we should kick the "Russkies" in the ass, what his divorce was costing him.

Louis left his stool and stood over Dalbey and admired the gun.

It was a 20-gauge Winchester, an old pump action with a 14¼-inch pull that fit like a third arm, and Dalbey never cleaned it without thinking of the Judge and the day they went to the ramshackle Winchester factory in New Haven to have it custom-fitted by Dave Carlson.

"Durkin," Louis said, displaying his expertise. The checkering on the Tonelli stock was an elegant fleur-de-lis, a trademark of the famous John Durkin, whom Dalbey remembered as a smiling, quiet man who had spent most of his life in the Winchester custom shop and seemed amused by his fame.

"Beautiful work," Louis said.

Dalbey nodded, accepting the compliment for Durkin. The Judge had come to visit him at Yale in 1948, the first time he had ever done such a thing. They had lunch at Morrie's, then drove out to the factory in the Judge's Ford. A surprise visit, a surprise gift of a special shotgun. In six months the Judge would be dead. God, he thought, was it really thirty-five years ago?

He figured the pump action had cost him the national skeet championship. He was tiring when he missed his

ninety-seventh target. But he wouldn't think of shooting
with anything else. It was the only gun he owned. And
quite frankly, he hadn't thought the championship all that
important.

Finished with the cleaning, he placed the shotgun
carefully in the padded case and snapped it shut. He took
a small canvas carryall from the locker, put the shooting
vest inside, and zippered it shut.

"Nice seeing you, Louis," he said.

"Bye, Mr. Dalbey."

He stepped out of the gun room and into the heat.
The sun was in the southeast, probably an hour before
noon, and it was already at least ninety degrees. He
followed the walk to the parking area that ran the length of
the clubhouse and beyond. He went to his car, a dark blue
1979 BMW 2002 sedan, opened the trunk, placed the
cases inside, and slammed it closed. He climbed the four
steps to the wide, long veranda of the Pelican Point Gun
Club and entered through the front door.

There was no one in the lobby except the steward at
the desk. He looked up and said, "Ah, Mr. Dalbey. A
message from your wife. She'd like you to call her at home."

"Thank you." Dalbey went to a bank of telephone
booths, rummaged in his pocket for a coin, and dialed the
number in New Canaan. It rang several times before
Eleanor answered.

"Hello," she said in the measured, finishing-school
tone that was Eleanor.

"Hi, this is Phil."

"Oh, Philip." Her voice brightened a degree. "You
got my message."

"I did. I'm at Pelican Point."

"Are you coming by today?"

"I was thinking I might. I was going to call."

"Good. I want to talk to you."

"About an hour. I'm having a drink with Harry

Markham." He could see her glancing at the clock, disapproving.

"I'll be here," she said, then added quickly, "Oh, Philip, you had a call from New York, a man named Steffinelli. He said it's *very* important that you get in touch with him."

Dalbey scowled at the phone. Vince Steffinelli. They hadn't been in touch for ten years, not since the Allende business in Chile. "He leave a number?"

"I have it here somewhere . . ." He heard her fumbling with papers. "Must be in the other room."

"It's okay," Dalbey said. "I'll call him from there. Thanks, El, see you in a bit."

He hung up and went to the bar. It was a Wednesday, a working day even for those who could afford Pelican Point, and there were few people in the club.

"Flip," Markham called from the table next to a window, "over here."

Dalbey didn't like being called Flip. It was the prep school nickname for Philip. Dalbey was used to the name, had even liked it when he was at Trinity-Pawling, but he didn't like toy names for adults. Markham, however, was a Choate old boy and there was no stopping him.

The barman came to the table and Dalbey ordered a Perrier and lime. "Not drinking?" Markham asked.

"Too early." Dalbey didn't drink at lunch anymore, found that it made him sleepy in the afternoons.

Markham lifted his gin and tonic. "Never too early." He drank from the glass, put it down. "Well, how's it going, old buddy?" His confidential account-executive tone.

"Keeps going," Dalbey said.

"Kids good?"

"Fine." They weren't all that good.

"Wife?"

"Couldn't be better." He hadn't seen her for three weeks and wondered what she wanted to talk about.

The television screen over the bar caught Markham's

attention, and he listened to interviews with the U.S. Marine force in Lebanon. They were in battle dress, hunkered behind sandbag bunkers bristling with weapons.

"Goddamned Russkies," Markham said. "They're behind this whole Lebanon bullshit. I mean, they oughta just turn those marines loose and let 'em kick some ass."

There was something on about the town of Glen Cove, Long Island, denying beach passes to members of the Soviet delegation to the U.N. who lived in the town, claiming they were spies. The U.S. State Department was upset.

"Run them suckers out," Markham said. "Get rid of that damned United Nations. Take our money, give us nothing but crap."

Dalbey was amused by Markham's diatribe. His approach had an appealing simplicity. One adversary, one solution. He was glad, however, that Markham was selling soap and automobiles and not setting foreign policy. He finished his Perrier and pushed back his chair, rising. "I have to run." He extended his hand to Markham.

"I'm just getting started," Markham said.

"I know." Dalbey thought Markham was a complete fool. The most remarkable thing about him was that he had graduated from Choate and from Brown, two tough schools. There had to have been something smart about him once, but there was no evidence of it now. He didn't know why he liked him.

Dalbey went to the bar and signed the check. He waved to Markham, acknowledged a few other members, and left.

He opened all the windows in the car. It was rare that he used the air-conditioning. He drove through Bridgeport, picked up the southbound Connecticut Turnpike for a few miles, then headed north on Route 25. He got on the Merritt Parkway and drove south and got off at the New Canaan exit, then drove north on Route 124, a two-lane blacktop. He followed the double yellow line into town—a few blocks of chic, expensive shops and restaurants—then out again and into what was known, generally, as the back country.

A mile out of town he turned onto Cat Rock Road, a narrow, twisting blacktop without shoulders or guardrails. Dalbey didn't like the road. It was a maze of blind, hairpin turns, bumpy and poorly engineered; a horse-and-carriage road grown quaint. In the winter it was treacherous. Teenagers used Cat Rock for joyriding, straddling both lanes and negotiating the turns at sixty mph. Dalbey drove it because it was the most direct route to his house.

The road climbed gradually but steadily through woods that were supposed to look natural and untouched. Low stone walls paralleled the road. Occasional mailboxes leaned on the edge of the road, close to driveways that snaked into the woods and disappeared into carefully casual plantings that hid the houses.

Dalbey honked the horn as he approached a particularly sharp curve on the climb up Conklin's Hill. He hugged the inside right lane around the curve. There was a steep forty-foot drop off the outside lane, and a small brook at the bottom studded with granite boulders. A flimsy wooden guardrail protected the curve. He topped the hill, then wound through a densely wooded area that broke into open meadow where a few horses grazed, then lawns and houses.

Dalbey's own house was set back from the road. It was a two-story white clapboard Colonial on three acres. Shrubs and well-tended flower beds surrounded the house. The second floor was gabled; the wood-shingle roof was weathered dark brown. Dalbey remembered when the shingles were new, when Eleanor was in the full fury of remodeling what was known in those days as the Bascom place, when Arthur was a baby.

Eleanor's mother found the house. Eleanor was a Worthington and the Worthingtons had lived in New Canaan for ten generations, as Dalbey had learned when he wondered, aloud, why anyone would want to live in New Canaan.

They had been married for three months and were living in his apartment in New York City.

"It's the old Bascom place," Eleanor had said. "You'll love it. It's just a half mile from Mother's."

"I like New York," he had said.

"But you're away so much." It was true, he traveled a great deal. "I don't like being here alone. It frightens me." She had lived in New York for two years, but with a roommate.

"I don't think I'd like commuting."

"Daddy does it," she said. "He doesn't mind."

They bought the house, but Dalbey also kept the apartment. He lived in New Canaan, but when he worked late, which was often, or arrived on a late flight, which was often, he stayed in the city. It was not unusual for him to be in Europe for two weeks at a time. When the kids were small he tried to be in New Canaan as much as possible, but his absence was expected and accepted.

Dalbey shifted down and turned into the drive. A boy was cutting grass, crossing the lawn on a tractor mower. Dalbey drove slowly up the drive, past the side of the house, and parked in the wide, black-topped space between the rear of the house and the two-car garage. Eleanor's red Toyota wagon was in the garage.

He got out of the car and closed the door. The busy noise of the mower competed with the labored whir of an air conditioner in an upstairs window. He stood for a moment looking at a huge, old elm at the rear of the house, a climbing tree with stout, welcoming limbs. One spring when Arthur was eight, he had hacked at the tree with a hatchet, leaving a network of gashes that began to bleed sap. The tree actually seemed to be in pain, and Sharon, five then, had wailed hysterically until a tree surgeon came and painted the wounds with tar. It had a sad, lonely look now; empty of children.

Dalbey entered the house through the back door, letting the screen door announce him.

He moved through the small alcove they always called the mud room, into the large kitchen. He listened, heard a radio softly, the muted sound of a vacuum cleaner in an upstairs bedroom. Wednesday. The cleaning woman. He went to the doorway and called, "I'm home."

Eleanor answered from the second floor, but he couldn't make out what she said. He went to the refrigerator in search of a beer. He always kept several cases of Budweiser in the basement. Eleanor hated beer, so there were usually a few cans in the frig. He swung open the door. The Budweiser was on the bottom, but there were five bottles of Amstel Light on the top shelf. Odd, he thought, scowling. He reached for the can of Budweiser, closed the door, and had snapped the top open when Eleanor came into the kitchen.

"Philip," she said, advancing. "How nice." She turned her head slightly, offering her cheek. Dalbey responded, kissing her lightly. "How was the shooting?"

"Hot," Dalbey said.

"Oh, isn't it dreadful."

It was always the same small talk. It seemed strained without the buffer of kids to give it substance, but they kept it going, moving around each other politely, careful not to crack the veneer of civility that would reveal the void beneath the surface. This was Eleanor's life, patterned after generations of Worthingtons, and she maintained it carefully. He fit into it as the husband, the successful businessman who traveled, the father of her children. She never probed his life outside of New Canaan. It simply wasn't part of her rigid patterns. There were no surprises with Eleanor. He felt sorry for her without fully understanding why.

"Your friend's number is in the study," she said.

"Friend?" He couldn't really call Steffinelli a friend.

"Well, he called on your private number. I assumed."

He'd had the private, unlisted number installed in his study when Sharon turned fourteen and took over the family telephone. That was eight years ago. He hadn't seen Steffinelli for ten. How could he have gotten the number? He answered his own question, smiling. Easy. They got whatever they wanted.

"I'll see what he wants." Dalbey took the beer with him, went through the dining room, the formal living room, then down a short hallway with the study on the left and a guest bedroom on the right. He opened the door on the left and entered, leaving it ajar.

He read the slip of paper on his desk, lifted the telephone receiver. He punched the area code for Manhattan, then the next seven digits. He waited for two rings, then a female voice said, "West Development Company."

"Mr. Steffinelli, please."

"Who's calling, please?"

"Philip Dalbey."

"One moment, please."

Steffinelli came on the line. "Phil Dalbey," he said in the nasal voice that Dalbey remembered well. "Jesus, man, it's been a long time."

"Ten years."

"That long? Jesus."

"You left a message to call."

"Yeah, listen, Phil, very important that we talk." Dalbey waited through several beats of silence, then Steffinelli said, "Not now, not on the phone. In the office. Tomorrow."

"Well, Vince," he hedged. "I don't know—I—"

"It's important," Steffinelli went on, talking over him. "Phil, this is Crisis One."

The telephone code talk triggered a disturbing pulse-surge in Dalbey. It brought back things that he thought were permanently buried. "Crisis One" meant that whatever Steffinelli wanted to talk about was considered life or death.

"You still at the same place?" Dalbey asked.

"Jesus, no. We seem to move every three months." Steffinelli gave an address on West Forty-sixth Street. "Between Ninth and Tenth. How about ten o'clock?"

"What floor?"

"Just look for West Development."

"See you at ten."

He hung up, staring at the phone, still hearing Steffinelli's voice. What the hell could be life or death? He knew there wasn't going to be an answer until the next day, so he shrugged it off and went back to the kitchen, still carrying his beer.

Eleanor was seated on a stool at the counter listening on the phone, taking notes. She smiled, waggled her pen at the round oak table. Dalbey took a seat and drank some beer, watching her.

There were streaks of gray in her dark blond hair, and he thought, she's getting older. She wasn't pretty, but handsome, with the kind of face—skin taut over high cheekbones—that improves with age. He would describe her as patrician, the product of private schools, expensive orthodontics, and two-hundred-year-old houses. Her hair was swept straight back and twisted into a bun at the nape of her long neck. Her nose was straight, the eyes pale blue, and she had a wide smile of perfect teeth. Her body was still good, and Dalbey wondered what she did for exercise. She was fifty, and he pondered, a bit sadly, what would become of her.

When she hung up the phone she said, "Sorry about that. Local politics. John Steiner, remember him, that awful man, owns the plumbing service? He's going to run for school board. Incredible! He's never read a book."

"You wanted to talk to me," Dalbey said.

She caught her breath with a little "ah" sound, said, "Yes," and came to the table, changing her expression slightly, and sat opposite him. "Philip, I'm getting a divorce."

He had been lifting the beer can and he stopped,

holding it a foot off the table. His mouth opened and closed. He lowered the beer can to the table. She was waiting for him to say something, but he didn't know what to say.

"Well?"

"I—" He lifted his hands. "I—"

"Surely you're not surprised."

"As a matter of fact I am."

"Now, Philip, don't tell me you're going to be difficult."

"No, I don't mean *that*. I mean, it's just something you've never said before."

"Well, it's time. The children are grown. You've never liked any of this." She included the house and the twenty-six years in her gesture. "It's time."

"I guess so."

"I wanted to tell you before you got the papers in the mail. I certainly don't want it to be unfriendly."

Dalbey realized he was acting stupidly, but he didn't know what was expected of him. His relationship with Eleanor had solidified into such predictable patterns that he knew the required response to all situations, and if there were deviations, they were so minor that adjustment was easy. Not this time. He leaned back in his chair and gripped the edge of the table with both hands. He must have looked odd, because Eleanor smiled.

"I do think you're a little upset. I'm surprised, and I'm flattered. You're a very nice man really," she said. Then she became practical. "I'm sure you'll agree I should have the house. The car, of course. I have my own money, as you know, so there's no problem there." She paused, as though thumbing through her mind for what she had planned to say next. "I'll be selling the house. It's too big for me. Bertha Keillor says she can get close to half a million. Isn't that amazing?"

She's already talked this over with a real estate agent, Dalbey thought, and yes, it was amazing. They had paid ninety thousand dollars and thought it was high.

"I have to go into town," Eleanor said. "There'll be plenty of time for you to get your things, and you're welcome here anytime. I don't suppose you'll be staying over."

He shook his head, mumbling, "No, I have to . . ." but she wasn't listening.

She was back at the counter gathering her purse and keys and notebook. Then she was at his side to peck her lips on his cheek. "We'll talk. Lock the door when you leave." Then she was gone.

He rose from the chair and went to the kitchen window to watch her stride to the garage. "Well, I'll be goddamned," he said to himself. He chuckled softly, shaking his head slowly from side to side. "I'll be damned."

When the Toyota disappeared down the drive he went back to the table and lifted the can of beer.

That's that, he thought. Just like that. "You'll never leave Eleanor," he remembered Marianna saying. "Not really, not completely. As long as there's an Eleanor, you don't have to make a commitment. She makes it too easy for you. I think about us sometimes as . . . well, you know, but I know it's not possible. She has you, Philip, and you like it that way." Maybe you were right, Marianna.

He walked through the house, stopping in each room and slowly looking around. None of the furnishings were his, none of the bric-a-brac, but there were memories in every room. He went through, touching this and that. Twenty years of kids. Although he hadn't realized it before, there was a lot of his life in the house.

The study was his room, but there was very little in it that he would take away. He went through the guest bedroom where he had slept the past eight years. Some clothing he would want, but that's all. He went back to the study and called Bill Shoreham, his lawyer in New Canaan.

A receptionist said Shoreham was lunching at the Racquet Club. He called there and had him paged.

"Shoreham here."

"Bill, this is Phil Dalbey. I'm out at the house. I'd like to see you."

"Here or at the office?"

"The club will be fine. I can be there in about fifteen minutes."

"I'm on the patio," Shoreham said.

"On my way."

He hung up the phone, took a last look around, and left the room. The vacuum cleaner was wheezing in the living room. He passed through, saying hello to a woman he didn't know, and left through the back door.

It was going to be a relief not to have to work at a relationship that didn't really exist, but he also knew that he was going to miss something about it.

He backed the car around, stopping for a long look at the old elm, then swung out and down the drive. He stopped at the end of the drive to check the traffic on Cat Rock Road. There was a white van parked off the road next to a utility pole about fifty yards to the right. There was a lineman at the top of the pole, leaning back against a leather belt, supported by climbing spikes. Dalbey stared at the man, thinking, hot work on a day such as this. The man's face was turned, so Dalbey only saw his white hair. Old for a lineman, he thought. He made another check for traffic and pulled out to the left.

About a mile down the road it suddenly occurred to him that he hadn't seen a lineman climb a pole in years. They always seemed to use cherry pickers nowadays. He slowed the car, thinking of going back, not sure why. The call from Steffinelli had him jumpy, of course. The guy was probably with a cable TV company. They used the same poles. He shifted down, speeded up, shifted again.

He drove through the town, then south to the turnoff for the Racquet Club, another membership he wasn't going to need.

The patio was half-filled with lunch guests, and Bill Shoreham was alone at a table under an umbrella.

"You eating alone?" Dalbey said, dropping into a chair.

"Finished," Shoreham said. He was average height, sandy-haired with a reddish mustache, and a face that was lightly freckled. He was younger than Dalbey, but his waist was spreading and a mound of belly strained against the buttons of his shirt.

Dalbey ordered a Budweiser and noticed that Shoreham was drinking Amstel Light. "Popular beer."

"Beer of the month," Shoreham said. "Actually it's not bad."

"I think I need a lawyer."

"So I hear."

"You hear?"

"I'm also Eleanor's lawyer."

"You're handling it for her?"

"No, I'm not."

"Well, then—"

"No, I can't. And if I could, I wouldn't."

"Conflict of interest?"

"Not that exactly, but I've known you both too long. I couldn't do a fair job for either side."

"It'll be friendly."

"That's how they all start," Shoreham said. "Then the lawyers start earning their fees."

"What do you suggest?"

"Eleanor has retained Peet, Hogson and Trilby. I think she went to school with Don Trilby's sister. I would suggest you have your New York lawyers make arrangements after you've been served. It's clean, it's business-like, and you'll know you're not being pushed around by Worthingtons."

Dalbey's beer came. He waited for it to be poured. He took a swallow, then said, "You make it sound grim."

"It can get very unpleasant. Right now Eleanor doesn't

want anything but a divorce. When a lawyer explores your finances, he might convince her differently."

"Swell guys."

"It's just a good idea to gear up for the worst and be glad when it doesn't happen."

"Well, what do *you* think of it?"

"Of what?"

"The divorce."

"I'm amazed it took this long."

"Never thought she'd do it. Never entered my mind."

"Well, that's the way it goes. You live with some-body twenty-five years and suddenly you're dealing with a complete stranger."

Dalbey knew Shoreham was talking about his own unpleasant divorce, but what he said could apply to Eleanor. The woman he had just talked to wasn't the Eleanor he knew. She was so positive, so in charge. She was like an emerging chrysalis about to fly, and Dalbey had to admit he kind of envied her.

Shoreham signed the check and said, "I've got to get back. We have a closing at three." He got to his feet. "Can't imagine why anyone would buy a house on a day like this." He leaned forward, extending his hand.

Dalbey reached up and grasped the hand. "You're a friend," he said. "Thanks."

"Yeah, well . . ." Shoreham seemed about to say some-thing more, but thought better of it. "See you around."

Dalbey watched him walk away. He had been a friend for a long time, had known Eleanor most of her life. His sister had been Eleanor's closest teenage friend. Dalbey lifted the empty Amstel Light bottle, turning it in his hand.

Chapter Three

The cab dropped him on Ninth Avenue at nine-fifty
A.M. It was already hot, the temperature eighty-one degrees and rising. The heat wave was making news, and the
pale, cloudless sky said that no relief was in sight. He
walked west on Forty-sixth Street. It was shabby residential, what used to be known as Hell's Kitchen. Four-, five-,
and six-story tenements for the most part, their fronts
draped with black metal fire escapes. The brick was
painted red, yellow, or gray, but mostly red.

Dalbey walked slowly past the neat rows of battered
trash cans that sagged against iron fencing, their lids
chained to window grillwork. Clusters of black and green
plastic trash bags were piled at the curbs around frail,
slender trees. He stopped at Hartley House and read a
hand-lettered announcement that the Forty-sixth Street
Block Association would be holding a rally. Then he
crossed the street.

No parking was allowed. The street sign said it was a
tow-away zone, but there were vans parked in front of
Acme Plumbing Supplies and New Day Laundry, and a
few cars.

Two kids sat on a stoop in the middle of the block
with a portable radio the size of a Hammond organ tuned
to WLIR "Rock Around the Clock."

Dalbey walked to the playground near the end of the
block. He stood outside the high fence and watched a few
kids play one-on-one, then retraced his steps to Dario's
Grocery. Number 447 was across the street.

It was one of the few brownstones in the block. The facade bore the signs of unskilled remodeling, pale blotches of patching painted over, the crude scars of window ledges removed. The three upstairs floors looked residential. Windows framed with curtains, green plants, a white bucket of flowers on the top-floor fire escape. Air conditioners, like trophy heads, jutted from windowsills.

He crossed the street and climbed the five steps to the entrance. A sign to the right of the door announced: WEST DEVELOPMENT CO. He pushed through the doorway and stepped into a shabbily carpeted foyer with a closed door on the left, a stairway straight ahead, and an opened doorway on the right. He went to the doorway and leaned into a cluttered office with three desks. One was occupied by a middle-aged woman typing. The walls were painted gray and decorated with a Caterpillar bulldozer calendar and large pictures of building-remodeling projects in progress. The woman looked him over and asked, "Can I help you?"

"Mr. Steffinelli?"

She reached for a telephone. "Your name?" He gave his name. He watched her fingers dance over the touchtone keyboard. Six one one, he said to himself. The woman spoke his name into the phone, the hung up and said, "Someone will be down for you." She went back to her typing.

There was no place to sit. He glanced up and around at the high, sculptured ceiling. He stepped into the hallway and was wondering what was behind the closed door when a young woman appeared at the top of the stairs. She started down, and when he looked up, she stopped with a hand on the banister and said, "Mr. Dalbey? Won't you come up, please?"

She waited for him to reach her, then led him the rest of the way. On the second-floor landing they were stopped by a heavy metal door. On the wall, to the right of the door, there was a digital panel with ten numbered keys. She reached out and punched a code into the panel. Eight four two two eight, Dalbey committed it to memory. The door buzzed and she turned the knob, pushing it open, holding it while he passed through.

He followed her into a bright, empty hallway with closed doors on either side. She opened the first door on the right and Dalbey followed her into a prototype outer office of plain beige walls, Formica-covered desks, gray filing cabinets. The large print on the wall, an early Braque, was typical government-office decor, the kind of thing GSO bought by the gross. The few green plants were a personal touch. Just inside the door were three soft leather chairs and a circular coffee table carefully decorated with copies of *National Geographic*.

"Would you please wait?" The woman indicated the leather chairs while she glanced at her desk. The light on her phone was lit. "He's still on a call," she said. "He knows you're here. Would you like coffee?"

"No, thank you."

Her duty completed, she smiled a patent smile and circled her white Formica desk. She concentrated on the paper in her typewriter. Dalbey had been trying to place her accent. There was a tinge of Wisconsin, but it was more Western than Midwest.

The intercom buzzed. She lifted the phone. "Yes?"

When she replaced the receiver she swiveled her chair around to face the computer terminal behind her. She pulled open a shallow drawer in the console table, studied something inside, then punched the keys on the computer. Her body blocked the keyboard, but Dalbey assumed she was entering the access code to the mainframe computer at Langley. When she had the information she wanted, she called on the intercom and said, "In 1958 he was teaching at Temple University in Philadelphia."

Dalbey reached for a magazine and had turned to an article on Montana when the light on the secretary's desk went dark. Seconds later the door to the inner office opened and Vince Steffinelli, grayer and heavier, appeared.

He advanced on Dalbey, grinning widely. "Hey, hey, look at you. Jesus, you look good."

Dalbey stood and intercepted the extended hand. "Vince," he said.

"Goddamn, you look great." Steffinelli released his hand and guided him toward the inner office. "Janet," he said, stopping Dalbey with a touch on the arm, "this is Phil Dalbey."

The young woman at the desk smiled. "We met."

"He's one of us," Steffinelli said, and Dalbey noticed a slight change in the woman's expression, as though suddenly recognizing him. "One of the best," Steffinelli added, then he nudged Dalbey forward. "No calls."

The office was not large, but big enough for a couch against one wall, cabinets along another, and a large wooden desk. There were the usual photographs: a middle-aged woman, two college-age girls, a smiling young man in cap and gown. On one wall was a framed Mercator map of the world. The floor was carpeted in deep blue. There were two chairs facing the desk, and Steffinelli offered one of them to Dalbey.

"It's been a long time," Steffinelli said, taking the chair behind the desk.

"Ten years," Dalbey said, but he was thinking, I rarely saw Vince. They did everything through the blind drop Dalbey had worked out.

"We really missed you. I know why you left, but I figured you'd sort it out and come back."

Dalbey shrugged. It was old territory. He had been over it in his mind a hundred times. He didn't want to talk about it. When he had decided he was helping the bad guys, he had quit.

"I was never an employee," Dalbey said. "I was just helping out."

"For twenty years."

Dalbey didn't answer. Nineteen years to be exact. He had trouble with time these days. He noticed, more and

promote weight lo__ __
the Boston accounting execu__ __ __
lost more than 60 pounds, exercises
four to five days a week (basketball,
squash, yoga and strength training
are favorites) and needs only very
minimal insulin.

Insulin is the hormone that moves
sugar out of the blood and into the
body's cells. With diabetes, the body
either can't create the hormone
(type 1) or, more commonly, becomes
resistant to its effects (type 2). In
both cases, insulin injections are a
common treatment. (January marks
the 100th anniversary of insulin's
first use in a diabetes patient.)

A type 2 diagnosis is frequently
met with a mixture of fear, dread,
guilt—and drugs. "People with type 2
diabetes often end up with four or

UB
t-
oll.
go
Recipe:
hred-
cup raw
soning
marina-
–faced
l. *528*
t,
dium,

○ *LIGHT*
cheese
eatballs.
a layer
spinach
or fiber.

↑ *BETTER* TUNA MELT
After draining water, mix
tuna with diced red onion,
celery and pickle, and
1 teaspoon each mayo and
lemon juice. Top bell pep-
per halves with tuna and
½ slice cheddar. Bake at
300°F for 7 minutes. *327
calories, 13g fat, 673mg
sodium, 4g fiber*

*Kelsey Ogletree writes on
food and health for* Bon
Appétit, Shape *and other
magazines.*

more, that the past seemed to be compressed. Twenty years blended into twenty weeks. It was like ancient history and it was like yesterday.

"Crisis One," Dalbey said.

Steffinelli was looking at the map on the wall, his mind somewhere in the past, and Dalbey knew that it was a map of "out there," a place of friends and enemies, bravery and treachery. To the people who sat in the offices and lived with their computers, it was a fantasy world like Tolkien's *Lord of the Rings*. Steffinelli might have been thinking about that time in Prague when Dalbey almost walked into it, when everything went haywire and they were waiting for the messenger.

Dalbey's voice brought him back and Steffinelli said, "Oh, right. Right." He opened the manila folder that lay in the center of his desk. He pursed his lips, as though deciding where to start, then lifted a newspaper clipping and held it out to Dalbey. "You hear about this?"

Dalbey leaned forward to take the clipping. It was *The New York Times* story about the murder of Daniel Cassidy and his family. He had already read it.

"He was one of us," Steffinelli said.

"That's what it says."

"You remember him?"

Dalbey stared hard at the face in the newspaper clipping. It was a file photo and showed a man in his fifties, balding, wearing steel-rimmed glasses. "Should I?"

"You were on a mission with him."

Dalbey scowled, studied the face. "Not possible," he said. In the first place he had never been on a mission with anybody. "I never saw this face before."

Steffinelli looked at the folder on his desk. "July twenty-third, 1943."

"That was forty years ago." Dalbey worried his lower lip with two fingers and looked hard at the face of Daniel Cassidy, thinking back. "I was eighteen."

"Holland." Steffinelli watched for Dalbey's reaction.

"Code name Calico."

"I remember." What Dalbey remembered was terror and confusion.

"Cassidy was in command," Steffinelli said.

He had dark, curly hair, Dalbey remembered, damp from the spray that exploded over the blunt end of the landing craft. He was the only one who laughed.

"Twelve in the team," Steffinelli read. "Ten were going ashore."

"I was just the gunner," Dalbey said. "It was my first time out." He had been trained as an aerial gunner then transferred to G-2 before he ever flew a mission. He was in London, had learned to his surprise and chagrin that intelligence work was paperwork, when he heard that OSS was looking for an experienced rock climber. He signed on and found himself volunteered as a gunner.

He met Cassidy and the others, a blur of names and faces, at a final briefing. A ship would take them to within five miles of the beach, the landing craft the rest of the way. Ten would go ashore, the rest would return to the ship. "Don't screw around on that beach," Dalbey remembered a Navy commander saying. "We wanna get our asses outta there." It was a touchy mission because nothing as big as a landing craft had ever been brought ashore. The Dutch underground had set it up, and the section of beach, way in the north between Callantsoog and Juliana-dorp, was not mined. They were due ashore at 0100. A swinging red lantern would spot the landing area and announce that it was clear.

Dalbey was assigned to man both guns on the LSD, the twin-50's that he knew, and a 20mm cannon that he figured he could handle in a pinch.

"It's coming back?" Steffinelli asked.

"Yeah, it is, but I don't see what that's got to do with anything."

"You got the shit kicked out of you."

"You're not kidding. They must have had a god-damned panzer division on that beach."

He remembered they came in through the surf, steering on the red light. There was no moon. It looked like a piece of cake, but the landing team was tense, silent, huddled in the bow. When the war was over, the Allies would learn that the Dutch underground had been penetrated by the Germans from the beginning. The sand ground under the boat, and the forward ramp dropped away and landed with a thud. The ten men bounded down the ramp, through the surf, and were barely on the beach when the Germans, eager to grab the landing craft as a trophy, opened fire.

Floodlights bathed the scene with a stark, eerie light. The ten men on the beach stopped in their tracks. Machine-gun fire broke out and Dalbey leapt in his seat behind the gun, startled, his heart pounding. There was the sound of hail rattling on the hull of the landing craft. Then the men were running through the surf and Dalbey was shooting. The LSD's engines started to roar in reverse, and some-one was screaming at the Navy bos'n to wait for the team.

"We were lucky to get out of there," Dalbey said.

"Left one man on the beach."

"He was down. Nine made it back, which was amazing. The one guy, Slattery—he was dragging himself across the sand. But I tell you, there was no waiting. Those Navy guys were already pulling out."

"We believe Slattery murdered Dan Cassidy and his family."

Dalbey stared. He heard what Steffinelli said, but his mind was still on that beach forty years ago.

"It is the opinion of the Agency," Steffinelli went on, suddenly sounding official, "that he also killed Jonathan Steach, Howard Benjamin, Arnold Westman, Art Wilson, and Sean McCarthy."

"I knew Steach. He was my European contact for years." Dalbey might have added that Jon Steach was a confidant, the closest thing he had to a friend in the sixties. "He was killed by a car bomb in Munich."

"That's right."

"Terrorists."

"Official explanation," Steffinelli said. "We now believe it was Slattery."

Dalbey had the feeling he should also know the others, but he had to ask, "Who are the others?"

"All were Operation Calico."

"Calico. I don't remember any of them. I can't believe Steach was there. We never mentioned it."

"That kind of a mission, you don't get to know the people. You forget them."

"Except for Slattery," Dalbey said.

"That's right."

Dalbey had to take a deep breath. "You're saying that Slattery is killing everybody who was on that mission forty years ago."

"That's right."

"For leaving him on the beach."

"That's right."

"What committee at Langley came up with this brilliant concept?"

"A computer," Steffinelli said. "We had three people killed in two years, no motives, no suspects. All about the same age, all near retirement. Benjamin and his wife shot by an intruder. Neighbors in next apartment hear nothing. Silencer. McCarthy stabbed in the street in Athens. No witnesses. When Cassidy got it, we started matching their files, looking for a common thread."

"Calico."

"And old OSS guys, and the fact that they stayed in the service."

"Coincidence," Dalbey said.

"Okay, but then we ran a follow-up on the whole Calico team." He looked down at the file. "Roger Hall missing in action in 'forty-five. Stowe killed with the

Rangers in 'forty-four. One died of a heart attack in 'sixty-eight. Jon Steach you know about. Arnold Westman became an accountant in St. Paul, Minnesota, killed in a car bombing in July 'eighty-two, no suspects, no motive. Three still alive . . ." His voice trailed off.

They sat for long seconds, staring at each other, letting it register.

"It's crazy," Dalbey said. Steffinelli nodded. "Doesn't make sense."

"Does when you get to know Slattery. A real sweetheart." Steffinelli consulted the file, turned a sheet of paper. "British found him in Sachsenhausen in 'forty-five. He was a mess. The Gestapo had worked him over real good. Spent six months in a military hospital. Stayed in Europe. Made Amsterdam his home base. Used his separation money and back pay to get into the black market. Contract killer, they say, but no proof. No arrests. Turns up in the Congo and Biafra as a mercenary. Spotted in Hong Kong in 'seventy-one. In Greece in 'seventy-two. Word gets around that he'll hit anybody, anywhere, for the right price. In 'eighty-one he drops out of sight."

"He's got to be in his sixties," Dalbey said.

"Sixty-three."

"It's too outlandish to believe."

"I'd agree, except we got a lot of dead people. And the computer picked him."

"How would he know who was on that mission? He was just one of the team."

"Records. There's records on everything. He had connections. You want to find out bad enough, you can get the names."

Dalbey knew that was true. "Nobody has seen him?"

"Nobody. We had watchers on his house for a couple months. Nothing. Not even a phone call."

"The house in Amsterdam."

"Right. His wife is there, but she hasn't seen him,

won't talk about him. We figure he was in Maryland last month."

"And you figure I'm next in line," Dalbey said. "How about the other two still living?"

"Calvin Graham and Peter Evans. Graham is retired in Tucson. Evans runs a dive operation in Key Largo."

They sat back again for more long, silent seconds, then Dalbey said, "What am I supposed to do?"

"Be careful."

"That's it? That's all the United States government has to say? Be careful?"

"No proof," Steffinelli said. "It's still a theory. One of you gets it, we hope to be close enough to bring him down."

"Jesus." Dalbey looked more closely at the newspaper clipping, scanning the details. He whistled lightly through his teeth. "It's crazy."

"I never said the guy was sane."

"Incredible." Dalbey stared at the floor, then put his head back, taking a deep breath that he blew at the ceiling. When he finally looked back at Steffinelli, he said, "You're serious about this."

Steffinelli nodded, and Dalbey sat back, crossed his legs and absently straightened the seam of his trouser leg, mentally adjusting to the situation. "I take it the guy's really good."

"Has to be."

"Has to be," Dalbey repeated under his breath.

"At least you know he's coming."

"That's a comfort." Dalbey's fingers strayed to the seam of the expensive tropical worsted jacket, under the left-hand sleeve, and he was slightly reassured by the hard line of the foot-long baton he carried there in a heavy-duty pocket.

Steffinelli picked up on the unconscious gesture. "I got something for you." He reached into a drawer and brought out a holstered revolver. He placed it on the desk and pushed it over to Dalbey. "Take this."

Dalbey raised a hand, palm out, but Steffinelli was back into the drawer. He added a box of cartridges, a federal permit, an official ID. "In case you get picked up."

"No thanks," Dalbey said. "I've never been any good with a handgun."

"You'd be surprised how good you can get when it's important."

Dalbey had to smile. Having barely qualified as marksman with the M-1911 .45-caliber semiautomatic pistol, it always amazed him to read in the newspaper how some 120-pound female had picked up a .38 Special for the first time in her life and placed five shots in a neat one-inch pattern in the back of a husband or lover who was running like hell. They always said, "I did it because I loved him." Dalbey pulled the jacket aside to show the baton.

Steffinelli knew that the baton was an effective weapon, but he said, "We're not talking about some mugger looking for subway fare back to Brooklyn. This guy's a pro." He pushed the revolver forward a few inches. "Take it. I hope you won't need it."

Dalbey reached for it reluctantly. He dropped the spring holster in his lap, examined the pistol, a .32-caliber Smith & Wesson. Chrome-and-pearl handled. He broke the action, spun the chamber. "Nice little gun. Got something I can carry this in?"

Steffinelli called the secretary and she brought a large manila envelope. She didn't seem surprised to see the gun and held the envelope open while Dalbey slipped the holstered weapon inside. She smiled and withdrew.

Dalbey checked his watch. "Meeting my son for lunch," he said. They were both standing in the middle of the office. They shook hands.

"We'll be in touch." Steffinelli handed Dalbey a folded sheet of paper. "These are the numbers where I can be reached. You call me for anything, you hear?"

Steffinelli walked him to the metal door and let him out. "Good luck, Phil." He closed the door when Dalbey was halfway down the stairs.

As Dalbey reached the bottom step, the front door opened and a young man entered. He said nothing to the woman in the downstairs office, just nodded as he passed Dalbey and went up the stairs. Dalbey poked his head into the office where the woman was typing. She looked up when he said, "Good-bye, thank you," and she said, "You're welcome."

He stepped into the street with the deep-rooted instincts of the field man that ten years could not erase. The quick scan to find the odd pattern or what was *too* normal, the workers not quite busy enough, the hot dog vender in a residential street, the car seen too often, the moving curtain in an empty window. The dread of the unexpected hand on his shoulder and the softly spoken, "Would you come with us please."

He paused to allow a professional dog walker to pass with her string of unruly clients, then walked east.

He felt strangely serene. He knew he should be feeling anxiety or concern, but he was one of those people who react to elemental stress with a fatalistic calm. It went beyond the will to survive. Faced with real danger, he reacted instinctively to master the situation, control it and subdue it.

Dalbey was a careful man, but if pressed, he would have to admit that it was in those situations when the adrenaline was pumping—the knockdown at sea, the avalanche, the skidding car—that he felt the most alive.

If he couldn't avoid Slattery, he could at least cut the odds in his favor. His mind raced with plans and possibilities, and he realized that he knew nothing about Slattery, a condition he would have to remedy.

Chapter Four

Dalbey arrived early at the Overseas Press Club. His son was not waiting in the lobby or the small alcove with the chattering wire service teletypes, so he went into the lounge to wait.

There were half a dozen lunch crowd regulars at the bar that ran the length of the east wall. It was a large room with oak beams and paneling. A huge chandelier hung from the two-story ceiling. A fireplace and grand piano dominated the south wall. There were several tables with straight-backed chairs adjacent the bar, then a four-foot-high wooden divider, and the rest of the room was filled with leather couches and easy chairs and tiny veneer tables for drinks. It smelled of furniture polish and old age.

He went to an easy chair that gave him a view of the doorway and the lobby beyond. He glanced at the manila envelope in his lap, thought of checking it, and changed his mind. It felt like a gun. He glanced at his watch, then studied the men at the bar. They were mostly public relations men in lightweight gray suits, white shirts, and silk ties, one-time journalists who had wearied of always being behind in the rent and changed sides for a shot at the pot of gold. They tended to drink too much and laugh too loud. They were like cheerleaders turned prostitute, doing the same thing they always did and wondering why it wasn't fun anymore.

Dalbey joined in the fifties when he managed the Paris office of the International Press Service. He had no journalism background and didn't need it. He had been hired to run IPS like a business, and that's what he did. In those days the club had been a convenient meeting place on trips to New York; he wasn't sure why he still belonged, but each year when he decided the membership fee was a waste of money, he sent in his check and argued that it was a legitimate tax deduction.

He saw Arthur enter, glance around the lobby, and start for the bar. He was tall and favored his mother, light-haired and strong-boned, a few months past twenty-five. That's my son, Dalbey thought. He has my genes. I taught him to ride a bicycle. I bought him a dog. I taught him to shoot. We should be friends and we're not.

Arthur smiled from the doorway and lifted a hand. Dalbey pushed out of the chair and crossed to the doorway.

"Hi, Dad."

"Arthur."

Dalbey shifted the manila envelope to his left hand and took Arthur's hand in his right.

"Shall we go up, or do you want a drink down here?"

"Let's go up," Arthur said in the deep voice that always surprised Dalbey. He hadn't paid much attention to things such as changing voices. "I've got to get back downtown."

They climbed the wide, sweeping staircase, making comments on the weather, the good reports on the stock market. Dalbey noticed that the red carpeting was getting threadbare. It was two flights to the dining rooms, and they went to the left where they could sit and eat under the stern gaze of Edward R. Murrow.

A tuxedoed maître d' led them to a small table against the wall, and Dalbey took the seat on the banquette, facing the room. Arthur made a joke about his keeping his back to the wall.

A waiter took their order for drinks and they both asked for Perrier and lime.

"No beer?" Arthur asked.

"Puts me to sleep."

Arthur studied the large menu and Dalbey said, "I would suggest—" and Arthur said, "Smoked trout."

Dalbey smiled. It was the only thing he ate at the club, the only thing he thought was edible. The clubs of New York are not famous for their kitchens.

"I'll have the London broil," Arthur said. "I need the protein."

Dalbey was thinking that the trout would have more protein, but he knew Arthur was just making small talk. He was careful about what he said to Arthur. They both seemed to avoid anything that might expose the truth of their relationship and let loose the flood of . . . what? Dalbey wondered. Discontent? Resentment? Hatred? Certainly not hatred. But there was resentment for sure, some anger. Sure, Dalbey had been an absentee parent, but hell, there are lots of absentee parents. He could tick off a list of careers that kept men away from their families. It had never affected his relationship with his daughter. No, the problem with Arthur went deeper than that.

"I'm thinking of getting into option trading," Arthur said. He worked for a New York bank, trading currency on the world market.

"It's a tough field."

"It's all research. It's where you can make the megabucks."

Dalbey wrote their luncheon order on the blank form, along with his name and ID number.

"Have you talked to Sharon?" Arthur asked.

"Not since we last had lunch."

"I worry about her sometimes."

"About what?"

"Well, we don't know who her friends are, what she does."

"She works at the Boston Museum of Art. She shares an apartment in Cambridge with two girls. And she's spending weekends in Rockport. I had a postcard a month ago."

"With who?"

"What do you mean, with who?"

"Who she's spending the weekends with?"

"Arthur, Sharon is twenty-two years old."

"She could be staying with some guy."

"So what?"

"So *what*?"

"Yes, so what. She's an adult. She's living her own life in Boston."

"It doesn't bother you that she might be involved with some married man?"

"Is she?"

"I haven't talked to her."

"Arthur, I don't know what you're driving at."

"I'm just surprised that you're not more concerned about her."

"There's nothing to be concerned about. Your mother talks to her at least once a week. If Sharon was in any trouble, your mother would tell me."

"Would she?"

"Of course she would."

The waiter brought the Perrier and placed the tall glasses on the table. He reached for the luncheon order and pencil and accidentally brushed the manila envelope off the table. It landed on the floor with a thud. The waiter's reaction was a growl of annoyance. Arthur leaned over before Dalbey could move and picked it up. He seemed surprised by the weight, and when he felt the contents, his eyes widened.

He handed the envelope to Dalbey. "What's that for?"

"Collector's item," Dalbey said, placing it at his side.

"I didn't know you collected—"

"It's for a friend."

"Why are you carrying it around?"

"I just picked it up."

"Isn't it against the law to—"

"It's an antique," Dalbey said.

Arthur mulled it over, obviously not fully believing, but not sure. Dalbey took a drink to fill the uncomfortable silence.

"Mom thinks you work for the CIA."

"She's kidding you," Dalbey said.

"I don't think so."

"Well, you know what I've done for a living. And it sure as hell wouldn't leave time for a second job."

By the time Arthur was old enough to remember, Dalbey was president of IPS and working in New York City.

"You sure traveled a lot," Arthur said.

"It was that kind of job."

"But you still travel a lot."

"I'm a consultant now. I work for different people. They pay me to look at trouble spots and help solve their problems. I go to where the trouble is."

"She says you just won't grow up."

Why, Dalbey wondered, do women want to believe that? Dalbey found it annoying, but it was obvious that Arthur was fishing for something, for a reaction at least, and Dalbey was determined to keep a lid on it.

"She says that's why you're shooting all the time."

"Shooting is a sport." Dalbey had tried to teach Arthur, but he wanted the boy to love it, the way he did, the way the Judge had. He remembered hunting the fields around New Paltz with the Judge, the good smells of October, the antics of the clumsy, crazy bluetick hound that the Judge had trained on birds and that did everything wrong. He saw himself walking the same fields with *his* son, but the boy wasn't interested, and Dalbey lacked the patience of a good teacher.

The waiter interrupted the conversation with their

lunch, and Dalbey was glad. Damned if he was going to apologize for his trapshooting.

They talked while they ate. Dalbey sensed that there was more than the usual tension between them and he steered the conversation off the family.

"What do you think of the America's Cup?"

"I think it's a disgrace."

"The secret keel, you mean?"

"I mean the idea of spending twelve million dollars on a boat race."

"They spend more than that on a bad movie."

"It's not the same thing. Have you seen Mom?"

"Yesterday."

"How is she?"

"She's fine."

Arthur fell silent, concentrated on his plate. Dalbey didn't like the conversation

"How's the Street feel about the AT and T breakup?" Dalbey asked.

"They figure AT and T will make a bundle of money and telephone service will go to hell."

Dalbey lifted the bones from the trout with his fork and carefully placed them at the side of his plate.

"I'll call Sharon," Arthur said.

"Oh?"

"Maybe I'll go up there for a day."

"That would be nice." Dalbey was trying to push Slattery into the back of his mind so he could concentrate on what was eating Arthur, but it was difficult. He had known tension in his lifetime, had felt the nauseous tremors of fear, even the humiliation of being robbed at knifepoint; but to be the possible target of a lunatic killer, this was new.

A busboy took their dishes and the waiter delivered coffee, rattling the cups and saucers onto the table and pouring from a silver coffeepot.

"I talked to Mom last night," Arthur said.

Then you already knew I saw her yesterday, Dalbey thought. He wanted to ask, What's your game, Arthur? But he stayed silent, stirred cream into his coffee, and waited. When Arthur realized the Dalbey had no intention of adding anything, he said, "She told me about the divorce."

"Yes?"

"Well . . . ?"

"Well, what?"

"What are you going to do?"

Dalbey wondered if it was any of Arthur's business, and decided it probably was. "Were you surprised?"

"Of course I was surprised," Arthur said, agitated.

"So was I."

"What are you going to do?"

"See my lawyer."

"Your lawyer? See your lawyer?"

"That's right."

"You're not going to stop her?"

Dalbey spread his hands, then laced his fingers and stared down at them. When he looked up, he said, "Arthur, your mother didn't ask for a divorce. She didn't ask my opinion, She simply told me that she was getting a divorce."

"You could stop her."

"She has a right to do anything she wants to do."

"You won't."

"No, I won't."

"Jesus." Arthur was trembling. "You'll just let it all crumble?" He gripped the edge of the table. He spoke through clenched teeth: "You never did give a damn about her, never had time for any of us."

"Arthur, this is not the place."

"You sonofabitch." He was talking fast, his face contorted. "You had your house in New York, your whores—"

"Arthur!"

"Jesus!" He came to his feet and the chair fell back-

ward, clattering. The room was already silent, staring.
"You're a cold bastard." He turned on his heel and walked
from the room, flinging away the large white napkin when
he realized he was carrying it.

Dalbey stared after him, stunned. A waiter moved in
quickly and righted the chair. Conversation picked up,
tentative at first but quickly back to rhythm, and the gap
was filled. Dalbey knew that something had been ticking
away inside Arthur for a long time, but he was still
surprised and shocked by the vehemence of his anger.
Now he knew why, at least, in the three years that Arthur
had lived in New York City, he had never come to the
house on Seventy-fourth Street.

He felt weary. He pressed back against the cushioned
vinyl and stared at the table. He wants to like me and he
can't, Dalbey thought.

He tried to remember exactly when his relationship
with Arthur had taken a turn, when the boy had sensed the
polarization between father and mother and felt the need
to choose sides. Dalbey had noticed it when Arthur was
thirteen, but it might have started before that. The sad
thing was that Dalbey had ignored it when he might have
changed things. But he had thought it was just a growing-
up kind of thing that would work itself out.

It had never occurred to him that Arthur's needs
might be greater than his own, that Arthur couldn't just
relax and let things flow, that he had to be reassured.
Dalbey's background had not prepared him for that. The
Judge had never said I love you. Dalbey could not recall a
single embrace or affectionate kiss. But there had been an
emanation of love, an aura transmitted with a glance, a
smile that said, You and me, kid.

He was glad, in a way, that Arthur had finally blown
up. In time they might be able to talk it out.

Relax, he'd like to say. No law says you have to like
your father. Guilt, anger—that's bullshit, a waste of time.
If I made you miserable, I'm sorry. I didn't mean to. I'm

neither a god or a villain. I'm just a man like you. I don't know any more than you do.

He was thinking, kids are a pain in the ass, when the waiter asked, "More coffee?"

"I beg your pardon?"

"Coffee."

"No, thank you."

The waiter moved on. Dalbey glanced at his watch, then rose. Life goes on. He had things to do. He shifted the table slightly, reached for the manila envelope, and sidestepped out from the banquette. He felt the furtive glances of the men he knew, the bold inquisitive looks of the men he didn't.

A former network correspondent who now published journals for the frozen-food industry lifted a hand and said, "Flip."

Dalbey nodded. He didn't know Jerry Call well, but he remembered him as a tough competitor for IPS. He had run into Jerry Call in Amsterdam the night Jerry quit journalism. Jerry had wired New York demanding a raise in pay, or else. He figured that after twenty years he had leverage. They wired back: *WHAT ARE YOUR PLANS?* So much for leverage.

Stopping in the hallway, Dalbey apologized to the maître d' for his son's outburst. The maîre d' palmed the ten-dollar tip, smiled uncomfortably, and mumbled appropriate sounds. Dalbey descended the stairs and stopped at the bank of telephone booths to call his security man, Dan Curran.

Then he walked to Madison Avenue and hailed an uptown cab. The fifteen-minute ride took thirty-five, and by the time Dalbey arrived at East Seventy-fourth Street it was three o'clock and ninety-four degrees. The cab dropped him on York Avenue and he walked the half block to number 513.

The short, dead-end block was the last before the East River Drive and the East River. It was a commercial

street, the north side dominated by a four-story Con
Edison substation, a solid wall of yellow brick, windowless,
the brick relieved at mid-block by a large, corrugated-
steel door. On the opposite side were three- and four-story
warehouses and lofts that housed an odd collection of
businesses: a United Parcel terminal, three floors of theater set builders, a TV commercial studio, a loft building of
interior designers, an architectural firm, a custom-furniture
manufacturer.

Dalbey's building preserved the three-story warehouse look on the outside, complete with a garage-size
steel roll-door that was sealed and covered on the inside
by a plaster wall. A small sign next to the solid entrance
door said: DALBEY ASSOCIATES, 513.

Opening the door, Dalbey stepped into a steel-and-
glass enclosure. The large vertical window on the left was
three thicknesses of bullet-proof glass in welded frames. It
looked onto the reception desk where Mossy Stern surveyed
all visitors and pressed the button beneath her desk that
unlocked the steel door with a buzz. There was another
button to activate a two-way voice communicator. The
door buzzed. Dalbey pushed it open and stepped into the
shock of cool air.

Mossy handed him a small pink bundle of telephone
messages. "Dan Curran is in the conference room."

"Thanks, Mossy."

"Your mail is on your desk."

He leafed quickly through the messages. "Larkin
didn't call back?"

"No."

Dalbey had bought the building in 1973, the year he
left IPS to become general manager of the Kapler newspapers. The price was right and he was attracted by the
location, the odd commercial street in the heart of the
fashionable Upper East Side, and the amount of space. He
paid a quarter million, then added two hundred thousand

for remodeling, giving a free hand to the architect, a young woman recently graduated from Pratt Institute.

The first floor beyond the reception area contained three offices, rest rooms, a conference room, a computer room, and beyond a solid door at the end of the hallway, a two-story squash court. The architect had managed to retain the warehouse look, upgraded with fabric-covered walls and modern lighting. A steel stairway with pipe railings led to the second-floor living quarters, where the hallway floor was open steel grillwork. The living space was simple and modern, a large kitchen planned for a serious chef with adjacent dining area, two bedrooms, two baths, and a comfortable leathery lounge with a large window overlooking the squash court. The third floor was a fully equipped gymnasium with a small sauna, showers, and dressing rooms.

Dalbey stopped at his secretary's office and leaned in the doorway. "I'm back. I have to see Dan Curran, then we'll talk."

Curran was seated at the large conference table drinking coffee. He was a large man with a jowly Irish face, and thinning, unruly hair that always seemed to need trimming, as did the gray tufts in his ears. Twenty years of police work had left their mark. His clothes had a baggy, thrift-shop look, and he smiled with his mouth while his eyes waited and doubted. He was retired and now ran his own successful security company. Dalbey had hired him after the second burglary.

Curran lifted a hand in greeting. He stayed in his chair.

"Thanks for coming right over." Dalbey leaned on the table to shake Curran's hand.

"You'll get by bill."

Dalbey pulled out a chair and sat. He waited a moment for Curran to pose a question, but the big man was waiting. "I'd like to review our security," Dalbey said.

"How do you mean?" There was a slightly defensive edge to Curran's voice.

"If someone were determined to get into this building, could he do it?"

"How determined?"

"Very determined."

"He could blow out the wall with dynamite. He could use chain saws on the roof. They have a new saw that will go through that steel door. They got a—"

"Quietly determined."

Curran leaned back in his chair. "Quietly determined." He linked his hands behind his head and stared at the soundproof ceiling tiles. "Not a chance."

"You're absolutely sure?"

"Positive."

"I'm talking about a professional."

"We figured on professionals." Curran took a sheet of paper from an inside pocket and spread it on the table. "Let's see what we got." He took a pair of reading glasses from a hard, snap-open case and put them on. "All first-floor windows are barred. No skylight. Front and back doors are secured with Fox police locks. Nobody's coming through them. Fire escape windows on second and third floors have steel gates locked from the inside. You probably won't be able to get out in a fire, but nobody's coming in." He took a breath and read on. "A time-delay alarm system goes into effect when the last person leaves the office and it's monitored in our central office." He studied the list another minute. "Nobody's coming into this building quietly."

"How about the roof?"

"No skylight. No way in."

"I'd like to know if he's there."

"Who?" Curran asked suddenly. "Phil, is this something the cops should know about? I can talk to some old friends."

"Nothing for the police."

"You want to tell *me* about it?"

"There's really nothing to tell."

"Okay, the roof." Curran knew when not to push a good customer, but he made a mental note to have his surveillance teams make a few nightly passes on East Seventy-fourth Street. "An infrared scanner system," he said. "A wide-angle camera turns on a three hundred and sixty and covers the whole roof. Monitor inside the building. It's expensive."

"Sounds good."

"A pressure-sensitive alarm system covering the whole roof. Anybody steps on there, you get the alarm the same time we get the alarm. Then you check the TV monitor."

"How about razor ribbon? I see it around."

Curran looked over the top of his glasses. "You sure you don't want to talk about this?"

"Razor ribbon," Dalbey said.

"A pro will go through it like butter."

"It will slow him down. He'll have to cut it. Maybe wire an alarm to it."

"We'll be chasing every goddamned cat in the neighborhood," Curran said.

"Just have it buzz inside here. Then I can check the scanner."

"And watch him coming through the ribbon."

"Right."

"Phil," Curran said, close to anger, "will you tell me what the hell this is all about? It's my business thirty years, for crissake. I can maybe save your ass."

"Honestly, Dan, there's nothing to tell. I'm being cautious. It's the way I am. There's an implied threat against my life, but that's all it is, implied. How about the razor ribbon?"

Curran gave a loud sigh and shook his head. "You'll get the ribbon." He wrote in his notebook and tore out the page. "This is my number at home. Call me at any hour. I'm not home, the wife knows where I am. We're both out, I check the answering machine on the hour. I'll be charging you double time, plus a bonus, so don't be bashful." He pushed his bulk out of the chair, groaned, and stretched. "I sit more than ten minutes I can't move. We'll start on the roof in the morning."

"Thanks, Dan."

"We could put a dog in here."

"No thanks. I've seen your dogs. I live here, remember?"

"Yeah. Well." Curran stood and waited, but he finally decided that he had all the information Dalbey was going to give him.

When Curran left, Dalbey went to his office and looked through his mail. There wasn't much. A few bills. Two requests for donations to save the whales and the Penobscot River. A letter from a forgotten Yale classmate trying to find a job for his son. A sales pitch from American Express offering to insure all his credit cards for one low fee that would be billed later. He had expected to find a letter from Peet, Hogson & Trilby, attorneys-at-law, announcing the divorce action of Eleanor Chance Dalbey, née Worthington.

He felt strangely disturbed by the idea of the divorce. His son's anger heightened the feeling of failure, of course, but it seemed to be more than that. In a sense he had cheated three people. By paying the minimal attention to the family, he had kept Eleanor and both kids on hold while he lived the career life. He hadn't played by the conventional rules, and they were finally rebelling. There was the nagging feeling that he had missed something that couldn't be retrieved. He was about to lose the sense of stability and continuity that the family represented, and he was already feeling slightly adrift.

Mossy interrupted his thoughts with a long-distance call from Bob Larkin in Columbus, Ohio. Larkin was negotiating the purchase of a chain of small daily and weekly newspapers in West Texas and New Mexico, and Dalbey had been analyzing the chain's growth potential.

The newspapers were in good shape, a sound investment, but Dalbey didn't think Bob Larkin was right for the newspaper business. Larkin had made a fortune moving in and out of businesses: real estate development, a catalog company, oil leases during the crisis, an athletic-shoe company during the running boom. There was no doubt that he had the Midas touch. But newspapers were slow growth, and they were a personality business that demanded involvement, especially in small cities. Larkin saw eighteen properties and a balance sheet. Dalbey saw eighteen editors, arrogant and underpaid, more than a few of them idealists devoted to their communities, and they could give the wrong owner a large pain in the ass.

He assured Larkin that he would have a complete report in his hands by the following week, then called for his secretary.

Alice Walder strode into his office carrying a file, a notebook, and a pen and took the seat opposite Dalbey's desk. He noticed for the hundredth time that she was getting gray, and slightly, comfortably overweight, and he thought as he always did, if she was getting old, what the hell did that make him?

Alice had gone to work for Dalbey the same week she graduated from Katharine Gibbs. She had long since advanced to executive pay, but always refused a title. "Jerry's comfortable with a secretary," she said in her wisdom, referring to her husband, a New York City fireman. She knew the business as well as Dalbey, got things done without fuss, and typed ninety words a minute on the word processor.

"How we coming on the Larkin report?" Dalbey asked.

"Michael's running the 1982 figures through a new program he wrote." When Dalbey raised a quizzical eyebrow, she added, "It's good. He makes a five-year profit projection based on Department of Labor statistical projections and GNP projections for the same period. Then he does a five-year comparison with Kapler and McKnight and comes up with a lot of beautiful charts and graphs."

"How long is it going to take?"

"It's done. He's running it now. It's beautiful."

"Does it mean anything."

"Bob Larkin's committee will love it." She tried not to smile.

"And he'll figure he's getting his money's worth."

"Exactly."

Dalbey knew she was right. His report would show the fiscal logic of the acquisition, and he would emphasize the pitfalls without saying outright that Larkin should stick to the fast turnaround and stay away from newspapers. But he knew that Larkin probably wouldn't take his advice anyway. Like most successful entrepreneurs, he was confident he could operate in any field. It was the kind of thinking that kept bankruptcy lawyers in business. Larkin had probably already made up his mind, but Michael's printout would give the committee something to read.

He closed his eyes and pressed his fingers against the lids. "I don't like this part of the business," he said.

"We have to eat."

"You're right." Larkin's fee would be in the neighborhood of one hundred thousand dollars. "Will we have the report by next week?"

"No problem."

"I promised it. Anything else?"

"Harmon Kapler called."

"Kapler?" He flipped through his telephone messages.

"For me," she said.

"For you?"

"Wants to have lunch next week."

"You're serious."

"I'm serious."

"Are you going?"

"Lunch at Le Cirque? Of course I'm going."

"Le Cirque! He's going to make you an offer!"

"I know."

"You wouldn't."

"Well" she said, teasing. "I don't know. I'll listen to what he has to say."

"Harmon Kapler. I can't believe this. I thought he was my friend."

"How come you never take me to lunch at Le Cirque?"

"Costs too much."

"Guess I can't argue with that."

Mossy buzzed to announce that Mr. Odako had arrived and was waiting.

"Tell him to go up," Dalbey said. "I'll be right along."

Alice stood in the doorway. "Ta-ta." She turned to leave, then turned back. "Will you be here tomorrow?"

"Think so."

"I'll have the cover letter ready for your signature."

"Harmon has a terrible reputation with women."

She left, smiling, and Dalbey gave his desk a final once-over, checking his calendar. Then he left the office and climbed the stairs to the third floor where Kenji Odako was getting ready for their workout.

In 1978 Dalbey had been mugged, a common enough occurrence for a New Yorker, but he had been shaken and demoralized by the attack. He was unlocking his front door at midnight when a teenager pressed a knife against his side and emptied his pockets. He stood there, palms pressed against the door, the kid kicking his feet out to keep him off balance, and he was trembling, sick with fear. He felt helpless, humiliated, and furious.

The next day he met Kenji Odako, 8th Dan Black Belt, master of *ninjutsu*, and began learning the ninja art of attacking with a bamboo cane called a *rambo*. The baton that Dalbey carried was Odako's carbon-steel version of the cane.

Their weekly workout lasted an hour, but because

Dalbey had missed three weeks, this time they went until six o'clock, and Dalbey went to the shower sweating and weary.

The water revived him and he dressed in a gray sweat suit. He felt better. It was still light when he bowed Odako out of the building, but the office staff was gone.

He was installing the long bar of the police lock that fitted into a plate in the floor when he heard noise from the computer room.

"Michael?" he called.

"Yo!"

He walked back to the computer room and stood in the doorway. Michael Durso was hunched over the keyboard. He was close to Arthur's age, but totally different. A nice boy. He was disheveled and brilliant, what they called a computer nerd. Dalbey knew he often stayed late, using the modems to communicate with other computers. Dalbey suspected him of belonging to the network that broke computer codes for the fun of it, even though it was illegal.

"I was locking up," Dalbey said. "How long will you be?"

"Another half hour." Michael peered at the columns of figures on the screen.

"Holler when you leave. I'll let you out."

Dalbey went back to install the lock, then went up the stairs and into the large, white kitchen, where he turned on the lights and took some boned chicken breasts and fresh green beans from the refrigerator. He began the preparation of chicken tarragon, savoring the smell of the finely chopped shallots, and trimmed the beans to be cooked in a bamboo steamer. While the chicken simmered in the aromatic sauce, he took a small bottle of *chenin blanc* from the refrigerator and removed the cork. It was a nice wine, a 1969 vintage from the Simi vineyards in California, and he had ordered two cases of splits on a friend's recommendation. He filled a wine glass and sipped it while he cooked.

"I'm ready to go," Michael called from downstairs.

Dalbey checked the flame under the chicken and went down to the front door to let the boy out and lock the door after him. Then he went to a small panel of numbered keys mounted on the wall and activated the alarm system. Anyone now entering would have ten seconds to enter the code that would keep the alarm from sounding at Curran's control center.

He went back to his dinner and had tuned in some Mozart on WNYC-FM when the phone rang. It was his sister calling from Westport. It annoyed him that her speech was already slurred. He carried the phone to the stove and turned the chicken.

". . . and since I have to be in town, I just know you'll want me to stay over. And we have so many things to talk about. You haven't been up to see Mama for at least four months, Philip. I talked to Marcus and he said—"

"Emmy," he interrupted, "I'm in the middle of cooking dinner. When are you coming in?"

"Tuesday. I have a million things to do. They're having an August sale at Saks; I want to catch the Kandinsky show at the Guggenheim, then there's—"

"Emmy, I'm cooking dinner."

"Cooking dinner? For yourself?"

"See you Tuesday."

"Philip, are you trying to get rid of me?"

"Good-bye, Emmy."

"You're horrid."

"Good-bye."

"Philip?"

"Yes, Emmaline?"

"Do you know I love you?"

"Yes, I know that."

"Good-bye, Philip."

Dear, dear Emmaline. How did the girl who finished

third in her class at Vassar College become such an idiot? Poor Emmaline. Having trouble with being fifty-four. Divorced. Kids grown and gone. The dream faded. Nothing left but the vodka and the shopping.

He served his dinner on bone china and lit a candle. He turned the Mozart down and sat, eating, sipping the wine, enjoying the quiet. He thought back over the day and it tired him. Thank God they weren't all like that. If Alice was seriously considering a job with the Kapler newspapers, he might just pack it in and think of something else to do. He really didn't like consulting work. He had plenty of money. He wanted to do something that would bring back the enthusiasm. When he finished eating, he carried his wine to the study, where he stretched out on a leather couch to read.

It was eight forty-five when Eleanor's brother telephoned from New Canaan. "Phil, this is Frank Worthington."

There was something in the voice that alarmed Dalbey. He felt the quickening of his pulse. He sat upright. "Frank, what a surprise."

"Phil, I have some bad news."

Frank's announcement was confused and rushed, but Dalbey registered the key words: "Eleanor... accident... Conklin's Hill..." When Frank was finished, Dalbey said he would be there in an hour.

He stared at the silent telephone, then carefully replaced it in its cradle. He took a deep breath and let the air rush through his open mouth. He filled his lungs again, hyperventilating. A confusion of thoughts rushed through his mind. It just didn't make sense.

Eleanor was dead.

Chapter Five

He didn't want to go in there. He was parked in the street down the long walk from Frank Worthington's rambling white house. He had been sitting there for five minutes. The house was brightly lit and there were people inside. Death brings people out; they have a need to huddle together. He had seen Frank Worthington pass one of the lighted windows.

I just want to be alone, Dalbey thought. He would have to go to the house, but he didn't move, just sat there, his hands gripping the wheel.

Things would have to be done. He had never dealt with the details of death. He had not called Arthur and Sharon. Somebody should. He wondered what they had done with Eleanor's body, but there it was. Eleanor's body. Where was she . . . it? Jesus!

It was a warm, soft night. For some reason he thought of summer nights in New Paltz, long ago when people sat on porches and rocked, disembodied voices and muted laughter, the sudden flare of a match and the glow of a cigarette. He glanced again at the house. The porch light shone on the trees, two old oaks and a towering black walnut, casting shadows. The lawn in darkness looked cool. It would be a good night for night walkers. Soak the lawn with water. By midnight the grass would be crawling with the fat, oversize earthworms. Just go around with a flashlight and pick up all you could use. In some places they called them night crawlers, and then he thought, Jesus Christ, Dalbey, what are you doing?

He got out of the car. He walked into the light. He climbed the three steps and crossed the porch, and Frank Worthington appeared behind the screen door before he could touch the bell. Frank pushed open the door and stood aside to let Dalbey into the house.

"Phil."

"Hello, Frank."

They were in the hallway. There were a dozen people in the large living room. Dalbey recognized some of them.

"Let's go into the library," Frank said, his voice appropriately lowered.

Frank closed the oak-paneled door. The dark, book-lined room was lighted by a green-shaded desk lamp. Dalbey sat in a deep leather chair, and Frank took out his pipe and poked around in a plastic tobacco pouch. Dalbey was surprised that he still smoked; most of the people he knew had quit. He waited for Frank to tamp the tobacco and light up.

"Terrible thing," Frank said.

"How'd it happen?"

Frank puffed dramatically and sat opposite Dalbey in a wing chair. "She went off that turn on Conklin's Hill. Rolled down the embankment. Police say she must have been traveling too fast."

Not like Eleanor. She knew that road. Dalbey started to say, "Did she—"

But Frank interrupted. "She was . . . gone when they got her out of the car." He couldn't say "dead." "The car was totally wrecked."

Dalbey sat forward and stared at his hands. "Where did they take her?"

"Norwalk hospital. It's routine. The police went to your house, then they called me." Frank waited, then said, "I made arrangements with the Hoyt funeral home. I figured it would be the right thing."

Yes, Dalbey thought, Frank would know the right thing. He was the unofficial head of the Worthingtons, the keeper of traditions.

"It's good of you, Frank. I'm kind of in shock."

"Of course."

"When did it happen?"

"The police said about seven forty-five. They were there in ten minutes. They called me at eight-ten."

"I should call Arthur."

"I called him," Frank said. "He'll be here in the morning."

I should have brought him with me, Dalbey thought. When am I going to start doing the right thing?

"I couldn't reach Sharon," Frank said. "Her roommate will try to reach her."

"She has a weekend place in Rockport."

"Her roommate said she was out to dinner."

They talked about what Frank called "the arrangements," and when Frank offered to handle everything for him, Dalbey gladly accepted.

There was a tap on the door and Elise Worthington entered. "Frank, the Colemans have to leave." Her voice was apologetic and funereal.

"I'll see them out. Excuse me, Phil." Frank left the room and Elise stayed. She was a pale, colorless woman, but eternally pleasant.

"Poor Philip," she said. "This is so tragic. We just loved her so."

He stared at his hands. Yes, it was tragic. That's the exact word. Eleanor was finally about to break loose and this had to happen.

Frank returned. "You'll stay with us tonight."

"Oh, no," Dalbey said. "I'll stay at the house."

"You shouldn't," Elise said. "You shouldn't be alone tonight."

"I'll be fine. What did they do with the car?"

"It was towed into town. I think it was the Gulf station. I have it written down somewhere."

"That's okay," Dalbey said. "I'll get it later."

Elise ducked her head and brought a handkerchief to

her mouth. She closed her eyes tightly and her body trembled.

"She knew that road like the back of her hand," Dalbey said.

Elise blinked her eyes, surprised. "But she was run off the road."

"Lise!" Frank said.

"Oh—" She caught her breath.

"Run off?" Dalbey said.

"Well . . . it—"

"Frank, tell me. What do you mean, she was run off the road?"

Frank glared at Elise. He took a deep breath and said, "Bill Shoreham said someone deliberately ran Eleanor off the road."

"Bill Shoreham?"

"He was with Eleanor."

"Bill Shoreham?"

Elise said, "Oh, dear," in a tiny voice and pressed the handkerchief over her mouth. It was plain that Frank did not want to talk about Eleanor and Bill Shoreham.

"What happened to Shoreham?" Dalbey asked.

"Scratches, bruises. He was thrown clear of the car." Frank's shoulders sagged and he looked old. He wouldn't like the kind of gossip that a place such as New Canaan feeds on.

"Where is he?"

"They took him to the hospital. I don't know where he is now." He didn't add that he didn't care, but it was implied in the tone of his voice.

"Now, exactly, what did he say happened?" Dalbey was suddenly alert.

"I didn't see him," Frank said. "It was in the police report. Shoreham claimed someone forced them off the road. I don't know what to think. You know that road."

"What kind of car was it?"

"What kind . . . ?"

"The car that forced them off."

"I have no idea."

"Didn't say what color?"

"I have no idea."

Dalbey wanted to see the car. But there were things that had to be settled with Frank. Elise excused herself and hurried from the room. She went back to their guests, friends, Eleanor's sister and her husband.

"We could do this tomorrow," Frank said.

"I'm okay, Frank. I really appreciate what you're doing." He wondered if Frank knew about Eleanor's plans for a divorce. Probably not. Wasn't the sort of thing Eleanor would talk about.

Friday would be spent gathering the family and notifying friends. The viewing would be on Saturday. Frank would take care of announcements and flowers. There would be a Monday afternoon service at First Presbyterian and burial at Crestlawn. All the Worthingtons were buried at Crestlawn.

And back to work on Tuesday morning . . . Dalbey chastised himself for being critical. Frank was being more than helpful and he should appreciate it. Dalbey agreed that it was a good schedule, and he wondered whom he would call, who his friends were who might want to know.

Elise was back to tell them that Sharon was on the phone. Dalbey froze in place. Frank waited for him to move, then reached for the extension on the desk. Dalbey raised a hand. Frank stopped and Dalbey lifted the receiver.

"Sharon, this is your dad."

"Oh, Daddy." She was crying. Arthur had already spoken to her. Leave it to Arthur. Dalbey was developing a feeling of genuine antipathy toward his son. He told her what he knew of the accident. Yes, it was terrible. Yes, she was too young to die. Yes, he was in New York when it happened. All alone, poor Mother. Well, not exactly alone, Dalbey thought. She would come by train in the morning. It was already arranged that Arthur would meet her. Good old Arthur.

Dalbey said good-bye and returned the receiver to the cradle. Frank placed a hand on his shoulder. "She's okay," Dalbey said.

They left the library and went to the living room, where Dalbey suffered through the condolences. He was already learning his role: eyes downcast, a small smile. "Thank you, you're very kind ... yes, she was very special ... yes, one of a kind ... a great loss."

When it was possible, he excused himself and left. They would be saying that he seemed to hold up very well. He sat for a moment in the car. There was something unreal about it all. As though it had nothing to do with him. He started the car and slowly pulled away from the house.

He went to the police station, which was on South Main by the new high school, and identified himself to the sergeant on duty behind the glass. He was told to wait, and in a few minutes a lieutenant came out and escorted him to an office.

He read the accident report. No skid marks. Drove straight through the wooden guardrail and rolled down the hill. Hit the boulders at the bottom. Shoreham was trying to get Eleanor out of the car when the police arrived. Shoreham claimed a van overtook them and tried to pass on the curve and deliberately ran them off the road.

The officer was polite, but it was plain that they didn't fully believe Shoreham's story. Police have a lot of dealings with lawyers, and Shoreham had been drinking.

Dalbey used the phone in the lobby to call Shoreham's home. Since his divorce, he lived alone in a small house near the train station.

Shoreham answered and he was obviously well on the way to being very drunk.

"Bill, this is Phil Dalbey."

"Oh, Jesus, Phil," he blubbered, "it's awful. Oh, it's awful. Oh, my God, how can you ever forgive me? She's dead, Phil. Damnit, she's dead."

"I'm coming by, Bill. I have to talk to you." He hung

up. He didn't want to have to listen to Shoreham, especially a drunken Shoreham. But there were things he had to know. He thanked the police sergeant sitting in the glass enclosure and left the building.

He drove back to town and stopped at the Gulf station. It was closed, but Eleanor's car, what was left of it, was there. He parked with his headlights on the wreckage and got out to look.

The car must have tumbled end over end, landing upside down on the rocks. The roof was flattened and the glass shattered. The wheels faced in off directions. The sides were waffled and the right door canted on the twisted hinges. The interior was a shambles, the steering wheel jammed against the roof. Bill Shoreham had been incredibly lucky.

Dalbey crouched next to the battered left front fender looking for paint from the van that might have scraped against the car. A lot of red from the Toyota was missing, but no paint was added.

He made another circle of the wreck, then got back into his BMW. He was just four blocks from Shoreham's house. He was there in less than ten minutes and Shoreham answered his first ring, knocking over a chair in the process.

Shoreham's eyes were puffy and red. He smelled of bourbon. He stood in the doorway, weaving, holding the door for support.

"Oh, Jesus, Phil, it was awful." He shook his head, tears spilling down his cheeks. "You hate me, I know, but that's okay. I understand." He was slurring his words, running them together. He pushed away from the door and lurched across the room, tripping over a rug and landing in a chair.

Dalbey entered and closed the door. Shoreham had his drink in his hand. "I didn't mean it . . . honest to God, I didn't want anything like this"

Crossing the room to the sideboard, Dalbey poured

two inches of Martell into an old-fashion glass and added two cubes from an ice bucket. He took a chair facing Shoreham.

"Phil, you know I didn't mean it. . . ."

"Take it easy, Bill," Dalbey said softly. "It wasn't your fault."

"Oh, God, I wish it coulda been me."

"I know that." Dalbey wasn't enjoying this. He didn't like to see people lose control. It was something he found difficult to sympathize with. But he wanted Shoreham to remember and to talk. "How did it happen, Bill?"

"Through the rail. Jesus! Spinning. Went flying. Crashing. I flew. . ."

"Where were you going?"

"Wha?"

"Were you going to dinner?"

"Yeah, at the Club."

"You were being followed," Dalbey said.

"Oh, that goddamned van!"

"Tried to pass, right?"

"Oh, Phil, it was crazy! On that curve. Christ, the van came right into us!"

"What color was it?"

"Wha?"

"The color of the van," Dalbey said.

"White. It was white."

Dalbey had to take a deep breath. His chest felt congested. He looked at the ceiling and breathed deeply. A white van parked off the road. A lineman up on the pole. Watching. He had scouted that road. Knew that curve. The son of a bitch, whoever he was.

"What did he look like, Bill?"

"Who?"

Dalbey was getting annoyed with Shoreham. He had minimal patience with drunks. He could wait until the next day to talk, but he wanted to know now.

"The driver of the van. What did he look like?"

"I didn't see him. It was so fast. I didn't see him."

Dalbey sat back in the chair, tired and deflated. He was exhausted and his nerves were raw as hell. He couldn't believe that just twelve hours ago he had been talking to Vince Steffinelli. He took a good swallow of the brandy. He closed his eyes, rolling his head on his neck. He needed sleep.

"Jesus, I hope you don't blame me, Phil."

"Get some rest," Dalbey said, rising. "I'll talk to you tomorrow."

Shoreham stared at nothing. He leaned to one side, his jaw slack. The glass tilted in his hand.

Dalbey left him sitting there and walked to his car. He opened the door and looked up at the sky. It was going to be warm all night, what Eleanor called a single-sheet night. It was a quarter moon and a haze blurred the panoply of stars. The last Metro North shuttle from Stamford was pulling into the station. Poor Eleanor.

He was ready to wager anything that the driver of that van was a man with white hair.

Chapter Six

There were only three lightweight suits in the closet, so Dalbey didn't have to think about what to wear. He took out the dark blue tropical worsted and hung it on a doorknob. He chose a wine-colored rep tie and a white shirt and dusted off a pair of black shoes.

While he might spend a week choosing a pair of hiking boots or a sleeping bag, he gave no thought whatsoever to dressing for business or social situations. His suits were tailored by J. Press, as they had been since his days at Yale, in blue, brown, and gray. His shirts and ties were ordered from Brooks Brothers, and he went there just once a year to make a selection.

Frank, as promised, had taken care of the arrangements. Dalbey wondered why that word—"arrangements"—annoyed him. He felt that it described the Christian burial process as well as anything, but it avoided the fact of death.

The wake had been easier than he had thought it would be. He had arrived at the funeral home early to see Eleanor alone, thinking it might be an emotional moment, but it wasn't. Eleanor seldom wore makeup, so the face exposed in the coffin was a painted mannequin in a bed of white satin that merely resembled her, a waxen figure in repose.

He felt nothing beyond a twinge of sadness. It was the same years ago when he saw the Judge, except that he was appalled to see the Judge with rouged lips. He had the feeling at the time that there must be something wrong with him that he felt no grief. It hit him a week later when he was crossing Yale Common; tears welled in his eyes and he said aloud, "God, I'm going to miss you."

Arthur and Sharon had arrived at the wake with Frank and Elise. Arthur had elected to stay with Frank and had not spoken to Dalbey as yet. Sharon was staying at the house.

It had been a strange day. He called his office. He called Vince Steffinelli, who seemed genuinely shocked. He asked Steffinelli to pull some strings and check on the white van. Vince called back in the afternoon to report that the van had been stolen in Hartford and had been abandoned in Bridgeport, a few blocks from the train station. It had collided with something red.

Dalbey had asked Steffinelli for a picture of Slattery. He said he would check with Washington. When he called in the afternoon, he said they didn't have a photo.

"That's hard to believe."

"That's what they said. He wasn't the kind of guy wanted his picture around."

"But if he was wanted, somebody would have a picture for crissake."

"He wasn't wanted. He was dangerous, but there was nothing on him."

"The French must have a photo."

Steffinelli said that he'd check further. Dalbey had called his sister and brother. Marcus would serve as a pallbearer. He tried to think of others he should call. He paged through their personal telephone book, but they were Eleanor's friends. He knew many people, but he drew a distinction between friend and acquaintance, so he had very few friends. He didn't find anyone he wanted to call. So he sat in Eleanor's house, among the mementos of twenty-six years, and consoled his daughter with talk of the past. And when he went to see his wife to tell her he was sorry—for everything—there was just the waxen image.

And now he was dressing to attend her burial. He had shed no tears and he felt bad about that. He had tried to find some logical explanation for Eleanor's death, but there was none. It was obvious that Slattery had stalked her carefully, and it was equally obvious that he didn't care whether or not she died. It was too sloppy. A pro would never do that unless all he wanted was an accident. Dalbey couldn't fathom the sense of it.

He was sitting on the edge of the bed. He had heard the shower stop, knew Sharon would be dressing. He sat unmoving, wondering what he should do next, when Sharon tapped on the door and said, "Daddy, the limo will be here soon."

"I'll be right along."

He dressed, and when he came through the living room and into the kitchen, Sharon was standing by the window, gazing at the old elm. She was tall, like Eleanor, and blond, but she was prettier. He stood next to her and said, "I was remembering the other day the time we had to get the tree doctor to save that elm."

"Oh, Daddy." She turned to press her face against his chest. He patted her back, and she said, "I'll ruin your suit."

"I don't care."

The limousine driver came to the front door. Dalbey and Sharon followed him to the car. They sat in the back and Dalbey held her hand as they were driven to the church. The driver took the long way around, avoiding the scene of the accident. Frank was taking care of everything.

A black hearse, the rear door ajar, was parked in the circular drive at the church entrance. The driver passed it and pulled to the curb, letting them out. Stepping from the air-conditioned car, Dalbey noticed the extreme heat for the first time. An attendant led them into the church and they walked slowly to the front pew, where members of the immediate family sat facing the closed casket, which sat on a wheeled cart, surrounded by flowers. Arthur was already there with Frank and Elise, and he moved over to make room for Sharon. Dalbey sat on the end.

It amazed Dalbey that the church was filled, that Eleanor knew so many people. He wanted to turn around and look over the crowd, to see who was there, but he didn't. He wondered who would turn out for his funeral, and he couldn't think of more than a dozen people.

The service was not long. A soloist in the choir, a contralto, sang "Amazing Grace," then the minister asked the mourners to turn to page 39 in the hymnal, and they sang "All My Trials." The minister, who it turned out had attended school with Eleanor, delivered the eulogy, and Dalbey listened carefully. If the man had known anything special about Eleanor, it didn't come out. Just the usual: A life ended too soon, but the ways of the Almighty were strange, indeed, and He knew what He was doing. It ended with a prayer for the departed, then an announcement that interment would be at Crestlawn Cemetery.

The pallbearers filed out of their pew and took their places on either side of the casket as attendants moved the flowers. The side door was opened.

Dalbey took Sharon's arm and they stepped in behind the casket as it was wheeled down the aisle then through the side door to the hearse. An attendant guided Dalbey and Sharon to the first limousine and opened the door. Sharon crouched and stepped inside. Dalbey held the door for Arthur, but Arthur glared at him, curling his lip, and went to the second car. Frank regarded the scene with a pained expression and shook his head. Dalbey took a deep breath and entered the car.

He wondered what, if anything, he was going to do about Arthur. It was strange. Both children had grown up with him with the same amount of attention, but Sharon was warm and loving, while Arthur seemed to hate him.

The hearse pulled away from the curb. The limousine fell in behind and the funeral cortege was under way. It seemed like a lot of trouble to bury a person and Dalbey had never understood the need for it in a modern society. It was convention, of course. It was the ritual of passing, different in all religions, regions, and tribes, but all to the same purpose. It was a kind of exorcism for the living, making death official and final. And as he was carried slowly along, Dalbey thought of more primitive rituals and decided that what they were doing was nothing compared to a tribe in Australia that burned the village where a death occurred, never again spoke the name of the deceased, and performed painful tortures on the widow and relatives to ensure that the dead felt properly mourned.

"Are you thinking of Mom?" Sharon asked.

"Yes."

"It just doesn't seem real. I have the feeling she'll be home when we get there."

Dalbey nodded, but said nothing. He patted her hand. It was cool in the car. They were silent for another ten minutes, and the hearse turned and passed through the cemetery gate. The cortege wound through the narrow roads, and when they reached an older section on a hill, the limousine came to a stop. The hearse turned and drove on to the grave site.

The driver opened the door and Dalbey followed Sharon into the bright sun and heat. Cars were pulling in and parking on both sides of the road. Dalbey saw Bill Shoreham and wondered if he should tell him that he was right about the white van, but decided, to hell with it. Frank stepped to his side and asked in a low voice, "Are you okay?"

"I'll do."

It was a short walk up the hill, following a path that snaked around a lot of Worthingtons. Dalbey wondered what they'd do when they ran out of space. There were flowers on many of the graves, and the grass was carefully trimmed. Dalbey had been here twice before, for the burials of Eleanor's parents. It was a pretty spot, and he remembered that Eleanor had mentioned the view, a thought that had seemed mildly amusing at the time. He glanced at the stone for one of the illustrious ancestors: *ELIJAH WORTHINGTON 1840–1865. 1st Connecticut Inf. Reg. HE SERVED. R.I.P.* He had been wounded in the famous stand at Little Round Top at Gettysburg and had come home to die. The Dalbeys had a similar plot in New Paltz, and he wondered if he would wind up there, a part of history.

There was an awning over the grave site, and the casket, draped with flowers, sat on a metal frame that would lower it into the ground after everyone left. The ground around the grave was covered with green outdoor carpet, and the pile of dirt was hidden beneath a green tarp. The minister stood at the head of the casket. His Bible was marked with narrow strips of white paper.

Dalbey stood in the front between Frank and Sharon. Arthur had moved away. It was a large group of mourners. The minister read from the Bible. Dalbey heard the voice, but the words didn't register. Sharon's shoulders shook and he put his arm around her.

He had always felt somewhat detached from groups, an aloof observer, hearing and seeing everything but not a part of it. It was getting worse with age. Now he seemed to be standing outside his body, watching. It made him think of a primitive painting by Emil White that he had seen in California many years ago. Childlike in its stiff and meticulous execution, it was a picture of a deserted street in San Francisco that conveyed a haunting feeling of loneliness and despair. One little man stood in the middle of the empty street, a suitcase in his hand, tall buildings rising on either side. The picture was titled: "I'm a stranger here, myself." He felt like that.

Frank nudged him and flickered his eyes at the casket. Dalbey glanced at his hand and he was holding a white carnation. The minister was silent, looking at him, waiting. Dalbey stepped forward and placed the flower on the casket. He let his hand rest there a moment, and said, under his breath, "Sorry, kid. I wish it could have been better." He stepped away and others followed his lead. He shook hands with the minister and said, "Thank you."

That was that. He stood to one side and waited for Sharon. She was weeping and Elise held her. He remembered that his sister Emmy had begun to cry at the Judge's funeral, and his mother had said sternly, "Emmaline, we don't do that."

People drifted away, then he and Sharon were back in the limousine, this time with Emmy and her two kids. They drove to Frank Worthington's, where a large buffet supper was waiting.

The mood shift was sudden. The house quickly filled with people. After a hesitant start the conversation quickly became party talk of stock market and career gossip, local politics and children. Dalbey found it healthy, but also slightly disturbing. He had glanced across the room at

Arthur, who looked outraged. When he looked back, Arthur was gone.

"I went to school with Eleanor," a woman said, and Dalbey turned to face an attractive brunette. "I don't believe we've met. I'm Angela Purdy."

"How do you do," Dalbey said, shaking her hand.

"The last time I saw Eleanor she seemed very happy," the woman said.

The conversation soon exhausted itself. A couple stopped to offer their condolences. Dalbey introduced them to Angela Purdy and made an escape.

He found Sharon, who seemed to be enjoying herself, and he took her aside.

"Will you be staying tonight?" he asked.

"I have to get back."

"When's your train?"

"Seven."

"I'll drive you to Stamford," he said.

"You don't have to do that."

"I don't mind."

"Arthur said he wanted to drive me."

"Oh."

She placed her hand on his arm. "What's wrong between you and Arthur?"

"I don't know."

She searched his face to see if he was telling the truth. "Daddy, what's happening to our family?" Her voice broke on the last word and tears glistened in her eyes.

"It's a bad time," he said.

"I've never seen Arthur so bitter."

"We'll have to work it out." He squeezed her arm and kissed her cheek. "I'll call you."

"I love you, Daddy."

"I love you, too, hon."

How easily that was said. But I do, he thought. I don't suppose I show it too well, but I do. He wondered if Sharon was in danger from Slattery and decided she probably wasn't. He thought he might tell her to be careful, but she wouldn't know what he meant, and he didn't think he could explain it. "Take care," he said. "I'm going back to the house."

It occurred to him that he didn't have a car. He needed a ride. He went looking for Frank and entered the library. It was quiet in there and he closed the door. He thought Frank was sitting in the wing chair facing the window, but it was Arthur.

"Oh," Dalbey said, surprised. "Arthur."

"Hello, Father. Having a swell time?"

"Not particularly. I'm leaving."

"Rushing back to New York?"

"As a matter of fact I'm going to the house." He didn't know why he was answering Arthur's questions.

"Your house now."

"It always was my house, Arthur."

"Yes. Well, we had a tendency to forget that."

Dalbey didn't answer. It seemed rather pointless. Arthur had a full craw, however, and he wasn't going to let it rest. He rose from the chair and started to move past Dalbey to the door. But he stopped and said to Dalbey's face, "Well, you're rid of her now. You can do any damn thing you want."

Perhaps it was the insolent tone of his voice. A sudden rage welled up in Dalbey. "You little shit!" he growled as his hands came up and bunched Arthur's lapels. He spun him off balance and lifted him off his feet, propelling him across the room, and slammed his back against the wall, holding him so he had to stand on his toes. "Just who the hell do you think you're talking to?"

Arthur held his breath, terrified. The ease with which Dalbey manhandled him was startling, the explosion of violence unexpected.

Dalbey saw his son's fear and damned himself for a fool. He released his hold. He took a deep breath and let it out slowly, his arms at his sides. Recognizing Dalbey's defeat, Arthur gloated, the suggestion of a smile curling his mouth. Dalbey looked at him sadly and left the room.

His hands were trembling. He wanted to be away. The Judge would *never* have done a thing such as that. On the other hand he would never have talked to the Judge like that. He heard Frank's voice from the dining room or the kitchen, but by then he had decided to walk.

It was only a mile and a half. When he was clear of the house, he removed his suit jacket and loosened his tie. It was hot and he was perspiring, but it felt good to be alone after all the people. There were no sidewalks and he walked against the traffic, stepping off the blacktop when a car passed.

He supposed he would sell the house. Seemed a shame, but there was no way he would live in New Canaan. Maybe he should keep it for Arthur or Sharon. He wasn't sure. It was still too early. He would have to think about it.

The time went too quickly and he found himself approaching the house. He stopped to look up at the telephone pole where the man had stood, canted out on the climbing spikes. If he had just come back. He had known something was wrong.

He crossed the lawn and entered the house. The phone was ringing. He answered it.

"You're there," Frank Worthington said.

"I'm here."

"You didn't say anything. Are you okay?"

"I'm fine, Frank. I just wanted to walk. You understand."

"Well, you call if you want anything."

"I will Frank. Thank you for everything."

He hung up the phone and went to the kitchen for a beer. He took out an Amstel Light and opened it, decided it wasn't bad, but no better than Budweiser. He carried the beer to the living room and dropped into a chair. He got up and went to the fireplace and studied the framed photographs on the mantel. He climbed the stairs and went into Eleanor's bedroom, where he sat on the bed and drank the beer. Eleanor's scent was in the room. He had to do something about Slattery.

But what? He left the bedroom and descended the staircase to the first floor. He went to the study and slumped into a deep leather chair.

He needed help, but he was having doubts about Steffinelli. His answer about the photograph had been evasive. Field people were considered pawns by the desk people, and he wasn't even a field man. At best he had been a courier, and that was ten years ago. He had always liked Vince, but ten years was a long time. He remembered that when he had asked point-blank about the involvement in Chile, they had lied to him. The sons of bitches lied about everything.

He held the beer up to the light, squinting through the amber glass. Slattery was moving on him. He couldn't imagine how Eleanor's accident fit into Slattery's plan, but the killer had gone to a lot of trouble to run her off the road. He wasn't sure where to start. Christ, he thought, I can't even figure out my own son.

He went back to the kitchen and opened the refrigerator. Everything was as she had left it, expecting to return. He stood there for five minutes staring inside. Skim milk. Low-fat cottage cheese. Broccoli. Cauliflower. Lettuce. Apples. The larder of a woman conscious of her weight, careful about her health. But it hadn't kept her alive. He closed the door and stood with his hand on the handle.

He had been avoiding the obvious because he didn't want to face it.

He had to find Slattery and kill him if he could.

Chapter Seven

Dalbey was up early the next morning. He made coffee, showered and dressed, and sat in the kitchen making a list of things that would have to be done about the house.

When he felt certain he had missed the rush-hour traffic, he locked the house and drove to New York City.

He left the BMW at his garage on Seventy-fourth Street between First and York and walked to his office. Mossy buzzed him in, watched him nervously, and said, "I'm sorry about Mrs. Dalbey."

"Thank you, Mossy."

Alice heard him arrive and was waiting in her doorway. There was little about his personal life that she didn't know, and her eyes searched his face for signs of his response to the tragedy. "Sorry about Eleanor," she said. "She was a nice lady."

"Yes, she was. Thank you, Alice."

He went into his office and sat at his desk. His mail was opened and carefully arranged. Unopened, on top, was a small square envelope addressed in Marianna's perfect script.

He turned the envelope over in his hands. Odd that she would know so soon, but then again, maybe not. Bad news travels, and they still had mutual acquaintances. For his part, Marianna was seldom out of mind. He knew the relationship had ended before it was over, prolonging the nostalgia, but there was more to it than that. They had been an almost perfect match in the wrong times of their lives. She was thirty-four, neither young nor old, but he was keenly aware of the age gap. "When I'm seventy you'll only be forty-six," he argued, but she had answered with a smile, saying, "You better stay in shape."

The note was short and formal. But he knew that she was reminding him she was there. He stared at the plain blue paper for a long moment, then placed it aside.

He went through the rest of the mail quickly and at the bottom, discreetly submerged by Alice, was the divorce action from Peet, Hogson & Trilby. He was about to drop it into the wastebasket, but he stopped. There might be a will. There was the house and Eleanor's trust fund, which should be transferred to the kids. He didn't think Bill Shoreham should handle it. He kept the cover letter and made a note to call Don Trilby.

Dalbey crossed the hall to ask Alice about the Larkin report. It had been sent on time; she had signed his name to the cover letter. Then he stopped by the computer room.

Michael Durso was totally absorbed in what he was putting on the screen. Dalbey tapped on the open door. Michael started and looked around. "Mr. Dalbey." Taken by surprise, he stammered awkwardly, "I was sorry to hear about your wife."

"Thanks, Michael. Do you have a minute?"

"Sure."

Dalbey stepped into the room and closed the door. "I need your help." He pulled out a chair and sat facing Michael, who was sitting back, toying nervously with his beard, frowning. It wasn't like Dalbey to close an office door to talk, and he seldom asked for help.

"I have to get into the CIA computer," Dalbey said.

Michael's hand froze in mid-motion, the fingers holding a small tuft of beard. His mouth dropped open and he blinked. "Jesus," he said.

"It's probably illegal."

"No kidding."

"Can you do it?"

After the initial surprise Michael was only marginally stunned by the idea. He knew the great "hackers," the wizards who could break just about any computer code known to man. He had been into a lot of computers himself, mainly for fun, for the challenge, but he had avoided the high-risk government computers.

"I only want the personnel file," Dalbey said. "I think I can get the mainframe access code."

"You can?" Michael's look of disbelief slowly became a smile, as though he were seeing Dalbey for the first time and liked what he saw. "All right," he said, his enthusiasm climbing. "We might do this." He put his head back and closed his eyes. "The computer will want a name. That's the person authorizing entry. Then there will probably be a ten-digit access code for the file, and then a password."

Dalbey had been making notes. He whistled softly. "They don't make it easy."

"The password will generally change weekly or daily," Michael said. "Routine personnel is probably weekly. The real secret stuff would have a daily password."

Dalbey ran over his list again. "What will this ten-digit code look like?"

"Three letters, probably, then three numbers and four numbers."

"Like a phone number."

"Sort of."

Dalbey glanced at his watch. It was ten-twenty.

"If you're going after something really sensitive, the computer will blow the whistle on you," Michael said.

"Blow the whistle?"

"It will be programmed to let someone know that somebody from outside is digging into the file."

"Then what?"

"Then we'll be up to our asses in FBI agents."

"This should be fairly routine."

"Let's hope."

Dalbey rose from the chair and said, "This is between us."

"Right on."

Dalbey went back to his office and dialed Vince Steffinelli's number. While he was waiting, he reached out and activated a recorder. He got the West Development Company, then the secretary, and finally Steffinelli in a somber tone.

"Phil, how are you holding up?"

"It was difficult."

"I can't tell you how sorry I am."

"Vince, I need your help."

"Anything, old buddy. Anything at all."

"I saw Slattery, Vince."

"You what?"

"I saw him, Vince, I'm sure of it. I can describe him."

"That's a break."

"I don't want to talk on the phone," Dalbey said. "I want to meet in the old place."

"When?"

"Noon today."

"Today is tough."

"It's important, Vince."

"I'll be there. Noon."

Dalbey hung up and stopped the tape. He checked his watch again. It was ten forty-five.

He ran the recording tape back and replayed the conversation. He ran it back and played it again. "I saw Slattery, Vince." "You what?" He stopped the tape and ran over that exchange again. "You what?" Again. "You what?" Was there a note of panic in the voice? Was he being paranoid? There was no question that Steffinelli had leapt at the bait. That in itself didn't mean much, but it was enough to make him think. He didn't mind paranoia. It had been a way of life for many years. Paranoia could keep you alive.

He left the office and went to the second floor to see

if Dan Curran's people had been there to secure the roof. As he'd expected, Curran had moved fast, and there was a new TV monitor suspended from the ceiling in a corner of the hallway.

When he returned to the first floor, Mossy said, "Dan Curran wants you to call. They installed the TV camera on the roof."

"I saw. I'll call him after lunch."

He left and walked to York Avenue, where he hailed a southbound cab.

"Forty-sixth and Tenth Avenue," he said to the driver. "Go through the park."

Ninth Avenue would be easier and closer, but he didn't want to chance running into Steffinelli on the street.

The cab dropped him on Tenth Avenue and he walked east, taking his time. When he reached Dario's Grocery, he went inside and browsed, staying close to the window to watch the entrance to number 447.

After ten minutes the store owner was staring at him. "Can I help you with something?" he asked.

"Thank you, no. Just looking."

The owner, probably Mr. Dario, shrugged and muttered something under his breath and kept staring. A customer entered to keep Mr. Dario occupied, then Vince Steffinelli came out of the brownstone and walked east. Dalbey checked his watch. Eleven forty-five. Vince was probably going to be late. He might get a cab on Eighth Avenue; it would still take ten to fifteen minutes to get to the main library on Forty-second and Fifth; walk inside, take the elevator to the third floor, walk to the main reading room. Another five minutes, maybe six.

The library had been his New York message drop in the old days. He would fill out a call slip for *Memories* by William Linton, the 1895 biography of a long-forgotten nineteenth-century wood engraver, and mail it to Steffinelli. It was a book that would always be a part of the library's collection, and one that would rarely be used. He would plant the material in the book and send it back to the archives to await the call slip delivered by Steffinelli.

Dalbey was feigning interest in a can of Italian plum tomatoes when Steffinelli's secretary emerged from the building across the street with another woman. They came down the steps, laughing and talking, and walked east. He returned the can to the shelf and left the store.

He felt lucky. The girl might have lunched in the office. He had been prepared to lure her out with a phone call, but this would be better. He stepped into the street, checked for traffic, and crossed. He went straight for the steps, glancing at the WEST DEVELOPMENT CO. sign as he went up. He went in through the door as though he belonged. He went up the stairs, walking naturally, and stopped at the top.

If the woman down below was listening, this would be the test. He reached for the digital panel, closed his eyes a moment, then punched: eight four two two eight. The door buzzed; he turned the knob and opened it. He stepped inside and let it close behind him.

He turned into the empty hallway, praying that the office door was not locked. It wasn't. He opened it and closed it after him. He went straight to the secretary's desk and opened the small drawer beneath her computer terminal.

The codes were typed on a piece of paper that was taped to the bottom of the drawer for easy reference. Like hiding a key under the doormat. He put on his reading glasses and copied them all. There were no names and no password.

He went through her desk and found the personnel directory for Langley and copied down the names of the personnel director, the head of the computer section, the head of the office of logistics, and the Deputy Director for Support. He replaced the book and closed the drawer.

Where would she keep the password? He searched around her desk—under the blotter, beneath the typewriter pad. It would be in an obvious place. There was a second small drawer under the terminal. Nothing there. He was about to risk checking the terminal in another office when he noticed a tiny slip of paper Scotch-taped to the keyboard. He peered through the glasses perched low on his nose. *DYNASTY.* He copied it.

He looked at his watch. It was twelve-twenty. He had to move. He pocketed his notes and folded the glasses. He went to the door and listened. He opened the door and stepped into the empty hallway, wondering how many employees they had here and where they were. He walked quickly to the stairway and had his hand on the doorknob when he heard voices from the other side. The women were back. They didn't go to lunch. He could probably brazen it out with the secretary, but he didn't want to have to explain things to Steffinelli. He glanced around. There were several closed doors. He went to the nearest door and opened it. It was a tiny utility closet that contained the telephone relays. He squeezed inside and pulled the door, leaving it slightly ajar. He heard the buzzer and the opening of the door. The two women entered. They passed his narrow line of vision, then one said, "That damn door," and footsteps approached. He held his breath, wondering what he would say, but she pushed the door closed and he was in darkness.

He waited several minutes, then slowly turned the doorknob and eased the door open a crack. He could hear the muffled voices of both women in Steffinelli's office. He quickly slipped into the hallway, went out the door and down the stairs. When he reached the front door he breathed a sigh of relief, knowing he was home free.

Pushing hard on the door, he strode through and almost collided with Vince Steffinelli.

He felt the heart-stopping adrenaline rush of complete shock. For a moment he couldn't speak. Fortunately Steffinelli was just as surprised, giving Dalbey the seconds needed to recover and ask, "Where were you?"

"Where were *you*?"

"Second-floor reading room. I waited. I came here looking for you."

"We never used the—"

"Let's walk."

He had to keep a step ahead. He had the advantage of ten years absence and the death of his wife to account for his confusion and cover his lie, but Steffinelli was in a suspicion business, even if he was a desk man, and Dalbey had always been know for decisiveness and precision. He guided Steffinelli down the steps and led him across the street.

"I looked for you in the third-floor reading room."

"Damn, Vince, I forgot." Dalbey shook his head. "You're right. It was always the third floor. I don't know what's the matter with me lately." A weak excuse, but Steffinelli seemed to accept it.

Dalbey led the way to the playground on the south side of the street and sat Steffinelli on a bench in the sun. It was too hot for basketball players. There was no breeze, and the heat shimmered above the blacktop.

"Christ, it's hot." Steffinelli took out a handkerchief to wipe his face.

"Were you able to come up with a photo of Slattery?" Dalbey asked. He suddenly wanted to trust Steffinelli, to stop playing the game. There was no reason for this. For twenty years he had trusted the Agency with his life, for crissake. It seemed ridiculous to treat Vince like the goddamned KGB all because of a tone of voice.

"Nothing," Steffinelli said. "You said you saw him."

"At the funeral," Dalbey lied. Steffinelli's answer gave him the same feeling as before. It was too evasive. There had to be an old file photo, something. He wasn't going to make a judgment, but in that instant he decided to continue on his own. "There was one person who didn't seem to belong," he said, making it up as he went along. "A heavyset man with dark hair. He had a large nose and a mustache. When the service was over I looked for him, but he was gone."

Did Steffinelli lose interest when the description obviously didn't fit Martin Slattery? Dalbey had been watching closely, but he couldn't tell.

"Is that all?" Steffinelli said.

"You don't believe me."

"Of course I believe you. But the man could have been anybody."

"I thought you'd be interested." He decided to put Vince on the defensive.

"I'm interested. But it's not a lot to go on."

Dalbey rose from the bench. "I've wasted too much of your time."

"It's no waste." Steffinelli stood and followed Dalbey out of the playground.

A cab was coming down Forty-sixth Street and Dalbey raised his hand to stop it. He had been putting Steffinelli on, but he decided to be serious. "I gotta tell you, Vince. I don't think the guy meant to kill Eleanor. He wanted an accident, that's all. I don't know why. But I'm going to find out."

The cab pulled into the curb and Dalbey opened the rear door. He shook Steffinelli's hand. "Thanks for everything," he said. He slipped inside and closed the door. As the cab pulled away, he watched Steffinelli, who stood there, his expression blank.

When he got back to his office he went straight to the computer room, where Michael was eating a sandwich and reading a copy of *Creative Computing*.

Dalbey closed the door and said, "I got it. At least I think I have it." He handed the slips of paper over to Michael and looked over his shoulder as he studied them.

"Steffinelli would probably authorize the request from that terminal," Dalbey said. "These other people are in Washington."

Michael wheeled his chair to the computer and activated the modem. He entered the entry code and the computer asked for authorization. He typed in Steffinelli's name and the computer flashed back: INVALID IDENTIFICATION.

"Damn!" Dalbey said.

"Might be too long." Michael tried STEFF, but it was rejected. He tried the list of names, and each time the screen said: INVALID IDENTIFICATION.

"We got a problem," Michael said. "It might be code."

"A code that could be used for any terminal and would be easy to remember."

"Why so?"

"Otherwise it would have to be written down. We're dealing with clerical help."

"Maybe I can get it through one of the billboards," Michael said. "There's a hacker calls himself Ghostrider, says he can get in anywhere."

"Try KUBARK," Dalbey said.

"What is it?"

"Years ago it was the cryptonym for CIA."

Michael typed KUBARK and the screen accepted it for authorization and asked for the access code for the file. "I think it still is," Michael said, grinning. He consulted the slip of paper and entered the ten-digit code. The computer then asked for the password, but when he entered DYNASTY, the screen said: PASSWORD INVALID.

"Shit!" Dalbey said. He punched a fist into his palm. "We were almost there."

"Probably last week's password," Michael said.

"Now what? I could probably go back tomorrow. I know where she keeps it."

Michael had been studying the password and he said, "Let me try something." He exited the CIA computer and entered a new entry code.

"What are you doing?" Dalbey asked.

"Checking the Nielsen ratings for the week before last."

"*Dynasty?* Think it's possible?"

"People have fun with passwords."

Michael was into the Nielsen computer with such ease that Dalbey wondered why anyone would bother to subscribe. The list of popular television programs appeared on the screen. *Dynasty* did not head the list, but it was the top series. Michael then called up the most current listing. *Dallas* had edged out *Dynasty*.

"Whatta you think?"

"Try it," Dalbey said.

Michael went back into the CIA mainframe, selected the personnel file, and entered the password: DALLAS. The computer asked for a name.

"Michael, you're a genius."

"What name?"

"Slattery," Dalbey said. "First name, Martin."

Michael typed the name, pushed the command button, and the screen filled with data on Martin Slattery. "There's your man," Michael said. "You want a printout?"

"Yes."

Michael switched on the printer, pressed the command, and the printer clattered into action, transferring the data from the screen to paper.

When it was done, he handed the printout to Dalbey, who slipped on his reading glasses and sat back to study it. The information was pretty much as Steffinelli had outlined it. There was Slattery's home address in Amsterdam and the first name of Mrs. Slattery.

"Well, I'll be damned," Michael said. Another Agency personnel file was on the screen.

"What's that?" Dalbey looked up from the printout.

"You're a spy."

Dalbey spun and glared at the screen. He pushed his spectacles up on his nose. My God, he thought, they've got a file on me. They had files on thousands of people, he knew, but the information on the screen said he was ACTIVE.

There was a CA after his name, and to the right of that WE. He couldn't believe it.

CA meant covert action. WE was Western Europe.

Chapter Eight

The existence of the file infuriated him. It was a lie, planted for God knows what reason. He felt compromised and defenseless. He wanted to call Steffinelli immediately, but he resisted.

Vince was obviously lying about the Slattery photo. Dalbey was well aware of the scope and ingenuity of the Agency's photo surveillance. He knew that when the Agency was interested in someone, particularly an enemy, they had pictures, every conceivable kind of picture. It was part of the routine. If there were no photos of Slattery on file, it was only because the Agency had caused them to be moved or destroyed. If this was true, and Dalbey believed that it was, then Vince was lying and Dalbey was being used.

He didn't know how or why, but it no longer mattered. He wouldn't barricade himself in and wait. He had never liked still hunting, and he wasn't going to start. Whatever was going on, the key was Slattery. If and when he brought Slattery to bay, everything else would fall into place.

In the meantime he would give rein to paranoia, assume that he was bugged and watched. It didn't matter by whom.

He had Mossy make a flight reservation from LaGuardia to Columbus, Ohio, for that night. She booked a room at the Airport Hilton. Then he went to Gleason's Tavern, a brown-walled saloon at Seventy-fifth and York, where he used the pay phone to call KLM and get a seat on their night flight to Amsterdam. He then made a credit card call to the Doelen Hotel. They were full of course. It was August. But there was always a room for Mr. Dalbey.

He had a sandwich and a beer at Gleason's, taking a table in the rear where he could think. His plan was simple. While Slattery stalked him in New York, he would go back to the source. He had to study the game he was planning to hunt. There would be patterns, habits, and, he hoped, weaknesses.

Startled in a clearing, a deer will run, zigzagging, for cover. When there is no pursuit, no following shot, no frantic action, the deer will stop, short of escape, flanks quivering with the musky excitement of flight, and look back. He will do it every time.

Dalbey returned to the office by three P.M., and Dan Curran was waiting to explain the operation of the roof camera and the alarm on the razor ribbon.

When Curran left, he called Peet, Hogson & Trilby in New Canaan and spoke to Don Trilby. The lawyer was unusually reserved, which Dalbey attributed to the divorce action, but when he broached the subject of handling Eleanor's estate, Trilby's tone was even more guarded.

"I'm sorry, Dalbey, I couldn't possibly."

He was one of those who used last names and affected an accent that Dalbey called Boston Gothic. He instinctively disliked the man and wouldn't retain his services under any circumstances. But his curiosity was aroused.

"Why couldn't you possibly, Trilby?"

"Sorry, old boy, I'm not at liberty to discuss that."

Dalbey managed to curb his irritation and remain civil. He called Bill Shoreham and learned that there was a will. It was several years old and would undoubtedly have been redrawn after the divorce, but it was still in effect and would be sent to probate. "She left everything to you," Shoreham said. "Arthur has retained Don Trilby to contest it."

Oddly enough, Dalbey was no longer surprised or hurt by what Arthur might do.

"How'd he find out so soon?"

"He asked me and I told him. He doesn't have a case."

"Doesn't matter."

"Will you fight it?"

"No." He'd be damned if he would go to court against his own son. The Judge would spin in his grave. He asked Shoreham to see that Eleanor's trust fund was divided between the two kids.

"Do you think I should be handling this?" Shoreham asked.

"It would be a favor to Eleanor."

Shoreham was silent for a few seconds, then he asked, "What about the house?"

"The house is in my name."

"I know that, but I can't see you living in New Canaan."

"I'd like to sign it over to Sharon. She can do what she wants with it."

When he was finished with Shoreham he had an hour for his workout on the third floor, then he showered and packed a small bag with enough clothes for a couple of days, adding a camera, compact binoculars, and his baton.

He usually called a limousine to take him to Kennedy Airport, but this time he walked to York Avenue and hailed a cab.

He checked in at the KLM counter at the International Departures Terminal, charged a round-trip ticket, and went into the VIP lounge to wait.

It was the typical airport lounge. Boredom and Muzak seemed to emanate from the walls and drift through the room with the air-conditioning. More than a dozen senior businessmen, middle-aged and beyond, in three-piece suits artfully tailored at the waists, were scattered about on sofas and easy chairs. They busied themselves with the contents of their briefcases or stared at magazines or drinks or each other. There were several expensively dressed women travelers. Conversation was sparse and quiet. The smiling hostess waited by the door. The red-jacketed waiter leaned on a corner of the small bar and talked to the bartender in Spanish. A bank of TV screens listed the status of departing flights.

Dalbey sat alone with a beer and studied the woman who was crossing the room.

She moved with easy assurance, aware of her beauty, but not overly impressed with herself. She was tall and long-legged, with a good body. Her white linen dress and red accessories were a dramatic contrast to the wheat-colored hair and simple makeup. Besides her purse she carried a slim leather briefcase.

He regarded her as he might a painting, seeing a reflection of his own concept of beauty. But even while his interest was subjective, it was also impersonal. He was just looking. It was not in his nature to pursue a woman. There had been many times when he felt the desire to initiate a conversation with a strange woman, but it would have been inconceivable for him to make the first move. As he got older, he had less and less interest, could predict in detail the inane opening dialogue, the blissful awakening of a relationship, the moment of boredom, and the painful recrimination of separation. On the other hand, he agreed with the Judge, who had once told him: "When you stop looking, you can just lie down in the old buryhole and wait for the dirt." He preferred a more athletic, outdoors type, but there was no denying she was a damned attractive woman.

He was amazed to see her continue straight to where he was sitting and smile down at him. Her voice, when she spoke, was low-keyed. Her accent was British, unmistakably High Church.

"Philip Dalbey?"

He was surprised to hear her speak his name. He rose to his feet. "Yes?"

"Oh, dear," she said, "you don't remember me. I'm Claire Paige. We met in Rome . . . several years ago . . . at your embassy." She studied his expression and kept adding clues. "You were with the Pattersons."

"I remember," he said, remembering the occasion, at least, and hoping to save her further discomfort. He shook her hand.

"No, you don't," she said, laughing lightly. "I'm terribly chagrined, but I forgive you." She glanced at the chair facing his. "May I?"

"Please."

They sat, the waiter appeared, and she ordered a gin and tonic. "I feel such a fool," she said. "You must think me frightfully bold."

"No. No. I should have remembered. I'm sorry."

"You're kind." She preened, arching slightly and using her right hand to reach over her shoulder and pull the hair away from the left side of her face, a move that was self-conscious and sensuous. "We're on the same flight," she said.

When he didn't answer, she added, "I saw your name on the passenger list. I hope you don't mind, but I took the seat next to you."

He didn't mind at all. They renewed the evening of the embassy party. He had been in Rome for a business conference and had attended as a guest of George and Emily Patterson. She had a remarkable memory for trivia and recalled the events that had highlighted the party: the Italian actress in the embarrassing dress, the orchestra playing "Bring on the Clowns" just as two oil sheikhs arrived with their colorful entourages. She even remembered that he wore a dark suit instead of the customary tuxedo.

They walked to the departure gate together and took

their seats in the business section on the intimate upper
deck of a 747, which Dalbey preferred to first class.

She was with the United Kingdom's mission to the
U.N., on her way to a conference on monetary policy at
Den Haag. Dalbey figured her to be about thirty-eight.

For the first hour after takeoff they talked. She loved
her career. She preferred living in London, but New York
was nice if you had a great deal of money. The situation in
Lebanon was distressing, and Reagan had made a mistake
sending in the marines. They agreed on many things, and
he found her exceptionally bright and informed. She asked
for his business card because, "I don't want to lose you this
time," and he gladly handed it over. When she asked
where he was staying in Amsterdam, however, he lied,
telling her the De L 'Europe, a popular deluxe hotel two
blocks from the Doelen.

He had no reason not to trust her, except that he was
positive he had never met her before.

They picked at the airline food, drank chilled white
wine, watched a boring movie, and slept. Dalbey awoke in
the middle of the night. The cabin was darkened except
for one reading light. Claire Paige was curled in her seat;
her head rested on his shoulder and her right hand was
curled over his arm. He was careful not to disturb her,
enjoying the contact, but he was reminded of what he
called Dalbey's Law: *When a beautiful woman under forty
makes a move on a man of fifty-eight, she's either weird or
she wants something.*

He had no idea how the law applied to Claire Paige,
but he would find out in time.

The plane was approaching Schiphol when Claire
Paige awoke, rubbed the sleep from her eyes, ruffled her
hair. She said, "I must look a frightful mess." She didn't as
she padded, shoeless, down the aisle to the rest room.
When she returned, she was smiling and radiant.

They landed at six-thirty and it was another thirty

minutes before they cleared the crowded plane and rode the beltway to the main terminal and customs.

The glare of morning swept away the romantic glow of the crossing. In the capsule above the earth, motionless except for the hum and tremor, with no awareness of speed or progress, time and reality were suspended, and the trip took on a reality of its own that ended with the tires on the tarmac. And now their conversation, once intimate and intermingling, was hesitant and awkward.

"Will I see you again?"

"I hope so."

"I'll be back in New York in a week."

"I'll call."

"You have the number?"

"Yes."

A driver was waiting with a diplomatic clearance to whisk her past customs. They touched hands briefly. Smiles. And then she was gone.

He stood for a moment staring at the door through which she and the driver had passed. She seemed to be what she said she was, but he doubted it. He didn't trust coincidences, and he had few illusions about himself. He saw an aging businessman with failing eyesight and thinning hair and crowned teeth who was a little weary of it all and had to stretch out the aches in the morning and sighed with pleasure when he put his bones down at night to read and wait for sleep: not your average romantic idol.

Since he had nothing to declare, he moved quickly through customs. The inspector was curious about the baton, which was packed, but when Dalbey explained that it was a unipod for the camera, he was satisfied.

Dalbey had his passport stamped and he carried his bag to the taxi ramp just beyond the main entrance of the towering, cathedral-like terminal building. He passed up the first three cabs and took the fourth. He gave the address: 24 Nieuwe Doelenstraat, and the driver was pulling away when he realized that he had neglected the

money exchange. The driver wouldn't mind taking U.S.
dollars, he knew, but he would have to get a supply of
guilders. He could go to the American Express office,
which was within walking distance of the hotel, on Damrak,
and there was a bank on Vijzelstraat, near Reguliersdwars,
which was closer.

The cab negotiated the sweeping airport cloverleaf
and joined the northbound traffic on the six-lane highway
that bordered the Bosplan, the vast sports park that
stretches from the airport to the outskirts of the city. To
the right, beyond the neatly harrowed squares of cultivated field and the grazing milk cows and the two-story,
red-brick houses, was the grassy barrier sloping upward
that is never far from sight in Holland, the wall of a canal.

By the time he reached the Doelen, Dalbey was
numb with fatigue. The fare was thirty-five guilders and
he gave the driver fifteen U.S. dollars.

His room was ready and he went immediately to bed
and slept until noon. He awoke still feeling tired, but a
cold shower revived him, and he stood by the window
looking down on the canal, pleased that he had been given
one of the rear rooms reserved for special guests. Jon
Steach had recommended the Doelen back in the sixties.
It was a unique blend of Old World civility and modern
conveniences, and Dalbey stayed there whenever he was
in Amsterdam.

He debated whether or not to call Slattery's wife and
decided against it. He dressed in a lightweight twill suit
with an oxford button-down shirt and striped tie, an outfit
that clearly labeled him an American. The Dutch may be
reserved, even hostile, to one another, but never to a
foreigner.

Leaving the hotel, he went to the bank to change his
money, then chose a nearby *pannekoekenhuisje*, where he
lunched on crepes stuffed with a sauced chicken. It was
midafternoon when he walked to a taxi stand and engaged

a cab to take him to 35 Van Hogendorpstraat in the northwest section of the city.

It was an old street, narrow and cobbled, running adjacent to one of the dozen or more canals that lace the city, with cross streets on each end of the block arching over stone bridges. The house was four stories, brick, with a steep tiled roof and gabled windows.

Dalbey paid off the cab and crossed the brick sidewalk to the street-level door that was painted green. He rang the bell and waited until the door opened and a man stood in the opening.

"*Ja?*"

"*Goeden dag!*" Dalbey reached out to shake hands, which is the Dutch custom. "Philip Dalbey."

"*Goeden dag! Pieter van Dresser.*" The man grasped Dalbey's hand.

"I'm looking for *Mevrouw* Slattery," Dalbey said, using the bit of Dutch to be polite.

"*Ja,*" the man said, acknowledging Dalbey's query, but offering nothing more.

"Is she here?"

"*Neen.*"

"She doesn't live here?"

"She moved away." His English was accented, but good. With the exception of the northern provinces, such as Friesland, English is the second language in The Netherlands, and most educated people also speak French and German.

"Do you have an address?" Dalbey could see that the man was going to balk. "I was a friend of her husband. During the war. We served together. I came from New York to see him." The Dutch still hold a fondness for the Americans who liberated the country from the Germans, and they still feel that New York rightly belongs to them— especially when they're in New York.

The man looked him over carefully, then he said,

"Almeer." He stood aside, holding the door. "Come in, please. I have the address inside."

Dalbey stepped into a narrow hallway and followed the man through a doorway on the right that led to a small living room crowded with heavy furniture and bric-a-brac and lace doilies. The man went to a walnut secretary in the rear of the room and searched through an address book. He wrote the address on a slip of paper and brought it to Dalbey.

"She moved several months ago," he said.

"Thank you." Dalbey read the address. "*Dank U!* You're very kind."

"Nice to meet you." Van Dresser smiled and once again extended his hand.

They shook hands and after many *dank U zeer*'s Dalbey was able to make his exit. He walked to the nearest bridge and crossed the canal, pausing to gaze at the houseboats lining the quay. He stopped a pedestrian and was directed to a taxi rank a few blocks away. He didn't find a cab waiting, but there was a direct-line telephone.

He felt suddenly weary, remembering the days when he could fly all night, work all day, and still be ready for dinner and a pub crawl. Not anymore. Almeer was twenty miles to the southwest of Amsterdam; not far, but the way he felt it seemed like light years. He needed sleep. He returned to the hotel. It was early and the bar was empty, but he had two Heinekens to relax. When he went to the desk for his key, there was a message to call his office.

He stared at the message slip, not believing it. He placed a call from his room and spoke to Alice. Yes, she had tried to reach him—but in Columbus. Where was he? Bob Larkin was taking his advice not to buy the newspapers and he wanted to meet. Where was he calling from? He said he would see her in a couple of days, and to himself, he hoped it was true.

The message had been left to make him aware that

they knew where he was and what he was doing. He put his head back on the pillow and closed his eyes, massaging his temples with his fingers. They wanted him to know that they were two steps ahead of him. He kept thinking *they* when he had no idea who or what *they* meant.

There had to be a *they*. He didn't give a damn how skilled Slattery was or how deranged he might be; he could not have known he was staying at the Doelen Hotel in Amsterdam. There was no way a single assassin could have monitored his phone and tailed his every movement in New York and got to Amsterdam ahead of him. That took an organization with people and contacts. It was almost as though they knew he would go to Amsterdam. His mind's eye conjured up an image of Claire Paige. Jesus, he was never out of their sight for a moment.

He was getting a headache. He took two aspirin with water. Did his part in Calico really have anything to do with this? It was such an outlandish idea. But people were dead; a lot of people if he could believe Steffinelli, and he knew that he was being drawn into it, whatever it was.

He put the doublelock on the door and propped a chair under the doorknob. He checked the locks on the windows. Whoever he was up against, he would probably face a single assassin. He wanted to be awake if someone forced the door. He had to keep thinking Slattery.

Chapter Nine

The hotel was in the centrum, walking distance from the train station, one of those nondescript places that offered anonymity and little else. It had its share of regulars: traveling men, pensioners, a few prostitutes,

Arab students who glowered and whispered in the elevator. They accepted cash, the name you preferred, and seldom pressed for a passport.

He was registered as John Miller, a name that matched the American accent that he clung to even though it had been years since he had lived in the States and usually conversed in French. He was in room 31, which faced a dismal central courtyard, but was equipped with a minibar and a telephone. He was sitting by the window, holding a photograph of Philip Dalbey to the light, when the phone rang. He crossed to the bedside table and lifted the phone.

"Yes?"

"He was here," a man's voice said.

"Who is this?"

"Van Dresser. I gave him her address."

"How long ago?"

"Ten minutes."

"What took you so long?"

"I had to call them. They told me to call you."

"Thank you." He replaced the receiver and returned to the chair by the window and studied the photograph. He reached for another picture that had been taken the day before, an eight by ten that showed Dalbey at the taxi stand at Schiphol airport. He squinted, staring hard, trying to associate the man in the photograph with the eighteen-year-old boy on the landing barge, but he made no connection. He raised a hand and brushed absently at his short-cropped white hair. He remembered the kid shooting, but that was all.

Forty years ago. He gathered the photos and slipped them into the folder with the Dalbey background. They had studied their man, no doubt of that. It was a part of the job he usually preferred to do himself, but he had to admit that they were accurate so far. He would never have relied on a computer to predict a target's behavior, but the machine had pegged Dalbey's reaction to pressure with unerring accuracy. In the same way the computer can momentarily process thousands of chess variables to thwart human skills, it had digested every known fact about Philip Dalbey's background and life performance to date, producing a psychographic model to be run through the maze of statistical probability. The thought of it made him feel old.

He rose from the chair and stretched. He was impressed by the new technologies, but not convinced that they were infallible. He preferred to believe that the right man was better than the best machine. What would the god-damned computer have done at the Cassidy house? There wasn't time to consult a million variables. You had to decide.

Bending to touch his toes, he felt the pull in the back muscles and groaned aloud. It got tougher every year. He sat in the middle of the room and went through a series of yoga stretching exercises that he did several times a day. He was winding up, working on the neck muscles, when the phone rang, and he broke off to answer it.

"He's back in his hotel," a voice said without preamble.

"Any visitors?"

"None."

"Calls?"

"One. A message to call his office in New York."

"Did he?"

"Yeah, but they seemed to think he was in Ohio."

"So the call must have originated here."

"Possibly."

"Male or female?" he asked.

"Male."

"Probably him." He gave it a moment's thought. "He's being cagey. Might be a code."

"Code my ass. Dalbey doesn't know anything about this. What now?"

"Maybe you ought to ask that computer."

"Don't knock the computer, wise guy, you haven't

been winning gold stars lately. They're not exactly thrilled with how you handled the business in Connecticut. There's talk you might be getting a bit long in the tooth."

He resisted the goading. What the hell did they know? They were clerks. They bugged telephones, for crissake. They were break-in artists. They were shadows, watchers, gumshoes. Sure, they had muscle. They could bribe and harass and threaten. They had their computers and endless money. But when it came right down to taking somebody out, doing it right so there was no trail, that took a pro. There had been static about the woman in Connecticut, but what the hell, it worked. They wanted Dalbey threatened, stressed. That's what they got.

"Keep the surveillance on," he said. "But when Dalbey heads for the house, call everybody off. I'll take it from there."

"We'll see."

"You went to a lot of trouble to get Dalbey over here. Don't screw it up."

"We'll see. *Ciao*, old buddy."

He replaced the phone and stretched out on the bed. This job was getting to be a pain in the ass. Too many people involved. Too complicated. He preferred the jobs where he had a name and address, period. No connections. A clean hit and payment in cash. The criticism about Dalbey's wife rankled him. They wanted an accident to push Dalbey over the edge, he gave them a goddamned accident. The woman was killed. What the hell did they think happened in accidents?

The knock on the door had been expected, but when it came, his body tensed involuntarily and his hand went to the gun under the pillow. There were three knocks. He waited, then there were two knocks. He relaxed, but continued to wait until there was just one knock. He moved to the door, the gun in his hand. "Who is it?"

"Mr. Kodak."

He opened the door and admitted a short, bald man in a rumpled tan suit, who carried a professional photographer's case that looked like a medium-size aluminum suitcase. The man nodded as he entered and went straight to the bed, where he deposited the case. He had nervous hands and he pushed at his steel-rimmed eyeglasses. "This is a beauty," he said, releasing the catch and opening the case. His business was producing specialty weapons. Inside the case, nestled in sponge-rubber cutouts, was a camera body, a long telephoto lens, a heavy-duty tripod, and an oversize tripod handle.

"Spotting scope," the visitor said, pointing to the lens. "Five hundred millimeter." He touched the camera body. "Light refracting eyepiece." He took the camera body from the case, turned it over in his hand, and moved a small lever to its "on" position. "Infrared for night vision." He replaced the camera body and removed the tripod, holding it up to show a trigger mechanism at the top of one leg. He used his finger to trace the fourteen-inch gun barrel that looked like part of the adjustment handle. He had built a Super fourteen Thompson Contender into the tripod. He turned it over to display the opening for an eight-shot clip. "Forty-four magnum." He lifted the oversize handle and screwed it onto the end of the barrel. "Noise suppressor." He patted the weapon, delighted with the ingenuity of it. "It's zeroed to the scope at three hundred yards."

"Very nice, as usual. How much?"

"It's taken care of."

He expected that so he didn't pursue it. It was unusual for a client to get so involved, but this outfit wanted control of everything.

"Drop it at Sid's," the visitor said as he left. The man nodded and closed the door. He went to the bed and completely assembled the weapon, carrying it to the window to practice sighting through the camera body.

When he was satisfied that it would function, he took it apart and returned the parts to the case. He checked his watch, then went to the phone and requested a number in Almeer.

His party answered and he spoke to him in French.
"My name is Laugier. I reserved a skiff for three days. Yes.
That's fine. No, not fishing. I'll be doing some photogra-
phy. Just have it ready for me."

This was the part he liked. The feeling of moving into
action. He went to the small refrigerator and took out a
bottle of white wine, a 1982 Puligny Corton that he liked
for its dry, lemony taste. He drank a toast to his success.

It would be tricky because they insisted that he take
them out together. Dalbey was easy. He could have taken
him ten times in the past week. The other guy, now, he
was something else. He knew what was coming down, and
he was being very coy. But the two of them had to get
together sometime. When they did, he'd be there.

Chapter Ten

Dalbey had decided that the CIA was behind the
surveillance. It made sense that Steffinelli and his friends
would track the target, hoping to move in on Slattery
when he made his move. It should have made him feel
secure that Uncle was there to help, but it didn't. He felt
like bait and he didn't like it. He had his own reasons for
going after Slattery. He wanted to do it alone.

He was up early. He showered and dressed and took
the elevator to the lobby. He had coffee and glanced
through the *International Herald Tribune*. He assumed
that the switchboard was monitored, so he had the desk
call the Godfrey Davis Agency to hire a car and driver for
the day.

When he reasoned that the watchers had been alerted,

he left the hotel and walked for a mile, returning in thirty minutes. If he had been followed, there was no sign of it.

He took breakfast in the hotel dining room. When the hostess came to his table to tell him that his car was at the entrance, he sent a message for them to wait. He dawdled over coffee, and then left through the kitchen.

He ran down the alley that paralleled the canal and caught a tram on Amstelstraat that took him to the taxi rank at Nieuwe Markt. He engaged a cab that left him at the Van Wijk auto rental agency on Prinsengracht.

He used his American Express card to hire a car and driver and gave Den Haag as his destination. The driver was heading south on the *autosnelweg* when Dalbey changed the destination. The driver shrugged and left the highway on the first exit. It was all in a day's work to him. They headed east for Almeer. It was not until they were crossing the causeway over the Gooimeer that Dalbey handed the address to the driver: Westerparkgracht 12.

They left the motorway on the Almeer turnoff, avoided the town, and followed a series of blacktop roads until they were on a narrow dirt road that took them through neat farmland that could have been Ohio or Indiana. The driver turned along a canal dotted with jachtyards, then pulled over and stopped.

Dalbey climbed a white wooden stairway from the road to the top of the canal bank. There, on the edge of the water, was a small white cottage with a gracefully sloping roof and tall French windows that opened onto a large slate patio. An impressively large weeping willow shaded a portion of the patio and dipped feathery limbs into the water.

Herring gulls scolded and drifted on the light breeze that rustled the clusters of gorse and the stiff, brown grasses of the salt marsh that stretched beyond the far side of the canal. The air smelled of wild rosemary. A solitary photographer drifted among the marsh grass in a flat-bottomed skiff, his long telephoto lens trained on a stately

oystercatcher that bobbed and weaved through the grasses
with delicate precision.

Dalbey concentrated his attention on the photographer hunched over the camera and tripod, noting the
bulging pockets of the safari jacket, the white hair showing
beneath the straw planter's hat. He was getting paranoid
about white hair. The man was totally absorbed in the bird
and he didn't show his face. Dalbey watched the man for
several minutes, probing for some indication of threat, but
finally gave it up.

He turned his attention to the house, listening for a
stir of life. A window was open on the second floor and a
wayward curtain danced over the sill. Slattery might be in
there. If he had anything to do with the message at the
hotel, he could be in there waiting, watching. Dalbey felt
a moment of misgiving. He touched the hard line of the
baton against his side. Was he doing something foolish?
He climbed the steps and rang the bell, a startling musical
chime that shattered the silence. He heard footsteps from
within and he braced himself as the door opened.

"*Ja?*"

"Mrs. Slattery?"

"Yes."

"My name is Philip Dalbey."

"The American." She smiled at Dalbey's expression
and added, "Pieter called."

"Yes. Of course."

"What can I do for you?"

She was about Dalbey's age, perhaps a year or two
younger, and had obviously been quite pretty in her day.
Her face, now, was pleasantly attractive, with sad blue
eyes and neat gray hair that curled above the collar of her
light summer dress. She was medium height for a woman
and slightly overweight. She stood with one arm out-
stretched, holding the edge of the door. It was obvious
that she was not going to invite Dalbey into the house,

which was understandable if she was alone—or even if she wasn't.

"Your husband..." Dalbey started, not clear in his mind just what he wanted to ask.

"Yes. Pieter said you were friends in the war."

"Served together."

"In OSS."

"Yes."

"He never spoke of you." She raised a hand and brushed the hair from her face. "He didn't have many friends." She stared into space a moment, as though transported to another time, then she brought her eyes back and said, "What do you want, Mr. Dalbey?"

"I'm looking for your husband, Mrs. Slattery."

"Looking for him?"

"I'd like to know when you saw him last."

"I don't think that—"

"When?" He didn't mean it to sound so abrupt.

She frowned, seemed slightly offended, and said coldly, "It was October 1981."

"'Eighty-one? You haven't seen him for two years?"

"Mr. Dalbey, who are you?" There was anger in her eyes and she pressed her lips together.

He brought a leather wallet from his inside pocket and produced the Central Intelligence Agency identification that Steffinelli had given him.

She bowed her head to read it, then lifted her eyes and stared at him, perplexed. "I don't understand."

"I must talk to you about your husband."

"Mr. Dalbey, my husband is dead. You must know that."

He stared dumbfounded, unable to make sense of what she had said, totally disconcerted. He said the only thing that came to mind. "No."

"He died of cancer in 1981."

Dalbey was shaken. He didn't mean to speak what was in his mind. It came out involuntarily. "Not possible."

Her eyes widened and color rose in her cheeks. Aroused by his impertinence, her mouth tightening, she said sharply, "I was there."

"I'm sorry, Mrs. Slattery. I just—I don't understand."

"Why don't you ask your people," she said, still annoyed, regarding him with cold disdain.

"My people?"

"I don't know what game you're playing, Mr. Dalbey, and I don't care. But if you're really with the CIA, you must know that Martin worked for your organization all his life."

It was a blow. He thought, Vince, you son of a bitch, what are you doing to me? Her revelation left him bewildered, shaking his head. His distress was apparent and it softened her.

"The CIA," he said.

She nodded.

"You know this for a fact."

"I was his wife. I live on his pension."

He pursed his lips and blew out an audible breath of air. Wow. He ran a hand through his hair and shifted on his feet. He didn't know what to make of it. Who killed Dan Cassidy and his family? If not Slattery, who? Why? Was Eleanor's death really as accident? What the hell was he doing in Amsterdam?

"Mrs. Slattery, did Martin have white hair?"

She smiled suddenly and said, "Why do you ask?"

"It could be important."

"You're a very stubborn man, Mr. Dalbey. Just a minute." She left him standing there and disappeared into the house, leaving the door ajar. A moment later she reappeared and handed him a framed photo. "This was taken in 1980."

Slattery was standing on the deck of a sailing barge. He was laughing, waving with one hand and patting his nakedly bald head with the other.

Chapter Eleven

It was still early in the day when Dalbey returned to the city. He paid off the driver near the Muntplein and walked to City Hall, where he had a clerk search through the death certificates filed for 1981. They quickly found what he wanted. It was in Dutch, but easily translated: *Slattery, Martin B. October 13. Natural causes.*

He lunched at a sidewalk cafe, overstaying his welcome, then he walked. He stopped by the Herengracht to watch the excursion barges pass. A young girl waved and he waved back.

They had purposely led him to a dead man and he didn't know why. There was no longer any doubt in his mind that *they* was Steffinelli and the Agency, and it annoyed him to think that they were playing games with him. He wanted to know what was going on, he wanted facts that he could grasp. The only unmistakable fact so far was that Eleanor had been murdered. But was it a fact? It was Steffinelli who confirmed it. It was Steffinelli who had brought him into this, Steffinelli who was leading him through the maze. Was Slattery really dead? His wife said so, the death certificate said so; he knew he could find the attending physician who would swear to it, and it still wouldn't mean a thing. They created their own reality. Dental records? Nonsense. Dental work could be duplicated in hours.

He wasn't used to cavalier treatment from anybody, let alone his own government. Steffinelli, more than anyone, was well aware of just how much of himself he had given, and it burned his ass to think that they were setting him up for something.

For twenty years he had been a dutiful courier. Beginning in the Eisenhower years. The Cold War was on, the last clear and simple conflict: good guys versus bad guys. He had been asked to help because he was trained and because he traveled. Just pick up a small package from Frau Kessler at Wilhelmstrasse 32, a piece of film in Budapest, a number code to be committed to memory and delivered by drop in New York. He had felt patriotic and had wanted to help. But when it became more and more difficult to tell the good guys from the bad guys, when he finally agreed with Jon Steach that the maniacs and adventurers had taken over, he had quit.

Now, leaning on a railing, looking down at a sun-dazzled reflection in the lazily drifting water, he could still hear Steach, angry and disillusioned, saying, "They won't let you go, Flip. They can't. The old gentlemanly days are gone forever. They've gotten too paranoid for that. Did you ever have to deal with Ed Wilson? You've heard of him? Frank Terpil? Oh, they're beauties. They oughta be in a bughouse, for crissake. Our brethren. They want to blow up the whole goddamned world. One way or another, Flip, they'll hang on to you."

"I don't work for the Agency," he had said. "I don't get paid."

"Oh, for crissake, Flip, do you think anybody does this for money? Jesus, man, come on. There's a million weird reasons, but it's never for money."

That was ten years ago, in 1973. A few months later Steach was killed. Dalbey remembered the TV footage. A hole in the street. The engine lodged in a tree. Steffinelli had blamed it on Slattery. More bullshit. Steach was on to something and somebody blew him away. Incredible that Steach and he had been on the Calico thing together and he had never known it. Not until Steffinelli told him.

Good old Steffinelli.

He had some hard questions for Vince. It made him want to be on the next plane back to New York. But that's what they'd expect. Everything he had been doing to this point was predictable. It embarrassed him that the woman had known exactly where to find him at Kennedy Airport. He had been trained better than that. He was already improving, sharpening his edge. Today had been good. He caught them off balance. He smiled at the thought of someone having his ass chewed for losing him.

He wanted to stay lost. It wasn't that he felt threatened. He realized only too well that if they wanted him dead he'd be dead. They were maneuvering him around for some reason. He was offended that they assumed he was some kind of idiot who could be handled at will. If he didn't show at the hotel, they would assume that he was running. It was their turn to wonder what the hell was going on.

The high-speed train to Den Haag took two hours. He called the Doelen Hotel from there, told the desk man where he was, and asked him to hold his room. He smiled, enjoying himself. He listened carefully and was rewarded with a soft click just before he hung up. The hotel was tapped. He was trying to think two steps ahead of them. Why would he go to Den Haag? Claire Paige? Possibly. If they were tracking him in Den Haag, they wouldn't be looking elsewhere.

He took the bus to the airport at Rotterdam, where he called Howard Bestor, the IPS bureau chief in Paris. He caught the six-thirty NLM City Hopper to Paris. Bestor met him at Orly and they drove to his apartment on Rue de Boucheries.

"The reservation is in my name," Bestor told him. "We can make the switch when you buy your ticket."

"Perfect."

Bestor's wife and children were traveling in Sweden, so Dalbey stayed the night.

In the morning he boarded the TWA flight to New York while Bestor called the CIA resident at the U.S.

embassy, said he was Philip Dalbey, and made an appointment to meet for lunch.

Dalbey wasn't sure they would have a telex out on him, but if they did, the phones between Amsterdam, Paris, and New York would be busy. When he didn't show for lunch, there would be some annoyed people. He leaned back and savored the moment.

He tried to read, but couldn't keep his mind on it. The time dragged, as it always did for him on a flight. The pilot gave the ETA and the temperature in New York. The heat wave was still on. He had chicken for lunch. He drank a small bottle of white wine.

Fragments of thought crowded into his mind. The events of the past week still didn't make sense. Even Eleanor's death was unreal. He had to do something about Arthur. He thought about Claire Paige and found himself comparing her to Marianna. Dick Bennett wanted to meet in Bishop for a week of climbing on the Palisades Glacier. Might be good to get away. He wondered if maybe he was getting too old for climbing. He should let Arthur and Sharon have the house between them. It was small of him to cut Arthur out, and it wouldn't solve anything. He wondered if Claire Paige would call and what he would say. He wondered what Bob Larkin wanted to talk about. He was becoming more and more bored with his work.

It was eleven A.M. when the flight landed at Kennedy. He went through customs without baggage, had his passport checked, and took the first cab in the rank. He arrived at his office just past noon as Mossy was leaving for lunch.

"Mr. Dalbey, where have you been? The calls. We couldn't tell them anything."

"Sorry, Moss, I didn't know where I'd be."

"Do you want me to stay? I was just going to lunch."

"You go ahead."

He went to his office. Alice appeared in the doorway. "You were very mysterious on the phone."

"I was in Amsterdam."

"Amsterdam."

"Right."

"And you don't want to talk about it."

"Not right now."

"Larkin has called every day," she said, changing the subject. "He's really eager to talk to you."

"I'll call him."

"Are you okay?"

"I think so. I'll let you know."

She stared hard, frowning with concern. He winked to reassure her and she left. He riffled through the mail and telephone messages. Bill Shoreham had called. Marianna had called twice. He picked up the phone, took a deep breath, and dialed Steffinelli's number.

He got a recorded message: *The number you have dialed is no longer in service. Please consult your directory.* He hung up and dialed again. *The number you have dialed* . . . He dialed again, carefully selecting each number. The same recording. He replaced the receiver.

He rose abruptly and strode out of the office, calling, "I'll be back," and rushed out into the intense heat. He hurried to the corner and hailed a southbound cab.

"Forty-sixth between Ninth and Tenth," he said. The driver dropped the flag and started away. "Through the park," Dalbey added. "Might be faster."

What did it mean, phone disconnected? He knew damned well what it meant, but he didn't want to think about it. He tried to relax but couldn't. He sat forward and directed the driver, who tried to ignore him. They ran into heavy traffic at Columbus Circle and he groaned. Ninth Avenue was moving. The driver turned off onto Forty-fifth Street, and halfway down the block they were stopped by a garbage truck.

"Oh, shit," Dalbey snapped.

The driver leaned on the horn. The two men wrestling with the battered trash cans shouted, "Hold your water," and took their time.

"C'mon, for crissake, I gotta fare."

"Up yer ass, buddy."

They climbed into the truck, inched forward, and made room. The cab leapt forward and roared down the empty street, jumping a red light at the corner, where they made a right turn, went north to Forty-sixth and made another right.

"Four forty-seven," Dalbey said. "Middle of the block. On the left."

The driver picked his way along the street reading house numbers. When he passed Dario's Grocery he stopped. "I don't see it," he said.

"I'll get out here." Dalbey paid the fare, added the tip, and bowed out through the door.

The brownstone was gone. Dalbey stood on the sidewalk and stared. A yellow bulldozer whined and rattled over the pile of rubble, pushing it together for the front-end loader to gather up and bring to the large dump truck waiting at the curb. There was a gaping hole where the building had been.

Dalbey wandered into the street, transfixed. Son of a bitch, he mumbled to himself. I don't believe it. Tires squealed as a car braked to a stop, and Dalbey jumped. He retreated to the curb. He turned and entered the grocery store.

"When did that happen?" he asked, pointing across the street.

"Monday," the store owner said, happy to find a new listener. "Early. Never saw nothing like it. One day—bam—the goddamned place was down. Dirt. You should see dirt. Trucks. Couldn't move on the goddamned street. Never saw nothing like it."

Dalbey returned to the street and crossed over. He stepped gingerly over the rubble, but the bulldozer operator waved him off.

"Who do you work for?" Dalbey shouted, but he couldn't be heard over the noise of the bulldozer. The driver pointed to his ears and shook his head, but he didn't stop working. Dalbey stepped back to the sidewalk. The lettering on the door of the truck said CECIO BROS. DEMOLITION. There was a Long Island telephone number. He went back to the grocery store.

"Is there a phone I could use?"

The store owner pointed to a wall phone in the rear. Dalbey inserted a coin and dialed the number. The operator asked for additional coins, which he counted out and inserted to a chorus of bells and gongs. He got Cecio Brothers and learned that the building was owned by Keystone Realty in Manhattan. He found them in the yellow pages and called. They were out to lunch.

He returned to the street and stood in the sweltering heat, staring at the space where the building had been, remembering the elaborate office setup and wondering: Was that put together just for me? Jesus, the CIA had a budget like every other government agency. How the hell could they justify that kind of expense?

When he got back to his office he called Keystone again and got the office manager. Yes, their building at 447 was being demolished. Previous tenant? It had been a short-term rental to a film company. Paragon Films. He had no idea what they used it for. They paid in advance with a certified check.

Paragon was listed in the Manhattan book, but when he called their number, he got his favorite recording: *The number you have dialed is no longer in service.* Son of a bitch.

Why would they go to all that trouble? He called the CIA field office in downtown Manhattan and asked for Vincent Steffinelli.

The operator took a minute to consult her directory and said, "I'm sorry, I show no listing. I will transfer you to personnel." He waited and another woman came on the line.

"I'm looking for Vincent Steffinelli, please."

"One moment." More waiting, then, "Would you spell that name, please." He spelled it and she went back to her directory. She came back on to say, "I'm sorry, Mr. Steffinelli is no longer with the agency."

"When did he leave?"

"I'm sorry, I am not at liberty to give that information. If you wish to write you may—"

He hung up. That couldn't be true. Vince was too young to retire. And deskmen didn't quit when they had twenty-five years in. He leaned his head back, stretching, and closed his eyes. Damn, he wished to Christ he knew what was going on!

Leaving his office he went to the second-floor apartment. He switched on the TV monitor and watched pigeons on his roof for a few minutes. He went to the bedroom, opened a bureau drawer, and took out the .32 Smith & Wesson that Steffinelli had given him. He broke the action and ran his finger over the firing pin. He took out his reading glasses and gave it a close look under the light. It had been filed away just enough to make it useless. Thanks, Vince.

He dropped the gun back into the drawer. He decided to call Dan Curran and get some handgun training. He'd need a new gun. But then he thought it might be better to get a new hammer for the Smith & Wesson.

When he returned to the first floor he went to the computer room, where Michael Durso was engrossed in a project for Alice.

"Hey, Michael."

"What's up, Mr. Dalbey?"

"I need another favor. I'd like you to get into that computer again and get these files." He wrote the names on a sheet of paper. *Martin Slattery* and *Vincent Steffinelli*.

"I still have the printout on Slattery."

"Try it again."

"Done." He took the sheet of paper, then consulted his notes for the codes.

Dalbey returned to his office. When there was a break in this, he felt he would be able to handle it. He functioned well in crisis. The important thing was to be ready.

In the meantime he had to live his life. He picked up the telephone message slips. He fingered the two from Marianna and wondered if it would be right for him to call. No one had ever touched him as she had, and he wanted very much to talk to her. He could use some support. But he placed the slips on the desk and called Bill Shoreham instead. He told Shoreham that he wanted Arthur to have an equal share of the house.

"Arthur feels the same way," Shoreham said sardonically. "He's planning on suing for his half."

"Oh, no."

"Oh, yes."

"Jesus Christ, what's that goddamned kid up to?"

"I think he just wants to have it out."

"Well, he's not going to have it out over his mother's property. Let him have it."

"He won't be satisfied," Shoreham said. "He wants a fight."

"Just so it's private," Dalbey said wearily. "Give him half of everything and we'll see what happens."

Shoreham rang off. Dalbey held the phone, debating again whether he should dial Marianna's number, then hung up. It wasn't the right time.

He was tired. Things were piling up and that damned Arthur wasn't helping a bit. He stretched and glanced at his watch. It was still on Paris time. Nine o'clock. But it was three o'clock in New York. No wonder he felt drained.

Michael knocked and entered. He held a sheet of paper at his side and he looked bewildered and worried.

"Find anything?" Dalbey asked.

"I couldn't get in."

"Couldn't?"

"Codes didn't work. Nothing."

"They changed everything."

"I don't think it's that," Michael said. "The fact is, I don't think we were ever talking to the CIA computer."

Dalbey sat up in his chair. He had gotten the code from Steffinelli, the same code he had seen the secretary use on her computer terminal. "Why do you say that?"

"I just made contact with Ghostrider."

"Ghostrider?"

"The hacker I told you about. His thing is to drive the bureaucracy crazy. He breaks computer security, spreads the word, and the government has to spend another million for tighter security."

"Our money," Dalbey said.

"Anyway, I gave him our codes, and he said it's not for the CIA computer."

"You believe him?"

"He gave me the codes for the CIA. I went into the computer and got Steffinelli." He held up the sheet of paper. "He resigned."

Dalbey took the printout. Steffinelli's life story. Married with three kids. Dalbey had never known that he had graduated from Notre Dame. The agency had recruited him in 1958. He had resigned in 1980. That was all.

"That's it? You tried Slattery?"

"Nothing there. Nothing on you, either."

It was all a setup. If Vince wasn't working for the Agency, then who the hell was he working for?

"What computer were we talking to?"

Michael raised his palms and shook his head. "There's no way of knowing."

Mossy buzzed and said, "There's a man on who says it's very important that he talk to you, but won't give his name."

"I'll take it." He expected it to be Vince Steffinelli. He said, "This is Dalbey."

"Flip, don't use names. I have to see you."

He couldn't speak. He sat rigid, gripping the phone, a look of disbelief on his face. That gravely voice, what they used to call a whiskey tenor. He suddenly felt like laughing.

"You there?" asked the voice from out of the past. "You know who this is?"

"I'm here. I know."

The familiar chuckle. "You're supposed to be in Amsterdam. Them folks are pissed. Is this phone secure?"

"I don't think so."

"That's okay. I need your help. This is Crisis One, good buddy. You're the only person I can trust. I'll be in touch."

Dalbey listened to the click and the dial tone. He was still holding the phone when Michael said, "Are you okay?"

"Yeah, I'm fine." He hung up the phone, stunned. It was beyond his comprehension, but he knew the voice as well as he knew his own.

It was Steach—alive!

Chapter Twelve

Dalbey couldn't sleep. He lay on his back with his eyes closed, the pillow punched up to raise his head, his arms spread, concentrating on the magnified sounds of New York at night, trying to get Steach out of his mind.

The air conditioner labored. He isolated the movement of the fan and tried to count the revolutions. Traffic on the East River Drive made a steady rush of sound like . . . like what? A strong wind, he thought . . . no, more the roar of a distant cataract, maybe a waterfall. The horns had different notes, different tones. There were sirens. He listened to the painful mesh of gears and the rumble of an eighteen-wheeler on York Avenue; the maddening Klaxon of an ambulance.

Steach was alive! What made Steach such a good field man was his unpredictability. But this was overdoing it. Dalbey opened his eyes and stared at the ceiling, shadowy in the half-light. Where the hell has Steach been for ten years? And why? How did Steach know he was in Amsterdam? Steach and Steffinelli? He couldn't sleep. He switched on the light. He lay for another minute, then rolled off the bed and stood and stretched. He dressed in a pair of athletic shorts and court shoes, went to the squash court on the first floor and spent an hour slamming a ball off the polished wooden walls, and was glad he didn't have neighbors.

He had showered and was carrying a small glass of sherry to the den when the phone rang. He glanced at his watch. Two-thirty A.M. It was probably Marianna.

The ringing was insistent, agitated. He counted the rings until it stopped. Eleven. Had to be Marianna. It was like her to call in the middle of the night and ask, "Do you want me to come over?" He felt a pang of regret, remembering, but he knew it was too early to deal with a commitment.

Dalbey, come off it! You buried your wife five days ago, for crissake! But there was nothing there; we'd been strangers for years. Decency, my boy, the Judge said, there's such a thing as decency.

He finished the sherry and stepped into the hallway. He stopped to switch on the TV monitors and watched his roof through the infrared lens. Dullest show in town. He went back to bed.

This time he resorted to an old problem-solving device that usually brought on sleep. He took the pad and pencil he kept on a nightstand next to the bed and wrote down the one problem he wanted most to solve, *Find Steffinelli*, in bold script. He studied the page for a full minute, trying to eliminate everything else from his mind, then he turned off the light. He lay in the dark considering the avenues to locating Vince, but an outside thought kept intruding: *If Steach is alive, who died in the car bombing?*

Sleep finally came and it was well past eight in the morning when he awoke. His small staff, including the cleaning woman, would soon be arriving. He arose, still tired but anxious to get moving.

He dressed while the coffee was brewing, then went to the ground floor to turn off the alarm system and pick up the *Times*, which was delivered to the front door. He had his usual breakfast of bran toast and juice and was at his desk, reading the paper, when he heard Alice arrive.

"Good morning," she called from her office.

"Morning, Alice."

She appeared in his doorway. "Are you up to something weird?"

"Not at all." He looked up. "Why do you ask?"

"Why do I ask, he says. You call from Amsterdam and won't tell us where you are. TV cameras on the roof. You got Michael working on something he won't talk about. The telephones are making breathing noises. And two men are watching the building."

"Two men?"

"In a blue Ford. Across the street and down a ways. Two men. They look like cops or salesmen. They were there yesterday when I came back from lunch. They were there when I left last night. They're out there right now."

"I'll check it out."

"You're not going to tell me," she said.

"Nothing to tell. Now I wonder if you would try to get Barry Sheehan for me?"

"Congressman Delacourt's in Europe."

"No doubt. But Barry will be watching the store."

"I'll try."

He returned to the newspaper until she said over the intercom, "Sheehan's in a meeting. He'll call back."

That he could count on. Barry Sheehan was senior administrative assistant to Congressman Robert Delacourt from New York's Thirty-seventh District, a man who owed his job, in part, to support from Dalbey and the Kapler newspapers. Delacourt was a senior member of the House Select Committee on Intelligence, and Dalbey was about to call in a chit.

He left his office and went to the second floor where he could look down on the street from the kitchen.

The blue Ford was parked between a brown UPS truck and a silver Datsun 280Z that was a regular on the street. It looked like a fleet car, plain with no options, dirty and dented, the kind NYPD detectives rattle around in. It could also be a rent-a-wreck, or just a plain Ford suffering the abuses of New York street life. The two men in the front seat were clearly watching Dalbey's building, however, and they were doing nothing to conceal the fact.

Alice buzzed the kitchen phone to say that Barry Sheehan was on line two. Dalbey pressed the button. "Barry, this is Phil Dalbey."

"Phil. It's been a while. What can I do for you?"

"You can help me cut a little red tape. I have a friend used to be with the CIA. I haven't seen him in ten years. He left the Agency in 1980, and personnel refuses to say where he went. They want me to write letters."

"What's the name?"

"Steffinelli."

"Spell it."

"S-T-E-F-F-I-N-E-L-L-I. Vincent."

"What was his job?"

"He was field director for New York when I knew him."

"Okay. You gonna be there? I'll call you back."

"I'll be here."

Dalbey hung up and returned to the window. One of the men had left the car and was walking west. He was short, balding, and red-faced, and his blue seersucker pants were bagged and wrinkled from sitting. He was not wearing a jacket, and the white short-sleeve shirt bulged at the waist. His arms were fat and hairy and unusually short, extending just to his hips. He was young, about thirty, but he seemed to walk with effort. When he reached the corner, he stepped into a phone booth. Dalbey glanced back at the parked car. He couldn't see much of the driver, but he had a large mustache.

They were reporting to somebody and the car was not equipped with a radio. Dalbey made a mental note of the license number.

When he returned to his downstairs office, he called Dan Curran and told him that the building was being watched. He gave a description of the car, the number, and what he had seen of the occupants. Was it an official stakeout of some kind? Curran would check it out with his contacts still on the police force. In the meantime Curran would put a watcher on the watchers.

There was nothing to do now until he heard from Barry Sheehan. He was considering the confrontation with Steffinelli when Mossy buzzed the intercom to announce that Bob Larkin was calling from Columbus, Ohio.

Dalbey took the call with a mixture of irritation and relief. He didn't want to be distracted from thinking about Vince and what he had begun to think of as "the problem," but he also welcomed the refreshing clarity of discussing business in which the motives, at least, were easily understood by all sides: greed.

Larkin wanted to buy Southwest Newspapers, Inc. after all. "Too good a deal to pass up."

"There are problems," Dalbey said.

"The main problem is me," Larkin said. "Don't worry, I got your message."

"I didn't mean to imply that."

"Of course you did. That's what I was paying you for. I agree with you. But I have a solution."

Larkin wanted Dalbey in as a partner. A new corporation. They would each invest one million in cash. Larkin had the banks ready to invest in a bond issue that would raise another sixty million, and Wolcott Hambler, the sole owner of Southwest Newspapers, was agreeable to a friendly buy-out and would continue to hold twenty percent of the stock in the new company. Besides the newspapers, Southwest owned two local television stations, a radio station, and a cable TV franchise.

"We'll break up the property," Larkin said. "I'll package the radio and TV with a couple TV properties I already own, sell 'em off for enough profit to retire the bond issue. So we actually get the newspapers for under ten mill, and you run them."

"Why me?" Dalbey asked. Larkin was inviting him into a situation where he could become very rich.

"Wolcott Hambler wants you. He's agreeable to a friendly buy-out for sixty million, but he wants the newspapers protected. Doesn't give a damn about the TV, but his father started the papers. I mentioned you and he went for it."

"Why the million each?"

"That's to keep us interested. I don't usually use my own money. Well, what do you think?"

"I think I'd like to think about it."

"Not too long. We gotta move."

"A week," Dalbey said.

"No more than that. Then we'll talk."

It was a lot to think about. What happens, for instance, when Larkin gets bored. That, of course, could be hammered out in the legal agreement, but it was going to be a tough negotiation. Dalbey was tempted. But why bother? He didn't need or care about the money. He had enough to live comfortably for the rest of his life. He was bored, true, but did he want the hassle of running a chain of newspapers? He had been there before and had been glad to leave it. Okay, he missed the involvement, the feeling of being in the middle of things, and yes, admit it, the power. But if he said yes it would have to be a commitment for the next fifteen or twenty years—the rest of his life. For what? Ego gratification? Did he want to live in New Mexico?

Mossy interrupted his thoughts with a call from Barry Sheehan. "I ran your guy down," Sheehan said.

"What's the story?"

"Routine." Sheehan shuffled paper, cleared his throat. "He resigned in 1980, as you said, and went to work as head of security for Tel-Tech International."

"That's it?"

"Only odd thing is that the CIA has a lid on the guy. I had to go all the way to the deputy director's office to get this."

"He's working at Tel-Tech now?"

"That's what they say. It's a big job. He's a senior vice president."

"Where's he work?"

"Corporate headquarters is Denver. I suppose he works out of there. Good enough?"

"Barry, you've been a great help. I owe you one."

"Don't think about it."

Dalbey knew he wouldn't have to think about it. He'd be getting two tickets for the next fund-raising dinner.

He leaned back in his chair and stared at the dead phone. He steepled his fingers and blew on them. It was eight A.M. in Denver. Too early to call. He didn't know what to make of Sheehan's revelation. Tel-Tech was one of the world's most powerful conglomerates. Dalbey remembered the *Time* cover depicting the company as a malevolent-eyed octopus embracing the world. It wasn't surprising that Steffinelli had left government for a lucrative job in the private sector. That was common.

The disturbing thing, the element that nettled and confused, was trying to connect Tel-Tech with the charade of the CIA safe house, the Calico nonsense, and the accusations against Slattery that had drawn him to Amsterdam.

Dalbey buzzed the computer room through the intercom and spoke to Michael Durso. "Michael, I'd like you to check Dun's for a company called Tel-Tech."

"Tel-Tech International?"

"That's right. I want a printout on everything they own, their annual report, the works. Probably be in the billion-dollar listing."

Dalbey drummed the desktop impatiently with his fingers. He needed a plan, but it was difficult to know where to begin. He rummaged in his past, trying to make some connection with Tel-Tech. The only link he could think of was Steffinelli. How did Steach fit in? He had questions but no answers. There was a connection, there had to be a connection.

Reaching for a yellow legal pad, he wrote at the top of the page in his careful penmanship: *Daniel Cassidy*. And to the right of the name he wrote: *murdered*.

Was there a connection here, as Steffinelli had suggested? He had been on one mission with Cassidy forty years ago, barely remembered him, had never seen him since. He remembered the newspaper story of the murders only because it involved a retired CIA official and the motive was cloaked in mystery.

He wrote: *Calico*.

Odd, he now realized, that he had never questioned how Steffinelli had connected him with the Calico mission, or how Vince knew the details of the mission as though he had a copy of the debriefing. Was there really a record of every OSS operation in World War II? He recalled Vince's saying, "We ran a follow-up on the whole Calico team."

That had to be bullshit. Come on, if Vince was with Tel-Tech, he didn't have access to government computers, and why would that ancient history be in anybody's computer file? Not a chance. Vince knew about Calico because somebody told him—somebody who had been there.

He was thinking that the detailed debriefing of Calico was probably filed somewhere in the National Archives in Washington when Bill Shoreham called from New Canaan.

"Bertha Keillor has a buyer for the house," Shoreham said.

"Already?"

"Well, Eleanor had it listed with her about six weeks ago."

"Oh?"

"You didn't know?"

"She mentioned something about it."

There was an uncomfortable silence, then Shoreham said, "The price is good, and the people are ready to make a deposit."

"How much?"

"Five thousand, I believe."

"No, I mean how much for the house?"

"Half a million."

"Amazing."

"Well, that's what properties are going for around here," Shoreham said.

"Have you talked to the kids?"

"Couldn't reach Arthur. I talked to Sharon. She says it's up to you. She doesn't want the house."

"Then I guess we ought to sell it and put the money in the trust."

"That's what I'd do."

"You'll tell Bertha to go ahead?"

"I'll handle it. Now, what about the furniture?"

"Oh, Jesus, the furniture. I guess there should be an auction."

"More money in a tag sale."

"Bill, I don't have time for that."

"I'll take care of it. There are women here who handle the whole thing."

"That would be great." He was about to say that he would come to New Canaan during the Labor Day weekend when he remembered that his phone was probably tapped and his building was being watched. "I have to be in Washington for the weekend," he said. "I'll talk to you next week."

When Shoreham disconnected, Dalbey telephoned his daughter at the Boston Museum. She was getting ready to leave for the weekend. She had already removed many personal items—including her mother's jewelry—from the house. She had been through the attic, but there was nothing she wanted to keep. He repeated, for the benefit of the telephone, that he would be in Washington for the weekend.

When he called his son, Arthur, at his bank, he was put through to his supervisor, who informed him that Arthur had resigned on Wednesday. "Came in here," the man said, an edge to his voice, "said he was leaving. Cleaned out his desk and was gone the same day. A very poor show, if I do say so. No notice, nothing. Left us in a terrible bind."

Dalbey was surprised. He wouldn't have expected Arthur to leave a job without notice. There was a lot about his son that he didn't know. He dialed Arthur's apartment on East Eighteenth Street, but the line was busy.

"Tel-Tech International," Michael said, placing the printout on Dalbey's desk.

"Thank you, Michael." Dalbey reached for the printout, then said, "Oh, Mike, just a minute." He pulled open a desk drawer. "I want you to do me a favor." He shuffled a small pile of business cards. "There's a guy . . ." He finally selected the card he wanted. "A freelance researcher in Washington. Here, make notes." He handed over a notepad and a pen. "The National Archives. Year is 1943. I want to know anything he can find out about an OSS mission code-named Calico. European Theater, out of Great Britain. I want the names of the team members, the debriefing report, anything. A rush job."

"Everything closes by noon today."

"Damn, that's right. Okay, try to get him now. If you can't, try him on Tuesday."

When Michael left the office, Dalbey leaned back to study the report on Tel-Tech. He opened the four folds of the printout and whistled softly to himself, shaking his head slowly. He knew they were a major multinational, but he'd had no idea how big.

He went down the list, counting the corporations Tel-Tech controlled or owned outright. Sixteen. It was mind-boggling. He knew Colorado Mining, of course, and Fromson Tool, which produced diamond bits for oil drilling. Inter-Tel Communications was well known, as was Pecos West Oil. But Tel-Tech was also into chemical paints and pharmaceuticals, hotels and resorts. He had no idea what Bowser Industries made, but with annual sales of $4.7 billion, it had to be military. Westcott Data Group, whatever that was, had annual sales of $685 million. It surprised him that Tel-Tech owned seventy percent of Royal Belgian Shipping. What did Magnum Development Company develop? Danscorp Ltd.? Overseas Charter Company? Well, he knew Overseas Charter, at least. That was the charter airline favored by the CIA. He began to see Steffinelli's connection. There was also something vaguely familiar about Phoenix Exploration, Inc., but he couldn't place it. My God, they even owned one of the country's major brokerage houses.

The printout told him in detail what he already knew: that Tel-Tech was a huge corporation with a lot of money and great power.

It didn't tell him who was watching his building or who was listening on his telephone.

He reached for the phone and called Dan Curran. When he got through to Curran, he said, "Dan, this is—"

"I can't talk," Curran snapped, cutting him off. "I'm coming over." Before Dalbey could reply, Curran disconnected, leaving him with a dial tone.

Scowling, Dalbey pressed the disconnect button to silence the irritating noise, then punched in Arthur's number. It rang once, then he got the *bah-bah-bah-bah-bah-bah* busy signal.

He glanced at his watch: eleven thirty-five. He was about to call information for Tel-Tech's Denver number when he noticed it was included in the Dun's report. He called and asked for Vincent Steffinelli and waited until a carefully modulated female voice with no accent said, "Mr. Steffinelli's office."

"Speak to Vince, please? This is Colonel John Keating."

"I'm sorry, Colonel Keating," said the corporate voice, "Mr. Steffinelli is not in the office at this time. If you'll leave your number, he'll be calling in."

Dalbey left a fictitious Washington number. The phone tap would be reporting to Vince, he knew, but it might make them wonder what he was up to. He tried Arthur's number again and got the busy signal. Could the phone be off the hook? He was beginning to worry.

"We're closing at noon."

He looked up at Alice Walder who was standing in the doorway. "Going away?"

"Jerry's on duty," she said.

He nodded. "Well, have a good weekend."

"I will," she said, but she didn't leave. "You're all right?"

"I'm fine."

She nodded, pursing her lips. "Okay."

"By the way, how was your lunch with Harmon?"

"Very nice."

"He make you an offer?"

"Yes, he did."

He waited, and when she didn't go on, he said, "Well?"

"Well what?"

"What was the offer?"

She folded her arms and leaned against the doorjamb, a coy smile playing across her face. "You tell me what those men are doing out there, and I'll tell you what Harmon said."

He grinned, shaking his head. "Jesus, even you're getting difficult. I don't know why those men are out there. That's why I've been calling Dan Curran."

She studied him skeptically, deciding whether he was being evasive or telling the truth. "Harmon offered me a management position," she said finally. "I'd be in charge of syndication."

"You'd be good at it."

"Good pay, stock options, the works."

"I thought you weren't interested in any of that."

"I'm getting interested."

"So, you're considering it."

"I'm thinking about it, yes."

"What's Jerry think?" Dalbey was referring to Alice's fireman husband.

"Oh, that wouldn't be a problem now. Jerry knows who he is. You spend twenty years running into buildings that everyone's running out of, you stop worrying about your manhood."

"I don't suppose you'd consider moving to New Mexico."

"Where's New Mexico?" she said like a true New Yorker.

"Larkin says he'll buy Southwest Newspapers if I come in as a partner and run it."

She moved into the room and sat gingerly on the edge of the chair facing Dalbey's desk. "When did this come up?"

"Today. That's why he called."

"You're not seriously thinking about it."

"I don't know."

"When you left Kapler you said, 'Never again.'"

"Things can change."

"You want my opinion?"

He could tell from her expression that she was against the move, but he was curious to know why. He often sought her counsel. He could dissect a problem logically, personally weighing the pros and cons, but she had known him a long time and she added an intelligent, dispassionate viewpoint that he found invaluable in making important personal judgments. "As a matter of fact," he said, "I would like to know what you think."

"Don't do it."

"Why do you say that?"

"You'll be going backward, covering old ground that has gotten attractive because you've been away."

"Could mean a lot of money."

"You're not interested in money and you know it. If you want to make a change, you should do something entirely new."

"Like what?"

"I have no idea, but I know you, and I know how bored you got running the Kapler newspapers."

He leaned on his elbows, propping his chin with both hands. He gazed at her for a long moment, thinking, then he said, "You're probably right."

"Who needs another million or two?"

"Right, who needs it."

"Don't tell Jerry I said that," she said, laughing. "Oh, Lord, that reminds me. I have to get to the bank before they close for the weekend. I don't have enough money for groceries."

Mossy interrupted to announce that Dan Curran was at her desk and was in a hurry.

"Do I get to eavesdrop?" Alice asked.

"Go to the bank."

Curran came along the hallway before she could

answer and she retreated. Curran entered Dalbey's office and handed him a typewritten note that read: *Don't say anything about surveillance until we sweep for bugs*.

In the hallway, behind him, were two men in shirtsleeves carrying oversize briefcases. Curran waved them into the room. Dalbey was standing, frowning at the note. The two men opened their cases, which were fitted with UHF sensors to monitor the presence of electronic listening devices. Curran waggled a finger at Dalbey and led him out of the room.

Curran took the lead, and they climbed to the third-floor gymnasium. Curran went straight to the dressing room, where he turned on one of the adjacent showers.

"Okay," Curran said. "That's enough background noise to garble anything." He sat on the bench against the bare wooden wall.

"What's this all about?"

"There's a court order for the phone tap," Curran said.

"Who?"

Curran raised both hands shoulder-high and waggled his fingers. "Not sure. I found out that it's federal, but that's all. I'd say it's either the FBI or Treasury."

"Couldn't be a private company?"

"Not with a court order."

"Why would the government tap my phone?"

"I was gonna ask you that."

"I can't imagine. Who are those people watching the building?"

"They're not cops." Curran pulled a dog-eared note-book from a side pocket. "Car is registered to a"—he flipped a page—"William Demeny in Binghamton, New York. No report of its being stolen or missing. Could be anybody. The federals play by their own rules. But it's not a local stakeout."

Curran pushed himself up with a grunt. He gestured with a sideways nod of his head and left the dressing room. Dalbey followed him to one of the windows overlooking the street. Looking down, Curran broke into a grin and pointed. "Enjoy this," he whispered, "you're paying for it."

A police car was parked in the street parallel to the blue Ford. The heavyset man was standing on the outside, leaning against the car, hands on the roof, his legs extended and spread-eagled. He raged at the young police officer who was patting him down. The driver was still inside the car, and the second officer stood next to the open window looking over the registration and the man's driver's license.

"That's a couple of very angry dudes," Curran said, chuckling. "They don't know they're on their way to the precinct."

Curran left the window and started down the stairs. Dalbey followed. When they reached the first floor, the electronics men were working over the reception desk. Mossy was gone.

"Clean so far," one of the men whispered to Curran.

Without answering, Curran led the way along the hallway to Dalbey's office. Alice and Michael had also left for the weekend. When they were inside the office, Curran closed the door and said, "Okay, we can talk in here."

"What will they do about those guys?"

"Nothing. Maybe find out who they are, who they're working for, but I doubt it. They'll be legal."

They talked for almost thirty minutes. Curran probed for information, Dalbey pleaded ignorance. The two electronics men returned to say that the building was clean.

"Okay, we'll get out of here," Curran said. "Don't say anything on that phone you don't want taped."

"Dan, thanks again."

"I hope you realize this is serious. For a judge to override the Fourth Amendment there's got to be a damned good reason. You might want to call your lawyer."

When the three men were gone, Dalbey locked the

door and went to the second floor. He went to the window and looked down. The blue Ford was still parked at the curb, but the two men were gone. He went to the phone and tried Arthur's number. It was still busy.

Chapter Thirteen

It was one-twenty P.M. Dalbey turned down the air-conditioning, set the alarm, and left by the front entrance, carefully locking both doors.

Visiting Arthur posed a dilemma. If he was there, something would have to be said about his leaving the bank. Dalbey would then be accused of meddling in his son's life. If Arthur wasn't there, he was going to have to look for him, which could be worse. Whatever he did he was bound to annoy Arthur.

The blue Ford remained empty, but that didn't mean much. Such an obvious stakeout could be a decoy. The real trackers would be a lot more difficult to spot, and if it was a Tel-Tech operation, as he assumed, they could afford the best. Steffinelli was aware that Dalbey had been trained to recognize and avoid surveillance.

Dalbey walked the eight blocks to Seventy-seventh and Lexington and took the downtown subway to Grand Central. He was careful to be in the rear of the last car, which he knew would drop him at the foot of the exit stairs. Six other pasengers had boarded the car at Seventy-seventh Street, three men and three women. He discounted the women and one of the men, a Hispanic wearing a silver hard hat and soiled working clothes.

He left the train at Grand Central, weaving through the press of waiting passengers on the crowded platform, and bounded up two long flights of stairs. He jogged along the busy concourse and slowed to a fast walk when he reached the vast, domed rotunda of the main terminal.

It was already crowded with the crush of people fleeing the city for the last summer holiday. Dalbey stopped at the information counter, a glass-enclosed rococo octagon topped by an ornate clock, giving his pursuers—it had to be a team—time to catch up. He picked up a New Canaan train schedule, then climbed the sweeping marble staircase and exited onto Vanderbilt Avenue.

He walked to Madison Avenue, where he stopped to look at a window display of men's hats. He picked up on one of the tails, the Hispanic in the hard hat. He went into the store and bought a straw Stetson with a colorful band. He came out wearing the hat and walked to the mid-Manhattan branch library at Fortieth and Fifth Avenue. He entered from Fifth and took the escalator to the second floor. He looked up Daniel Cassidy in the *New York Times* file, found the listing for the murder story, and filled out a call slip, which he took to the publications desk.

He glanced across the room to where the Hispanic construction worker was leafing through a volume in the section labeled ETYMOLOGY.

Dalbey took the copy of the *Times* to a copy machine and reproduced the article. He returned the newspaper and rode the elevator to the fourth floor, then hurried down the exit stairs to the Fortieth Street entrance, where he slipped into a phone booth and called Dan Curran.

"Can't find out a goddamned thing on the stakeout," Curran said. "There's a lid on it; nobody's talking."

"How about the guys they took in?" Dalbey asked.

"One phone call and they walked."

"Find out anything?"

"Phony ID, phony names. No car registration. But after that phone call all hell broke loose in the precinct."

"You don't know the connection."

"I don't wanta know that kinda connection."

"What should I do?"

"Call your lawyer, then take a trip."

"I'm being tailed right now."

Curran was silent a moment, then he said, "Well, look at it this way: at least you won't get mugged."

"Thanks." Dalbey hung up. He left the building and walked to Park Avenue South and took his time about hailing a cab. He still hadn't made a second tail. Didn't really matter, but as an exercise it was interesting. There had been a time, in the old days, that he went through this routine daily: the involved, erratic movements until he was satisfied that he wasn't being followed.

This time he was enjoying himself; he had already decided where and when he would lose the tail, and in the meantime he was going to make them work.

He took a cab south to Union Square. Radio WINS was reporting: "... *traffic already backed up in the Midtown Tunnel. An overturned truck has blocked the Bruckner Expressway, so if you're heading north you should try the Major Deegan. Temperature is ninety-one degrees at Central Park, with a seventy percent likelihood of evening thunderstorms....*"

He walked south through Union Square Park, then dodged traffic to beat the light crossing Fourteenth Street. He paused to see who might be willing to risk their lives to follow him, and when the light changed, he crossed again. He walked north, circling the park this time, proceeded to Eighteenth Street and east to number 138, where he mounted four steps and entered a tiny vestibule to look for Arthur's name on the register.

It was in the second row, typewritten, apartment 3-C. He pressed the tiny black button after the name. He waited for the buzzer to unlock the door or a voice to question him, but there was no answer. He tried it again, waited, then again. Still no answer.

He then did what every New Yorker knows how to do

and does often. He took a credit card from his wallet and
slipped it between the door and the jamb, pushing the
bolt back, and opened the door. He stepped into the
empty hallway. It was a walk-up. He climbed the steep
stairway to the third floor, found 3-C, and rang the bell.

There was no answer. He rang several times. He
sensed that someone was behind the door, but there was
no response. He rang again. Then a female voice asked,
"Who is it?"

"I'm Arthur's father," Dalbey said loudly.

A magnified eye appeared in the fish-eye in the
center of the door. Dalbey knew she could see about
two-thirds of him, and he removed the straw Stetson to
expose his face.

"Arthur's not here."

"I've been calling all day. Can we please talk?"

She was hesitant. He took his driver's license from his
wallet and slipped it under the door. He heard her pick it
up. She then began unlocking the door, an involved
process that took at least ten seconds of clanking and
banging. The chain lock was last and she opened the door.

"Please come in," she said, handing back the license.
"I'm sorry, but you have to be careful." It was a soft voice
and he picked up a slight accent that was Maryland or
Delaware. He stepped past her into a modest-size living
room, and she closed the door. She touched her hair and
said, "I must look awful."

Dalbey smiled. "You look wonderful." He extended
his hand. "I'm Philip Dalbey."

She took his hand. "I'm Helen," she said with a shy
smile that dimpled the left side of her angular face. She
was barefoot and wore faded blue jeans and an oversize
T-shirt that said GOUCHER across the front. She was young,
maybe twenty-three, medium height with a slight, trim
body.

He gestured toward a sofa and said, "May I?"

"Oh, please."

He sat and she said, "Can I get you something?"

"No, thank you."

She said, "Well," and took the chair opposite him. She broke the uncomfortable silence with, "So, you're Arthur's father."

"Yes."

There was another stretch of smiling and then they both said, "I—" at the same time and stopped abruptly. She said, "Sorry."

"No, please, you were saying."

"I forgot what I was going to say." She placed the back of her hand against her mouth to suppress the laughter, and he had to smile.

Then he said, "I was wondering, how long you and Arthur . . ."

"A year. Longer actually. Fourteen months." She smiled and added, "And eleven days."

So this was Arthur's girl. Sitting there, struggling with the clumsiness of chance encounter, he realized that he had never met a girlfriend of Arthur's. It seemed strange to him now, but he had never thought about it before, had just assumed that Arthur had a social life. He had written the checks for the skis, the tennis racquets, the club dues, the car payments, the weekends on the Vineyard, reasoned he was discharging his paternal responsibility and let it go at that. When they did talk it was:

"What'd you do last week?"

"Nothing much."

"Sailboarding?"

"A little."

"Who with?"

"Some of the kids."

"Anybody I know?"

"Don't think so."

In time Dalbey stopped asking. Arthur didn't seem to require guidance, and Dalbey stopped thinking about it.

He and Arthur never had a problem. Now he was beginning to realize they never had anything. It had never
entered his mind that Arthur might have a special girl.

After a tentative start Helen talked. Dalbey interjected
the occasional question, but mostly he listened. As she
relaxed she became animated, and a wry sense of humor
surfaced. She talked about her family, her yodeling dog,
and her job as a TV production assistant. She embroidered
her short saga with anecdotes that made Dalbey laugh. He
enjoyed listening to her.

"I'm surprised we never met," he said.

"You're never home." He recoiled slightly and she
added quickly, "That's what Arthur says. You weren't in
New Canaan the two times I was there."

"You met Eleanor."

"Yes." Her expression was pained. "I'm sorry. I would
have been at the funeral, but Arthur..." She paused,
unsure. She began again, more tentative. "He didn't think
it would be wise."

"I don't understand."

"He thought—" She bit her lip. "I shouldn't be saying
any of this."

"Like what?"

"He said it was going to be unpleasant."

"It was."

"I'm sorry."

"Families," he said, looking at his hands and nodding.
"We'll have to work on it."

They were quiet then, absorbed in their own thoughts,
then he said, "Where is Arthur? I called the bank. They
said he quit his job."

"He's in Denver."

"Denver?"

"He got this incredible job offer. Doubled his salary.
He hated to quit the bank like that, but they insisted he
decide immediately."

"They?"

"An investment firm. Batson, Batson and Harbrace. They're very big."

"They're in New York," he said.

"The corporate headquarters is in Denver."

He didn't have to ask. He could see the printout, the name near the bottom of the list.

"Tel-Tech International."

"That's right," she said, surprised. "Do you know them? They're awfully big."

"I'm getting to know them." It could be a legitimate job offer, but he didn't think so. He didn't like coincidences.

"I better be leaving," he said.

"Oh, no. I'm just getting to know you."

"I'm afraid I must. I have to..." He was about to say "go to New Canaan," but he thought of Arthur's working for Tel-Tech. "I have to be in Washington."

Chapter Fourteen

When Dalbey left the building, he stopped on the top step to adjust the new hat and carefully surveyed the street. A young woman was standing in front of a plumbing supply store, and when Dalbey appeared, she turned and studied the window display of valves and T-joints with interest. He hadn't expected a woman.

He walked to Third Avenue, looking for the Hispanic, and spotted him talking to a hot dog vendor. As he reached the corner, an uptown bus pulled into the curb and he stepped aboard. He dropped seventy-five cents into the padlocked fare box. As he took a seat near the rear, the young woman from the plumbing supply store came on board and paid her fare. She went to the rear of the bus and sat alone on the seat that stretched across the back.

Dalbey stole a glance through the rear windows and saw the Hispanic frantically waving for a cab. As the bus approached the next stop, Dalbey rose and walked gingerly to the front, then turned and started back. The woman had risen from her seat, and she sat back abruptly. Dalbey went to the rear and sat next to her and watched her fidget uncomfortably for twenty blocks.

The tail was too obvious and he found this disturbing. Steffinelli was not a fool. He would have ordered a couple of real pros to follow Dalbey . . . unless—unless there was a third person who liked to work alone. An incompetent two-man team to make him overconfident and relax his vigil, making it easy for a third man.

He left the bus on the south side of Forty-second Street and crossed with the light. He joined the crush of commuters and holiday travelers entering Grand Central Terminal and followed the flow to the main rotunda. His route was already planned. It was an old trick, simple, but always effective. He knew his followers would now be used to zeroing in on the colorful Stetson. In the center of the milling, pushing mob he removed the hat. The old magician's sleight of hand. He virtually disappeared. He moved through the crowd, working his way west. He turned down the concourse to the shuttle, then down the ramp to the Oyster Bar. He went down the stairway to the lower-level tracks, where he dropped the hat into the trash bin and waited. If he was still being followed, this would be a good quiet place to find out who it was.

A train rumbled into the platform and he moved off, walking the full width of the lower level to track 113, where he took the elevator back to the upper level. He made a right turn and entered the marble-lined underground passageway that leads to the Roosevelt Hotel at Forty-sixth and Madison. Of the dozen exits from Grand Central, this is the least known. He was positive that he had eluded his followers, but he had never picked up on a third person, and this continued to bother him.

When he emerged on Forty-sixth Street he found a cab immediately, a minor miracle in New York.

"One twenty-fifth and Park," he said.

The driver nodded and lowered the flag. The rush hour traffic was heavy, but Dalbey didn't mind. The cab was air-conditioned, and it gave him time to consider his next moves.

The government had a legal tap on his telephone, a privilege usually reserved for top-level mobsters, the drug traffic, tax evaders, or suspected enemy agents. He was under full surveillance by agencies that the New York cops wouldn't even mention. His wife was dead, and he believed that Vince Steffinelli knew why. How did Tel-Tech International figure in this? Why the Calico story? Why Slattery and why did Steffinelli want him in Amsterdam? Didn't Vince realize he'd have questions to answer when Dalbey got back?

And the answer to that is, *No, because they didn't expect you to come back*.

Jesus! He took the copy of the newspaper story from his pocket and carefully reread the account of the Cassidy murders. The assumption was that it was a hit on Cassidy, and the women were just in the way. No robbery. Nothing touched.

Why was Cassidy killed? The story alluding to his CIA background left the impression that he had either been silenced or was a casualty of the secret war. But Dalbey knew that the latter could not be the case. A retired agent is inviolable. It's an unwritten rule, the last vestige of a gentlemen's code. The head of Britain's MI6 could walk out of Whitehall one day, leaving behind his crew of bodyguards, and go raise roses in Devon without a backward glance or a moment's fear for his safety.

So it had to be something that had surfaced from the past. Not Calico. No, Dalbey was more inclined to believe that it had something to do with a more recent period—a period when Steffinelli and Steach and Cassidy were all working for the same company, and Dalbey was their volunteer delivery boy.

Such as what? Dalbey had never wanted to know what he was carrying. It seemed safer that way. But the connection had to be the courier work. It was the only thing that made sense.

"Which corner?" the driver asked. They had pulled up on the south side of 125th Street.

"This'll be fine," Dalbey said.

He paid the fare and bowed out of the cab into the oppressive heat. He crossed the street and climbed the steps to the elevated Metro North platform, where he waited for the next train to Stamford, Connecticut. He stood out of the sun, but the heat, now ninety-three degrees, and the heavy, humid air made breathing difficult. He slung his linen jacket over his shoulder, but even that was too warm, so he held it out to the side, hooked on one finger, hoping in vain for a circulating breeze.

A loudspeaker announced his train as it rumbled into the station. He waited, watching the stairway. If there was someone still following, he would appear now. No one came. The conductor raised his arm and Dalbey stepped aboard.

The train was crowded, but the air-conditioning made it relatively comfortable. He had to stand as far as Greenwich. The train emptied at Stamford, and he crossed the station plaza to the Avis office and rented a small Chevrolet.

He would have preferred his BMW, but he assumed that they were watching his garage.

It was six-fifteen when he passed through the center of New Canaan. He took the road north and turned onto Cat Rock Road. He negotiated the twisting curves carefully, still adjusting to the rental car. When he passed through the hairpin turn at Conklin's Hill, he noticed that the broken guardrail had been replaced by spring steel.

He slowed to a crawl, and on the crest of the next turn he found room to pull off the road and park. He left the car and walked back to the guardrail.

It was quiet. The sun was low, but the pale sky, dappled with scudding clouds, was still bright. The slope betrayed scant evidence of the crash, the abrupt end of life. Some torn brush, a slice of plowed dirt, the glint of overlooked pieces of glass or chrome near the bouldered creek bed with its trickle of water.

He wanted to know what Eleanor felt by imagining the rending metal, the catapulting plunge, the scream of terrified finality, but he failed. It was too quiet, too unreal.

An approaching automobile intruded upon his reverie. A dusty, red Datsun descended the hill, the tires agonizing on the curves, then droned out of sight and sound. He walked back to the car, feeling disheartened, and drove off, climbing the steep, winding hill.

As he approached his house—Eleanor's house—he noticed that the grass was newly cut. Who . . . ? Probably the same boy he had seen on the tractor. He felt the hand of Frank Worthington. He would have to make arrangement through Frank to pay the boy. He had owned this house for twenty-six years, had raised two children here, and he had no idea how the damned grass got cut.

He turned into the driveway, geared down. There was a car parked in the space between the house and the garage: a gray Mercedes sedan. He drifted in next to it and killed his engine. He opened his door quietly, slid out of the car, and closed the door without a sound. He had second thoughts and reached in through the open window to get his jacket—and the baton.

The door to the mud room was unlocked. He let himself into the kitchen and stopped to listen. He moved through the dining room, his steps muted by the thick carpeting, and stopped again in the living room. There was a sound from the study, and he moved cautiously down the hallway. He stopped at the open doorway.

A man was busily going through the top drawer of the file cabinet. His back was to Dalbey, and he was totally engrossed in his search. He was oddly dressed for a burglar: faded Breton red yachting slacks with a navy-blue stretch belt, a green Izod shirt, and beige leather Reeboks. He worked fast, pulling up the manila folders and riffling through the papers. He stopped to push up his black-rimmed glasses and clucked his tongue.

"What the hell are you doing?" Dalbey snapped.

The man leapt, crying out. He slammed the metal file drawer and spun away, startled out of his wits. He tripped over a chair, banging his shin. He grimaced in pain and cursed, "Goddammit to hell!" He danced on one foot, holding his shin, and snapped at Dalbey, "Jesus Christ, man, why did you do that?"

"Who are you?"

"Attorney for the deceased."

Dalbey was taken aback by the man's rejoinder. "You're what?"

"Attorney for—"

"Trilby!"

"That's right. Who might you be?" The senior partner in Peet, Hogson & Trilby was still in pain, but was fast regaining his arrogance.

"I live here," Dalbey said. "I'd like to know what the hell you're doing in my file cabinet?"

"Dalbey?"

"That's right."

"But you're not supposed to—" He stopped abruptly, clearly rattled, and clamped his lips.

"I'm not supposed to be here. That's right. Now what were you doing in that file?"

"This is terribly embarrassing."

"It's also burglary," Dalbey said. "Just stand over there." He stepped into the room and reached for the telephone.

"Now see here!" Donald Trilby moved forward as

though to leave the room, and Dalbey reached for the baton. He stopped Trilby with the foot-long steel rod pressed against the tender intersection of the rib cage.

"Why don't you just relax," Dalbey said calmly. He increased the pressure on the baton and Trilby stepped back.

Dalbey dialed 911 and got the police dispatcher. He gave his name and address and said, "I've got a burglar here, and if he moves a muscle, I'm going to kill the son of a bitch." He hung up.

"Really, Dalbey, this is ridiculous."

"Why don't we move this into the living room," Dalbey said.

Trilby was getting worried. He was considering the legal ramifications of his position and it wasn't good. "You can't—" he blustered, but Dalbey cut him off with a broad smile.

"Sure I can." Dalbey waggled the baton like a truncheon. "Let's go."

Trilby moved to the doorway and slipped through, apprehensive eyes fixed on Dalbey, who didn't really consider the man a threat, but was damned curious about what he was looking for. He gave Trilby a prod with the butt end of the baton to move him along the hall.

"Over there, Trilby." Dalbey pointed to the oversize sofa. "It would give me great pleasure to knock you on your ass."

Trilby sat, tense, perched uneasily on the edge of the cushion. Dalbey stood eight feet away.

"We can talk," Trilby said.

"Good. Tell me what you're looking for."

"I can't discuss that."

"Cut the bullshit, the cops are on the way."

"You're not really serious about this."

"We'll see."

"Dalbey, for God's sake, I'm a respected attorney in

this town. My family has lived here for generations. My great-grandfather was the governor of this state."

"Red-handed," Dalbey said. "I believe you legal boys call it flagrante delicto, or haven't you been keeping up on your jurisprudence?" He smiled. "It means, literally, while the crime is blazing. Caught in the act of committing a misdeed."

"I know what it means," Trilby said sourly.

Dalbey wanted to press the advantage, but he wasn't sure how far to go. He knew he would never prefer charges. Hell, there was nothing in the files worth stealing, and he was already feeling sorry for Trilby's predicament.

"Why don't you just tell me what you're looking for and we can forget the whole thing."

"Financial records," Trilby said. "I thought you might be hiding assets."

"From Arthur?"

"Yes."

Dalbey gave it a moment's thought, but it didn't wash. Trilby knew that Arthur and Sharon were going to share the full value of the estate. And even if there were a lawsuit, a routine court order would force Dalbey to make a full financial disclosure. No, Trilby wasn't looking for anything that had to do with his problems with Arthur. "Who are you working for?" Dalbey asked.

"I already told you."

He was going to be stubborn. Dalbey was wondering if Tel-Tech International could coerce a respected attorney into burglarizing a house. What the hell could they be looking for? He was wondering how to proceed when an unmarked police car with a portable red light flashing on the roof turned off Cat Rock Road and roared up the driveway, sliding in behind the parked cars.

Dalbey stepped to a window and peered through the curtains. Two plainclothes detectives were standing by the car looking at the house. They walked to the back door and rang the chime.

Dalbey hung his jacket on a chair and placed the baton on a sideboard in the dining room. He went to the back door to admit the two policemen.

"Mr. Dalbey?"

"That's right."

"I'm Sergeant Parella." He was about forty. He wore gabardine slacks, a plaid sport shirt, and a brown-and-white check sport jacket draped over a short-barreled .38 in a brown spring holster. His partner was younger, early thirties, pale-skinned and freckled, and he wore a white short-sleeve shirt with a dark tie and dark blue slacks. "You reported a break-in."

"That's right. Come in, please."

Dalbey led the way to the living room, explaining to Parella, "I came home unexpectedly and found a man" —they had reached the living room—"this man, searching through the files in my study."

Trilby sat back on the sofa, relaxed, his legs crossed.

"Mr. Trilby," Parella said, surprised.

"Hello, Lou," Trilby said. "Hello, Martin."

The second officer nodded. Sergeant Parella turned to Dalbey. "I don't understand," he said. "This is Don Trilby."

"That's nice to know," Dalbey said. "Now I'd like to know why he broke into my house."

"I didn't break in."

It was Dalbey's turn to be surprised. "How'd you get in?"

"I have a key."

"You have a key to my house?"

Trilby spoke to Sergeant Parella. "I was the attorney for Mrs. Dalbey. She was suing for divorce. I am also the attorney for Arthur Dalbey, this man's son. I was given the key by Arthur Dalbey."

"Did he tell you to search my files?"

"As a matter of fact, he requested I look for certain documents in what he called the family files."

Dalbey couldn't deny that the files contained mostly

family business: old tax records, correspondence on Eleanor's trust, insurance claims, letters to friends, stock transactions, automobile records, medical records, that sort of thing. Trilby had obviously noted the contents and knew he was on strong ground with the two police officers, but Dalbey knew it wasn't what he had been looking for.

"I don't believe he had any right in this house without a court order," Dalbey said, annoyed that Trilby had scored a checkmate.

Sergeant Parella took the tone of a policeman long used to the domestic aberrations of the suburban rich. "Anything missing?" he asked.

"I don't know. I don't think so."

"It sounds more like trespassing," Parella said, acting the arbitrator. "We'll see that Mr. Trilby leaves the premises, but this is a civil matter between you two gentlemen." He kept his gaze on Dalbey. When there was no objection, he turned to Trilby and said, "Shall we go, Mr. Trilby?"

"A pleasure."

"I'd like that key," Dalbey said.

Trilby produced the door key, which he gave to the policeman, who handed it to Dalbey.

"You should see your lawyer if you want to pursue this," Parella said.

"Thank you, Sergeant. I'd also like to request that you keep an eye on the house during regular patrols."

"So noted." Parella scribbled in a small spiral notebook.

Dalbey walked them to the door and watched them drive away. He returned to the living room and dropped into a chair, noticing for the first time that the air in the house smelled stale. He opened some windows and turned on the air conditioners in the study and the guest bedroom. He went to the refrigerator for a beer.

He went back to the window, drinking from the can, and stared at the space where Trilby's car had been parked. It was time—past time—to think seriously about this. He turned from the window and went through the house to the study and studied the open file drawer.

When a lawyer has to do something nasty like a search, he hires somebody to do it. Somebody told Trilby to handle it himself, somebody with the money and clout to make Trilby jump. What was it he said? *You're not supposed to be here.* Of course, the phone tap expected him to be in Washington, so did Arthur's girl.

Would Tel-Tech have the influence to initiate a government wiretap? Does McDonald's sell hamburgers?

Steffinelli and Tel-Tech. Arthur working for Tel-Tech. Trilby representing Arthur. But he, Dalbey, had no connection whatsoever with Tel-Tech. Then why the hell were they searching his house?

He dropped into the leather swivel chair and leaned back, pressing a hand over his eyes. The first meeting with Vince. He was easy for Vince to manipulate. Vince knew him, knew he would never sit and wait for a killer to make his move. They had offered the bait that would take him to Amsterdam, and he had taken it. Dumb, he supposed, but he had assumed that Vince was a friend.

But why Eleanor? Sure, it had made him move, but they could have done it without that. And Vince must have known that when he learned that Slattery was dead, he'd be back looking for blood.

Unless they were sure he wasn't coming back, and that didn't make any sense at all. He uncovered his eyes and stared at the ceiling. He was giving himself a headache and all he had was more questions.

He left the study and walked through the house to see if there was anything he wanted to keep. On the second floor he found three photo albums and put them on Eleanor's large double bed. He climbed the steep, narrow stairs to the attic. Musty, it smelled of old cedar and camphor and was oppressively hot. Eleanor saved things. He sat on an overturned wooden box and sipped his beer. He picked up an old pair of hockey skates, size three. Here were the good but outmoded appliances, a vacuum tube radio, a rack of old clothes, suitcases that no one would ever carry, camp trunks, school papers and old prints, toys, a chemistry set, golf clubs. A junkyard of discarded hobbies and musical instruments that no one learned to play, remnants of birthday parties, a deflated football. He hadn't been up here in years.

It was too hot. He descended the stairs and closed the door. He picked up the photo albums and carried them downstairs and back to the air-conditioned study.

His instinct told him that Don Trilby had to be working for Tel-Tech, but why would they be interested in old tax records, a house full of furniture, and an attic full of junk? It didn't make sense.

He had to move. The possibility that Trilby had already called people in New York was too great to ignore. He switched off the air conditioner, took a last look around without feeling anything except relief that he was leaving, and went across the hallway to the bedroom. He took a canvas flight bag from the closet and emptied the bureau drawers of socks, underwear, and casual polo shirts. He took the few slacks and jackets from the closet, still on their hangers. He turned off the bedroom air conditioner, gathered everything up, and carried it to the car. He returned to retrieve his jacket and baton from the living room and closed the windows. He took a slow look around. It would probably be the last time.

There was a framed photo of Eleanor on the mantel and something compelled him to take it. He locked the rear door and walked to the car without looking back.

He drove to the Worthingtons', where Frank and Elise were cleaning up their dinner dishes and making plans for a Labor Day barbecue.

Dalbey sat at the kitchen table and Frank brought him a beer, pouring it into a frosted glass.

"I'm selling the house," Dalbey said.

"Bill Shoreham called."

"I'm storing some things for Sharon. Eleanor's silver and china, the linens. She says she doesn't want them, but she might later. Bill has arranged a professional tag sale for everything else, but I'd like you to go through the house and take anything you want."

"We couldn't possibly," Elise said.

"Take a look. It's what Eleanor would want. There might be some family things that I don't know about."

Dalbey produced the door key and placed it on the table. "This is for the back door. Shoreham will have a key."

"Seems a shame to sell that house," Elise said. "Something wrong with a house passing out of the family."

Dalbey nodded, but didn't comment. "I owe somebody money for cutting the grass."

"Jim Parson," Frank said. "I've been taking care of it. When the house is sold, I'll let you know how much."

Dalbey stayed for what he considered a polite interval. He had little in common with Frank and Elise, but he had always considered them pleasant enough, and he was careful not to offend them by appearing indifferent. He finished the beer and pushed up from the table, saying, "Well, I've got to get back to the city."

"I don't know how you can stay in that awful city," Elise said.

"I'm beginning to wonder myself," Dalbey said.

"Will you be here for the sale?" Frank asked.

"I think not. Bill's going to handle it."

"We'll be glad to help."

"I'll tell Bill."

"When is it?"

"Next weekend."

Dalbey made it to the front porch over their polite protests that New York was no place for a holiday weekend, and he retreated to the rental car, looking back once and waving a hand before sliding into the car.

It was after eight o'clock and getting dark. Summer

was winding down, but the sounds he loved were still part of the warm night. The trilling and sawing of myriad insects, the cries of night birds. Moths flung themselves at the porch light, and somewhere in the distant dark a dog barked.

Dalbey made a U-turn and drove into town, passing through the small business section and on to Bill Shoreham's rented cottage.

Shoreham was dressed to go out, but he led Dalbey into the living room. "I didn't expect you."

"I'll only be a minute."

"I'm taking my kids to dinner."

"I just wanted to make sure the sale was all set."

"Next weekend," Shoreham said.

Dalbey unfolded a sheet of paper and handed it to Shoreham. "Here's some things I'd like to have placed in storage for Sharon."

Shoreham glanced at the small list. "No problem."

"Well, I'll talk to you after the holiday."

"I'll be here."

"By the way, do you know if Don Trilby does any work for Tel-Tech International?"

"Oh, sure, Westcott Data is one of his biggest clients. They're in Hartford. Why?"

"Just curious." Could he talk to Shoreham? He felt confused and alone, but he didn't know whom to trust. "Well, look," he said, "I'll let you go."

"Staying at the house?"

"No. I have to head back to the city."

"Will you be here for the sale?"

"I'd rather not."

"I'll take care of it."

"I told Elise and Frank to go through the house and take what they wanted."

"Fine."

Before he left New Canaan, Dalbey stopped by the police station and spoke to the duty officer, the same lieutenant who had shown him the report on Eleanor's accident.

"I was wondering, what have the Bridgeport police found out about the white van?" Dalbey asked.

"The white van?"

"The van that ran my wife off the road. I was told the Bridgeport police found it abandoned near the railway station and there was red paint on the fender."

The lieutenant frowned. "Let me get the file." He scraped his chair back. He left the room and was gone for almost five minutes. When he returned, he placed a file folder on the desk, tapping it with his finger, and said, "Mr. Dalbey, there's nothing here about any white van being found. I called the Bridgeport police, and they don't have anything either."

Dalbey was beyond surprise. He bowed his head, massaging his forehead with the fingers of his left hand. "Damn." He felt foolish and angry and tired. He looked up, shaking his head. "I guess I was misled." He stood up and extended his hand. "Thank you. Sorry to bother you."

"No bother." The officer shook Dalbey's hand. "I'm sorry. Whoever told you that, it was damned cruel."

Chapter Fifteen

Dalbey left New Canaan, driving south on the Merritt Parkway toward New York City. He turned off at Route 684 and drove north. He connected with Route 84 west and crossed the Hudson River at Newburgh to finally mesh with the northbound New York Thruway. The weekend traffic was still heavy, but it was only fifteen miles to the New Paltz exit.

It was after eleven o'clock when Dalbey came off the Thruway and into town on Route 299. It was quiet, as he expected, only the bars and a few restaurants still open. It's a short drive through New Paltz; nine blocks to the Wallkill River bridge and out of town. Dalbey turned right on Chestnut Street and parked at Barnaby's, where he knew they would still be serving food.

He took a booth in the bar and ordered a chili burger. He drank a Budweiser while he waited. There was a small group of rock climbers at the bar, young, long-haired, and mustached, plus a few girls, and one of them was telling about his problems on Sky Top, while the others chided and laughed.

"I thought I was on Grey Face, but I took that hand traverse on the seventh pitch and expected to go around the corner and find that big crack, and the damn thing wasn't there. So I traverse back and take a good look, and I'm on Minnie Belle and the ledge will take me to Jekyll and Hyde, where I sure as hell don't want to be. . . ."

Dalbey liked climbers and enjoyed their talk; a good thing if you had to grow up in New Paltz, where the two landmarks were the college and the Shawangunks. The college has been there since 1828, the Gunks, as they are called, about 400 million years. Geologists call it the Shawangunk Conglomerate, a tilted shelf of sedimentary rock thrusting out of the ground to form 150-foot cliffs that surround and overlook the Wallkill River valley. The Gunks have been a mecca for rock climbers since 1930.

Although he hadn't climbed seriously for fifteen years, and he was never the best, Dalbey had mastered most of the routes in the Gunks, and as he listened to the young man's story, he could actually recall almost every crack and toehold of his own climbs on Sky Top.

When he left the restaurant, Dalbey crossed the river and drove north on 299. The family home, where his mother still lived, was in town. Dalbey owned a cabin on two hunded acres that bordered the Mohonk Preserve, an area owned by the Mohonk Trust that encompasses the Gunks and is legally designated as permanent open space.

Eight miles from town he turned right onto Route 44, a winding narrow road that climbs into the Preserve, winds around the western end of The Trapps, the most popular climbing area, and plunges down a long hill to Route 209 and Lake Minnewaska. As he approached The Trapps, Dalbey slowed and turned onto a single-lane dirt road, where he was stopped by a heavy chain draped across the road between two stone pillars. Signs on the trees warned: *Private Property. No Hunting. No Fishing. No Trespassing. Violators Will Be Prosecuted.* He left the car to unlock the chain.

He drove on, the headlights illuminating a corridor through the dense overgrown forest.

The Judge had called this place The Camp. It had been the homestead of four generations of Taggarts, the last being McNeil Taggart, whom Dalbey remembered as a ragged, unkempt old man, unmarried and childless. He trapped for pelts, fished, hunted, and worked at odd jobs when he needed extra money. He was not a recluse. He was often seen fishing the Wallkill or driving the back roads in a battered pickup. But he avoided the town as much as possible and the town shunned him, except for the Judge, who considered Old Mac a master of the dry fly and the second-best wing shot in the Hudson Valley. When the Taggart place was on the block for back taxes, the Judge settled the arrears, bought the place from Mac at a fair price, and let him live there until he died. Then the Judge had the place cleaned from top to bottom and it became The Camp. Dalbey was working in Paris when he heard that his mother had the place up for sale, and he bought it.

It was an isolated property, bordered on all sides by state land or the five-thousand-acre Preserve. The nearest house was three miles away.

The mildly rutted driveway meandered through the

property, taking the easiest route through the trees. It emerged into a meadow and lifted gently to end at a grove of tall pines where three buildings stood: the house, a small barn, and a woodshed. The only original artifact remaining from the Taggart days was the rusted engine of a 1928 Hudson that hung from a tree. The Judge said it gave the place character and Dalbey agreed. The property ended at a barbwire fence about fifty feet beyond the rear of the buildings. From there the land rose steeply through a stand of live oak and dense brush, which gave way to a spill of talus. Still climbing, the terrain was interrupted by a low stone retaining wall that supported a wide hiking trail, and then ended abruptly at the high, perpendicular wall of The Trapps.

Dalbey parked facing the front porch of the slope-roofed, one-story house. He left the headlights burning so he could see the flat rock where he kept a key hidden.

He opened the front door and stepped inside to switch on the lights, including an outdoor floodlight mounted in a tree. He carried his clothes from the car, then opened the doors and windows. The house had been closed since April when a visit to his mother had coincided with the opening of trout season. He had a caretaker who came by a couple times a week to check things, make repairs, and plow the road in winter, but he rarely came into the house.

Dalbey came to New Paltz maybe four or five times a year, but he wanted the cabin ready. The telephone was always in service, electricity always connected, minimum heat all winter, and cold beer in the refrigerator.

The main room and the large stone fireplace remained from the original house. Dalbey's workmen had eliminated the attic, giving height to the room and exposing the lodgepole beams. He had added two bedrooms, two baths, and a modern alcove kitchen. The furniture in the main room was a long, rectangular table of rock maple big enough to accommodate eight captain's chairs; there were two leather easy chairs facing the fireplace, a color television and stereo system in a corner. The walls were studded with wooden pegs from which hung coils of red and blue climbing ropes and slings of mountaineering hardware. Over the fireplace was a rare split-bamboo fly rod that had belonged to the Judge and a framed sepia photograph of the Judge fishing the Wallkill. There was a special cabinet behind a locked wooden door that held half a dozen shotguns, including an old Ithaca double and the Judge's 12-gauge Remington autoloader.

Another closet, unlocked, was for coats, and it held a collection of hiking and climbing gear, leather boots and harnesses, day packs, alpenstocks, a collection of *kletterschuhe* for rock climbing, and even several pairs of the new Fire Rock Boots that cling to rock like the feet of a lizard.

Dalbey was tired, too tired even to bother with a beer. He doused the lights and fell into bed, groaning aloud and savoring the luxury of not having to move, and in minutes he was asleep.

He was awakened by a banging and hello-ing from the front, and he recognized Jim Crowther's bullfrog bass.

"Okay, okay!"

He slipped into faded navy sweats and an old T-shirt that said *OCEAN DIVER Key Largo* on the front, and he padded through the house barefoot to find his caretaker at the screen door.

"Ah, Mr. Dalbey. Didn't recognize the car."

"Rental." Dalbey yawned and blinked sleep-puffed eyes. "What time is it?"

"After nine. Day's half gone."

"Or at least half started. How about some coffee?"

"Can't stay. Thanks just the same. Making my routine run through here, saw the car is all. Thought I better check."

"Glad you did. How you been, Jim?"

"Taking nourishment. Hear old Mary Beth was raisin' hell at the Town Council."

"Oh, yeah?" Mary Beth was Dalbey's mother.

"They say she cussed out Old Man Miller." Crowther was grinning.

Warren Miller was president of the water company, among other things. Mary Beth Dalbey, once the paragon of polite English usage, had taken to mild profanity when she passed eighty. "Running out of time" was her excuse. "Makes 'em listen." She was not fond of Warren Miller.

"Well," Crowther said, chuckling over the local gossip but not elaborating, "gotta get a move on."

"Nice to see you, Jim."

"Be up all weekend?"

"Probably. Any fish in the crick?"

"One or two. Weather's too warm."

Dalbey watched Crowther return to his pickup truck and drive away. Then he made coffee. He rummaged in the bedroom closet for a pair of running shoes. When he finished the coffee, he left the house and ran five miles, averaging ten minutes per, which wasn't fast, but it made him feel good. Then he showered, dressed in chinos and a polo shirt, and drove into town for breakfast.

It was almost noon when he parked in front of the family home on South Chestnut Street. It was a modest two-story clapboard house, white, with a bay window and green shutters. It was on a rise with two narrow terraces of cropped grass. Concrete steps climbed to the front portico. A paved driveway at the side led to a single-car garage at the rear of the house. A Dodge station wagon was parked in the drive. Farther on, near the garage, was a small yellow Toyota with battered fenders.

Dalbey climbed the three sets of steps, rang the bell, then opened the front door and stepped inside. "Anybody home?"

"Who wants to know?"

"Your son."

"Philip Dalbey, as I live and breathe."

He followed the sound of the voice into the dining

room, where his mother sat on one side of the dining table and his brother, Marcus, sat on the end. The table was covered with neat stacks of printed literature and envelopes. He wondered what Mary Beth was campaigning for this month. In April it had been the sandhill crane.

She was eighty-four, and her short, wavy hair was snow-white. Her skin had a mottled-parchment look, but the blue eyes still sparkled with fun and her hands were as steady as ever. She tilted her head to receive Dalbey's kiss on the cheek.

"Sit, sit, sit. We need volunteers. Those sheets of address labels. Just peel them off and stick them on envelopes."

Dalbey took the chair and reached for the sheets of labels. "Do we get minimum wage for this?"

"You'll get your rewards in heaven." Her face clouded when she said that, and she pressed her fingers to her lips. "Oh, Philip, I'm so sorry about Eleanor."

"Thank you, Mother."

"I should have been at the funeral. This one"—she pointed at Marcus—"and that Emmaline. They act like I'm already in my grave."

"Tell that to Warren Miller."

She reared back and her eyes glittered. Marcus chuckled. "That old fool," she said. "Who've you been talking to?"

"It's all over town. Mary Beth Dalbey cussed out Old Man Miller at the Town Council."

"I never . . ."

Marcus was nodding his head and smiling. She waved a hand at him. "You stop that."

"Were you there?" Dalbey asked his brother.

"I was not, but I, too, heard a full report from a very reliable source. She definitely cussed him out."

"That foolish, aggravating man. Every time I rose to challenge his ignorance he would shout about Robert's

Rules of Order, Robert's Rules of Order! The damned fool."

"So what did she say?"

"Now, Marcus—"

"She said, 'Take your goddamned old Roberts and stuff him!'"

The three of them laughed together. "Is that all? By God, Mary Beth, you're getting soft in your old age."

"I think there was also something about Miller being a damned dried-up old fool."

Dalbey put his head back and shook with laughter. "What was this all about?"

Marcus opened one of the folders they were mailing, a funds appeal from the Open Trails Conservancy. "The water company land just outside the Mohonk Preserve," he said, winking. "She wants every acre she can get."

"Including the Taggart place," she said. "When are you going to give us that land?"

"You've already got it condemned so I can only sell to the state."

"She doesn't trust the state," Marcus said.

"Are you in this with her?"

"I'm her legal adviser. I keep her out of jail."

"Not always."

They laughed at that. In 1980 Mary Beth had been arrested during an antinuclear demonstration and had spent three days in jail, making the evening news in the process.

Dalbey looked for his glasses to read the flyer, but he couldn't find them. Without them the print would be a blur. "Damn, I'm getting so blind I need glasses to find my glasses."

"You don't need glasses to stick on labels."

"You mean you employ the handicapped?"

"Be careful what you say about the handicapped," Marcus said.

"We're all handicapped in some way," she said.

Dalbey was in awe of his mother. She was fifty when the Judge died. She went back to finish college, got her degree in one year, and then earned a master's in political science. She taught at the college for eight years, then retired to bedevil the Establishment. He knew that Marcus, who lived nearby, visited her every day. Looking at them now, working on a mailing and plotting new mischief, he envied their involvement.

"Where's Grace?" he asked.

"Helping out at the library."

Grace, Marcus's wife, was his mother's shadow, her partner in crime. When Mary Beth was arrested, Grace had punched a policeman to make certain she went to jail with her.

"How are the girls?" Dalbey asked.

"Fine." Marcus and Grace had three daughters; the youngest was Sharon's age.

"Where are they?"

"Midge is here, teaching at the college. Helen just had another baby, and she's talking about going to law school. Beth is working in Boston."

"Boston. Does Sharon know that?"

"Of course." Marcus looked at him strangely. "They're sharing a beach house for the summer."

"Sharon and Beth?"

"And Sharon's beau." You seldom heard that term used these days, but it sounded right coming from Marcus. "You knew Sharon was serious about a young man." It was partly a statement, more a question.

"No, I didn't."

"Beth says they're talking about marriage. You might be a grandfather before you know it."

His mother tilted her head up to regard him through her bifocals. "Do you good. About time you settled down."

"Mother, I was married for twenty-six years."

She arched one eyebrow and nodded her head, telling him what she thought of his idea of marriage.

He changed the subject, talking about Marcus's work as a Superior Court judge.

It disturbed him that Sharon had failed to confide in him, and he didn't understand it. He talked to her at least once a month. He thought they had a good, open relationship. Why did he have to hear from Marcus that she was sharing a house with her cousin? And this man. Not a mention. And they were talking about marriage. Grandfather? Jesus!

He left with Marcus after their mother announced, "Time for my siesta." The brothers parted on the sidewalk. Marcus drove off in the big station wagon.

Shopping for groceries, he decided to cook dinner at the cabin. He bought scallops of veal, shallots and fresh mushrooms, lemons, tomatoes, some basil. He stopped at the liquor store for wine and was surprised to find a Stony Hill Pinot Blanc. The dealer had three bottles and he bought them all.

It was still afternoon when he returned to his cabin—hot, but nothing like the city. He put the wine and veal in the refrigerator. He changed into shorts and hiking boots, took a pair of binoculars, and climbed over the rock debris to the wide trail that ran beneath the cliffs. There were a lot of climbers, a lot of watchers, and a lot of hikers. He took the trail to Sky Top, an easy forty-minute hike, and found a good perch where he could watch the climbers through the binoculars.

He bored quickly, so he did a circuit of Sky Top until he was overlooking Mohonk Lake and the Mohonk Mountain House beyond. He trained the binoculars on the sweeping front porch of the lodge.

It was a sight he loved. It was always startling to see the Mountain House, a towering seven-story lodge of spires and gabled roofs, one of a handful of the great mountain hostels remaining from the early 1900s, when all these hiking trails were carriage roads bringing guests from the train depot at New Paltz Landing.

Dalbey hiked back along the trail. Two strands of barbed wire on his fence were down. It made it easy to climb over, but he made a mental note to have Jim Crowther fix it. He sat on the porch, rocking, listening to bird talk, and watching the clown capers of the squirrels and the hyperbusy chipmunks while the afternoon faded. He cooked scaloppine with a mushroom and lemon sauce, linguine with a fresh tomato and basil sauce. He ate at a small table on the porch, keeping the wine chilled in a bucket of ice cubes.

He judged it a close-to-perfect day, but perfect days, damn it, were not much fun alone. You could be sailing, rail down, sails driving, the tiller thrumming in your hand, the water curling away from the bow, flung spindrift glittering in the sun, but if there wasn't someone to share the elation, someone to grin at and shout at "How 'bout this?" it was deflating, incomplete somehow, as though it wasn't really happening.

He made it an early evening, cleaned up the few dishes, finished the wine, and was in bed by nine, the alarm set for four A.M.

When the alarm went off—*bee-bee-bee*—he reached out and caught it on the fourth ring. He threw off the covering sheet and swung his feet to the floor. It was still dark. The air was cool and he felt good.

The Judge could give his shoulder a single shake and whisper, "C'mon, Phil, they're waitin' for us," and he would be awake and on his feet a minute later, pulling on old clothes. The smell of coffee perking and toast. Wide-awake. School days they had to pry him out of bed.

An hour later he was on the river, down east of Hugenot Street where there were some good deep pools. He wore chest waders and a canvas fishing vest over an old checked flannel shirt. A pair of magnifying glasses—for tying flies to the leader—hung from his neck. He glanced up and around, checking for trees, as he worked the 6-weight line off the reel with an eight-foot graphite rod.

He pumped the line out until he had a good loop working overhead, and then brought the tip down to drop his wet fly in the current above a cutback. When it drifted through the pool he snapped the rod up, lifting the line and the fly, letting it drift overhead, then pumping it into a controlled arc while he felt his way carefully along the rocky river bottom to try another spot.

The water was probably too warm. Trout like it cold. But he didn't mind. He liked being on the river and he enjoyed the casting.

It was light now. The birds had been busy since false dawn, a steady trilling and chirping punctuated with occasional riffs that made him scan the trees for the singer. The sky was not yet showing blue, but the high, windblown cirrus was already reflecting a yellowish glow. It was going to be a network-quality sunrise and another hot day. Working the line overhead, feeling the wash of water against his boots, Dalbey savored the clean damp odors of earth and dew and grass, letting the thoughts tumble through his head.

His mother was wrong about one thing; he wasn't about to settle down. He thought of all the trout streams he'd never had time to fish: the Snake and the Salmon, the Kootenai, the Yellowstone, the McKenzie, the Flathead north of Kalispell, the Roaring Fork in Colorado. And he had never sailed for any length of time without searching for the next telephone, his umbilical to New York. He wondered what it would be like to cruise without a schedule, no landfalls at island airports to rush back home.

When the sun was up he reeled in his line, removed the fly, and returned to his car. He stopped in town to buy *The New York Times* and went home to a breakfast of scrambled eggs and toast. He ran his five miles, showered, and sat on the front porch to rummage through the newspaper. He discarded the classified and real estate sections. The magazine and book review were put aside for later. He glanced at the sports headlines. He was leafing through Arts and Leisure when he stopped to read a promotional advertisement in the TV section. Major General Hugh Winston, retired, chairman of Tel-Tech International, was the scheduled guest on *Face the Nation*.

Dalbey glanced at his watch. It was almost ten-thirty A.M. He dropped the newspaper and went into the house to turn on the television. He switched to channel 4 and went to the stove to pour coffee. He waited through an interminable series of commercials, the introduction and more commercials, and then the camera was on the humorless, square-jawed face of General Winston.

The face was impassive during the introduction. He fiddled with a pencil, twirling it between his fingers, and when the interviewer welcomed him to the program, he nodded and forced a smile.

Dalbey tried to fathom why Winston was appearing voluntarily on national television. He had been known for keeping a low personal profile, but in the past year he seemed to be increasingly visible. His photograph, usually limited to the business magazines, was now appearing in the news publications. Dalbey had listened to him speak at the National Press Club, and his normally hawkish, conservative views had been greatly tempered. Winston was heavier than Dalbey remembered him, and the extra weight seemed to age him.

"It's been rumored, General, that you have always maintained close ties to the CIA."

"That's nonsense. I'm a businessman."

"In 1976 you supported the military coup in Argentina. It's been suggested that the CIA—"

"That's not true. We do business in Argentina. We welcome stability in government. Every businessman does. But we steer clear of internal politics."

"Speaking of politics, can we explore your relationship with Richard Nixon?"

"I don't have a relationship with Richard Nixon."

"You supported his candidacy."

"So did a majority of Americans. I personally contributed money to his campaign. He thanked me. That's not a relationship."

"One of your subsidiaries, Bowser Industries, is a major supplier of weapons systems to the Pentagon."

"We do some of that work, yes."

"Four point seven billion in 1981."

"Could be. I don't deal with figures."

"Is it true you named Bowser Industries after your dog?"

Winston almost smiled. "A golden retriever, yes. A very noble animal."

"May I ask why?"

"Why?"

"Yes. To name a seven-hundred-million-dollar company like that seems, well, whimsical. Why the dog's name?"

"Because the cat's name was Tinkerbelle."

The reporter smiled, but she was just playing an old reporter's game before she went for the jugular.

"The French newspaper *Le Figaro* reported that Bowser Industries supplied Syria with weapons in the recent Lebanon crisis."

"Not true. That, I believe, would be a treasonous act. We have marines in Lebanon.

"The weapons were sold to France, a NATO ally. We have no idea how those weapons got to Syria."

"The evidence suggests—"

"If you have evidence of someone in France passing NATO weapons to Syria, I would suggest you put it in the hands of the State Department. That's a very serious allegation."

Dalbey stared hard at the screen. The man was tough and quick, and if you believed the interviewer, ruthless. Vince Steffinelli's boss. A man who could make wars happen. It was difficult to imagine that kind of power.

The interview ended and the names of the production staff crawled over the face on the TV screen. Why, Dalbey wondered, is this man having me followed? He was in Winston's way, for some reason, and it was something that couldn't be settled with a buy-out or a lawsuit. But why weren't they moving on him? This was puzzling. They seemed to be hanging back, content to just watch and listen, as though they were waiting for *him* to make the move.

What move, for crissake? Vince would know. He had to flush Vince, rattle him, get him to talk or make *his* move. Dalbey knew that he was up against rough company, but he was tired of the bullshit, goddamnit, so he was going to shake the tree.

Chapter Sixteen

Dalbey drove back to New York early on Labor Day to avoid the traffic. He dropped off the rental car and took a cab to Seventy-fourth Street.

The stakeout seemed to be gone. The street was empty except for parked cars, and he knew most of them.

He let himself in and punched in the code to deactivate the alarm. We went to his office to take the calls off the recording device. Nothing much. His sister wanted to visit. An obscene remark from a friend in Florida. A few calls with no message.

To alert the listeners that he was once again in residence, he called Marianna. There was no answer, but he let it ring long enough to awaken the poor devil monitoring the tap.

He called his son's number and there was no answer. The last summer weekend and everybody out of the city. He called Emmaline. She wanted to visit that week, but he told her he was going out of town and put her off for a week.

When he felt hungry he walked to a small French restaurant on First Avenue. He noticed that his surveillance was in place, a middle-aged man in a rumpled tan suit. He did nothing to lose him on the walk back to his building.

On Tuesday, with the country back in business, he had Mossy book a morning flight to Denver for Wednesday and reserve a room at the Brown Palace hotel.

Michael Durso reported that the researcher in Washington would be spending the day at the National Archives.

"You terribly busy?"

"Nothing critical," Michael said.

"I'd like information on Hugh Winston, the chairman of Tel-Tech. Personal stuff. How he got started. How much he's worth. Marriages. Politics. Gossip. Call Bill Henley over at Kapler Newspapers. Tell him you're working for me and we want to use their files."

"Got it."

He called Davidson's Gun Room in Yonkers to make sure they still did repairs. They did.

The morning mail brought an envelope from Bill Shoreham. It contained a newspaper clipping about Eleanor's accident. The photo of her was several years old. There was a note attached: *"Thought you might want to keep this. Bill."*

He hadn't thought of using a clipping, but it was perfect. He went to the copy machine and made several copies on eight-by-ten sheets.

When he passed Alice Walder's office, he stopped and looked in. "I have to drive to Yonkers. I'll be back."

"We have to talk," she said.

"This afternoon. Soon as I get back."

"Promise?"

"Scout's honor."

He climbed the stairs to the second floor and got the

.32-caliber Smith & Wesson with the filed firing pin. He checked to make sure he had the federal license to carry it.

When he was ready to leave, he had Mossy call the garage to bring his car down. He wanted to make sure they followed.

He walked the block to pick up the BMW. The heat was already building and he carried his suit jacket. The revolver was in a small flight bag. It was a forty-minute drive to Yonkers. He got off on Broadway and ground through the small-city congestion until he saw Davidson's sign on the left.

There was a parking lot in the next block. He pulled in and left the car. He carried his jacket and the flight bag.

"How long?" the attendant asked, marking the ticket with his plate number.

"Hour at the most."

Dalbey took the proffered ticket and walked back along Broadway, crossing over to enter Davidson's.

He asked for repairs and was directed to the rear. It was a large store, comfortably air-conditioned. The walls were lined with racks of rifles and shotguns. The police section displayed riot guns and semiautomatics. There were posters and flyers for everything short of machine guns. The handguns were in a long row of locked glass cases. There were shelves of ammunition, and racks of leather holsters and gun cases and camouflage clothing. The clerks wore shooting vests with DAVIDSON'S on the back and nicknames on the front.

"Help you?" a clerk labeled DUKE asked.

"Hope so." Dalbey unzipped the case and brought out the Smith & Wesson, breaking it before handing it over. "It needs a firing pin."

Duke ran a finger over the pin. "Needs a whole new hammer. Might have one." He used a magnifying glass to check on the serial number and the model number. He went back to a workshop area in a wire cage and rummaged through some drawers. He returned with a chrome-plated hammer. "You're in luck. We can fix it right now if you like."

"How long?"

"About twenty minutes. It's just a replacement. I'll need your license."

Dalbey handed over the federal firearms permit. Duke looked it over and wrote down the name and number, as New York State law required. He handed it back, appraising Dalbey, then took the weapon to the workshop and discussed it with a gunsmith wearing a green eyeshade and a soiled blue apron.

With time to wait, Dalbey strolled through the store, looking at the stock. A clerk was extolling the merits of an Armalite semiautomatic to a worried home owner: "And much better than a handgun. Thirty-two-shot clip. You don't have to know how to shoot. Just point it and spray."

He looked over a section of black-powder muskets and a small replica of a Civil War cannon. He went to the shotguns and asked to see a ten-thousand-dollar Purdy double. It was beautiful workmanship, and the clerk, a man with a huge handlebar mustache, said, "We don't sell many of those." Dalbey passed it back and the clerk carefully wiped it down with a chamois before putting it away.

When the pistol was ready, Dalbey bought a spring-loaded belt holster to fit it and a box of ammunition. He left the store carrying everything in the flight bag. He crossed the street and glanced back to see the man in the rumpled tan suit hurry into the store. Steffinelli would soon know that he was armed.

He drove back to Manhattan and left the car at the garage. He walked back to the office carrying the jacket and the flight bag.

Mossy greeted him with his reservations. "You're on United flight two-o-two, leaves Kennedy at nine. You'll be in Denver by noon. Open return. Hotel is confirmed."

Alice wanted to discuss the job offer from Kapler Newspapers, and Dalbey knew she wanted to take it. He waited until she brought it up, then said, "I think you have to give it a trial. You'll always regret it if you don't."

"What will you do?"

"I don't know."

"Buy those newspapers?"

"Not sure. I'm about sixty percent against it. But I've got to make up my mind. I promised Larkin an answer this week. Have you told Harmon?"

"I'll call him tomorrow. I wanted to talk to you first."

There wasn't much more to say. There was a moment of silence, then she asked, "Do you want to talk about anything? Is something wrong?"

"Nothing I can't handle." She frowned and he patted her hand. "Thanks for asking. Now I better get handling."

He went to his office and called Marianna. He had decided over the weekend not to renew their relationship. There were a number of reasons. Her youth, for one, but more importantly he had decided that he really wanted to live alone and unencumbered. On the other hand, she had been a good friend and he wanted to bring her down gently. She answered and he said, "Hi, this is Philip."

"Flip, I just got in from the Hamptons. I've been trying to reach you."

"Sorry, it's been a rough week."

"Flip, I have wonderful news. I'm getting married."

"Married?"

"A wonderful man. A lawyer. Very rich. Are you happy for me?"

He told her he was happy for her. Akron? Marianna living in Akron? Not possible. The intended groom was fifty. Did he think that was too old? What could he say? Yes, he would like to have lunch or dinner with her. He had to go to Denver, but he would call in a week or two.

When he disconnected, he replaced the phone and

held his hand on it, staring. Well, he thought, how do you like that? He didn't like it at all.

He made a person-to-person call to Denver, was given another number, and called that. When he finally got his party, he explained who he was and where they had met, and he said he was looking for some professional advice.

"You want to talk."

"That's right."

"Hundred dollars an hour, two-fifty minimum."

"That sounds good."

"Cash."

"No problem." He made an appointment to meet the man in the rotunda garden of the Brown Palace.

When he hung up, he had to smile. This one was going to rattle old Steffinelli.

The rain began at four P.M., desultory showers at first that just raised the humidity, then a cloudburst. The sky darkened and was rended by lightning and rumbling, reverberating thunder. The wind rose and the rain came down, lashing the windows and pelting the sidewalks. He called a fish market on York Avenue and ordered fresh salmon fillets to be delivered.

Later, with the staff gone and the rain reduced to a steady drizzle, he worked on a salad of greens to go with the caper dressing and the salmon, which was charbroiling on his vented indoor grill.

He uncorked a split of the chilled *chenin blanc* and ate in his dining alcove. He decided that eating alone was not all that great, that food tastes better when the experience is shared. He wondered if Claire Paige had returned from The Netherlands.

When he finished, he rinsed the few dishes and put them into the dishwaster. He carried the wine to the lounge and watched the evening news.

As it often did, the news made him restless. He turned it off and went to the third-floor gym, where he changed clothes and spent an hour working out on the Universal.

He relaxed in the sauna, then spent a painful five minutes in a cold shower.

Back in the lounge he poured a glass of dry sherry and tried unsuccessfully to read. His mind was preoccupied with Denver. He reached for a manila file folder and took out a copy of Eleanor's accident story. With a red marking-pen he wrote on the bottom: *I'm coming for you, Vince.* He folded the sheet and slipped it into a blank envelope and sealed it. He wrote *Vincent Steffinelli/Personal* on the front.

When he finally went to bed he lay awake, staring into the dark, and thought about Jon Steach. Five days since he had called and not a word. What the hell was Steach into? He also thought about Claire Paige. With just a little imagination he could believe that they had really met at the embassy party in Rome. He wondered whom she worked for.

In the morning Dalbey packed a small carry-on bag and left before the staff arrived. He took a cab to Kennedy Airport, noting that he had company, and caught the United flight to Denver.

The morning headlines announced that the Russians admitted to shooting down the Korean airliner that had strayed over Russian territory with 269 people on board. The Russians claimed it was on a CIA spy mission. Dalbey was stunned. He listened to the excited talk around him, the anger against the Russians, the suspicions aimed at the CIA. Watching the flight routine, the passengers settling in, the flight attendants moving up and down the aisles, he couldn't help trading places with the terrified passengers on the doomed plane.

It was a tense but uneventful flight and they landed at Stapleton International Airport on time.

There were three security guards waiting when Dalbey emerged from the gate in Concourse B. They had obviously been shown photographs, because their expressions said, "That's him," and they closed in on him fast.

"Mr. Dalbey?"

"Yes."

"Philip Dalbey?"

"That's right."

"Would you come with us, please?"

"May I ask why?"

"Routine security check is all." They were polite but firm. They boxed him in and moved him along. It was a short walk. The leader went straight to a door labeled AUTHORIZED PERSONNEL ONLY and opened it, standing aside for Dalbey and the two guards to enter. He followed and closed the door. The room was white and bare, except for a table in the center and straight-backed metal chairs, and an odd-looking viewer that resembled a slide projector.

"Mr. Dalbey," the leader explained, "when you purchased your ticket you signed a waiver agreeing to a security search, if necessary. May we have your bag, please?"

They opened the bag on the table and examined the contents: a 35mm camera with a 135mm lens. Several boxes of fast color film. A shirt, underwear, socks. A pair of running shoes, shorts, and T-shirt. A leather bag of toilet articles that they opened and examined. An appointment calendar and a paperback copy of Plato's *The Last Days of Socrates*. Dalbey knew they expected a .32-caliber Smith & Wesson, and they were scowling over the contents of the bag.

"May we have your jacket, please?"

Dalbey removed his suit jacket and handed it over. They searched the pockets, removing his ticket and the envelope addressed to Steffinelli, and handed it back. The leader slipped the envelope into the viewer and switched it on. The picture on the screen showed the contents to be a copy of a newspaper clipping.

"Would you empty your pockets, please?"

"Could you tell me what this is about?"

"Your pockets, please."

He placed his wallet on the table, a comb, keys and change, some bills. The leader went through the wallet, glowering at the contents. When he didn't find a fake firearms permit or phony CIA credentials, he seemed disappointed.

"Maybe it's taped to my body," Dalbey said, then regretted the sarcasm, because they made him undress down to his boxer shorts.

There was no doubt now that Steffinelli had a direct line to a federal wiretap. He also had muscle with this airport security team, one of whom was a U.S. marshal. It was amazing what money could buy.

"You can get dressed."

"Maybe you have the name wrong," Dalbey said as he dressed. "I believe there was a Mr. Dolman on that flight."

The three men reacted without speaking. The leader nodded to one of the guards, who scurried from the room.

Dalbey finished knotting his tie. They had repacked the bag. He retrieved the things from his pockets.

"I hope we haven't inconvenienced you, Mr. Dalbey. You understand, I'm sure. Airport security."

Dalbey smiled and took his bag. The leader opened the door for him. "Have a good day, Mr. Dalbey."

He had to take a minibus to the auto rental offices beyond the parking lots. He used a credit card to rent a small red Plymouth.

"What's the best route downtown?" he asked.

The woman at the counter produced a small map. "Right out here." She traced the route with a pencil. "You go down here to Quebec. Turn left and down here to Colfax, where you make a right. That takes you right in."

Her directions were good, but he had to fight the noon traffic and an endless succession of stop lights. It took him forty minutes to reach Seventeenth Street and the Brown Palace hotel. He left the car with the doorman, handing over the keys and five dollars. "I'm just checking in," he said. "Ten minutes." It took fifteen, but the doorman had the car waiting.

He hadn't noticed a tail, but he was sure they were on him. He picked up Route 6 heading west and drove at a steady fifty-five. There was a state police car cruising about three cars behind. When he was beyond Denver, with the incredible panorama of the Rockies forming a solid, seemingly impenetrable wall straight ahead, he pulled off to the side to consult his directions. The IPS correspondent for the Western States, an old friend, was based in Denver. Dalbey had called from New Paltz for the addresses he needed. He was reaching into the small bag for the appointment book when the state police car pulled in behind him.

Dalbey wound down his window as the policeman, a tall, dark-haired man with a friendly smile, walked up, adjusting his hat.

"Howdy, sir, having a problem?"

"No, just pulled over to check my directions."

"What are you looking for?"

"Antelope Drive."

"Up ahead about five, six miles. It's well marked."

"Thank you."

"Don't mention it." He tugged at the brim of his hat. "Have a good day. Drive safely."

Dalbey waited until the officer had returned to his car, then he pulled back onto the highway and drove off. A few minutes later the police car passed him and continued gaining speed until it was out of sight.

About midway between Denver and Golden he saw the sign for Antelope Drive and he slowed for the exit. At the bottom of the ramp was a sign directing him to CORPORATE HEADQUARTERS. TEL-TECH INTERNATIONAL, INC. And parked next to the sign was the state police car and the same smiling officer.

The entrance was a quarter mile past the sign. He drove between two stone pillars and started up a long, sweeping drive that passed through terraced gardens of shrubbery and decorative floral plantings and sculpture. At the top of the hill was a windowless monolith of dark stone that seemed to have risen from deep in the earth. The entrance was a wall of tinted glass behind a marble courtyard of fountains and pools. Designed to project awesome power, the building resembled the mesas of the Southwest.

Dalbey parked in a space for visitors and crossed a marble bridge to reach the tall glass door that silently slid aside as he approached. He stepped into a towering atrium that was crisscrossed with escalators carrying office personnel to various levels. In the center was a receptionist's desk with an attractive white-haired woman. He counted the steps from the door to the desk. Sixteen.

"I'd like to see Vincent Steffinelli, please."

"Do you have an appointment?"

"No, I don't, but I'm an old friend."

"You name, please?"

"Philip Dalbey."

"One moment, please." She punched in an extension number and Dalbey automatically committed it to memory, a habit that was impossible to break. Six nine zero three. "A Mr. Philip Dalbey to see Mr. Steffinelli. Yes, of course. I'll tell him." She disconnected, and as Dalbey expected, she said, "I'm sorry, but Mr. Steffinelli is out of town and he won't be back until next week. Would you like to leave your number?"

He didn't expect to see Vince. He just wanted him to know that he had been there looking for him. He took the envelope with the clipping from his inside pocket. He handed it to the woman. "I wonder if you could see that he gets this?"

She looked at the name on the envelope, smiled, and said, "I certainly will."

"Thank you."

"You're quite welcome."

"A beautiful building."

"Oh, isn't it wonderful." She mentioned the name of a famous architect connected with Yale. "They say it's his favorite."

"Very impressive." He tried to imagine Arthur riding those escalators. Yes, he could see that.

"Well, good-bye. Thank you."

He acknowledged her smile and turned away. He crossed to the door in fifteen strides.

The next address was in Cherry Hills Village, an exclusive neighborhood in the south suburbs of Denver. He checked the map from the auto rental office against the directions in his appointment book. He wound down the long drive, took Antelope Drive back to Route 6, and headed east toward Denver. He picked up Interstate 25 south, a six-lane highway that was traffic-heavy but fast. He was making his usual check in the rearview mirror when he noticed the state police car, four cars behind, in another lane, keeping pace.

He used his blinker to announce he was going off at the Englewood exit, and he watched the state police car move into the outside lane. He turned left off the ramp. The police car went to the right. So there had to be a backup car working the tail. He studied the three cars behind him, but by the time he reached Cherry Hill Village, they were gone.

Dalbey found the address he wanted with ease, a large Tudor house on a cul-de-sac. It was relatively new. A sprinkler system delivered a spray of water to the carefully tended lawn. The property, about two acres, was well planted with trees and shrubs and a gardener was working on a flower bed. Vince was doing okay. A concrete driveway connected a two-car garage with the street. A red-and-tan station wagon waited in the driveway.

He found a place to park behind the landscape gardener's truck that gave him an unobstructed view of the house. He loaded the camera and aimed it through the open window, taking a reading on the automatic light meter. He adjusted the aperture to the film speed and shot several frames of the house. He had to wait another forty-five minutes, but he was finally rewarded. The front door opened, and an attractive woman wearing a tennis outfit emerged. She was followed by a teenage girl in jeans. Dalbey raised the telephoto lens and began to shoot. He stopped when they were both inside the station wagon.

They backed down the drive and into the street. When they passed Dalbey, the girl was talking animatedly and the woman was laughing. Vince Steffinelli's wife and daughter.

He wound off the unexposed film and removed it from the camera, slipping the small can into a pocket.

He made a circuit of the neighborhood. It was a carbon of exclusive, expensive suburbs from Philadelphia's Main Line to Shaker Heights. He wasn't followed, but when he was back on Interstate 25 heading for downtown Denver, the state police car was back in position.

Glancing into the mirror, he was having second thoughts about the wisdom of bearding Steffinelli in his own den. He was feeling vulnerable, the way he used to feel in East Germany years ago, knowing that one mistake and he could disappear.

When he reached the Brown Palace, he left the car with the parking attendant and carried his small bag to his room in the new Towers. It was almost time for his meeting, so he returned to the lobby and waited in the central garden.

He was staring up at the famed rotunda that rose all the way to the glass ceiling, the perimeter graced with balconies of bronzed filigree, when he was approached by Edgar Boice.

"Are you Dalbey?" The voice belonged to a tall, burly

man with short, gray hair and hard, bright eyes. He was fifty-one, Dalbey knew, much decorated in Korea and Vietnam, and he stayed in shape.

"Major Boice," Dalbey said, rising to shake his hand. "Thanks for coming."

Edgar Boice sat. "You wanted to talk." He was brusque in the military manner. He had once been a legendary Green Beret, a famous killer in uniform, and he was an instructor at Camp Peary when Dalbey took his CIA training. He had been quietly retired when he became hard to control and had bragged openly about pulling the trigger on the Central American revolutionary Esteban Ortega when the U.S. was denying any complicity in the execution. He was now considered a dangerous and unreliable psychotic.

"I have a problem you might help me with," Dalbey said. He assumed that the conversation was either being recorded or that Boice would be reporting to Steffinelli.

"You still working with those bastards?" Boice asked.

"No. This is a personal matter."

"What happened with you and the Agency?"

"Differences of opinion."

Boise smiled crookedly. "Yeah. They're a chicken-shit bunch. Well, what you got?"

"This is just exploratory, you understand."

"I gotcha. You got that money?"

Dalbey took two hundreds and a fifty from his wallet and handed them over. Boice stuffed them in his pocket.

"Are you available for work?" Dalbey asked.

"Depends on the work."

"I might have something for you."

"Like what?"

"I can't say just yet, but it will be worth your while."

"What does that mean?"

"I'm talking a million dollars."

Boice stared hard. "Why me? For that kind of bread you can get the goddamned Light Brigade."

"I happen to think you're better than a brigade."

Boice smiled that lopsided smile again. "I agree."

Dalbey had met other men who enjoyed killing. They made him feel that same way. He wanted the interview to end; he wanted to be somewhere else. He had planned to hand over the film can, imagining the effect on Steffinelli when he saw the developed prints, but he couldn't do it.

"Are you free to travel?" he asked. Now he was playing it by ear.

"Like where?"

"Could be anywhere. There's a man. A pro. I have an idea what he looks like. I'll know for sure who he is by next week."

"You want him hit."

"I want him stopped. But I want him alive. I want to know who hired him. I want him talking. I believe it's somebody very big, and I want to bring them down."

"Alive is tough."

"I know. That's why I came all the way out here." Dalbey rose to his feet. "You're interested?"

"I'd like to know more." Boice got up, realizing that the interview was ending.

"I'll be in touch." Dalbey extended his hand. They shook, and Boice walked away. Dalbey sat and pondered the situation. It might have turned out better than he had expected. If they believed that he was reaching for somebody above Vince, that he might be close to the identity of the Cassidy assassin, they would have to stop him.

He went to his room and called Chester Olney, his friend at International Press Service, who agreed to meet him for dinner. It wouldn't hurt to be seen with a wire service bureau chief. He slept for two hours, then showered and dressed, and met Olney in the lobby. They went to a small Mexican restaurant in the barrio and ate chili rellenos and refritos and drank cold Carta Blanca beer, and Olney dropped him back at his hotel.

The morning flight to Kennedy was delayed a half

hour, but they made up time with the help of the jet stream and he was back in his office by three P.M.

Alice had messages to call Bob Larkin. Michael's report on the chairman of Tel-Tech International was on his desk, along with an express mail envelope from Washington.

He telephoned Bob Larkin and told him he couldn't make up his mind.

"What's the problem?"

"I'm not sure I want to do it."

"Jesus!"

"Tell you what, why don't we fly up to Hayward, Wisconsin, and do some fishing for a few days?"

"Fishing? Are you serious?"

"We'll get away, where we can talk about this thing. They have northern pike up there you wouldn't believe. I know this Indian guide—"

"You gotta be kidding," Larkin exploded. "Fishing! Jesus Christ, man, I don't have time for fishing!"

"Bob, you have to make time. You have to relax."

"Relax my ass. I lose money when I relax. I'll get enough of that when I'm dead."

"Yes, Bob, but you won't enjoy it."

"Dalbey, cut the bullshit. Make up your mind. I'm working on other deals. Take another week."

"I've made up my mind," Dalbey said, suddenly remembering the sixteen-hour days, the twelve-city tours of endless meetings and hotel rooms and airports. "I'm going to pass."

"You mean, no?"

"I mean, no."

"You know this could mean a lot of money."

"I know. That's what hurts."

"A *lot* of money."

"Don't rub it in."

"You know I'll get somebody else."

"I know."

"Well, Dalbey, enjoy the fishing." He hung up.

Dalbey knew he might live to regret his decision, but it felt right, and what the hell. He already had enough money to live on.

He took up Michael's report on Major General Hugh Winston and learned that his rank was a Reserve commission. He had been discharged as a colonel in 1946 and had returned to Colorado, where he took over the bankrupt Colorado Mining Company. Within the year they discovered large uranium deposits in two of their defunct silver mines, and Winston was on his way to the first of his many millions. Dalbey riffled through the five-page report and put it aside to read that night.

The envelope from Washington contained the research on the Calico mission. It was a copy of the official report explaining the failure of the landing, and it began with the list of the team members that Dalbey wanted.

The first name took him by surprise. He scowled and sat back, muttering, "Son of a bitch," and wondered what it meant.

He went to his desk drawer to find the folded sheet of lined yellow paper on which he had listed the names Steffinelli had given him at their first meeting.

Dan Cassidy
Roger Hall
Bob Stowe
Martin Slattery
Peter Evans
Calvin Graham
Jon Steach
Arnold Westman
Howard Benjamin
Art Wilson
Sean McCarthy

He compared his list with the official roster. Cassidy, Hall, Stowe, and Slattery were dead or missing. Evans and Graham were supposedly living in Florida and Arizona. Steach was alive. He put question marks after Westman, Benjamin, Wilson, and McCarthy, the four Vince claimed had been murdered before Cassidy. He planned to check them out. His hastily scribbled notes said Westman had been living in St. Paul. He'd have to get a line on the others.

There were two names on the roster that were missing from Vince's list. Someone named Rudolph Batcher had been the ranking noncom, and the leader had not been Dan Cassidy, as Vince had claimed. He was listed as deputy commander. The officer in charge, the man Dalbey remembered only as someone with dark, curly hair, was Captain Hugh Winston.

Chapter Seventeen

On Friday he heard from Steach.

An envelope was delivered by messenger. It contained a single ticket to the musical *Cats* at the Winter Garden theater.

Dalbey knew immediately that it was from Steach. It was the system Dalbey had devised for clandestine meetings when Steach was his contact in Berlin. It was an orchestra seat near the right aisle, J-65, for Saturday night. Steach would have the ticket for the adjoining seat.

What would be important enough to bring Steach out of hiding? Dalbey still remembered the pictures of the car bombing. It had been blamed on terrorists.

Alice Walder interrupted his thoughts. "Your friends are back," she said. "Three of them this time."

Damn, maybe he had pushed too hard. He went to

the second floor where he could look down on the car that was parked across the street. They weren't trying to hide. Two men were in the car, and a third man, wearing a floral-pattern sport shirt with the tail out, was standing on the sidewalk talking to the man in the passenger's seat. They didn't seem to be planning anything, just waiting.

He returned to his office and Alice Walder said, "Well?"

"You were right. Three men."

"That much I know. Who are they?"

"I don't know."

"Philip, you're making me crazy. Who are they?"

"I have no idea. They could be government agents."

Her eyes widened. "FBI?"

"Why don't you just trot across the street and ask them?" He changed the subject. "Did you talk to Harmon?"

"I did. I'm starting there in two weeks. It will take me that long to get things straightened out around here. Do you want me to find a replacement?"

"I think not. What do I have coming up?"

"Berrigan signed the letter of agreement and he wants to set up a meeting. You're supposed to be in London in October, and Freeman-Hill wants to talk to you about the IPS merger."

"I think I'll probably wrap it up with that."

"What did you tell Bob Larkin."

"No."

"What did he say?"

"Said I was crazy."

"I think he's wrong. What are your plans?"

"I don't have any as yet." He leaned back in his chair and swiveled from side to side. "I'll wrap up these projects, I suppose, then I'd like to go someplace quiet and think about it." He clasped his hands and pressed the knuckles against his mouth, considering. "I'm fifty-eight. If you believe in longevity statistics, I have twelve years to live. I don't know what I want to do with it, but I don't want to waste it."

"You'll live to be a hundred."

"Why don't we settle for seventy-five?"

She got up to leave, then she asked, "Why are government agents watching you?"

"I said they *might* be government agents."

"Why don't you get that expensive law firm to find out. Get a court order or something. This isn't Russia, you know."

It hadn't occurred to him, but she was right. When she left, he called his attorney at the expensive law firm and told him that his phone was tapped by federal court order and that someone had his building under surveillance, and he wanted a court order to stop them or show cause. The attorney said he would look into it.

Then he called Dan Curran. He had to wait on hold through two minutes of Montovanni's strings, then a voice, deep and harried, cut in. "Curran here."

"Phil Dalbey."

Curran groaned. Two of his clients had been robbed the night before, but he could be there in an hour.

Dalbey had divided the Calico list into three categories: known dead, living, and question marks. He was working on living, so he called information for Key Largo, Florida, and asked for Peter Evans. He got the number and dialed, but there was no answer. He called the Chamber of Commerce.

"There's a diver named Peter Evans has a dive shop in Key Largo," he said to the woman on the phone. "Would you happen to know the name of it?"

"Peter who?"

"Evans."

"Just a minute."

There was a short wait, then a man came on the line. "Can I help you?"

Dalbey repeated the request and the man said, "That would be Deep Six. Do you want the number?"

"I'd appreciate it."

Dalbey got the number and called it. Peter Evans was out on the dive boat. He would be in the shop after two P.M. Dalbey said he would call back.

It took five calls to Tucson before Dalbey finally talked to Calvin Graham. He was retired from the post office. Yes, he remembered the Calico mission. Worst day he ever spent. No, he didn't remember any of the others. Wait a minute, one of the guys was hit, Slater, or something like that. No, he didn't remember a Hugh Winston. Rudy Batcher? No, didn't ring a bell. So damned long ago.

And they were going to be the easy ones. He started on the question marks. St. Paul, Minnesota, had two Arnold Westmans listed. He talked to the wife of the first one he called and learned that her husband had been too young for World War II. The second number didn't answer.

Dan Curran arrived, grumbling about the unfairness of professional burglars. "The sons of bitches disconnected the goddamned alarm system in the basement. It was like they had a goddamned schematic. How you gonna deal with people like that? They hit two apartments in a total in fifteen minutes. They knew exactly what they were after."

"How much?"

"Who knows? They're claiming half a mill. Probably more like a couple hundred grand."

"Not bad."

"Yeah. Everybody's asking, 'Where were you?'"

"Where *were* you?"

"Don't be a wise guy. What can I do for you?"

"I'm trying to track down some guys I served with in World War II. In 1943 to be exact. I don't know anything about them. I have their names and their army serial numbers."

"What unit?"

"OSS."

"You were OSS?"

"Occasionally. I was officially with the Air Corps G-two." Dalbey handed Curran a sheet of paper containing the names and numbers: Howard Benjamin, Arthur Wilson, Sean McCarthy, and Rudolph Batcher.

Curran studied the names. "You don't know where they were from?"

"No idea."

"When they were discharged?"

"They might have stayed in; transferred to CIA."

"Okay. First thing is to run them through the FBI computer."

"You can do that?"

"The New York PD can do that. Might cost you a couple bucks." Curran studied the page some more, then he said, "Then the Veteran's Administration. The serial numbers will help. They may have signed up for something. If we can get Social Security numbers that will make it easier. We can run them through the states' driver's license records. Unless they're trying to hide, we should be able to find them. I also have some friends at Treasury. Maybe we can bend the law a little and check tax records."

"How long will it take?"

Curran shrugged. "We could be lucky; no time at all. Or it could be tough."

A few minutes after Dan Curran left, Dalbey's attorney called to tell him that he had checked with official sources and that his telephone was not tapped and that no one was watching his building. Dalbey was tempted to invite him to meet the three men waiting outside, but he didn't. He said, "Thanks," and hung up. So much for expensive law firms.

He wanted to make some calls on his own, but this time he didn't want to alert Steffinelli. He gathered his personal telephone book, the Calico list, and some note-books into a leather briefcase, told both Alice and Mossy they could reach him at the Yale Club, and walked to York Avenue to get a cab.

It was a sunny eighty-eight degrees. Too hot for September in his estimation. After Labor Day he always expected summer to come to an abrupt end and autumn to come sailing in, with cool, crisp football weather.

The cab dropped him on Vanderbilt Avenue across from the Pan Am Building. He climbed the three steps and entered the high-ceilinged gloom of Ivy respectability.

He was crossing to the desk to book a room when it dawned on him whom he could call upon for aid. It had been in this same room that Colonel Archibald Terman had convinced him that it was his duty to help out in the Cold War. Shifting his gaze, he picked out the two chairs where they had sat, still in the same place after all those years. Terman was retired now, an old man, but Dalbey knew he would be no less a patriot and he would still exert a strong influence.

Dalbey booked a room using his membership number and took the creaky elevator to the fourth floor. It was a dull, uninteresting room, but it was clean and the telephone was secure.

He found the number in his book and called Colonel Terman in Annapolis, Maryland. A woman answered the phone.

"Colonel Terman, please?"

"May I ask who is calling?"

"Philip Dalbey."

"And what is this in reference to, Mr. Dalbey?"

"I was one of the colonel's people."

"Oh," she said, her tone changing abruptly. "One moment, please."

Dalbey waited for what seemed several minutes, then Terman came on the phone. His voice had the crackle of old age, and he had developed a habit of stopping to clear his throat, but the voice was strong.

"Is it really you, Philip?"

"It is, Colonel, how are you?"

"I will not trouble you with a list of my ailments and infirmities, Philip. Suffice it to say that I find myself in the clutches of an overbearing woman who protects me from myself, and I think that old age is for the birds. What can I do for you?"

"Colonel, you haven't changed."

"If only that were true." He cleared his throat. "Did you call to visit? That woman will be here any minute snatching the phone away."

"The truth is, I'm trying to track down four men who were on an OSS mission with me in 1943. I've been told they stayed on with the Agency. I want to know what happened to them."

"What are you working on?"

Dalbey paused, considering his reply, then he said, "You must have heard about Daniel Cassidy."

Terman took a moment to answer. "Yes. Terrible thing. I knew Cassidy very well. A fine man."

"This might having something to do with the murders."

"What do you want me to do?"

"Have the Agency run the names through their computer. I want Social Security numbers, addresses. If they're dead, I want to know how it happened, where and when."

"Let me have the names."

"First is Howard Benjamin. B-E-N—"

"Benjamin was one of my people. He's dead. Died of cancer last year."

"He wasn't murdered?"

"Died in a veteran's hospital."

"Okay," Dalbey said. "Next is Arthur Wilson." He paused, giving Terman time to write. "Sean McCarthy." He paused until he heard Terman grunt, then added, "Rudolph Batcher."

"Very well, Philip, I'll have this checked out. Where can I call you?"

"I'm calling from the Yale Club, but I won't be staying

here. My telephone is not secure. I'll call you tomorrow at noon."

Terman chuckled. "It's like old times, Philip. I miss it."

"Good-bye, Colonel. Noon tomorrow."

When he disconnected, he put a check after Benjamin's name. Another Steffinelli lie. He tried the number in St. Paul, but there was no answer.

All he could do then was to wait and see what Curran and Terman came up with. He wasn't even sure what he was looking for, but he believed that Calico was the logical place to start. It was the only lead he had. He was experienced enough to know that good intelligence work is the patient, painstaking accumulation of information and sifting and sifting, and checking and double-checking and triple-checking, until something doesn't fit. And then repeating the process ad nauseam. You had to expect a dozen dead ends before a door opened, and beyond the door might be another dead end. The great intelligence men were chess masters and puzzle solvers. If you were patient, relentless, and lucky—a picture might develop. In his own case he wanted it to be the face of a man with white hair who was trained to kill.

He called his son and his daughter. There was no answer at Arthur's apartment, and Sharon was still out to lunch. He checked his watch and thought, long lunch.

There was no longer any reason to stay at the Club. He packed his briefcase, dropped the key at the desk, and took the cab back to his office.

On Saturday morning he called St. Paul and spoke to Arnold Westman, Jr.

"Not me, Mr. Dalbey," the man said. "I'm just thirty-two, and I even managed to miss Vietnam. You might want to talk to my dad. He lives out at White Bear Lake now."

"Was he in the OSS?"

"He was in something like that. He didn't like to talk about the war. Let me give you his number."

Dalbey called the number and Arnold Westman answered. Yes, he had served in the OSS, and he recalled the Calico mission. No, it wasn't the only foul-up he remembered. It amazed him that the Allies had won the damned war. Just proved that the enemy was more incompetent.

Did he remember the other members of the Calico team? A couple. He had been with Stowe when he was killed in forty-four. Captain Winston, that son of a bitch, he was a big shot now. No, he never saw the others after that mission. Had he heard from Winston? Lord, no, why should he? Steffinelli? Never heard of him.

Dalbey thanked him and hung up. Arnold Westman was very much alive. Steffinelli had claimed he was killed in an unsolved car bombing.

When it was close to noon, Dalbey left the building and walked to the corner. The heat was building, and he wondered when the summer was going to shut down. He stepped into the first phone booth, then changed his mind and walked to his garage to use the public phone. He didn't mind Steffinelli's knowing that he was checking on Arnold Westman, but he didn't want him to know what he was finding out about the other question marks. He used a credit card to call Colonel Terman. He reached the housekeeper and had to wait for Terman to come on the line.

"Philip, by God, I've been waiting for your call."

"Were you able to—"

"I still have some influence. The admiral likes to humor the old boys. Anyway, Wilson and McCarthy are both dead. Wilson died of a heart attack in 1968. McCarthy was killed in March of this year. He was stabbed by an assailant in Athens. It's still an open case." He paused to clear his throat several times. "And that's all I have."

"How about Rudolph Batcher?"

"Nothing on Batcher. He was never connected with the Agency in any way."

"Well, that's it then. I'm left with just one question mark. Colonel, thank you very much, you've been a great help."

"Hope so, Philip. Drop in if you're down this way."

"I'll do that."

He hung up the phone and left the garage. He went back to the office. He put checks after two more names on his list. Besides Hugh Winston and himself, he now had four living and one question mark. He had an appontment to meet one of the living that night, and he thought he might make arrangements with IPS photo services to get pictures of the others.

Saturdays in the office were quiet, a favorite time for Dalbey. On a day like this he would ordinarily be putting in the most productive work time, but he was preoccupied with seeing Steach.

He went to the second floor and studied the men on the street. There were two of them in the car, and when he scanned the street, he saw the third man near the phone booth at the corner. He was going to have to shake them before he arrived at the Winter Garden.

Climbing the stairs to the third floor, he changed clothes and worked out for an hour, running three uphill miles on the treadmill and spending the rest of the time on chin-ups and upper-body weights. He relaxed in the sauna, showered, dressed, and went back to the first floor.

He telephoned the Four Seasons, one of New York's most expensive restaurants, and made a seven-thirty reservation for two. Then he went to the second floor, opened a beer, and went into the lounge to watch the Mets game on TV.

The temperature climbed to ninety-three degrees and there were thunderstorms at four-thirty that lasted for an hour and brought the heat down to a pleasant eighty-six. At six-thirty Dalbey shaved and dressed in a dark-blue

linen suit with a white shirt and maroon rep tie. He left
some lights burning, set the alarm, and went out through
the front door, locking up after him. He walked to the
corner and hailed a cab.

"Four Seasons," he said to the driver, then added,
"Fifty-second, between Park and Lex."

He arrived at seven twenty-five, gave his name and a
fifty-dollar tip to the maître d', and received an arched
eyebrow when he requested a table by the kitchen.

"By the kitchen, sir?"

"Close as possible."

"Yes, sir. Are you dining alone, sir?"

"I'm expecting a friend to join me."

"Yes, well, then, this way, sir."

A fact known to New York restaurant cognoscenti,
which he hoped his followers were not, is that the exclusive Four Seasons restaurant shares a kitchen with the
modestly priced Brasserie on Fifty-third Street. Dalbey
settled into his chair just long enough to give his drink
order, then he was up and into the kitchen. He carefully
picked his way through the orderly chaos of two kitchen
staffs and entered the Brasserie. He exited onto Fifty-third
Street and hailed a cab traveling west.

The Winter Garden is ideal for the Broadway musical.
It is a large theater, but the amphitheater is broad and
shallow, so it can accommodate the large audiences clamoring
to see a Tony Award hit such as *Cats*, but also offers an
intimate view of the stage from front row to rear.

Dalbey walked into the expectant atmosphere of a
milling audience preparing themselves. The theater was
half-filled. There was a babble of talk. Patrons sidestepped
to their seats. He was ushered down the right aisle to row
J, where the young woman leading him stopped and
returned his stub.

He moved into the row to find his seat. The seat to
his left was occupied by a large, overdressed, overcoiffed

woman who smelled strongly of perfume and leaned across her neighbor to discuss costume jewelry.

Dalbey waited and watched the row fill except for the seat on his right. He was wondering if Steach was going to show when a woman stopped at the end of the row and said to the person seated there in a carefully modulated British accent, "Would you mind, please? Terribly sorry."

Expecting Steach, he was surprised to see Claire Paige, and for a moment he thought it might be someone's not-very-funny prank. She edged past the four people standing, saying, "Sorry, sorry," and took the remaining seat next to him. She smiled and said, "Hello."

He was at a loss. He nodded his head and said, "Hello," in a half-whisper, but there were questions unasked.

"He was afraid to come," she said softly. "He wants to meet you someplace where you're positive you won't be followed."

Dalbey was cautious. He knew nothing about her. Their last meeting had not been accidental, and he was certain she had lied about meeting him in Rome. Was this going to be a trap for Steach? He asked, "Afraid of what?"

She looked around her, then groped in her purse for a small pad and ballpoint pen and wrote: *They want to kill him.*

Dalbey read the message, but he was careful not to react. He needed proof that she had been sent by Steach. His doubt was so obvious that she wrote: *You met like this in Germany.* She had her facts right, but she had also known details about the party in Rome. She could be legitimate or she could be well coached. He wondered about her relationship with Steach. His doubt was apparent to her.

"You don't believe me."

He shrugged. "I don't know you," he whispered. "The party in Rome. You were lying."

She considered that, looking straight into his eyes. Then she went into her purse and brought out a woman's leather wallet. She produced a black-and-white snapshot of a smiling man with his arm around a pretty young girl, then handed it to him.

The man was a youthful Jon Steach. The girl, although she could not have been more than twelve, was unmistakably Claire Paige. He turned the snapshot over. It was inscribed on the back: *Daddy. Devon. 1956.*

He returned the photo and reached for her notepad and pen. The houselights were dimming and the orchestra began the overture. He wrote: *Mohonk Mountain House. New Paltz, N.Y. Tuesday. 1 PM. Must Make Reservation.* He handed the pad back to her. She read it, then leaned close to whisper, "Thank you." She pressed her lips lightly against the side of his face and squeezed his forearm. As the curtain parted on the opening scene, she rose and left.

Dalbey was going to give her a five- or ten-minute lead before he followed, but he got caught up in the show and he stayed to the intermission. It was ten-thirty when he stopped at Gleason's on Seventy-fifth Street for a sandwich and a beer.

He sat in a booth and considered Steach and Claire Paige. Steach with a daughter pushing forty. Hard to believe. He had never known that Steach was married, would have sworn that he was one of the Company monks. So somebody wanted to kill Steach. Nothing new about that. Ten years ago he thought somebody had.

It was warm and pleasant when he left Gleason's, and the sky above the neon glow of the city was clear and dappled with stars. He walked down to Seventy-fourth Street and turned left into his block, angling across the street.

There were two men in the car parked directly in front of his door. When he stopped and inserted his key into the lock, both car doors opened and the occupants stepped out.

"Mr. Dalbey," the first man said, "we're FBI." Dalbey turned to face the two men. The speaker produced his ID and a gold badge. "We'd like to talk to you. We can do it inside or downtown."

The identification looked authentic, but so did the phony CIA document that Dalbey was carrying.

"Let's go inside," he said. He unlocked the front door, then the police lock on the inside door. The two men followed him inside. He closed the door, but left it unlocked. He led the way to his office, turning on lights as he went. He moved behind his desk out of habit and the man who had spoken before said, "Would you hold it there just a moment, sir?" He was holding a 9mm Walther. Dalbey glanced at the gun, at the man's expressionless face, and stood aside. He kept his hands where they could be seen.

The man checked the desk drawers, then asked Dalbey to remove his jacket, which he handed to his partner. When he was satisfied that Dalbey was not armed, he holstered his weapon and said, "Why don't we sit over here," indicating a couch and two chairs separated by a coffee table. He wasn't going to allow Dalbey the psychological protection of the desk.

They were not the men who had been watching the building during the day. They seemed cleaner, better dressed, and their shoes were shined. There was a uniformity about them: hair neatly trimmed, clean shaven, ties carefully knotted. They were about the same height, but the speaker was heavier and seemed to be in his forties, whereas the second man was younger and wore sunglasses.

When Dalbey was seated on the couch, the two men took facing chairs. The second man was examining the baton, turning it in his hands and thumping his palm, and the talker said, "That was cute tonight, Mr. Dalbey, very cute." Dalbey said nothing. He was not cowed by the two men, but until he had their credentials confirmed he was being careful. "Now, Mr. Dalbey, you know damned well what we want, so why don't we just put a screechin' halt to the bullshit and you tell us where he is?"

Dalbey wasn't absolutely sure whom they meant. It was probably Steach, but he figured if he kept his mouth shut they would tell him.

"You slipped out of that restaurant tonight to meet Jon Steach. We know you're involved with this man. For all we know, you may have been involved in the whole damn thing from the beginning. But I'm telling you now, we're going to find out where he is."

"I don't know where he is."

"Dalbey." The man's voice was flat but laced with angry undertones, and he had dropped the *mister*. "We want that son of a bitch. We're gonna have him. Before we leave here tonight, you're going to tell us where he is. We're getting really tired of your shit."

There was a commotion at the front door and both men rose from their chairs and instinctively drew their guns.

"Police!" a voice called. "Come on out! And come out slow!"

"My security service," Dalbey said. "If I don't deactivate the alarm they call the police. You know how it works."

"Son of a bitch!" the man growled.

"Do you hear me? Police!"

"I think you better say something," Dalbey said.

"Back here!" the man shouted. "Take it easy!" He replaced his gun and took out his ID folder. He stepped into the hallway holding his arms out away from his sides, the open wallet in his right hand. Two uniformed policemen came down the hallway cautiously, their service revolvers drawn. "FBI," the man said, extending the badge. Behind the police were two of Dan Curran's security patrolmen.

They talked to the FBI man in the hall, then followed him into the office.

"You're Mr. Dalbey?" one of the policemen asked.

"That's right. I'd like you to check their credentials."

"I did," the officer said. "FBI."

"I mean have the precinct check downtown. They could be phonies. Call in their numbers."

The young policeman was reluctant to tangle with the feds. Dalbey said, "Otherwise, get them out of here. They don't have a warrant."

"You invited us in," the man said.

"I'm inviting you out."

"Call," the man said, handing his ID to the policeman, who turned to the man with the sunglasses and held out his hand. The second man took out a plastic photo ID and handed it over. The officer scowled over the card and said, "This is Defense Department. How do I check this?"

"Just check the FBI," Dalbey said.

They sat and waited for the call to the precinct and the computer relay to the New York regional duty officer and a check against the duty roster and then the computer check with Washington that on weekends had to be relayed through the Boston regional office.

Dalbey studied the man in the dark glasses with renewed interest. A Defense Department spook. What was their interest in this?

The FBI credentials turned out to be legitimate, and the two policemen were ready to leave. Dalbey said to the security men, "I'd like you to stay."

"That won't be necessary," the FBI man said.

"They're staying," Dalbey said.

"We're on patrol," one of the men said.

"Call in and tell your office," Dalbey said. "This won't take long."

The man went to the front desk to call, and the FBI man, resigned to the fact that he wasn't going to interrogate Dalbey alone, took a more congenial approach.

"We realize, Mr. Dalbey, that this man is an old friend, that you served together in the war. We can understand that you want to help an old friend, but this is not the man you used to know." He paused for effect.

"This man is an outlaw. He went over the edge. When he disappeared in 1973, so did one hundred fifty thousand dollars belonging to the U.S. government. He was also insured for one hundred thousand, and that was paid to his beneficiary." He paused again, and from the pained expression on his face one would have assumed that the money came from his own pocket. "What's more, Mr. Dalbey, we believe that your friend arranged his own car bombing." Another long silence. "And you must not lose sight of the fact that someone died in that car."

The FBI man sat there nodding, the room silent except for the sounds of breathing.

"I haven't seen him," Dalbey said.

"You've heard from him."

"I really haven't."

The man in the dark glasses showed a small smile that was more of a grimace. The FBI man snorted. He didn't believe him.

"You're getting into something that's over your head, Mr. Dalbey. This man is dangerous. We want him for grand larceny and fraud. The German government is going to charge him with murder." He let the seriousness of the charges sink in. "You could be charged with harboring and abetting a fugitive. We can make it stick."

When Dalbey did not react, the man said, "My God, Dalbey, use your head. This man is a killer."

Chapter Eighteen

On Sunday morning the FBI man was back with six associates and a search warrant, and they "tossed" the office and the apartment.

"Just don't get in the way," Dalbey was told.

He wandered around watching the men root through file cabinets and desk drawers and bookshelves, even feeling cushions and furniture and exploring the water tanks of the toilets; checking anywhere documents might be hidden. Dalbey was figuring out what the government had to be spending on the surveillance, with three shifts on the phone tap and the people in the street, and now with double time for Sunday, and he wondered how the FBI budget could justify this for anything less than Public Enemy No. 1.

It was when they were near the end and he overheard one of the men declare the place clean and his companion say, "I'll call Steffinelli," that he began to wonder who was looking for what.

He leaned over a file cabinet and asked one of the searchers, "You a Treasury agent?"

"Nah, city marshal."

City marshals work on per diem, usually delivering official documents, but they can also be hired to help out a zealous FBI agent, and they could even be paid by a patriotic and benevolent private enterprise that was up to its balance sheet in government contracts. And Dalbey had just such a company in mind.

They went away empty-handed because, as Dalbey could have told them, there was nothing to find, leaving the place with a storm-tossed look.

Dalbey was annoyed, but he had no reason to complain. He had gone to Denver to prod Steffinelli into action and it had worked.

Steach had them running. Dalbey had done a lot of sleepless, middle-of-the-night thinking about Steach and had concluded that he knew virtually nothing about the man. He knew what he looked like ten years ago, that he was a career officer in the CIA, that he seemed to be good at his job, and that he liked him. Their friendship was the by-product of mutual deception and the fear of disclosure. And that was it.

Would Steach kill, as the man said? He was trained for it, certainly, and he had always carried a weapon that he would probably have used if it came down to it, but no, he would never have classified Steach as a killer, not one of the weirdos who considered it all in a day's work.

But he still had to consider the guy who went up with the car, with Steach's wallet among the scattered pieces. Dalbey had no answer to that, and the truth was that Steach could be a raving maniac for all he knew.

And Claire Paige. He had been thinking a lot about Claire Paige. Steach's daughter! Damn! Sure, every woman is somebody's daughter, but Steach . . . Jesus, he wasn't that much younger than Steach. How could he have been thinking about asking Steach's daughter to go trout fishing for a year?

He stood at the large window in the lounge looking down on the varnished wood floor of the empty squash court and wondered if Arthur would come by for a game. Hell, it was worth a try. He telephoned and Helen answered. Arthur was gone—an hour ago—to Denver. It was very sudden. Someone had called at eight A.M. and the ticket was waiting at Kennedy. Dalbey was tempted to invite her to play squash, but he didn't. Arthur might consider it inappropriate, to say the least. Then she asked, "Would you come to dinner some night if we asked?"

"Helen, I would love to come to dinner."

"You must be terribly busy."

"I'm not, as a matter of fact."

"Good. Soon as Arthur gets back. We'll call."

"I'll look forward to it."

She hung up and he smiled, pleased with his son's choice of women.

It was close to noon, so he walked to the restaurant on the corner for brunch. He passed up the champagne nd the Bloody Marys and settled for eggs Benedict and :offee.

He thought he might run in Central Park, but it was :oo warm. It was already ninety-three degrees and building. Before the day ended, it would hit ninety-nine, one of the hottest days of a hot summer.

And that's when Emmaline decided to commit suicide. The phone was ringing when he returned to the building and let himself in. He answered it at the front desk, and it was his sister, crying, close to hysteria, and blubbering unintelligibly.

"Emmy, now wait a minute, Emmy. Emmy, damnit, slow down!" He thought she was drunk. Christ! How could she be drunk by twelve-thirty? "Now, Emmy, tell me. Emmy!" He could feel the panic rising on a tide of anger, and he had to control it, to be calm, because she sounded more bent out of shape than usual and it could be serious.

He waited until she wound down and there was just the sound of sobbing, and he said softly and slowly, "Emmy, this is Phil. I'm here. Now tell me what's wrong."

This unleashed another flood of disjointed hysteria, but Dalbey was able to decipher her meaning. She had swallowed enough pills to make her dead, but then realized that the daughters would come home from the beach and find her body.

"Emmy, I'll be right there."

He disconnected and called information for Westport and got the number for police emergency and called and tried to be calm while he gave Emmaline's address and explained that his sister had taken an overdose of pills and no, he was calling from New York, and yes, she was there alone and could they please stop talking and get someone over there fast.

Emmaline, you goddamned crazy woman! The garage didn't answer. He slammed down the phone. He told himself that it would be okay. She was probably exaggerating. He didn't run, but he hurried.

It took him ten minutes to get his car and he was angry, but he tipped the attendant a dollar and took Seventy-fourth Street to York and then north to the East River Drive. He went out the Bruckner Expressway, empty on Sunday, and picked up the Thruway because it was faster and he could clip along at seventy. He stopped at the first toll plaza to call the Westport police. A sergeant told him that Mrs. Hamilton was unconscious when the emergency squad arrived, and they took her to Norwalk Community Hospital.

It took him another forty minutes to get to the hospital emergency room, and by that time Emmaline was recovering but groggy, and suffering embarrassment and a wide-screen headache in living color. They were going to keep her overnight.

She was still in one of the emergency alcoves, surrounded by a white curtain, and Dalbey leaned over her and bent down to kiss the onetime pretty face and said, "Hi, baby."

"Oh, Flipper," she said, strangling the end of the name, and squeezing her eyes closed so that tears oozed out under the long dark lashes that used to knock 'em dead, then dribbled over the puffy cheeks. "I can't do anything right." She choked and turned her head.

He held her hand tightly and said nothing, letting her weep, and when she stopped, he said, "Jesus, Em, you scared the hell out of me."

"I'm such a mess," she whispered. "Oh, Flipper, why am I such a mess?"

He had to admit it, she was a mess. Who knows why? She sure as hell wasn't alone.

"You're not a mess, Em."

"Do you mean it?"

"I mean it."

"You're such a liar."

He smiled and held her hand. The tears welled in her eyes again and she swallowed, and then a nurse came to say that they were going to move her upstairs.

"Oh, Flipper, the girls. Don't tell them. Don't . . . oh, God, they'll hate me for this."

"I'll take care of it." He knew the girls lived away from home and he assumed they were visiting. "I'll talk to them. A mild ulcer attack. How's that sound? Don't worry. They don't have to know."

He held her hand as far as the elevator, and the attendants took her away.

The two daughters were back from the beach and surprised to see him. He told his small lie, and they reacted about the way he expected, wanting to rush to the hospital. He convinced them to wait until evening when their mother would be rested.

It was four o'clock when he drove back to the city. The heat was draining him, and he gave in and used the air-conditioning. The radio was predicting thundershowers, but there wasn't a cloud in the sky. He left the car at the garage, told them to fill it with gas and oil, and dragged himself back to the apartment and stood in the cool blast of an air conditioner for five minutes before he went to the refrigerator and got a cold beer.

He drank half the can in one long swallow, then dropped into a chair, exhausted, and groaned aloud.

He left a trail of clothing to the bathroom and stood under a tepid shower for a full fifteen minutes, letting the stream of water revive him.

When he returned to his beer, he was wrapped in a terry-cloth robe. He felt that he might survive, but he was emotionally numb.

"Emmy, Emmy," Dalbey said aloud. "I love you dearly, but this was a rotten time for it."

He had to plan for Monday and he had lost a day. Getting to Steach without being followed wasn't going to

be easy. Not this time. It had to be perfect, and he was too
tired to think. He ate a salad, drank another beer, and
finally gave up and went to sleep.

In the morning the stakeout was gone. Dalbey left
the apartment to call Dan Curran.

Curran said, "Yeah, that figures. My friend downtown
says they lifted the phone tap yesterday. That search—I
think we better come make a sweep."

"Don't bother," Dalbey said. "Let them listen. Did
you get anything on those people?"

"I did. FBI had files on three of them. They're dead.
Benjamin, McCarthy, and Wilson. They were CIA like you
said. Nothing on Batcher."

"Nothing?"

"Not a thing. You sure he was an American?"

"You had his army serial number. Thirteen two double-
oh four four eight."

"There's no file for that number," Curran said. "My
guy at Treasury got really hot on it. Nothing at the
Pentagon. Nothing at VA. Immigration never heard of him,
and no Social Security number or tax record."

"Could have been killed," Dalbey said.

"Not according to Graves Registration."

"Could be MIA, could be a lot of things."

"Could be," Curran admitted.

Rudolph Batcher had been "scrubbed." Dalbey was
sure of it. He suspected that Steffinelli had performed the
sleight of hand while he was still with the Agency. Maybe
that big house in Denver was part of the deal.

Dalbey called Western Union and used a credit card
to send a telegram to Vince at Tel-Tech International in
Denver. It was just two words: RUDY BATCHER, and he
signed his name. If he was right, and if Vince assumed
that he knew more than he did, they might overreact,
giving him the edge.

He had to concentrate on getting to Steach. It was
going to mean a lot of driving, but it was a nice day for it

and his plan seemed perfect in its simplicity. He called the hospital in Norwalk and learned that his sister had already been released. Then he called New Age Electronics in Stamford, Connecticut, and talked to Eric Lewin, the young wizard who had installed the stereo tape system in his car. They made an appointment to meet.

He walked back to his office. Mossy admitted him and he went upstairs. He opened a bureau drawer and debated whether or not to take the Smith & Wesson and decided against it because he couldn't hit anything with the damn thing, anyway. He slipped the steel baton into a lightweight sport jacket and carried it downstairs. He said for the benefit of any electronic bugs that he had to go out for an hour, then gave a note to Alice Walder that said he would be gone for a couple of days, with the word *confidential* heavily underlined. He took some papers in a briefcase and left by the back door, something he rarely did. He had to use a key to unlock the gate at the end of the alley. He went to his garage and asked for his car.

When they brought the car down he used the key to unlock the trunk and examined the shotgun in the aluminum case. It looked untouched, but he made a mental note to shoot it later to make certain. He locked the trunk, tipped the garage attendant, and drove away.

He crossed the Triborough Bridge and passed through the grim worn-out neighborhoods of the Bronx, past Pelham and Co-op City, past the shabby suburbia of Mount Vernon and New Rochelle, where a toll basket demanded forty cents, and into the green wealth of Larchmont, Harrison, and Rye, the smooth hum and whir of Bavarian engineering carrying him along the six-lane concrete ribbon and over the line into Connecticut where the character of the landscape changes dramatically—mystically, it always seemed to him—from New York to New England.

The first turnpike service area was in Darien. He pulled off the highway and cruised the parking area until he spotted Eric Lewin's panel truck, then he passed along the next rank of parked cars, checking license plates, and pulled in next to a car from Massachusetts.

He climbed out of the car and stood by the rear bumper while Eric Lewin approached, a canvas tool bag slung over his shoulder. Lewin was young and he walked with a slouchy shuffle. His hair pushed out from under a baseball cap, and he wore round steel-rimmed glasses and a wispy mustache. His T-shirt was oversize and his blue jeans clung to bony hips and sagged, draping over a pair of unlaced red Converse All-Stars.

"Hey, man," he said.

"Eric."

"This it?" he asked, toeing the car.

Dalbey nodded and Lewin looked toward the entrance ramp and said, "Watch for a van coming in." He moved around the car and placed his tool bag on the hood. He took out a UHF monitor with earphones and a hand mike. He turned up the volume on the monitor and switched it on. "Wow!" he exclaimed, reaching to reduce the volume. "You weren't kidding." He worked his way around the car and found the transmitting device on the frame beneath the trunk. He took a large screwdriver, put down a drop cloth, and crawled under the rear.

"Can you put it on this car over here?" Dalbey asked.

"Which?"

"This Oldsmobile here. They're going to Massachusetts."

Lewin chuckled. "No problem." He was reaching up to pry loose the magnetic device. He gritted his teeth and grunted. He did it carefully. He crawled out with a black box the size of a cigarette package in his hand. He cast a furtive glance toward the restaurant, and when he was satisfied that he had the time to make the switch, he crawled beneath the rear of the Oldsmobile and pressed the signal transmitter against bare metal. "She'll stay," he said, rolling out and getting to his feet.

"Done?" Dalbey asked.

"Just about." Lewin went over the car again, checking

for a second transmitter, but found nothing. "You're clean, man." He was putting his equipment away when he said, "Hey, hey, here come your friends."

Dalbey looked up and a green, closed-panel van was coming off the ramp and into the parking area.

"See the directional antenna on top?" Lewin said. "These guys are high tech. They can stay a couple miles behind and still track you down."

"You mean track him down." Dalbey nodded at the Olds.

Lewin grinned. "I better split, man," He shouldered his canvas bag.

"How much do I owe you?"

"Fifty okay? House call, y'know."

"Bill me for a hundred."

"You got it." Lewin sauntered away and Dalbey sat in his car and waited for the driver of the Oldsmobile.

It was a man and a woman, middle years, overweight, their faces blank and bored, turnpike weary. There might be a little excitement in their lives when they got to wherever they were going. He was tempted to ask, but he just waited. The man picked at his teeth with a wooden toothpick. The woman talked, but he didn't seem to listen. They opened the doors on both sides at the same time. When they started their car, Dalbey reached for the key and started his.

He assumed that the men in the van knew that they were following a BMW. When the transmitter left the service area, a BMW had better leave with it. He backed out after the Oldsmobile and stayed on the car's bumper. As they paused at the turnpike and then eased into the right lane together, Dalbey glanced in his mirror to watch the van moving along the ramp, following the BMW and tuned in on the Olds.

Dalbey tailed the Oldsmobile as far as New Haven, where the turnpike picks up a confusion of local traffic and intersects with the northbound I-91. The van was out of sight. He made his move, passing the Olds and pushing the speedometer past eighty. If the driver of the Olds decided to save a dollar and head directly north to the Massachusetts Turnpike, Dalbey wanted to be out of sight.

He was through New Haven and approaching the exit before the Branford Toll Plaza when he glanced at the mirror and saw flashing red lights coming up from behind.

He muttered, "Shit!" and slammed a hand on the steering wheel. If the Olds had not taken I-91, if the van was still following, he couldn't be parked on the side of the turnpike with a police car behind him. He put the accelerator to the floor. The speedometer needle moved to ninety as the smooth power of the BMW rose to the occasion. It was a quarter mile to the exit. He hit the turn signal handle and the little green arrow blinked on the dash. He could hear the siren, but he ignored it. He shot off onto the down ramp, with the state police car closing on him, and made a show of looking into the rearview mirror as he pumped the brake pedal. He could see that he wasn't visible to cars passing on the turnpike. He pulled off onto the grass and waited for the angry policeman.

"Yes?"

'Your license and registration, please."

He produced both and handed them over. The officer carried them back to his car and spoke on his radio. Dalbey suddenly found himself wondering if Tel-Tech could have a pipeline into Hartford, and while it was possible, it seemed improbable. He got his license and registration back, a speeding ticket, and a lecture on safe driving. He listened politely and contritely, and when it was done and he was free to go, he drove to a diner and stopped for coffee.

When he felt that he had wasted enough time for the Olds and the van to be far ahead of him, he put the BMW back on the turnpike and took his time getting to Old Saybrook and the exit to Route 9, a four-lane concrete highway that runs north along the Connecticut River and is little used and oddly out of place. He swept down through the cloverleaf and out onto the highway.

His experience with the state police car in Denver had convinced him that even though he had ditched the transmitter, there could be a backup car following him. If that was the case, they were being overly cautious or very clever, because he was alone on the road, speeding north. He passed the signs for Essex and then Deep River, and then he got off onto Route 9A, a two-lane blacktop that dipped in and away from the river, swooping and curving through the lush, green countryside. He slowed and made a right onto the narrow lane that would take him to the Hadlyme ferry, finally stopping in a line of two cars facing a small dock and upright pilings at the edge of the river. He turned off the engine and got out.

It was a beautiful day. The water was dark gray and slow moving.

Dalbey walked to the river's edge and stood on the dock. Gulls were foraging upriver, and a chicken hawk hovered over the far hills and searched.

The ferry arrived and an attendant emerged from a small red cabin to help with the landing.

A yellow Datsun sedan pulled in behind Dalbey. The driver was a young woman with blond hair and her face half-hidden behind large sunglasses, and there was a small child—about two or three, Dalbey guessed—strapped to a car seat.

A pickup and a dusty Plymouth bumped off the end of the small, steel ferryboat, rolled off the dock, and disappeared down the narrow road. When the attendant was ready, he waved the cars forward and onto the ramp. The four cars lined up in two rows, leaving space for walking passengers. The attendant collected the fares and tossed off the lines, and the diesel gave a deep rumble that became a steady, forceful churning as the ferry pushed into the current.

It was only a six-minute trip. Dalbey stayed in his car for the ride. When they reached the eastern shore, the

ferry eased into the slip and tied up, then the cars
disembarked. The road curved through a small cluster of
red brick houses and climbed a hill. Dalbey was third in
line and he followed the two lead cars. They passed
several houses, and where the road curved to the left and
began to climb, Dalbey pulled off to the side and allowed
the yellow Datsun to pass. He made a mental note of the
plate number, and there was a sticker in the rear window
that said U OF CONN. Then he made a three-point turn and
drove back to the ferry. One car was waiting to board the
ferry. He followed it on board.

The attendant said, "Forget something?"

Dalbey laughed and said, "Yeah," and let it go at that.
They waited five minutes, but there were no more cus-
tomers, so they crossed the river with just two cars.

Convinced that he had eluded any pursuers, Dalbey
drove to the Pelican Point Gun Club and ran through a
box of shells on the trap range. He missed five out of
twenty-five, rare for him, but he had trouble concentrating.
He ate some lunch and drove to Westport to see his sister.
He had debated the wisdom of contacting Emmaline, but
he had no choice. She was going to be overwhelmed with
guilt; she was probably depressed. He had to see her.

She lived in an expensive house on a quaint street
with a small barn for a garage and a studio over the barn.

The two girls were watching a soap opera on the
big-screen television, and Emmaline was making a chocolate cake.

"Philip!" she exclaimed. "What a surprise." She held
a spoon coated with chocolate batter, so she leaned her
face forward and tilted for a buss, and he kissed her lightly
on the cheek.

"Look at me!" she laughed lightly. "A chocolate cake.
Don't say a word. It's for the girls. Sit, sit."

He perched on a tall stool at a counter and stared at
her until she frowned slightly and said, "What's wrong?"

What was wrong? Jesus Christ, the woman treated a suicide attempt like a visit to the goddamned hairdresser.

"Phil?"

"It's nothing. I've got a lot on my mind." He slipped off the stool. "I have to run."

"You just got here."

"I know. I wanted to look in is all. Wanted to be sure you're okay."

She smiled then, a small, warm smile that barely creased her face. Her eyes glistened and she whispered, "Oh, golly," and shook her head several times. She stepped over to him and touched his arm. "Thanks for yesterday," she said in a voice that was barely audible. He looked down at her hand, still slim and delicate but showing her age. He covered her hand with his and gave it a squeeze.

He heard it again, his mother's voice, the young Mary Beth, sternly, matter-of-factly. "We don't do that," she would say. Dalbeys don't cry. Dalbeys don't lose their temper. Dalbeys don't fall apart in public. Dalbeys don't let anyone know that they feel.

"I have to go," he said.

"We're coming in next week," she said.

"We?"

"The girls and I."

"Oh."

"We won't be any trouble."

"I just have the one extra bedroom."

"That's plenty."

Actually it would be good to have them there. The place could use some noise. The squash court wasn't used nearly enough. Maybe Arthur would come for dinner. Helen should meet some cousins.

Dalbey hugged his sister. "Next week." He called to the girls, then left.

He decided to avoid the main bridges over the Hudson River, so he took the Taconic Parkway and worked his way to the rickety old Bear Mountain Bridge. He stayed on

9W north, passing through all those defeated nineteenth-century river towns, Cornwall-on-Hudson, New Windsor, Middle Hope, Marlboro, Milton, all the cramped, weary, stoplight-studded main streets, waiting for revival.

It was almost six P.M. when he reached New Paltz. He had been driving all day and he was road weary. He stopped for dinner, then drove to his cabin and slept, confident that he would see Steach alone.

Chapter Nineteen

The morning was sunny, but cooler. Dalbey searched the radio dial until he got a weather forecast.

"A cold front sweeping down from Canada will bring cloudy skies and cooler weather, with highs in the seventies and a late-afternoon chance of rain."

Dalbey called the caretaker to tell him he was using the cabin, then he drove into town for groceries. When he returned, he sat on the porch and ate a breakfast of cold cereal and fruit.

It was eleven-thirty when he took his binoculars and climbed to the trail behind the house. He wore a light poplin golf jacket over a navy blue polo shirt, a pair of chinos, and hiking boots.

He crossed Rhododendron Bridge and took the Minnewaska trail, and even at a good pace it took an hour to reach Sky Top, where he had a view of the Mohonk Mountain House. At first glimpse, overlooking a patchwork of rolling hills and cultivated fields, with the southern Catskills in hazy pink and purple in the distance, it resembled a seventeenth-century castle or monastery, with turrets and towers and cupolas and steep, red-tiled roofs and gables. He hiked around the base of the cliff and sat on a huge rock slab to train the binoculars on the large front porch and second-floor veranda that overlooked the lake.

It was already off-season. The rows of rocking chairs were still and empty. He wasn't sure what he was looking for. Something out of the ordinary. Something that might mean trouble. He moved the glasses over the grounds, watched a few workmen who seemed to be working. Nothing was out of place. He studied the building a good ten minutes before leaving his rock perch to descend to the lakeshore road. He followed the edge of the lake and climbed the long, steep walk to the stone stairs that led to the porch. An arrow said ENTER HERE and pointed to a side door.

Passing through the door was like entering an Edwardian time warp. He stepped into the formal elegance of carved oak and velvet and floating cherubim and ornate beams and somber drapes and stiff, gilt-framed portraits of corseted overstuffed women and stern, bearded men. There was just one clerk at the main desk.

"Do you have a Mr. Steach registered?" Dalbey asked.

The clerk studied his list. "I'm sorry, sir, we don't."

"Thank you." Dalbey walked along the hallway, glancing into empty sitting rooms, a tiny snack bar and gift shop. He wondered what name Steach would be using. He returned to the lobby, checking his watch, then entered the Lake Lounge, a vast room with three fireplaces, dark wood paneling, and huge decorated ceiling beams that stretched the full sixty-foot width of the room.

He found Steach sitting under a six-pound rainbow trout caught by J. Fred Skinner on July 28, 1953. Dalbey didn't actually find him. Steach was sitting in a high-backed wing chair facing the porch and the lake, and he was hidden from view from behind. He had watched Dalbey enter the room through a small pocket mirror held in his hand, and he said, "Over here."

Since the cavernous room appeared to be empty, Dalbey was startled by the gravelly voice. "Steach?" he said, approaching the chair.

"Also known as William Trainor," the voice said.

Dalbey noticed the mirror in the palm of the hand, and he passed around the chair to face the occupant. He looked older, of course, and his gray hair was thinning. But it was Jon Steach, no mistaking that. He lifted a sinewy right hand. "Hiya, guy."

Gripping the hand, Dalbey grinned. He sat in the chair facing the wingback. "Jesus, Steach, it's good to see you." Dalbey shook his head. "You look great." Steach did. He had obviously been hiding out in the sun. His face was tanned, making the blue eyes luminous. He had a slightly hooked nose and a crooked way of smiling that produced a hawklike devilish look, and his body appeared hard and exercised.

Steach grinned back and said, "Long time."

They both sat there, smiling, not saying anything, just looking one another over. Then Dalbey glanced at the mounted fish on the wall and said, "Your taste in company hasn't improved."

"Around here that's lively," Steach said. "Where'd you find this goddamned geriatric home? They don't even have a bar, for chrissake."

"It's quiet."

"Jesus, you're not kidding. For entertainment tonight they're showing *Goodbye Mr. Chips*. And there's nobody here."

"It's off-season."

"The last season here was 1920."

"You wanted to talk."

"That's true. It's a good place to talk." Steach was serious for a minute. He said, "You're sure you weren't followed."

"I spent all day yesterday making sure."

"You were always pretty good at that."

"I like the game."

"Yeah, the game." He sighed and seemed to deflate.

"You're alive," Dalbey said.

"Yeah, I am, and I'm trying to stay that way."

They were quiet again and they sat there looking, locked in their thoughts, deciding how to proceed, how to bridge the gap of ten years. The questions roiled around waiting to be asked.

Then Dalbey said, "The FBI is looking for you."

Steach was genuinely surprised. "What the hell do *they* want?"

"They say you waltzed off with a lot of U.S. government money."

"Ah, that. But I'm surprised they brought in the FBI."

"You took it?"

"It was bribe money," Steach said. "We kept it around. Old bills. No records. Used it to pay agents, buy information, for anything that we didn't want traced." He smiled. "We didn't give receipts."

"But it was—"

"It was nobody's. I needed money. And at the time I wasn't sure who was trying to blow me up. I thought it was my own guys."

"You thought the CIA was trying to kill you?"

"Well, it wouldn't be the first time," Steach said. "I didn't know. I grabbed the money and beat it."

"But why? Steach, what the hell happened back there?"

Steach took a deep breath and expelled it noisily through pursed lips and shook his head. "I'm still not sure. I was blowing the whistle on Hugh Winston, the boss of Tel-Tech." He leaned forward in his chair and the hawk face was pained. "I didn't even think it was all that important, for chrissake. I sent through a routine report."

"About what?"

"Let's go outside." Steach seemed agitated and he

rose from his chair. Dalbey followed him through the side door to the rustic railed porch. Steach stood at the railing and looked out over the lake. "Pretty here," he said.

Dalbey leaned against an upright post that helped support the roof. "Well?" he said finally.

Steach talked, facing the lake. "Hugh Winston. Major General Hugh Winston. I found out Winston was up to his ass in intrigue in the Middle East. From the beginning he's been the chief financial support behind Colonel Muammar Qaddafi. He supplied the money for the coup that ousted King Idris and brought Qaddafi to power."

"Smart," Dalbey said.

"Hell, I agree. What could be worse than King Idris? I didn't give a damn who ran Libya, I was just concerned that Winston was using Phoenix Exploration to transfer all the dough."

"Phoenix?"

"Phoenix Exploration was a front the CIA used to shift large sums of money around. It was ostensibly a Tel-Tech company and they did some oil drilling, but the real business was getting the money where it was needed without a trace. You've heard of Overseas Charter?"

"The CIA air force."

Steach smiled. "Yeah. Okay, Overseas Charter was also a Tel-Tech company, and Winston was using it to ship freight all over the Middle East."

"Was that legal?"

"Legal?" Steach turned and held his hands shoulder-high. "Who gives a goddamn for legal? The Agency was being compromised. Phoenix money was behind Qaddafi's plot to overthrow King Hussein of Jordan and King Hassan of Morocco. Remember the twenty-five million Qaddafi loaned to Pakistan for the 1971 war with India? Phoenix money authorized by Winston. Phoenix, for crissake, was financing the Muslim rebels fighting in Ethiopia. Winston was Phoenix. Phoenix was CIA. I had it completely documented."

"So what'd you do?"

"What I was supposed to do. I sent in a report. I tell you, I personally didn't give a damn what Winston did. I wasn't saving the world. You know me better than that. I was just doing my job. Can you imagine the shit that would hit the fan if some half-ass reporter made the connection with the Agency? What India would say? Israel? Hussein? That bunch of Democrats in Congress? So I sent the report to Washington along with the documentation." He pushed away from the railing, flexing his shoulder muscles by hunching forward. He took a few steps, stretching, and stood looking over the hills, a hand poised on one of the uprights.

So they decided to eliminate him. They blew up his parked car. He was buying a bottle of wine when the windows of the vintners, a block away, were blown in.

"Who?" Dalbey asked.

Steach shrugged. He spread his hands and then clasped them. "My first reaction was terrorists. Then I thought it might be the Agency. Later on I began to think about how close Cassidy had always been to Hugh Winston."

"Dan Cassidy?"

"He was Chief of Operations for Europe. I sent him the report. I never heard another word. The son of a bitch must have taken it straight to Winston."

Dalbey took a copy of the newspaper clipping from his pocket and unfolded it. He handed it to Steach, who stared at it quizzically and dug into a pocket for a pair of reading glasses. "I saw this. Did you know Cassidy?"

"Not really," Dalbey said. "But I was on the Calico mission."

"You?" Steach glanced owllike over the top of his glasses.

"I was the gunner," Dalbey said.

"The gunner. I'll be damned." He laughed. "You were one scared kid."

"You're not kidding."

"So you know old Captain Winston."

"Never saw him before or since," Dalbey said. "After that day I went back to G two."

"Well, old Winston and Cassidy were close, and they stayed close after the war."

"And Cassidy sold you out."

"Had to be. I been over it a million times."

"I still don't see why Winston would give a damn," Dalbey said. "The Agency wasn't about to say anything."

"That's true, but could they count on me? I was never known as a team player."

"So what if you talked? One newspaper story and forgotten in a week."

"It was also right in the middle of that business about Winston's making secret donations to Nixon's campaign. The press was digging into that. There were rumors that he handed Maurice Stans eight million dollars."

"But a car bombing. C'mon, Steach."

"Flip, guys like Winston don't rig bombs on cars. They don't have to. They say, 'Eliminate that problem,' and by the time the order gets down to the street, you're dealing with people who'll take you out for the fun of it." He held up the newspaper story. "Do you think somebody up top planned to kill these women? They said, 'I think we have to do something about Daniel.' That's all. That's all it takes. And they don't want to hear any more about it."

Steach had the money and a half dozen passports, and since he spoke four languages, he got by easily and he could travel and even pick up odd jobs as a translator or importer, and the underground life wasn't all that bad. So why did he surface?

"I ran out of money. I got stupid." Steach dropped into a chair and leaned forward, his elbows resting on his knees. "I contacted Winston, let him know I was still alive."

"You're kidding."

"I wanted to negotiate," Steach said.

"Negotiate? For what?"

"I had copies of the old documents."

"Why would he care? That old stuff?"

"He's running for president," Steach said.

Dalbey had to think about that for a moment. It was true that Hugh Winston was taking a public posture. The interviews, the TV appearances, the speaking engagements. "Reagan's running for president," Dalbey said.

"'Eighty-eight," Steach said.

"He'll be too old."

"Don't kid yourself. Reagan's seventy-two. I'm telling you, Old Captain Hugh wants his chapter in the history books."

Assuming it was so, could the Qaddafi connection short-circuit a Winston run for the nomination? Dalbey considered the headlines, the clamoring TV reporters, the certainty of a public Congressional investigation, the possibility of federal prosecutors. Good-bye candidate.

Dalbey stared at Steach and tried to see him as an extortionist, a blackmailer. He couldn't; certainly not the Steach he used to know. But this man was how old now—sixty-three? Sixty-four? Broke, with no job, no retirement, officially dead and living underground . . . an old man running scared . . . grabbing at options . . . and he had only one thing to sell.

"What were you asking?" Dalbey asked.

Steach glanced down, embarrassed. "Does it matter?"

"I guess not."

So Steach offered to turn over his copies of the documents for a price, and he found himself dealing with Vince Steffinelli. The exchange would be made in Amsterdam because Steach felt secure there, but to really be on the safe side, Steach insisted that the swap be made by an old friend whom he trusted could not be bought or corrupted by Tel-Tech's billions.

"Me," Dalbey said sourly.

Steach grinned sheepishly. "Yeah."

"Thanks a bunch."

"Jesus, I thought there'd be nothing to it."

But why didn't Steffinelli just explain to Dalbey that Steach was alive and wanted to meet him in Amsterdam? Why the convoluted plot, why the Calico bullshit?

"I don't know," Steach said. "I guess they figured you'd ask too many questions. Better that you didn't leave a paper trail they'd have to clean up."

"Okay, I was in Amsterdam. What happened?"

"They were set up to take us both out," Steach said. "They owned Slattery's widow. They had a goddamned army over there. You were the bait to get me into the open. Once they had the documents, you and I were dead meat. Period. End of story. I left that message at your hotel to scare you off."

"You knew I'd be at the Doelen?"

"Claire said the De L'Europe. When you weren't there, I tried the Doelen."

Dalbey didn't speak for a minute. He was reviewing the events since his flight from Amsterdam—just two weeks ago. He asked, "What do you do now?"

"I want out," Steach said. "I'm too old for this. I just want to get the documents back to them. Once that stuff is destroyed, there's no case. I can disappear. They'll keep looking for a time, but they'll get tired of it."

Dalbey didn't think so. Why would they believe he was sending the only copy. But Steach wanted to believe it.

"So why don't you send them the stuff?"

"I don't have it," Steach said.

"What?"

"You do," Steach said.

Dalbey caught his breath. He blinked. He opened his mouth to speak, but closed it again. "That leather briefcase."

Steach nodded.

It had been a couple of months before the car bombing

in 1973, before Steach had made his report to Cassidy. Dalbey was flying home from Berlin, and Steach had given him the leather briefcase with the lock and the diplomatic seal and said, "Hang on to this until you hear from me." It had sat in his closet in New Canaan for a year, then gradually found its way into the attic. So that's why Don Trilby was going through his file cabinet, why they had tossed his office and apartment.

"You still have it," Steach said. It was a statement, but tentative, edged with question.

"It was in the attic. I haven't seen it in years."

"But it's still there, right? Flip, it has to be there. If they don't get those papers, they'll never stop looking."

Dalbey didn't want to tell him about the tag sale. Would anybody buy an old locked briefcase without a key? Would they even put a thing such as that up for sale? He didn't think so, but he'd have to go to New Canaan to find out. "I'll drive over today."

"I'll go with you," Steach said anxiously. It was clear that he was frightened.

It was curious about Steach. In his prime, in the years that Dalbey knew him, he had been scornful of danger. He didn't seem to know fear, and if he did, he didn't care. It was all a game, and if you lost, you'd be dead and so what? But now, with nothing ahead but boredom and breathing, with no future and no useful purpose, when it would seem that a vital man would say, "Enough!" he was desperate to live—simply to survive.

"I think we ought to keep you hidden," Dalbey said. "Let's get you checked out of here. I have a cabin about five miles over the hill. We'll stay there."

They checked out of the resort. Steach was traveling light, a single canvas bag that he carried on a shoulder strap. They took Steach's car, a Volkswagen Rabbit that belonged to Claire Paige.

"All those years, I never knew you had a daughter," Dalbey said. "I had no idea you were married."

"Well, I wasn't married very long. Wartime romance. We didn't know anything. Judith. Nice girl. She was only twenty-one when Claire was born in 'forty-five." He handled the two miles of sweeping, descending curves with the casual abandon of a European driver. He wasn't going to elaborate on historical marital problems, and Dalbey didn't ask.

"Where did Claire get the details on that embassy party in Rome? I know she was coached."

Steach glanced over and grinned. "I was there. I was working for the embassy."

"You're not serious."

"Interpreter. Hell, I'd been dead a long time. Why not? It was fun. I even had a State Department clearance."

"Dangerous."

"I didn't think so until I saw you that night. I gave notice the next day."

They drove past the gatehouse, past the golf course, down through the dense woods toward the town. The spires and tall buildings of the college could be seen in the distance, rising out of the green.

"Turn to the right up here." Dalbey directed Steach toward the cliffs and the secluded, private drive leading to the camp.

Steach parked the Rabbit by the barn and they carried his bag to the cabin. Dalbey showed him the spare room, the canned goods, the beer supply. Then he called Bill Shoreham in New Canaan, but Shoreham was in court.

"I'll run over there," Dalbey said.

Steach was standing by the large table, looking down at the papers that Dalbey had brought from New York. He was glancing at the list of names and could read the word "CALICO" at the top. "What's this?" he asked.

Dalbey came to the table and lifted the paper. "The Calico mission." He handed the list to Steach. "I got it from the National Archives. You're on there."

Steach had to dig around for his glasses before he could read the smaller type. He studied it and clucked his tongue. "Time's catching up to us, Flip." He sat in one of the captain's chairs and held the list at eye level. "Why the question mark after Rudy Batcher?"

Dalbey explained and Steach said, "There has to be something on him somewhere. He was discharged from the service. I know he did freelance work for the Agency. There had to be clearances. He must have had a Social Security card."

"Nothing," Dalbey said.

Steach pulled on his nose and scowled at the sheet of paper. He tossed it on the table. "You think somebody pulled all the records?"

"I do, and I think it was Vince Steffinelli. He mentioned everybody on that mission except Winston and Batcher."

Steach leaned his elbows on the table. He reached out and picked up an extra copy of the Cassidy story and read it again. "This could be Batcher," he said.

"That's what Batcher does?"

"That's *all* he does." Steach dropped the news clip. "And he does it better than anybody." He stared at the tabletop, then he looked up, and the blue eyes fixed on Dalbey. "If Rudy Batcher's in this I want to be outta here and long gone."

Chapter Twenty

It was three-thirty P.M. when Dalbey got to Bill Shoreham's office. The lawyer was there, but he had not received an accounting on the tag sale, and he had no knowledge of the briefcase. He gave Dalbey the address of the two women who handled the sale and called to make sure they were there.

Dalbey found the house, and two small children directed him to a basement office where he explained to Sherry Compton that the leather briefcase had been forgotten in the attic and that he now needed it.

Every item that had been tagged for sale was listed in a large ledger with a number and sale price, and Mrs. Compton was going through the list. "Here it is," she said, her finger poised on the green grid of the page, "but it wasn't sold."

Dalbey sighed with relief. "Good."

"It was donated to Helping Hands." The woman then added defensively, "Mr. Shoreham said you wanted everything to go except the items previously removed for your family. In that event, anything that isn't sold or put out on consignment goes to Helping Hands. They made their pickup on Monday morning." Dalbey groaned. She said, "Mr. Shoreham knew the policy."

"I understand," Dalbey said. "I just want to find it. Where do they take it?"

"I believe everything goes to their yard and warehouse in Bridgeport."

"Do you have an address?" He glanced at his watch. It was four-ten and he wondered what time the place closed.

It took him a half hour to get to Bridgeport and find the yard. It was south of the railroad and turnpike, among the fuel-oil storage tanks, power plant, truck depots, and scrap yards down along the harbor.

There was room to park a dozen cars in front of the boxlike one-story office of painted concrete block that was lettered in red: HELPING HANDS, and in smaller black letters: RECEIVING DEPOT. Attached to the white box and towering over it was a huge, gray Quonset hut.

Dalbey parked and entered a cluttered office that was furnished with scarred wooden desks and old chairs and filing cabinets piled high with books and papers. The office was staffed by one woman, a redhead in her fifties, who pecked at a typewriter and squinted at the page through thick glasses. She turned to face Dalbey and tilted her head back to aim her blank, myopic stare.

Dalbey explained about the leather briefcase to the woman, who stared at him open-mouthed. He had the feeling that he wasn't getting his story across.

When he finished, she said in a monotone, "You gotta see Mr. Van." She swiveled her chair and spoke into a microphone that amplified her voice through loudspeakers all over the property. "Mr. Van . . . Mr. Van, there's a man to see you. I'm sending him back."

She turned to Dalbey and used a pencil to point at the door. "Through there."

Dalbey said, "Thank you," and went through the door.

He was inside the Quonset hut. It was about the size of a football field and piled high with junk. There was furniture mimicking every conceivable period and style thrown together in soaring historical chaos, Louis upon Louis upon Queen Anne upon Italianate upon California Gothic upon Early American and so on up to the cross braces. There were discarded, outdated sporting goods, skis and skates and golf clubs and weary, sagging golf bags and unstrung tennis racquets and broken bikes and sleds, enough football pads to outfit a league and boxes of baseball bats and old gloves and hockey sticks and deflated basketballs. There was clothing, tons of clothing, and boxes of books forty feet high; lamps and utensils and dishes; the rejects of thousands of tag sales—in one large room a macabre monument to gluttony and consumerism.

Dalbey followed a dim, narrow corridor down the center of the building. He was drawn towards the sounds of a conveyor and voices. He passed narrow corridors that branched off the main thoroughfare. When he reached the center of the building, there was an open space where the

conveyor, wide and low to the ground like those that carry
luggage in air terminals, curved. In a large open door to
his left a truck was unloading. Boxes passed on the conveyor, turned where he stood, and continued down toward
the end of the building, where the doors were open and
he could see out to the water. Perhaps a dozen men were
pulling things off the conveyor and carrying them out of
sight. A man in dirty overalls stood at the curve of the
conveyor. He was stooped, his back twisted out of shape.

Dalbey knew that Helping Hands was created to
employ the handicapped. He approached the man and
said above the noise, "I'm looking for Mr. Van."

The man jumped back in surprise, but he recovered
and grinned. The man nodded his head, and Dalbey
assumed that he couldn't speak.

"Mr. Van," Dalbey said again.

The man raised his arm, pointed to the loading dock,
and said, "Van. Van."

Dalbey picked his way carefully to the open door on
his left and stood on a concrete loading platform. Three
men were unloading a truck, throwing the contents onto
the conveyor. The man closest to Dalbey was doing very
well with just one arm, and when there was a pause in his
work, Dalbey said, "I'm looking for Mr. Van." The one-
armed man pointed to a man in a blue work shirt standing
at the side of the truck. He was chewing on an unlit cigar
and pulling at the bill of a soiled red baseball cap as he
talked to the driver of the truck. His belly pushed out over
his leather belt and he had to keep hitching up his baggy
trousers.

Dalbey crouched down to vault himself over the edge
of the four-foot-high platform. He circled the truck and
addressed the man in the red cap. "Mr. Van?"

"That's right, what can I do for you?"

Dalbey explained about the leather briefcase.

Van said, "New Canaan, huh?"

"Right. Yesterday morning."

"Jeez, we've had thirty-five, forty loads in here yesterday and today."

Dalbey tried to imagine sorting through forty truckloads of junk. "Maybe I could look through what was brought in," he suggested.

"Jesus, you'd have to go through the whole goddamned place. We don't have that kind of system. Everything just goes where there's room. We separate much as we can. But mostly it all goes right on through and gets separated out at the end. Stuff can be fixed up and sold goes off to repair shop. Clothing gets separated; good stuff goes to stores, rest gets baled and sold for rags. For most of the stuff this is the end of the line. Most gets incinerated."

"Burned?" It was something Dalbey didn't want to consider.

"Yeah, see back here." Van led the way to the rear of the building. "We burn to salvage the metal." He pointed to piles of blackened metal waiting to be loaded aboard a barge. "We can sell the metal by the pound. We'd like to recycle everything, but it just don't pay." He stopped and pointed to a tall, square building of concrete block that stood off to one side. There were two stacks rising from the top, and a conveyor rose on a slant to an opening about two thirds of the way up the side of the blank gray wall.

"The incinerator!" Van shouted to be heard above the roar of a tractor that bumped across the yard. The tractor held a large steel hopper clasped in a forklike device that lifted the heavy load and carried it high. Dalbey watched the tractor roll up to a large bin at the base of the conveyor, then lurch forward and automatically dump the hopper. It backed away, returned the empty hopper to its place at the rear of the building, and went to pick up another.

An attendant at the conveyor pressed a large black button on a hand-held device and the belt whined and ground into action. There was a rending of wood and cloth and a screech of metal and the square buckets attached to the belt lifted the junk from the bin and carried it to the opening in the wall.

"We burn just twice a day," Van shouted. Dalbey nodded and Van touched his arm and led him to the open end of the warehouse. "Sorting goes on here." He gestured with the cold cigar. "All those different hoppers go to a different reclamation center every day."

A dozen men and two large women with their hair wrapped in kerchiefs worked at a fairly casual pace, unloading things from the conveyor and deciding the fate of a chair, a lamp, a Polaroid camera, a carpet, an electric mixer.

"We move through a lot of junk in a week," Van said. He glanced at a pocket watch. "We shut down at six." He waggled his thumb and Dalbey followed him back to the loading dock.

"What's your briefcase look like?" Van asked.

Dalbey tried to remember. He hadn't seen it for almost ten years. "Brown leather," he said. "Like an old-fashioned school bag. A flap came over the top and there was a kind of thick handle on the top. It was locked on the front with a brass padlock about so big." He used his fingers to show the size. "There was no key."

"No key," Van repeated. "Couldn't open it."

"Not without the key."

"So it was no good."

"Well, not unless you got the lock off."

"Anything else?"

"Yes. There was a sticker on it that said U.S. State Department."

"Oh, yeah?" His interest seemed to perk up. "This belonged to the U.S. government?"

"Not exactly," Dalbey said. "To a man who worked there."

Van lifted a hand and shifted his hat around on his head, then took out the cold cigar and examined it. "I tell ya, Mr. . . . uh . . . Mr. . . ."

"Dalbey."

"Oh, yeah, pleased to know you." Van shook Dalbey's hand. "Mr. Dalbey, there's no way of knowing where that briefcase might be. Could be inside, could be gone."

Dalbey reached for his wallet and took out a business card. "If it should turn up, I mean, if it should come out the other end of the building, I'll pay the person who finds it a reward of one hundred dollars. And I'll pay another one hundred to you." He wrote on the back of the card: *$100 reward for leather briefcase with brass lock*. He handed the card to Van. "You got that now? A hundred to you and a hundred to the finder."

"That's mighty generous."

"My number in New York is right here." He pointed to the face of the card. "Call collect."

"Mighty generous."

They shook hands again and Dalbey started to leave when a thought occurred. "Mr. Van," he said, turning back, "I wonder if I could have a couple of my people dig around in your warehouse for a few days. I'll still pay the two hundred if they find the thing, and I'll pay a hundred even if they don't."

"Why not? Send 'em by. We open at eight. Tell 'em to ask for Art Van. That's me."

"Thank you, Art."

There was hope. It wasn't going to be what Steach wanted to hear, but it was better than the incinerator. As he reached the BMW, he noticed a phone booth on the corner. He decided to call his office and offer Michael Durso a week or two in beautiful Bridgeport. He dialed and waited and the phone rang and nobody answered. He checked his watch. It was a quarter till six. Damn, the one evening Michael wasn't playing with the computer.

He left the booth, stopped, and stepped back in. He used his credit card to call Vince Steffinelli in Denver. He was going to tell Vince about the briefcase and the warehouse. He was put through to the secretary and was told that Mr. Steffinelli was out of town.

Back to square one. He would call Michael Durso in the morning and maybe send Steffinelli a telegram. It might solve the whole problem. In the meantime he could talk it over with Steach.

It was six o'clock when he backed the BMW away from the Helping Hands office and headed for the Connecticut Turnpike.

He drove south, and although it wasn't the most direct route to the New York Thruway, he felt it would be the safest. He cut down through the Bronx and crossed the George Washington Bridge, where he picked up the Palisades Parkway and connected with the Thruway west of Nyack. It was eight P.M. when he got off at New Paltz and stopped for a sandwich.

Since he knew Steach would be waiting, he made it a fast stop, then drove through, over the Wallkill and north on 299. He was bone weary when he finally reached the drive leading to the cabin. His headlights danced on the corridor of trees and cast moving shadows over the rutted and uneven road. When he topped the rise that brought him to the open meadow, he saw that there was a strange car in the yard. He slowed, letting the headlights dwell on it, a dark red Chevy sedan that looked like a rental. Steach's car had not been moved. The house was dark.

He was no longer tired. He felt the adrenaline rush, the ancient psychomotor symptom of flight or fight. He pulled into the yard, then backed around until the rear of the car was alongside the barn, hidden from the house. He doused the lights and removed the key. He opened the door and slipped out and moved in a crouch to the rear of the car. He unlocked the trunk and removed the shotgun from its aluminum case. He loaded it with four shells, released the safety, and pumped one shell into the chamber.

Crouching with the shotgun at port arms, he moved along the side of the car until he was in position to lean over the hood, the shotgun pointing at the front door. The hood was still too warm and he had to move back a step, but he rested the gun.

"Steach!" he called. He waited about seven seconds, then he called again, "Steach!" He waited in the dark, hearing only his own breathing, wondering what the hell was going on. He was about to call again when Steach answered from the back corner of the house.

"That you, Flip?"

"Jesus, Steach, you okay?"

"I'm okay. You alone?"

"Yes."

"Just checking now," Steach said. "Tell me where you were going today."

"New Canaan."

"Looking for what?"

"A briefcase."

"Okay, come on. Come to the back door."

Dalbey knew that Steach would have him covered, so he walked with his arms wide and the shotgun held high in his right hand. He still hadn't seen Steach, but when he turned the corner of the house he was staring into the barrel of a 9mm Walther. He stopped and Steach lowered the gun. "Guess I'm getting edgy," Steach said. He turned and entered the house. Dalbey followed.

Inside the kitchen Dalbey groped along the wall near the door and hit the light switch. The overhead light brightened the kitchen and cast light into the main room, where Dalbey could see that someone was sitting in one of the captain's chairs at the large table. He stepped into the room and flipped the switch that lit the standing lamp.

His mouth dropped and he said, "Arthur." He didn't move. His hand was poised by the light switch and the shotgun hung limply at his side. He noticed that Arthur was tied to the chair. He glanced at Steach for an explanation, but Steach just stared.

"Arthur, what are you doing here?"

"Why don't you ask that lunatic?"

Dalbey turned again to Steach, who shrugged. "He said he was your son. I didn't know. I thought we'd better wait until you got here."

"How long has he been here?"

"Couple hours."

"More like three," Arthur snapped.

Dalbey adjusted the safety on the shotgun and leaned it against the wall in the corner of the room. He crossed to where Arthur was sitting and untied the nylon cord that held his arms behind him.

Arthur rubbed his arms. He scowled, his mouth set in peevish anger. He glowered at Steach and said, "Who's he?"

"Jon Steach," Dalbey said. "An old friend."

"Steach?" Arthur frowned and rummaged into his memory. "Steach?" He was associating the name with the past. "Isn't he the one that was blown up? The one on television. A long time ago."

"That's him," Dalbey said.

Arthur was confused. He looked from Dalbey to Steach and back to Dalbey. "I don't understand."

"He didn't get blown up," Dalbey said. "It wasn't him."

"Then who was it?"

Dalbey turned to Steach and said, "Who *did* go up with that car?"

"No idea," Steach said. "Maybe the guy setting the bomb. I don't know. I didn't ask." He was glancing at the windows facing the porch.

"They said you were a spy," Arthur said.

Steach shrugged, but Dalbey blinked and asked, "Who said?"

"The TV. When it was on the news."

"That was ten years ago. How do you remember that?"

"You said he was a friend. I wondered why you knew

a spy." Arthur suddenly changed the subject. "Why has he been holding a gun on me?"

"He wanted to make sure who you were."

"Why? What's it matter who I am? What's he afraid of? Why does he keep looking at the windows? Is he still a spy?"

"Easy, Arthur, calm down. No, he's not a spy. There are some people . . . he has something some people want. It's hard to explain."

"Where is it?" Steach said, suddenly reminded. "Did you get it?"

"Not exactly." Dalbey explained about the tag sale and the warehouse. Steach listened in stunned silence as Arthur tried to make sense of what was being said.

"Gone?" Steach said.

"Maybe not," Dalbey said. "If it hasn't been burned, there's a good chance of finding it." He explained his plan to alert Winston's people and let them have the task of taking the warehouse apart.

"You think Winston will believe it?"

"Worth a try," Dalbey said. "I'll send Steffinelli a telegram."

Arthur had been forgotten in the exchange, but he interrupted to say, "Mr. Steffinelli wants you to get in touch with him as soon as possible."

Dalbey and Steach turned to the young man. "He says it's very important," Arthur said.

"You saw Steffinelli? Vince Steffinelli?"

"That's why I was in Denver."

Dalbey crossed to the table and sat in a chair facing Arthur, who was looking cautiously defensive. "And Vince gave you a message for me?" Steach sat on the arm of one of the leather easy chairs.

"He couldn't reach you, he said. You weren't in your office. He said it was absolutely essential that he talk to you."

"And he thought you could find me."

"I told him if you were in town, I could probably track you down."

"And you did."

"Yeah, I did."

Dalbey drummed his fingers on the table, considering the possibilities, then he looked up at his son and said, "Now, Arthur, I want you to tell me in detail what you did after that."

"After what?"

"After you left Denver."

"What's this for?"

"It's important, Arthur. In detail."

"I flew to New York," Arthur said.

"To Kennedy."

"Yes. I took a cab home. Helen told me you had called, so I called your office. There was no answer. I tried the house in New Canaan, but the phone was disconnected. I called Bill Shoreham. He wasn't there, but his secretary said the house was empty."

Arthur paused then, and Dalbey urged him on. "Then what?"

"That was yesterday. This morning I called Gramma. She said you'd been there a week ago. So I called Uncle Marcus."

"And?"

"And he told me the same as Gramma. But he gave me Jim Crowther's number."

"And he told you I was here."

"Right."

"So you drove up here."

"That's right. I picked up the car and I—"

"A rental car?"

"No," Arthur said. "Tel-Tech made one of their cars available."

"That was nice of them."

"Well, it's business. Mr. Steffinelli said it was of the highest priority."

"Did he also suggest it might be good for your career?"

"Not exactly. He said he thought I was being wasted as a stockbroker. He said there might be something opening at the corporate level."

"Do you know what Vince does? His job?"

"He's a senior vice president."

"Yeah, I know, but of what?"

Arthur appeared flustered. "I don't know. A senior vice president. I mean..."

"That son of a bitch," Dalbey said. He looked across at Steach, who had been listening carefully. "What do you think?"

Steach shrugged. "I think I wouldn't sit so close to that window."

Dalbey glanced at the window and pushed his chair back. Arthur watched them both, still not understanding. Dalbey said, "They probably bugged the car."

"Without a doubt," Steach said. "Old Vince bird-dogged you with your own kid."

"Damn!"

Steach got to his feet. He looked at Arthur, shaking his head, and walked into the bedroom.

"What is it?" Arthur asked.

Dalbey said, "They used you to track me."

"Why?"

"To get to Steach."

"What do they want with Steach?"

"They want to kill him," Dalbey said.

Arthur's eyes widened and he didn't have a rejoinder. It was beyond his comprehension. He didn't believe it.

Steach returned from the bedroom carrying a pillow. He took a piece of nylon cord and tied it around one end of the pillow, drawing it tight and then wrapping it around like a choker. He then stuffed the small end of the pillow into a wide-mouthed metal vase that resembled a spittoon. When that was finished, he took an old safari jacket from the closet and buttoned it around the pillow. He placed the dummy in a chair and moved it close to one of the windows facing the porch, then he adjusted the lamp shade for better backlighting. When that was finished, he said to Dalbey, "Where's he likely to be?"

Dalbey knew every inch of the property, but he tried to imagine where a stranger would position himself to hit the house.

"Might be more than one," Dalbey said.

"Not a chance. One guy knows, who cares? Two guys know, you got witnesses."

Dalbey nodded and pulled at his lower lip. "He's got to cover the front," he said. "That's the only way out. We've got the cliff blocking the rear. There's the trail, of course; he'd want to cover that." He took a pencil and pad from an end table and sat on the stone hearth to draw a rough sketch of the property. He had to squint to see the lines and Steach said, "Here, use my glasses." He penciled in the main features.

"There's high ground out here that gives an unobstructed view of everything," Dalbey said, tapping a spot on the sketch. "But it's too far away. Must be five hundred yards."

"Where?" Steach asked. Dalbey made a mark to show the place and handed Steach the glasses so he could study it. "Covers everything?" Steach asked.

"Yeah, but it's so far. I'd say he'd have to be down here in the trees."

"We'll see." Steach glanced at Arthur. "Better get him away from there."

"Right," Dalbey said. "Arthur, I think you better move away from those windows."

"I think you people are being ridiculous." Arthur didn't move.

Steach took a deep breath. He blew it out with an audible whooshing sound as he watched Dalbey, then he said, "I'm going to watch from the bedroom."

"You're sure he'll try something tonight?" Dalbey asked.

"I don't know. We're all here. Seems as good a time as any."

"We should think about sleeping in shifts," Dalbey said.

"Fat chance. No sleep tonight." Steach left the room to station himself at a window in the darkened bedroom.

"I'm leaving," Arthur said, rising from the chair.

"You are like hell," Dalbey snapped. He was losing patience, but he caught himself and softened his tone. "Arthur, for chrissake, if there is somebody out there, he's got to take all of us."

"That's ridiculous," Arthur said.

The window shattered, spraying glass. Arthur screamed and Dalbey jumped, his heart seeming to leap out of his chest. There was an echoing *BLONG!* as the bullet struck the metal head of the dummy and buried itself in the pillow, toppling the dummy from the chair. The wounded vase hit the floor with a metallic clang.

"Jesus!" Steach shouted from the bedroom. "Douse that goddamned light!"

Chapter Twenty-one

The moon was in the first quarter, a dim sliver of light obscured by a partial overcast. There was a slight breeze and it was cool, the first sign of the approaching autumn.

The sound of his shot disturbed a flock of roosting crows, which rose from a nearby tree with a loud rush of wings and raucous scolding, and a frightened deer broke from cover and crashed through the darkened brush below and behind the ridge where he sat.

He peered at the cabin through the big scope and smiled. The distant clang of metal that followed the shattering glass told him the shape in the lighted window was a dummy. That would be Steach. Very cute. He had fallen for the oldest ruse in the world. They had obviously tumbled onto the fact that the kid had been used to track them, and now they knew why. This could get interesting, he thought. He didn't know Jon Steach well, but he knew about him. Steach was an old pro who had survived the Cold War, when it was open season on field agents, so he didn't make many mistakes.

But it only takes one, he thought, and this is it, Steach, the end of the line. I don't know what you did to these people, but now you're mine.

The cabin was dark. The natural sounds of night had returned to the woods. He could still distinguish the outlines of the cabin and the barn, the dark bulk of the cliffs beyond, the driveway leading in from the road. He had followed close behind Arthur Dalbey, but had parked out of sight and had scouted the property on foot while there was good light. He had picked the high ground, choosing a location that gave an all-points view of the cabin and was beyond the range of sporting weapons. He still hadn't seen Steach, but he had heard the exchange when Dalbey arrived, so he knew he was there.

He glanced at the glowing dial of his watch and wondered how much time he had. The cabin was isolated, without neighbors as far as he could see, but there was occasional traffic on the nearby state highway, and the sound of gunfire carried, especially at night. A single shot wouldn't be cause for concern in a rural area where rifles were common, but if this turned into a firefight, there could be to the local sheriff or state police. It would be best to get it over with.

They had to know they were trapped, bunched together in a defenseless position. It was the worst possible predicament. And he had all the firepower. Steach was running scared, so he'd be off balance. The kid would panic. Dalbey was a question mark. They had warned him not to underestimate Dalbey, but he couldn't see the threat in a businessman whose big thing was shooting clay targets. He wasn't in the same league. No, Steach was the target. Once he had Steach, the others were just cleanup.

He lowered his eye to the scope and moved the rifle to scan the cabin. The weapon was mounted on a heavy-duty tripod. It was an M-21, the match-grade modification of the M-14 with epoxy-impregnated stock and free-floating barrel that is custom-made by a small staff of gunsmiths at Fort Benning for the U.S. Army sniper teams. In the hands of an expert the M-21 can explode a grapefruit at one thousand yards—more than half a mile. The scope was also U.S. Army, the big battery-powered Starlight telescope that gives the shooter daytime vision in hazy moonlight. At eight hundred yards, under normal nighttime conditions, the shooter can see the design in the target's clothing. It wasn't as good on a dark night such as this, but at five hundred yards it was still going to be like shooting ducks in a barrel.

Peering through the scope was like raising a shade. He saw everything clearly, could even read the numbers on the automobile license plates. He remembered once, years ago, when he had been examining a custom Mannlicher in the gun room at Abercrombie's in New York City. He had carried the unloaded weapon to the window to appraise its 9X scope and was sighting down onto Madison Avenue. He picked targets at random, placing the cross hairs on a strolling man or woman, trying to imagine the reaction if they had known they were in the sights of a high-powered rifle. He mentally squeezed the trigger. Bang, bang. He let some off, giving them a reprieve for no reason other than whim. He changed the rules of his game, holding the scope steady, taking out every fifth person who walked into the cross hairs. He was about to become more selective when the voice of the salesman roused him as though from sleep. "Sir? Sir? I'm sorry, sir, but we'd rather you didn't point the gun at the street."

He often recalled his feelings that day, especially on occasions such as this when he was waiting to make a kill, and it amused him.

There was no movement at the cabin. He moved the telescope from window to window. He had been tempted to take Dalbey out while he was behind the car pointing the shotgun at the cabin. He had the cross hairs on his back. But he had been hoping that Steach would step into the open, so he waited. The same thing in Holland. Dalbey stood there by the canal just waiting for it. Next time, buster, you go down with your friend.

His only concern was the rear of the house, which was out of sight, and he scoped the area. If they moved away from the house, he had them. He had a clear view of the path that cut through the woods, and he could make out the trail that ran horizontally below the cliffs. He panned the scope over the rock wall, seeing it clearly. There was no escape there. He brought his gaze back to the house and watched the window where he had placed the first shot. Nothing happening.

They would be trying to position him, wondering if they were up against one man or a team. Let 'em sweat. After the fiasco in Amsterdam he had insisted on working alone.

"You set up the target, I'll take it out."

"We'd rather you had a team."

"Alone."

"There'll be three of them."

"One that matters."

"Don't sell Dalbey short. He worked for the Agency nearly—"

"Twenty years, I know. He was a courier."

"Maybe just two good men."

"I go alone or I don't go."

Steach was in check. The stalking was done. The quarry was at bay. This was endgame, the real test of skill when the trapped player recognizes his peril, when the ancient predatory instincts of blood sport take hold. Next would come the flight, then checkmate—and the kill.

Like any chess master who has skillfully maneuvered his opponent, he approached endgame with relish. This was when it all came together—the intellect, the experience, the guts—and the higher the stakes the more sublime the win.

Steach would probably have a handgun. He knew Dalbey had a shotgun, and there might be a deer rifle in the cabin. He debated the logic of creating confusion by moving around to set up some fire from other positions, but decided against it. He wanted to flush them out, not pin them down. If they thought he was alone, they might assume they had the advantage of numbers and would try something stupid. He would stay in place and wait for that. If they decided to hole up in the cabin and go for stalemate, he had an Ingram M-11 for close combat.

He lifted his head from the eyepiece, grimacing as the cramped neck muscles recoiled. He sat erect, pressing the fingers of both hands into the small of his back. He massaged the muscles at the base of the spine and turned his head right and left. He rose to stretch, turning first onto his hands and knees, then rising on one leg before the other with a grunt. He spread his arms, swiveling at the hips, then slowly bent to touch his toes, his body limbering as the muscles and tendons warmed and stretched, and the dull pain abated. He could still run seven-minute miles and keep it up for an hour, and there was not an ounce of excess fat on the hard-muscled body, but this hard-earned conditioning didn't stop the muscles from protesting.

I'm getting too old for this shit, he thought.

He looked up at the panorama of stars stretching from

the cliffs to the far horizon. Using the bright glitter of Sirius as reference, he picked out some of the easier constellations: the great nebula of Andromeda, the bright six-star cluster of Cassiopeia on the edge of the Milky Way, the handle of Ursa Minor leading straight to the north pole. He sighed and brought his gaze back to the cabin. He thought, when this job is done, I could use a good long rest in some warm place.

He sat again, cradling the stationary rifle, and hunched forward to press his eye into the soft rubber cup of the scope.

"C'mon, Steach," he muttered aloud, "let's get this show on the road."

Chapter Twenty-two

They crouched in the darkness and spoke in muted voices. Arthur sat on the floor, huddled against the wall. "I can't believe this," he whispered. "It can't be."

"He's way out there," Steach said. "On the high ground like you said."

"That was some shooting," Dalbey said.

Steach gave a low whistle. "Incredible. You know what he's using."

"Sniper rifle?"

"Has to be," Steach said. "With a night-vision scope."

"Who are you talking about?" Arthur hissed.

"Whoever followed you here."

The conversation died, but the heavy breathing was loud in the room. Then Dalbey asked, "Did you see the flash?"

"No. But the sound was quite a ways off."

Steach crawled around the room until he found the metal vase he had used on the dummy. He crawled back to Dalbey and struck a match. They examined the bullet hole together. There was no exit hole. Steach found the pillow on the floor by the chair and felt around until he discovered the spent slug.

"Can you see this?"

Dalbey adjusted his reading glasses and Steach held another match. "Seven point sixty-two millimeter. U.S.A."

Steach fondled the slug in his fingers. "Boattail configuration. That's Army handload for the M twenty-one."

"Where would he get Army handload?"

"Hard to tell." Steach bounced the bullet in his hand. "That gun has a flash suppressor. You got binoculars?"

"Yes."

"A rifle?"

"Thirty aught six," Dalbey said.

"Let me have it. We'll draw another shot to get his range."

Dalbey used a key to open the gun closet. He brought out a scope-mounted, bolt-action .30-06 Savage, along with a filled cartridge clip, and handed them to Steach, who inspected them briefly in the light of a match, then slipped the clip into the breech and slammed it home.

"Okay," Steach said. "You remember how to count for range?"

"Three hundred yards a second. I've got a stopwatch."

"Great. Now use the binoculars. Even with the suppressor there'll be a small flash. Watch from the bedroom where there's no distraction. What's the effective range on this?" he asked, patting the rifle.

"About three hundred yards. Shoot high."

Steach moved to the broken windowpane and kneeled. He slipped the bolt to load the chamber. He pressed the button off-safety and rested the stock on the sill, the barrel extending through the broken window. Dalbey found the stopwatch and binoculars and entered the bedroom. He adjusted the binoculars to infinity and pressed them against the window, peering out above the trees to let his eyes adjust to the dark. He held the stopwatch with a thumb on the starting button and said, "I'm ready."

A moment later the silence was shattered by the reverberating explosion of the rifle in the other room. Dalbey tensed. He had to wait about six seconds, focused intently on the dark. Then the void was suddenly pierced by a distant flash of light. His thumb hit the button. He listened for the sound of the report that lagged behind the speed of light, and he hit the button again, at the same moment another windowpane shattered in the living room and Arthur screamed in surprise and fright.

"What the hell are you doing?" Arthur shouted.

"Take it easy, boy," Steach said.

"Easy, my ass! You're gonna get us killed!"

Dalbey felt his way into the room. He could make out the dark forms of Steach huddled beneath the window and Arthur against the wall by the closet. He trained a pocketlight on the stopwatch. "One point seven," he said, and snapped off the light.

Steach figured quickly in his head. "Just over five hundred yards."

"Then he's on that rise," Dalbey said. "That's on state land, maybe seventy-five yards beyond my fence."

"What kind of fence?"

"Three-strand barbed wire."

"Goddamnit!" Arthur cried. "Are you going to just stand there and talk? Why don't you get us out of here!"

"We're working on it," Dalbey said.

"Why doesn't he just go out there and give himself up? He's the one they want. Why doesn't he go out there?"

"Arthur—"

"I don't even know what this is all about! Why did you get me into this?"

Dalbey's voice was low and controlled, but laced with displeasure. "You're embarrassing me."

My God, he thought, I sound like the Judge. He knew the boy was frightened, as he should be, and he could remember that night on the beach when the Germans opened fire on Calico. He wondered if there had been a time when Steach had been that frightened, and he supposed so. He moved over to the fireplace and sat on the hearth. The room smelled of gunpowder.

They were silent then, except Arthur, who caught his breath in fluttering gasps the way a child will breathe after a crying tantrum. He was obviously seething with anger and frustration and impotent humiliation. "Damn you!" he snarled. But that was all, and then they sat in the dark and listened . . . and waited . . . for what? A sign, perhaps—something that would tell them what to do.

Dalbey rose suddenly and crossed to the kitchen doorway. He moved gingerly, a step at a time. He felt the eyes searching him out, following the sound of his movement. When he reached the wall-mounted telephone, he said, "I think I'll call the cops."

He held the receiver to his ear. "Dead." He hung it up. He returned to the hearth and sat. There wasn't going to be any cavalry arriving in the nick of time.

Dalbey was thinking that this would be a good time to be thinking about something profound, such as the meaning of life or the conflict of reason versus action, but his mind did its usual tap dance and projected a running kaleidoscope of junk. Sitting in the dark, waiting to be killed, he thought about an article in the *Times* tracing the history of the sweet potato and the yam. Jesus! He hated his brain at times such as that, but even when he forced himself to confront the seriousness of the moment, he merely imagined the man on the hill and wondered what he was thinking.

"What's this guy Batcher like?" Dalbey asked.

"Well, we don't know for sure that it *is* Batcher,"
Steach said.

"Let's say it is. What's he like?"

"He's a soldier. A worker, a working soldier. I knew
him in the war. Our war. He was solid. You were glad to
have him around. Some of us, when the war ended, we
just stayed in the trade. I joined the Agency. I guess
Batcher went freelancing. Scary thing about a guy like that
is that we don't mean anything. We're the other side.
We're just a night problem to him, an infiltration."

Dalbey was reminded of a disturbing conversation
with a master sergeant at Fort Benning, a marksmanship
instructor who had been a sniper in Vietnam and was
explaining the procedure for shooting up an unsuspecting
enemy patrol more than a half-mile away. "It's best to just
wound the officer," he said. "While he's thrashing around
on the ground, the others will crowd around to see what's
wrong with him, and you'll have a chance to take out two
or three more before they get spooked. Then you can
finish the officer." A dispassionate professional explaining
his job, and Dalbey found himself admiring the man in the
way that we admire any inspired mechanic.

"What do you think he's doing out there?" Dalbey
asked.

"Watching *us*," Steach said.

Dalbey thought about that. "Any ideas?"

"Nothing brilliant. But we can't stay bunched up in
here."

"Why not?" Arthur asked querulously.

As if in answer, there was the sharp report of another
shot, the splintering of wood, a tearing sound, and the
ring of metal as a slug entered the room and ricocheted.

"Holy shit!" Dalbey exclaimed, flinging himself to the
floor.

"We've got to split up," Steach said. "If he thinks
we're flanking him, he'll have to make a move."

Dalbey sat up. "But he can see and we can't."

"True, but he can't be looking everywhere. I'll make a run for the barn. Once I get into the woods I'll work my way over to the fence. Then I can follow the fence and come around on him."

"I'll go the other way," Dalbey said.

"What about me?" Arthur said anxiously.

"You'll stay here," Dalbey instructed. "You just fire in that general direction now and again and stay down."

"You have more rifles?" Steach asked.

"Shotguns."

"No range."

"Plenty of noise."

"True," Steach said. "If we can get him moving, range won't matter."

Dalbey brought out the 12-gauge autoloader and a box of shells. He handed Steach two filled cartridge clips and a box of cartridges. Steach had taken the safari jacket from the dummy, and he stuffed the extra ammo into the big pockets.

Dalbey turned to Arthur with the 20-gauge pump gun. "Come into the kitchen." He rose and crossed the room and Arthur followed.

They could safely use the pocketlight in the kitchen, and Dalbey explained the gun and led Arthur through a dry run.

"I'll need a diversion," Steach said. "You take the other corner of the house. You fire a few shots to hold his attention, and I run for it." It was only about twenty yards.

"Okay," Dalbey said.

Steach opened the back door and stepped out, with Dalbey following. Arthur gripped Dalbey's arm. Dalbey said, "I'm not leaving yet. I'll be right back."

When they were both outside, Dalbey cradled the autoloader. "Well, good luck."

"Yeah," Steach said, "right. Now let's count to ten slowly to get into position and fire when you're ready."

"Okay."

"One thing, Flip. I don't suppose you've done much of this, but if you get a chance on that guy, kill him. If you do any of that 'hands up' or 'don't move' shit on this guy, you're gonna be dead. Kill him. And don't shoot low. Remember what they told you at the Farm. From the shoulders to the belt buckle. Nail him. Now let's get counting."

Steach slipped away into the darkness, moving out to position himself at a corner of the house.

Dalbey counted under his breath and stepped carefully along the opposite side of the house. He finished counting by the time he reached the second corner. He brought the shotgun to his shoulder, pointed over the trees, and fired. A tongue of flame spewed from the barrel and the stock jolted his shoulder. He leapt back to the protection of the house.

He counted seconds, holding his breath, his back pressed against the house. One—two—three. He could hear Steach running. There was an answering shot. Steach cried out in pain and Dalbey heard him fall.

Dalbey gasped, catching his breath. His pulse raced. He whirled and stumbled around the rear of the house until he could make out the dark form on the ground that was Steach.

"Steach!" he hissed.

"Oh, shit!" Steach wailed.

"How bad?"

"Don't know. Goddamn, it hurts." Steach sucked air through his teeth. "Oh, Jesus, I can't move. Damn, I think he broke the hip."

"I'll get you—"

"No! Stay back. Jesus Christ, that's just what he wants."

"Don't move now," Dalbey said. "Just don't move."

"Son of a bitch."

Dalbey ran, stumbling and cursing under his breath, to the kitchen door. He lurched inside saying, "Arthur, I need help." He put the gun aside and felt along the wall until his hand touched one of the climbing ropes, and he slipped it from the peg. "C'mon!"

Arthur followed. They edged along the side of the house, then Dalbey kneeled and uncoiled the rope. He made a large loop in one end tied with a figure eight.

"Steach!" he called in a loud whisper and winced. Sounds seem to amplify at night and it was like a shout. There was no answer. "Steach, I'm going to throw a line." He waited for a reply. "Steach!"

"I hear you."

"Put the loop over your shoulders. We'll pull you out of there."

"Okay."

He coiled the rope in his right hand and held the bitter end in his left. He concentrated on the lumpish form on the ground, drew his right arm back as far as possible, and threw the rope with a grunt. It unraveled in the air and landed on the target.

"Steach. Get the loop. Feel for the knot. Get it over your shoulders."

The dark bundle was moving and they could see him struggling with the rope. Dalbey clenched his fists and coached him under his breath. The seconds dragged, but it looked as though he was getting it, and then he said in a weak, pained voice, "Okay."

"Arthur," Dalbey said, "take the rope. Pull slow and easy. When I say 'now.' Let's get it taut."

They pulled in on the rope until there was resistance, then they reached out as far as possible to take a grip. Dalbey said, "Now," and they hauled in. Steach moved about four feet. They took a new purchase and dragged him another four feet closer.

A loud report echoed with the rolling reverberations of small thunder and Steach cried out.

"Pull!" Dalbey shouted, unmindful now of the noise. "Pull!" And they hauled on the rope, hand over hand, gasping for breath, desperate in their haste, and Steach dragged across the ground.

The shooter fired again and again before they could haul Steach to safety behind the cabin.

Dalbey was on his knees and he rolled Steach onto his back. He leaned over him, bringing his eyes close to the face, and gripped one of his hands. "Steach!" He caught his breath and pressed his ear against the chest to listen for a heartbeat. He lifted his head and sat back on his heels and looked down at the inert, pained expression, the open, staring eyes. He reached out and closed the eyes.

"He's dead," Dalbey said.

He felt drained and sad and angry. The tears welled in his eyes and he felt a tightness in the chest, but he was still too shocked and disappointed by the suddenness of death to react. "Let's get him inside." He untied the loop in the climbing rope and pushed it aside. "Take his feet," he said to Arthur.

It was a struggle to carry him through the kitchen door.

"Where?" Arthur said.

"We'll put him on the bed."

"He's bleeding."

"That's okay."

Dalbey bumped into one of the easy chairs and cursed, but they managed to get the body into the spare bedroom and onto the bed. Dalbey took a clean sheet from the closet and covered him. Arthur had never seen a man die. He stared at the corpse he had helped carry, sobered and shocked. He realized now that there was someone out there who would kill him too—and his father. "Now what?" he asked.

"We gotta get out of here."

"Why don't we just stay here and make him come to us? We've got guns."

"I don't think we'd be a match for him. He's a professional. You just saw what he can do."

"But we'll have the advantage."

"I don't think so. When he comes in close, it won't be with a rifle. He'll have something shoots fifteen, twenty rounds a second. You'll think you're in the wrong end of a goddamned shooting gallery."

Arthur was silent then, and Dalbey led the way into the living room. "So what do we do?" Arthur persisted. "There's no way out." He was no longer blaming Dalbey for his predicament and that was an improvement.

"There's one." Arthur waited and then Dalbey said, "Up the cliff."

Listening in the dark, Dalbey heard the quick intake of breath. Arthur was afraid of climbing. Dalbey had tried to interest him when he was fourteen, but the boy would have none of it.

"In the dark? That's crazy."

"It's the last thing he'd expect," Dalbey said. "The last place he'd look."

"But it's crazy. I'd rather take my chances with the guy."

"It's not as bad as you think. If you know the rock, you can climb at night. Even as dark as this, when you know what's supposed to be there, you can see it."

"I don't know." There was apprehension in Arthur's voice, but that was better than the antagonism Dalbey had learned to expect.

"Right up behind the house is the easiest climb in The Trapps. Called Goldner's Grunge. It's easy and it's protected by bushes and trees. I could climb it blindfolded."

"That's you."

"You'll be roped in." Dalbey felt sure that Arthur wanted to be convinced.

"I don't think I could, not in the dark."

"Arthur—" Dalbey leaned forward and gripped both

of his son's forearms—"if we don't do this, we'll end up like Steach. We've got to try."

"I'm sorry, but—" He was still afraid, but he was wavering.

"I won't let anything happen to you. Trust me."

"I trust *you*," Arthur said. "I don't trust *me*."

Dalbey was at a momentary loss for words. That was the most his son had confided in him, ever. "You'll be okay. Let me show you the gear. It's all new stuff. It's so safe you wouldn't be able to fall if you wanted to." He went to the closet and groped inside. He brought out a webbed sling hung with at least two dozen carabiners, and from the "biners" dangled a selection of Chouinard wire stoppers, curved rocks and camming nuts, various sizes of hexcentrics, and several spring-loaded camming devices. He stuffed a day pack with gear, added small flashlights, and used the pocketlight to find boots.

"You still a size nine?"

"Yes."

"Here, take these." Dalbey pushed a pair of the new Fire boots into Arthur's hands. "You can walk up a wall with these things." He closed the closet door and felt along the wall to find another, longer, nylon climbing rope. "C'mon." He carried everything into the kitchen and dropped it in a far corner. "We'll need dark clothes." He went to the bedroom, where he rummaged in a bureau and came back with navy turtlenecks, black sweaters, and dark blue sweat pants.

They changed clothing and sat in the corner so he could use the pocketlight to explain the equipment. "You know what a biner looks like," he said, holding the carabiner in the light. He snapped the oval-shaped aluminum ring against the rope to show how the gate on the side gave way to admit the rope, then sprang back to lock. He pushed the gate open with his thumb and slipped the biner off the rope. He took up one of the wedge-shaped stoppers. "This jams into a crack, like this. Holds a couple tons. Snap a biner on, and the rope goes through."

He helped Arthur into chest and seat harnesses and buckled them together with carabiners. "You hook into the rope or you can hook into a stopper on the wall. You can't fall."

Dalbey went over things carefully in his mind. He knew he was rushing it, and he didn't want to miss anything. He changed his shoes. "One more thing," he said. He ducked back into the living room and got his 20-gauge pump gun and a box of shells. He took the nylon cord from the dummy and cobbled a makeshift sling for the gun. He loaded it and pumped a load into the chamber and engaged the safety. He dumped the box of shells into the small day pack.

"Now look. When we're out there we have to be very quiet. Sounds carry in this valley, especially at night. If you have to say something when we're climbing, you tug on the rope and I'll come back so we can whisper. Got it?"

"I think so."

"Here's how we climb. I'll go up about ten feet and make a belay. Then you climb up to me. If you slip, you won't fall. I'll have you. Just start climbing again. We're going to leave the hardware on the wall, so you'll just hook this biner, here, into the wire stopper or whatever we're using and wait. I climb again. Then you unhook and come up and hook in again."

"But I don't know how to climb."

"Arthur, if you can climb a ladder, you can climb this." Dalbey felt like shouting and shaking the indecision out of him, but he knew that would ruin everything. "I'm going to walk you up that cliff."

"How high is it?"

"Couple hundred feet." It was more like 320 feet, but that sounded too difficult.

"A couple hundred?"

"Arthur, you'll only climb ten feet at a time. It's a piece of cake, believe me."

Dalbey secured the rope beneath the flap of the day pack and slipped the pack over his arms. He slung the shotgun diagonally across his back. "I can't think of anything else," he said. "When we go out that door we crawl. You keep in touch with my feet. And no talking. If you want to stop, grab my ankle. Let's go."

Chapter Twenty-three

They stepped into the night and Dalbey leaned against the back of the cabin to orient himself, picking out the darker shapes of familiar trees and rocks. The brooding black wall of the cliff was sensed rather than seen, but it was there, a stone barrier shrouded in dark. Dalbey had never climbed at night, but he was sure that he could do the Grunge with a blindfold.

He picked out the worn footpath. That would be in the shooter's sights. He touched Arthur's arm and dropped to all fours. It was just twenty feet to the first stand of thick bushes. Dalbey crabbed apelike across the sloping ground, walking on hands and toes, moving quickly and low to the ground. It was painful on the hands and he wished that he had brought gloves. When they reached cover, Dalbey dropped to the ground and waited for Arthur to come up next to him. Then he whispered, "We can crouch from here to the scree. Stay down around the bushes. We have to save our hands."

Dalbey took the lead again and moved slowly and carefully. When they reached the barbwire fence, he was feeling pain in his lower back and he kneeled to straighten his upper body. He arched back, worked his shoulders, and rubbed his lower back with both hands. He stopped to listen carefully. He rose in a crouch and moved along the fence until he found the place where hikers had lowered the top wire, and he congratulated himself on forgetting to mention it to the caretaker. He climbed over and held the wire down for Arthur to follow.

It was another twenty yards to the scree, but Dalbey wanted to emerge from the trees directly below the Grunge, if he could. He felt that the trail at the base of the cliff would be exposed. He moved along the fence line for about thirty yards, then turned and made for the cliff.

The scree was an embankment of loose rock, and they climbed it on hands and knees and it hurt like hell. But Dalbey was pleased that Arthur was hanging in and not complaining. They reached the stone retaining wall and crouched there until Dalbey was sure he was looking at the lower pitch of Goldner's Grunge. Then they crawled over the top of the three-foot wall and crossed the trail to the base of the cliff, where they could huddle behind a stand of trees and bushes and get ready.

Dalbey unpacked carefully, silently. It was perfect. For the first thirty yards they would be protected by trees. He uncoiled the rope and secured one end into the tie-in loops on Arthur's seat harness with a friction knot. "Don't touch that knot," he whispered. "That stays there." He ran the line through the carabiner on the chest harness loops, then snapped a second carabiner to the first. "This is what you'll use to hook in and out of the hardware on the rock. You'll see how it works the first ten feet."

He took two turns around his own waist with the other end and tied off. He slipped the pack over his arms. He put the makeshift shotgun sling over his head, swinging the gun around under the small pack, then he added the nylon sling carrying his rack of hardware. He whispered close to Arthur's ear, "Try to watch what I do. When I tug on the line, it means I'm on belay and you can climb." He patted Arthur's shoulder and attempted a smile. Then he stopped for a moment to listen again, but he heard nothing unusual.

They were in a sort of gully. He stood close to the wall and placed his hands on the stone. It was cold and rough to the touch. He rubbed his hands over the rock, getting the feel of it. He looked up. It is always amazing how much you can see on a dark night. It's tricky, of course, and things look different, but with care and study you can see a great deal. He knew the route was like steps angling to the right. He ran his hand up the rock, feeling for a purchase, and he was oddly thrilled by the tactile sensation of searching the rock with his hands. His senses seemed to be magnified and he felt the changing textures of the rock, the minute cracks and knobs and pinch holds.

He took a hold and made his first step up, leaning out slightly to achieve a tripod effect against the rock. He reached up for another balancing hold, brought his foot up searching for a toe hold, then felt up along the rock for the next hold, pausing to make constant surveys. It was easier than he had expected. When he reached about ten feet, he searched for a crack in the rock above his head, felt it carefully with his hand to determine the holding power, then selected a stopper to wedge into the space and pulled it tight. He snapped a carabiner on the hanging wire loop and slipped the rope through the gate.

He ran the rope through the carabiner until it was taut and took a solid stance for a shoulder belay. He gave the rope a few tugs to signal Arthur and kept it taut as he climbed. He moved aside when Arthur reached him and showed him how to snap into the stopper loop.

"Very good," he whispered. "It's all just like that."

He turned to face the wall and start climbing, and the rack of hardware banged the rock. The jingling of aluminum alloy made him catch his breath, and he grabbed the sling of carabiners to muffle them. He let his breath out slowly and silently and listened, staring out into the dark.

He waited for a full minute before he began to climb again.

The next pitch was about fifteen feet, and he found a space between two rocks that took a large hexcentric. He strung the rope, established his belay, and tugged the rope to start Arthur. There were good, obvious holds, and Arthur reached him in about five minutes. This time Arthur snapped himself into the wire loop and gave a tug to test it. He nodded, and Dalbey went off belay and climbed the next short stretch.

On the fourth leg he stretched it out to twenty feet, and Arthur followed without a hitch. It was speeding up as Arthur gained confidence, but it was still painfully slow, and Dalbey knew they were working against time. The gunman would eventually tire of sitting on the hill and would come down to finish them in the cabin. When he found them gone and saw the climbing gear hanging from the wall pegs, he would soon be scanning the cliffs.

It took them forty-five minutes to climb ninety feet. They were on open rock, well above the trees. At one hundred and fifty feet they would reach a foot-wide ledge on which they would cross to the left about fifty feet to a deep chimney, and from there it was just ninety feet of easy climbing to the top. And with each short pitch, as their procedure became more routine, they picked up precious minutes.

Three more pitches and Dalbey reached the ledge. He debated the need for an aid, then inserted a stopper about chest high to be on the safe side. He was able to lean back and use a hip belay, which he preferred, and he waited for Arthur to climb, moving the rope in time with his progress.

The ledge was deceptive. It was littered with pieces of rock and soil and overgrown with seedling trees and brush, what climbers call dirty.

Arthur was roped in to a stopper and Dalbey was preparing to cross.

"You face the wall," Dalbey whispered. "Release the rope from here." He touched the carabiner. "I'll have you on belay halfway across. Place each foot very carefully. Get a solid footing before you shift your weight, and don't knock anything off the ledge. If you have to move a stone, nudge it closer to the wall." He paused, then added, "Don't let the brush trip you up, and don't hold on to the trees. Okay, here I go."

He stepped sideways with his left foot, balancing with his fingers on the wall. He placed his foot gently, slowly added weight until he was sure of his footing, then unweighted the right foot and brought it across. He repeated the maneuver, being careful not to dislodge any stones off the ledge. At one point the shotgun became entangled with a tree, and he had to come back a step to free it. The footing was better than he had expected, and he guessed that a full summer of climbers had cleaned it. When he passed twenty feet he felt for a spot to place an aid. He found a crack and wedged in a stopper. He attached a carabiner and then the rope. He drew it taut, letting it drape below the ledge, established a belay, and signaled Arthur to begin.

The five minutes seemed an eternity, but Arthur crossed without incident. "You're doing great," Dalbey told him. Then he moved out to finish the traverse. The brush was a nuisance and a few places were lumpy with mounds of dirt, but he made it across to the chimney and placed another aid to take a carabiner and the rope. He found a spot for a sound belay and signaled to Arthur.

He trailed the rope over his shoulder as Arthur moved. He could sense that Arthur was having difficulty with the brush. In a few minutes he could see him moving. He kept the belay taut. Arthur had crossed the mounds of dirt. He was maybe five or six feet away and seemed to be moving confidently when he fell.

Dalbey felt the movement in the rope and he tensed. He heard the scattering of dirt and stones. He saw the erratic movement and flailing of arms as Arthur slipped over the edge, then the anguished cry that echoed over the valley. Dalbey clamped on the belay, stopping the fall in two feet. Arthur hung out over the black abyss, dangling, and he called out in terror a drawn-out, desperate "Papa!"

Dalbey heard the metallic *click-clang* of an automatic weapon being cocked. It came from the darkness of the trees below and to the left. Oh, Christ! The gunman had been following the fence line to get behind the house.

Arthur turned slowly on the end of the rope. Dalbey held him, but a silent scream raged through him as he waited for the shot. He could see that Arthur's chest and arms were still above the ledge and he hissed through clenched teeth, "Climb, Arthur!"

A burst of firing racketed through the trees and bullets sang off the rocks where they had been ten minutes before.

"Jesus Christ, Arthur, get your ass up here!"

There was another searching burst of fire. The gunman wasn't using the night-vision scope. He was shooting by sound.

Terrified by the firing, Arthur got his hands on the ledge and levered his body up in one gasping lunge until his knees were up and he was using the rope to pull himself erect. Dalbey dragged him into the protective cover of the chimney as a short stitch of shots kicked up debris from the ledge.

Dalbey used a carabiner to hook Arthur's harness into the belay. They were safe for the moment, but they couldn't climb. Dalbey was considering what to do next when the gunman switched on a powerful flashlight and trained the beam on the wall. He assumed that they were unarmed.

In a swift synchronous movement, Dalbey swung the shotgun off his back, released the safety, braced himself

against the wall, and fired directly at the light. He knew
he was out of range, but the gunman doused his light.

Dalbey turned back and pressed Arthur hard against
the rock as the gunman answered with a burst of fire that
showered them with rock chips and left the whine of
ricocheting bullets echoing in their ears.

Dalbey felt pain in his chest and realized that he had
not been breathing. He swallowed deeply and eased away
from the wall. He slung the shotgun over his back and
reached out to remove the end of the rope from Arthur's
harness. He found a place to anchor a large hexcentric,
attaching a carabiner and the end of the rope with a
bowline. He released the rope from his waist and lowered
it down the face of the cliff.

He adjusted the pack and the shotgun. He gripped
the standing end of the rope and stood astride it, adjusting
the free rope around his body in a rappel sling. He leaned
close to his son. "When the shooting starts, you walk down
this rope. Then you run. That way." He jerked a thumb to
the right. "You get to the road and you keep going. Just
get away from here."

"I can't."

"Arthur, for Jesus sake"—he spit the words out in a
tense, tight-lipped whisper—"do what I say!"

"But Papa, I—"

Dalbey gripped the back of his son's neck to silence
him and pressed his forehead against the side of his head.
He said, "Arthur, I don't have a chance against this guy."
He squeezed Arthur's neck. There was more he wanted to
say, but it was too damned hard.

He leaned out, the standing rope in his left hand, the
free rope in his right for braking. He took a deep breath
and jumped backward off the wall, shouting to distract the
gunman from Arthur.

"Yaaaaaaaaaaa!"

The rope ran through his hands and slid over his
body. He had merely to close his hands to brake his

descent, and he swung into the wall with his feet extended. The gunman fired above him. He landed against the wall, bending his knees to absorb the shock, and pushed out for another drop. He bounded down the wall in four giant leaps, braking softly at the bottom. The gunman fired blindly and wildly, spraying the lower wall with a hail of bullets.

Dalbey touched the ground and ran. He unlimbered the shotgun and pumped it. He dived to the ground and rolled—once, twice—and he fired as he went over the retaining wall. He lay on the mound of loose rock, the shotgun blast ringing in his ears. He tossed a large stone into the woods below, then another and another and another. It sounded remarkably like a man crashing through the brush.

The gunman followed the sound and bullets tore at the trees. Then it stopped and it was deathly quiet except for the ringing.

Dalbey knew where the gunman had been and he listened for sounds of movement. He had tried to be quiet coming through the trees earlier, but without success. Too much underbrush and leaves, too many dry twigs. He knew he wouldn't have a chance in the woods. He listened and marveled. If the man was moving, he was awfully good.

Staring into the dark until his eyes itched, barely breathing, Dalbey's mind began playing tricks, amplifying the skitter of birds and small rodents, and transforming wavering tree limbs into grotesque, malevolent shapes. He heard the unmistakable snap of dry wood—out there—in the cover of the trees—ahead and to the right. He *was* moving.

Dalbey crawled onto the retaining wall. He cradled the shotgun infantry-style and inched along on elbows and knees. It was too painful. He stopped and listened. He heard something directly off to his right. He held his breath and looked—hard. Was there something there? He didn't dare move. It was the sound of a foot being placed carefully on leaves, an almost imperceptible *scrunch*, and then the *crick* of tiny twigs being crushed.

He swung the shotgun and fired, the flash and roar rending the dark silence. He leapt and ran for the cover of a rock. He hit the ground and rolled as the startled gunman answered with a volley of shots. Dalbey huddled behind the rock, breathing heavily. That was smart, he said to himself, now what?

His hand touched a loose stone. He gripped it and lobbed it into the trees. The gunman wasn't interested.

Dalbey dug into the pack for shells and reloaded the shotgun. He turned and peered over the rock, wondering what the gunman was doing. The man liked the protection of the trees. Well, why not? He moved like a damned ghost. If he knew Dalbey's position, which was likely, and if he was moving on him, he'd be about—where? Christ, he could be anywhere. Dalbey knew that there was no way that he was a match for that man. His only hope was the unexpected. He decided . . . he could be . . . there! And he fired.

He rolled to his feet, pumping another shell into the firing chamber, and ran, firing another round to the left of the last, and then another. He leapt the retaining wall, firing into the trees, and scrambled over the scree. He made it to the trees, crashed through some bushes, running scared and unchecked, and collided with the gunman, who was trying to avoid the lethal spread of the shotgun blasts that were tearing through the woods.

They came together on an angle and hit, grunting with the surprise and the force of the encounter. They caromed off one another, the momentum carrying them, and they fell, scrambling wildly to regain their feet.

Dalbey was up first by seconds, the shotgun leveled. He shouted, "Hold it!" just as Steach had warned him not to, and the man shot him.

He saw the dark shape of the weapon rise in the

assassin's hand, and still he hesitated. It seemed to explode in his face. Dalbey felt a sharp punch in his left shoulder, then he was reeling and he thought, Damn, I'm going to be killed, and he was falling. He saw the glint of a belt buckle and he remembered. He imagined a clay target rising. He led it about twelve inches and fired.

The searing pain meant that he was alive. Dalbey touched the shoulder and winced. The sweater was soaked with blood. He wiggled his fingers, and even though it hurt like hell, he could lift his arm. He cradled the arm and crawled over to where the gunman lay on his back.

Was this Rudy Batcher? The face was lined and drawn. He looked about sixty. Nothing special. An old man with white hair.

Dalbey picked up the Ingram. He turned it over in his hand, hefting it. Would the gun match the bullets from Dan Cassidy and the three women? He was willing to bet on it.

Chapter Twenty-four

They had a memorial for Steach in a little town in eastern Pennsylvania on the outskirts of Philadelphia, a crossroad place that was still listed in tiny print on the road maps, but no longer officially existed.

Oh, the houses were still there and Dunwood's grocery store and the flagpole and the volunteer fire company's red-brick fire house, but Dunwood's no longer handled the U.S. mail and the two hundred residents paid taxes to a nearby town.

It was just Dalbey and Claire Paige, and they carried Steach's ashes in a small tin box. Claire's idea. They had left New York early for the three-hour drive, parked the car, and now they were walking in the road. There were no sidewalks. There was no traffic, either, and except for a TV making distant soap opera sounds, it was quiet.

"He told stories about this place," Claire said. "I think he loved growing up here. But it's hard to believe, isn't it?"

It must have been a quiet country village at one time, but now it was blue-collar poor. There were maybe twelve blocks of small houses with slanting porches and small yards, the occasional neat white bungalow, some stucco left over from the thirties, a lot of asbestos shingle, and the inevitable mobile home with decorative aluminum awnings. There were the transmutations: imitation brick, imitation stone, and imitation wood siding—the flotsam of silver-tongued traveling salesmen. In one yard where a cutout wooden duck on a metal rod spun its wings in endless flight, there was a brightly painted old rowboat filled with dirt and geraniums. No, it wasn't exactly Jonathan Steach, but even a spy has to come from somewhere.

An old woman approached, towing a wire shopping cart on wheels, and they asked directions.

"What? What's that?"

"Could you please direct us to the creek," Claire said.

"The creek?" The woman regarded Claire with curiosity, taking in the expensive tweed skirt and English walking shoes, the suede jacket and silk scarf, the accent. "Why do you want to go to the creek? Nobody goes to the creek anymore. It's polluted. They put in a dump. The city did. Way up there, ruined the creek. Used to be beautiful. Kids went swimming there. Not now."

"Have you lived here long?" Claire asked.

"Since 1928."

"Did you know the Steach family?"

"Of course I did. Lived over on Avenue A. Nice people. Two nice girls and a terrible boy. A bad mouth, that boy, and wild."

Claire smiled broadly. "That was my father."

"Oh, dear!" The woman pressed a hand to her mouth and laughed. "I'm sorry." She shook her head, chortling. "Well, we can't pick our parents. Maybe he improved."

"We wanted to find a place called the Rocks. It's where he used to swim."

"Oh, the Rocks," the woman said. "All the kids swam at the Rocks." She turned and pointed south. "You go down that hill. There at the next corner. At the bottom there's a railroad bridge. You cross that, go down the steps, and take the dirt road. That will take you to the creek. Turn left and you'll come to the Rocks."

"Thank you," Claire said.

"You're welcome. You tell your father Mrs. McNamara says hello. He'll remember." She chuckled and laid a hand on Claire's arm. "He was a devil."

Dalbey and Claire walked to the corner, went down the hill, and crossed the railroad. It was about a half-mile to the creek, a sluggish, muddy, trash-fish creek about fifty yards across. Trees and dense brush grew along the scummy banks. They followed a footpath, pushing aside tree limbs and vines, dodging mud puddles.

Another half-mile and the path opened onto a clearing and there, before them, was a formation of huge boulders that rose out of the water to a height of about seventy-five feet. It was a beautiful spot, despite the obvious pollution of the water, and it was easy to imagine the rocks covered with young bathers a half century ago.

Dalbey's left arm was in a sling, and he carried the tin box in his right hand, but it was easy to walk up and over the boulders. Claire went ahead, looking for something, and Dalbey followed. He stopped halfway and watched her scramble over the rocks, seeing another side of her that he liked. She seemed to be checking the path to the water, then she'd go higher.

"Are you okay?" she called down. "Want me to carry that?"

"I'm fine."

She smiled and he was taken again by what a beauty she was. She continued to climb, looking back at the water, and when she was near the top, she cried, "Here it is! I found it! I can't believe it's here. I thought it was just a story."

Dalbey took the easiest route around and over the boulders, and when he reached her, she was pointing to an inscription on the rock. It was in white gloss paint, hand-lettered with a small brush. The letters were not skillfully drawn, but they were clear: *J.S.* Under that, in smaller letters: *Dived from here. July 14, 1933.*

Claire raised on her toes and looked out toward the water. "He was the first to do it. In his time no one duplicated this. He was very proud of it." She touched the inscription. "He told me I'd find this here."

Actually it was quite a feat; not just for the height, which was about sixty feet, but because he would have had to launch himself out at least eight feet to clear the rocks on the way down. It was daring, even for a thirteen-year-old.

"You must think I'm balmy," she said.

"As a matter of fact I think you're quite nice."

Claire reached for the tin box and he handed it to her. She climbed down from Steach's rock and moved onto a huge boulder directly over the water, where she sat and smoothed her skirt around her legs. Dalbey followed and sat at her side. She stared soberly at the water. At length she said, "I suppose he wasn't much of a parent, but I loved him."

Dalbey sat quietly, listening. It was about all the eulogy Steach was likely to get. "He was just short visits and presents, the occasional holiday that was always interrupted by something pressing. I never even knew what his job was until that car bombing ten years ago. I thought he was a salesman." She was silent for long minutes, locked into the past, then she said, "Poor Steach, he was a good man. I wish I knew who killed him."

Dalbey didn't answer. They had already talked about it and there was nothing he could add. What did it matter?

When he went to the police after his release from the hospital, he found himself stonewalled. They refused to answer questions or discuss the shooting.

"It's out of our jurisdiction, Mr. Dalbey," the officer said.

"Is somebody checking fingerprints? That gun, the Ingram—"

"It's not our case."

"Whose case is it? I was shot out there, for God's sake."

"As far as we know, Mr. Dalbey, there wasn't any shooting."

"That's ridiculous."

"I know, but this is a national security matter. That's all I'm allowed to say."

Dalbey had to go to his brother, Marcus, who used his connections as a Superior Court judge to learn that federal agents had moved in quickly to put a blackout on the case and stamp it sensitive and top secret.

Both bodies had been cremated from a local mortuary: John Doe, unidentified, and William Trainor, foreign national on forged passport. All evidence, including weapons, had been confiscated.

"Jesus Christ, Marcus, how can they do that?"

"They can't."

"But they did," Dalbey said.

"Yes, it seems that they did."

"Who? Who moved in?"

"The cremation order was authorized by the National Security Agency."

"Incredible."

"Does seem a bit odd. To move that fast, I mean."

"Don't they have to notify the next of kin?"

"There wasn't any."

"Suppose there was?"

"Ah," Marcus said, "the sticky wicket. A close relative might have grounds to sue for damages, if they can prove those ashes are the long-lost relative."

"Five years in the courts."

"More like ten. The federal government doesn't like to admit mistakes. And ashes are ashes."

Dalbey checked with the Kent County sheriff's office in eastern Maryland and he learned that the National Security Agency had collected all evidence from the Cassidy murders and had taken over jurisdiction of the case.

"When was this?" Dalbey asked.

"Three days ago, sir."

But when Dalbey inquired further, he was told, "Sorry, sir, we have instructions not to discuss the case."

Claire had to be told, of course, and she wanted Steach's ashes. But Jonathan Steach had officially died in 1973.

"But that's not true," she protested. "You said yourself the FBI was looking for him for stealing funds."

"I think they were told to stop looking."

"But *we* know."

"Yes, we do, but that gets complicated. How long have you known he was alive?"

"A few years," she said. "He needed money."

"Did you collect on his insurance?"

She frowned. "Yes."

"And did you collect a death benefit from the U.S. government?"

She nodded, seeing the difficulties. If she knew Steach was alive, she was an accomplice to fraud—if he was alive.

"Why are they doing this? A week ago they wanted to arrest him."

"I think pressure is being brought to bear in high places," Dalbey said.

"General Winston."

"Smells like it."

It galled him that Steffinelli and Winston were walking away from this unscathed, untouched, triumphant in fact. So he sent Steffinelli a telegram: *LET'S TALK ABOUT THOSE RECORDS. WITH WINSTON.* He flew to Denver the next day.

Steffinelli was receiving this time, as Dalbey figured he would be. He had a large corner office, bright and modern with success written all over it. Vince was cordial. He came from behind his large desk when Dalbey entered, extending his hand. "Good to see you, Phil."

Dalbey looked down at the proffered hand, then raised his eyes to meet Steffinelli's. "Cut the shit, Vince. I didn't come here to play games. Where's Winston?"

As if on cue, the office door opened and General Hugh Winston entered. He looked softer in person, older, but he moved with the impressive arrogance of men used to dispensing power. He wore a gray suit, expensively tailored, and a blue silk tie. He eyed Dalbey suspiciously.

"General Winston," Steffinelli said, "Philip Dalbey."

Winston advanced and put out his hand and Dalbey shook it. "I've heard of you." The voice was strong and the sharp blue eyes measured Dalbey and took in the left arm supported by a sling.

"We were on a mission together in 'forty-three," Dalbey said.

"So I'm told."

"Not one of your finest hours."

"Oh? I thought I did rather well."

"So I'm told," Dalbey mimicked, and a slight trace of a smile cracked the corner of Winston's mouth.

"Can we get on with this?" The General lowered himself into a large leather armchair and crossed his legs. Steffinelli sat behind his desk and Dalbey was left standing.

"Steach is dead." Dalbey wasn't telling them anything they didn't know, but it had to be said, there in that room. He wanted them to know what happened to people when they pushed their goddamned buttons. "I killed Rudy

Batcher." When there was no reaction, Dalbey added, "I got him with a shotgun."

In a way he had to admire Winston's cool. The general sat there, relaxed, listening politely, and didn't blink an eye. Dalbey sat on the edge of a chair.

"Steach was trying to get those papers back to you. He tried something stupid, it didn't work. He just wanted out. Problem was, he didn't have the papers. All that time they were in my attic, and I didn't know about it. Incredible, eh? And now they're gone." He told them about the tag sale and added a small lie. "Somebody bought the briefcase with the papers inside. Paid five dollars. Good leather." He smiled. "No record of who it was. Paid cash." He paused, letting it sink in. "Probably some mechanic who won't even know what those papers mean. Maybe he'll look 'em over and throw them out. Or it might have been somebody who will hang on to them. An accountant, maybe, or a lawyer. Everybody goes to tag sales these days."

Dalbey glanced at Steffinelli, who looked horrified, but Winston seemed bemused.

"And when you run for president," Dalbey said, taking a long shot, "the records just might be out there, still floating around, waiting to be discovered. And if you get the nomination; who knows how important they could become. And you'll never know, will you? Your Qaddafi connection out there somewhere . . . like a time bomb."

Winston heard him out without a word. It was as though Dalbey was talking about someone else. When Dalbey paused, there was a long silence, then Winston said, "Yes, well . . ." He rose from his chair and said to Steffinelli, "Take care of this, Vincent." Then he took the several steps to Dalbey's chair and reached down to shake his hand. "Thanks for coming, Mr. Dalbey. Nice meeting you." And he left.

Dalbey stared after him until the door closed, then he turned back to Steffinelli.

"You could maybe run an ad for the briefcase," Dalbey said. "Offer a reward. Or maybe you could just kill all the people in Fairfield County who ever went to a tag sale." He was feeling furious and impotent. There was not a goddamned thing he could do, and he knew it and Winston knew it and Steffinelli knew it. "I'd like to have Steach's ashes."

Vince did not react.

"Did you know Steach had a daughter?"

Steffinelli's eyes widened.

"Surprised, huh, Vince? She's a high official with the British Mission to the United Nations. She wants her daddy's body for proper Christian burial, but it seems your guys have already burned it."

"Jesus," Steffinelli muttered.

"Might be a bit of a flap, Vince. Oh, I know you're covered, but the general's not going to like it."

He stood and leaned his good hand on Steffinelli's desk. "I want a release for those ashes. I want it delivered to my office. I want it waiting there when I get back."

Taking a deep breath, he rose to his full height. There was more he wanted to say, but it was personal and pointless. "See you around, Vince."

As Dalbey turned to leave, Steffinelli said, "Phil, about your son."

Dalbey stopped and turned back slowly. "What about him?"

"I want you to know that—that—" Steffinelli couldn't possibly admit to any knowledge of the gunman.

"Yes?" He enjoyed letting Vince squirm. Why not? The son of a bitch had sent Arthur back there to be killed. Was he remembering that he and Dalbey had worked together for twenty years? Maybe he was thinking of his own kids.

"I hope he's—"

"He's fine."

Actually he wasn't all that fine. When the shooting

stopped, Arthur was still on the cliff. It took Dalbey fifteen
minutes to coax him down the rope, and when he reached
the ground, he was sullen. He had been badly frightened
and shamed and shot at, and when Dalbey tried to reassure him with a smile, he said testily, "What's so goddamned funny?" Later, when Dalbey said that he should
resign from Tel-Tech, Arthur said, "I don't need your
advice. I have a contract. Those bastards owe me!"

Vince was saying, "I suppose he'll be leaving the
company."

Dalbey said wryly, "Don't count on it."

The release was waiting when he returned to New
York, and he drove to New Paltz to retrieve the ashes. So
he had had his say, and he got the ashes, and it didn't
make a damned bit of difference.

"It's a pretty day," Claire said.

He shifted on the rock. "Yes, it is." He felt vaguely
disconnected. It was over and it wasn't over. He had
talked to Art Van in Bridgeport, but nothing had turned
up, and it was Van's conclusion that the briefcase had been
burned. So much for that. He knew Steffinelli's people
would eventually find their way to the warehouse in
Bridgeport and they'd get the same story, and General
Winston would relax, maybe even become president of
the United States.

A chicken hawk circled over the rocks, dark against
the pale sky. It sailed down close to the trees on the far
bank, a swooping, effortless flight, then it worked its
wings, muscling upward to seek out the morning thermals.

"Sad, isn't it, the way lives turn out," Claire said.

"Some lives, I suppose," Dalbey said. "Steach didn't
do too badly. Certainly wasn't boring."

"No, I guess it wasn't."

There was a breeze blowing down and off the rocks.
Claire stood and opened the box and scattered the ashes.
The wind whipped them up like dust, and what was left of

Jonathan Steach was carried out over the rocks and the trees and the sluggish dank water of the creek.

"*Quid non mortalia cogis, auri sacra fames?*" Dalbey said.

Claire looked at him quizzically.

"From Virgil." He translated: "To what do you not drive the hearts of men, O cursed greed for gold?"

She stared at the water. "He was afraid of growing old."

"We all are."

"I suppose."

They hiked back to the car and drove south to the Pennsylvania Turnpike, which would take them to the New Jersey Turnpike and eventually to the George Washington Bridge and light years away from Steach's childhood.

"What will you do now?" Claire asked.

"I'm not sure. I've been thinking about maybe going fishing for a year."

"Fishing? For a year?"

"I think so. I want to think. I have to do something with the rest of my life. I want to do something different."

"Where will you fish?"

"All over. Winter's coming on, so I'd probably head for the Florida Keys and fish for bonefish on the flats. Next summer, out to Montana. There's a stretch of the Yellowstone, south of Livingston, that I've heard about."

"Is it hard to do? Fishing, I mean."

"Easy."

"Sounds marvelous."

He liked her voice, enjoyed her presence. Time passed easily with her, and he didn't feel that he had to talk or be entertaining. They were close to New York, on the stretch between New Brunswick and Newark, and he asked, "Would you like to go?"

"Go where?"

"Fishing."

"For a year?"

"Right."

"The two of us?"

"Yes."

"You're mad." She laughed. "I have a job, a career. I can't just pick up and go fishing for a year."

He let it drop. They sailed past the congestion of Newark and Jersey City, the refineries and chemical plants that plague the marshlands, and were approaching the Bridge when she said, "Could we try it for a weekend? I mean, isn't there a place close by where you could teach me to fish?"

New Paltz was out. He didn't want to go back to the cabin just yet. "The Beaverkill," he said. "It's a famous trout stream in the Catskills."

"Could we?"

"Absolutely."

"Oh, marvelous. What does one wear for fishing?"

"Waders. Huge rubber boots that come up to here." He thumped his chest.

"Oh, dear. How lovely. When shall we go?"

"Whenever you like. Why don't we talk about it over dinner tonight."

"Dinner. Yes." She sat back and peered out through the side window. She seemed to be smiling inwardly. "What time?"

"I'll pick you up at eight."

They crossed into Manhattan and took the Major Deegan south to the East River Drive and the United Nations Building, where he dropped her at her office nearby. Then he drove to his garage and left the car.

He walked to his building and Mossy buzzed him through the door and made a thing about his shoulder.

"It's nothing," he said. "A bad dislocation."

This brought Alice out of her office, and even Michael Durso appeared in the doorway of the computer room.

"It's nothing. Nothing at all." He escaped into the privacy of his office. There was a lot of mail. On the top of the pile was a message from Marianna. She had changed her mind, it said, she couldn't do it. She begged him to call her.

He was fanning the note, thinking, Christ Jesus, when Mossy interrupted to announce that a Mr. Van was calling collect from Bridgeport, Connecticut, and did he care to accept the charges?

"By all means," Dalbey said.

Then Art Van was on the line. "Mr. Dalbey?"

"Yes."

"This is Art Van. We found it."

Dalbey was on his feet, checking his watch. It was three o'clock. How long, if he left immediately?

"Hello? You there? Mr. Dalbey?"

"Art, don't let it get away. I'll be there in two hours."

ABOUT THE AUTHOR

STUART JAMES grew up in rural Pennsylvania and at fifteen went to work as a sports reporter and sometime Linotype operator for the *Delaware Valley Advance*. Later, while attending Temple University, he was a copyboy for the *Philadelphia Record*, after which he served a stint in an intelligence unit in the Army. Newspaper work took him all across the country before he abandoned journalism, invested in a used Royal typewriter, and wrote adventure stories "by the pound"—at the same time holding down such jobs as hunting guide, truck driver, bartender, rough carpenter, and ice cream salesman—as the rejections flooded in. At age twenty-eight, while working on a tuna boat out of Monterey, California, he sold his first story to a pulp magazine for $100. Several hundred stories later, when the short fiction markets started drying up, he became a staff writer, then executive for a series of magazines, including *Popular Mechanics* and *True*. Finally, he quit magazines to become a PR copywriter as well as ghostwriter and scriptwriter. "All the stuff any writer does," he says. James and his wife have two sons, "and we are all addicted to the outdoors. We spend a lot of time together sailing, kayaking, hiking, skiing, climbing, and scuba diving." He currently lives in Greenwich, Connecticut.

It was cold. An icy wind was blowing in off the North Sea. It roiled the dark water of the *Ijsselmeer* and blew across the marsh that separated the lake from the canal, rustling the stiff brown grasses and brittle berry bushes that leaned away and complained in dry whispers. It blew through the boatyard, lifting the canvas skirts of the stored yachts, and rattled the large sign that said: *VanVranken & Straalen, Jachtwerf*.

The boatyard was on the canal. It was quiet and dimly lighted, and the two men huddled in the dark shadows of a large, prefabricated metal building were barely visible. It was an unusually cold October, even for Holland, and the men were not dressed for it. They wore topcoats with the collars turned up and pushed their hands deep into the pockets.

"*Quelle heure est-il?* The shorter of the two men asked. His name was Verbeke. He was Belgian, but he spoke French. He also spoke German and Russian and American with a French accent.

The taller man lifted his arm and pulled back the sleeve to bring his watch close to his face. "Past midnight," he said. He was an American and his name was Garvey.

"Sonofabitch," Verbeke said. He stamped his feet and banged his elbows against his body.

"He's not coming," Garvey said. They had been waiting for two hours.

"Relax, Peter, he'll be here. He has nowhere else to go."

"I won't wait much longer," Garvey said, and

Verbeke smiled. It was just something to say. Garvey was a pro. If he was supposed to make a collection, he'd wait all night if he had to, and Verbeke knew it.

The wind shifted, coming from the corner of the building, and Garvey turned away from it, hunching his shoulders and shuddering. "Damn wind!" he muttered, blowing warm air into his cupped hands. "Goes right to the core."

"You're getting old, Peter."

"Tell me about it."

There were times when Garvey felt old, but he wished people would stop reminding him of it. Russ Campbell had brought it up when Garvey complained to the Geneva station chief about making a blind collection.

"It's a need-to-know, Peter," Campbell had said.

"That's what I'm talking about. I'd like to know what I'm collecting."

"Strictly routine. Verbeke's handling. You just sign for the goods and pass it along to Roger Kessler."

"I've never worked this way."

"Peter, get on the team. It's the way Washington wants it. This isn't nineteen-fifty-five. The Cold War's been over for thirty years."

"I'm not *that* old."

"You're acting like those snaggle-toothed veterans of the OSS, crying in their beer about how things used to be."

It was true in a way, and Garvey knew it. Although he was only forty, he went back to a time when a case officer worked his networks in his own way and answered to a station chief. Now the operations were directed from Washington, by people who didn't know the local situation, might never have collected a defector or held the hand of a guilt-ridden agent selling out his friends, and Garvey didn't like it.

"How come Verbeke's handling? He's a contractor. How do you know we can trust him?"

"He made the deal directly with Washington. They're sending Kessler to Amsterdam for the exchange, and you make the pickup."

"Why me?"

"Because you've done this before," Campbell said wearily, "and because Art Crowder said to send you."

Garvey remembered his shock when Campbell mentioned Art Crowder, and the mischievous smile on Campbell's face. "Maybe he's hoping you'll do something really stupid," Campbell said.

Arthur Crowder was Garvey's boss, the Company's deputy director for Operations since 1983. A political hack who had already held important posts at the Treasury and Commerce departments, he was appointed DDO during one of the congressional raids on the CIA, a "new broom" to bring the agency under control. Garvey didn't like the type, and when Crowder outlined his plan for "Open Secrets" to the Geneva station, it was Garvey who said, "You've got to be kidding," and walked out.

Garvey managed to get off with a citation for insubordination, but it was no secret that Art Crowder was gunning for him. That fact, plus the wailing cold wind and the long wait in the darkened boatyard were doing nothing to improve Garvey's disposition. He bounced on the balls of his feet to get the blood flowing. His breath blew warm over his lips and froze. "Whose idea was this goddamned boatyard?" he growled. He would have preferred a public place. A lot of pedestrian traffic was safer. Easier to get your guy lost in a crowd. No boatyards at midnight. You could get yourself killed in a place like this.

"He insisted on a quiet place," Verbeke said.

Garvey wanted to ask who "he" was, but he

couldn't admit to Verbeke that he didn't know, that his boss didn't trust him enough to tell him.

"Why didn't he just waltz into a U.S. consulate?" Garvey asked. "Why all this bullshit?"

"Somebody flagged him. He's been hiding."

Garvey caught his breath and let it out in a low, barely audible whistle. He recalled the E-code alert that had come through Geneva the previous month. The watchers at Orly had spotted two known KGB hit teams arriving in Paris on separate days. It had to be something special for them to ship in that kind of firepower, and Crowder's people had known. The sonofabitches probably set it up, Garvey thought. It's so simple. You've got a hotshot defector on the fence, leaning this way, that way, talking big bucks; you just leak. Suddenly the poor bastard's on the run, he has to jump, and you reel him in.

But he wasn't in yet. "Routine collection," Russ Campbell had said. Routine my ass, Garvey muttered to himself now. When the Soviets sent in the snuff squads it was because they were truly pissed. It had to be somebody important enough to stop, no matter what. Garvey's fingers instinctively gripped the cylinder of the short-barreled Smith & Wesson .38 in his right-hand pocket.

Verbeke sensed the movement and said, "*Tu as un pistolet?*" He seemed to revert to French when he was agitated or nervous.

Garvey showed the revolver in the palm of his hand. It was strictly business. Blue-black metal with a dark, wooden grip. He slipped it back into his pocket.

"I don't want any shooting," Verbeke said.

"Neither do I," Garvey said, and he meant it. On the other hand, if the shooting started, he knew from experience that it felt better to be shooting back. He would have wagered anything that Verbeke was armed. The Soviet hitters would be armed. He wished now, as a matter of fact, that he had accepted Oskar van Dressen's loan of an M-11 machine gun.

The boatyard was on the *Zijkanaal,* just a half mile off the highway that runs along the *Buiksloterdijk.* It was on the edge of a large *sportsplatz,* dark now and deserted. A narrow, unpaved road ran from the highway, twisting through patches of fenced pasture where cows grazed. It turned and followed the canal for a half-mile, passed the boatyard, and continued another five hundred yards before turning into the park. There, sitting in his darkened black Volvo, was Oskar van Dressen, Garvey's backup. Verbeke might be in charge, but that did not negate Rule 3 of Garvey's Law: *Never Commit Yourself Without an Exit.*

There was only one small light on in the yard. There were a number of halogen lamps mounted on tall poles, but they were dark. With the introduction of a potential threat, Garvey's senses went on red alert, filtering images, searching for the improbable, the unfamiliar, the deviations from the norm that would trigger an alarm. There was no watchman. Odd. In Holland there is always a watchman.

"What happened to the watchman?"

Verbeke smiled. He lifted his right hand from the coat pocket and rubbed the thumb and forefinger together. Bribed.

"When's he due back?"

"Three. We'll be gone by then."

There was a long, floating dock connected to the yard by wooden ramps. Small boats, sail and power, were strung along it. Halyards thrummed against hollow metal masts, and the boats pulled against the restraining lines. Verbeke's boat was there, a 22-foot Boston Whaler deep-vee with a center console and twin Mercury outboards. They were going to make the transfer by boat, a fast run across the *Het IJ* to *Diemenstraat*, just north of the *Centrum*, where Roger Kessler was supposed to be waiting to take delivery.

Garvey didn't like the idea of being on the water in this weather, but it wasn't a bad plan. Too complicated, of course, with too many details to backfire. But different enough to fool the Soviet goons if they were closing on their man. They'd be expecting a transfer by car.

An airplane droned overhead and Garvey looked, picking out the winking lights. Too high for the Schipol approach. He followed the lights across the sky and wished that he was in Geneva, or anywhere but where he was. He glanced again at his watch.

"Maybe they got him," he said to annoy Verbeke, to break the monotony.

Verbeke scowled and muttered something that Garvey didn't catch, but it amused him. Verbeke was getting worried. No delivery, no pay. One of the occupational hazards of being a free-lancer.

"Can't we wait inside somewhere, get out of this goddamned wind? I'm freezing my ass off."

"Everything's locked."

"Damn."

Garvey's practiced eye was now taking in the details of the yard. Besides the prefabricated metal building that dominated, there was a two-story brick building that housed a ship's chandlery and a small-boat dealership on the ground floor, offices on the second. The tarmac between the two buildings was filled with orderly rows of canvas-covered boats in wooden cradles.

Where would he position an ambush? The second floor of the brick building for sure. Where else? Inside the boats, perhaps, but that would be difficult. Just a single line of vision. Inside the big shed, ready to smash out a window? Maybe. There were too many obstacles in the yard, making it easy for a quarry to hide. Add the darkness and it wasn't a good place to spring a trap. On the other hand, if you just wanted to bring down one bird, a sharpshooter on the second floor could do the job easily with a good starlight scope.

"He's coming," Verbeke said, nodding toward the highway, and Garvey turned to look.

A pair of headlights danced along the unpaved road that led from the highway to the canal.

Garvey felt his pulse quicken. The cold seemed to leave him. He was alert. He pressed the button on the electronic signaling device in his left-hand pocket. One beep to alert Oskar that the collection was on. Two beeps would mean that the transfer was being made according to plan. When they were in the boat, he would signal with three beeps, and Oskar would take off and drive to Amsterdam, where he would park across the street from the Kessler rendezvous.

They watched the approaching lights. The car was running parallel to the canal. Garvey noticed for the first time that it was a taxi. The car stopped in the road outside the boatyard gate. A door opened and closed. Garvey heard voices. Verbeke moved away from the building and advanced on the idling car to make contact. Garvey followed for a few steps and moved into the shadow of a boat hull, out of sight of the brick building. The car shifted into gear, turned, and drove off, the headlights dancing and probing the dark.

The two men approached, dark figures, speaking in low tones in Russian. The defector was obviously irritated about something, probably explaining why he was late. Verbeke's Russian wasn't all that great, so he kept lapsing into French. The Russian was average height, he wore steel-rimmed glasses, and he was carrying a single suitcase that was heavy. Garvey didn't recognize the face and that surprised him. If the man was important, he would have been around awhile, so his face would have been on file.

Garvey stepped away from the cradled boat and the two men stopped.

"Peter Garvey," Verbeke said. He switched to Russian and began to explain who Garvey represented, but the Russian interrupted and said, in heavily accented English, "We know who is Colonel Garvey."

"Well, let's not waste any more time," Verbeke said. "They're waiting in Amsterdam. The boat's this way." He started for the ramp, then turned back and reached for the suitcase. "Want me to take that?" The Russian recoiled and did a half-turn to swing the suitcase out of reach. "I've got it," he said.

Garvey was about to send the second signal to Oskar when the yard was suddenly bathed in halogen light.

It was like being struck down. Brighter than daylight. Blinding after the hours of darkness. It stunned the senses. "Holy shit!" Garvey shouted. And then a bullhorn squawked and spoke like the voice of God.

"STOPPEN!"

Verbeke whirled around, startled. He did a full turn, off-balance like a marionette, his arms shoulder-high. He grabbed for the Russian's arm. "This way!" he shouted, pulling him toward the dock. The Russian was struggling with the suitcase, but he wouldn't turn it loose.

"You'll never make it!" Garvey had his gun in his hand. He reached out to stop Verbeke. "Don't," he shouted. "The road." He was too late. The two men broke for the ramp.

"STOPPEN! POLITIE!" the bullhorn blared.

There was a crash of glass and the sound of feet hitting the tarmac.

Garvey pointed the Smith & Wesson with one hand and shot out one of the lamps. It went with a flash of sparks and green smoke. He was taking aim on another when the general shooting began, and he was never sure who started it. Verbeke had a gun in his hand and so did the Russian. But he could have sworn that the first shots were from a submachine gun, a long burst, and then all hell broke loose and everybody was shooting.

"STOPPEN! POLITIE!" the bullhorn bellowed over the din, and for just a moment Garvey wondered why they were shouting in Dutch.

Garvey crouched in the shadows, against a boat, and took out two more lights. He saw Verbeke and the Russian crouched on the dock firing, trying to reach the boat and shooting on the wing. He shot out another light and ducked under the boat. He waited, took a deep breath, and made a run for the road.

"SNEL! SNEL! SCHIETEN!"

It was less than a hundred yards. He could hear the roar of the Volvo. Oskar would have heard the shooting and he was coming in. One of the great wheelmen. If Oskar was driving, you could count on that car being there. Garvey's breath came in gasps. He knew they were shooting at him because he could hear the bullets. He felt a punch in his left arm behind the bicep and he knew he was hit. But there was no pain. He made it to the road. The car was there, rolling slowly, the rear door open. He threw himself inside, shouting, "Get outta here!" He landed on his left arm and gasped with the pain, swearing through clenched teeth.

Oskar slipped the clutch, and the Volvo responded with a wail and screech of tires. It fishtailed, burning rubber, and Garvey was pressed against the rear seat.

They were firing at the car. The windows on the left side were shattered, and the rear window exploded in a shower of glass bits that fell like confetti. It was a hellish noise, like being inside a steel drum pummeled by hammers.

Garvey had been in a few shooting scrapes over the years, but never in a full-scale firefight, and he was surprised at his calm. He found himself thinking that Oskar's car was going to be junk and wondering how he was going to get Crowder to pay for it.

The barrage lasted maybe ten seconds, and then they were out of it, safe, gathering speed despite the unpaved road. The car bounced, rolled, and rocked. Garvey struggled to a sitting position and clung to the hanging strap with his right hand. He looked back, but there was nothing to see except the bright halogen lamps. He marveled at Oskar's driving, the courage of the man to drive into that mess to pick him up.

The car went into a slide as Oskar took the right turn away from the canal. He fishtailed it back on course, but Garvey couldn't take the slamming and jarring so he fell back and lay on the seat.

He wanted to laugh. He tried to hold it back. It seemed so damned inappropriate. Jesus, was he really enjoying this? It was a reaction to the tension, of course, like a sneeze gathering strength. He laughed. He lay back and punched his fist into the air and howled like some crazy kid. Oskar turned and grinned back at him.

The laughter subsided when Oskar shouted, *"Merde!"* Garvey grabbed the strap to haul himself up.

"Wha—?"

"Roadblock!"

"Holy Christ! How many people they got on this goddamned job?" The Soviets always had large foreign staffs, but this many gunmen to stop one defector didn't make sense.

Oskar gripped the wheel and increased the speed. There were lights ahead, but they couldn't see how the road was blocked or how many people were involved.

"What'll we do?"

"Run it!"

Garvey's fingers tightened on the strap. He held his breath. The bouncing headlights stabbed and flailed at the dark. There were people ahead and a large, dark shape on the road. They bore down on it at 70 mph.

"It's a truck!" Garvey shouted. "A truck! A truck!"

It was a military half-track. It straddled the road from shoulder to shoulder. There were ditches on either side of the road. There was a 20mm cannon mounted on the rear bed of the half-track. The man behind the gun was wearing a white helmet. The gun was trained on the road.

Oskar hit the brakes and twisted the wheel to put the car into a sliding 180. It was a sickening motion. Garvey let go of the strap and dropped to the floor. He landed on his left arm and grimaced with the pain, but he was still holding his breath, waiting for the crash.

The car came to a slow stop and it seemed to be tilted slightly. Oskar jammed it into first gear. He spun the rear wheels, attempting to make a try in the opposite direction, despite the cannon, but the rear wheel was in the ditch. The barrel of an assault rifle was pushed through the shattered window, and Oskar took his foot off the accelerator. The car was bathed in floodlight and someone was shouting in Dutch, "Out! Out!"

Garvey reached for the headrest on the front seat. He pulled himself up with effort. The rear doors were flung open and rough hands were clutching at him to pull him out. Oskar was already spread-eagled over the hood, being searched by uniformed Dutch police.

Dutch police?

Someone grabbed Garvey's left arm. He gasped as the pain rocketed to his brain, but before the spasm of light died and plunged him into blackness, he knew that something was terribly wrong, and he thought, the bastards set me up.

John le Carré

"John le Carré belongs in the select company of the best spy and detective writers. In all of his books, le Carré shows how endowed he is with the art of storytelling."

(The Times—London)

☐ 26757	LITTLE DRUMMER GIRL	$4.95
☐ 26487	SMILEY'S PEOPLE	$4.95
☐ 23693	LOOKING GLASS WAR	$3.95
☐ 26623	CALL FOR THE DEAD	$3.95
☐ 27437	THE HONOURABLE SCHOOLBOY	$4.95
☐ 26443	A MURDER OF QUALITY	$3.95
☐ 27995	THE NAIVE AND SENTIMENTAL LOVER	$4.95
☐ 26442	THE SPY WHO CAME IN FROM THE COLD	$4.50
☐ 26778	TINKER, TAILOR, SOLDIER, SPY	$4.95

LION'S RUN
by Craig Thomas
☐ (25824 • $4.50)

"When it comes to keeping the story moving and stoking up the excitement, Mr. Thomas knows his business."

—*New York Times*

"He knows how to make a chase scene drive the reader from page to page ... A damn good read."

—*Washington Post Book World*

"Not to be missed." —*London Daily Mirror*

Sir Kenneth, Director-General of British Intelligence, is the victim of an elaborate and brilliant KGB plot. At its heart is the murder of a British agent. Having discovered his role in it, the Soviets have found the one weapon against which Sir Kenneth cannot defend himself. The truth will convict him.

Time is running out as the KGB moves to bring Aubrey to Russia where he will quietly disappear. There are only two slender hopes for Aubrey's survival, one a persistent friend who refuses to believe the worst, the other Aubrey's bodyguard, who is only one desperate step ahead of the KGB assassins who are attempting to track him down before he can find proof of Aubrey's innocence.

In LION'S RUN Craig Thomas has created a masterpiece of suspense, a thrilling novel of intrigue, friendship and betrayal that has all the ingredients of a major Craig Thomas bestseller.

Also from Craig Thomas:

☐ 27702 **FIREFOX DOWN!** $4.95
☐ 27624 **FIREFOX** $4.95

Look wherever Bantam Books are sold, or use this handy page to order:

- -